Widow's Folly

MARGARET WESTHAVEN

D1558757

ZEBRA BOOKS
KENSINGTON PUBLISHING CORP.

ZEBRA BOOKS

are published by

Kensington Publishing Corp.
475 Park Avenue South
New York, NY 10016

First printing: May, 1990

Printed in the United States of America

The new Zebra Regency Romance logo that you see on the cover is a photograph of an actual regency "tuzzy-muzzy." The fashionable regency lady often wore a tuzzy-muzzy tied with a satin or velvet riband around her wrist to carry a fragrant nosegay. Usually made of gold or silver, tuzzy-muzzies varied in design from the elegantly simple to the exquisitely ornate. The Zebra Regency Romance tuzzy-muzzy is made of alabaster with a silver filigree edging.

A Whisper of Scandal

Maria's cheeks, already red, grew hotter as she wondered whether her friendship with Lord Abdul had completely shattered what reputation she had. No, surely not. She had simply been flirting, and everyone must realize that. But *had* she been merely flirting? Hadn't she been toying with the idea of flinging caution to the wind, of becoming the sort of fashionable, free-and-easy widow many thought she already was?

She dashed down the hall in distress, and ran headlong into Sir Stephen Wrackham.

"M'dame!" the handsome baronet said in surprise. "I've been looking for you—take you into supper—not feeling the thing?" Concern was written all over his countenance and Maria was accordingly quite touched.

"The headache," she whispered, staring into his concerned eyes. Here was one person who would always stand her friend.

"A bit to eat, just the thing for a headache," he said reassuringly as he led her towards the supper room.

Maria struggled to regain her calm. This was doubly difficult, for her happiness at being taken in to supper by this gentleman was quite out of proportion. Sir Stephen's friendship was no longer enough for her, but one of her dubious reputation could ask for no more . . .

THE BEST OF REGENCY ROMANCES

To Anne-Elizabeth Gibbons.
The circle comes to a close.

Chapter One

"Magnificent seat," said Sir Stephen Wrackham. "And a fine-looking woman."

Phillip Renshaw nodded, and both men stared after the dark-haired lady who had just thundered past them on a black mare. The rider galloped down a hill, a liveried groom following at a distance.

Renshaw's eyes glinted with mischief. "Well, it may be the oldest trick in the book, but why not? Don't you agree, Wrackham, that some maneuvers transcend the common to become classics? You must have learned that in the military. Come along." He urged his chestnut into action and flew off down the hill after the lady.

"What the devil?" Sir Stephen grumbled, not having understood a word of Renshaw's speech. Unless he wished to find his own way back from Richmond, though, he must follow along, and so he did, at the slower pace his sturdy mount demanded.

Lady Anne Hawley was in awfully good spirits. She had just ridden at her usual mad pace right past the picnic party her mother had wanted her to attend. Anne had declined the invitation, citing as her excuse that the duchess's refreshments would be poor and the company stodgy. Whenever dowagers and middle-aged matrons made up a good portion of a guest list, Anne skipped the entertainment if she could. After seven seasons, she qualified as a spinster, and ape leaders were allowed to be contrary. Lady Anne Hawley was nothing if not contrary.

At the age of twenty-five, and with a pretty independence inherited from her grandmother, Anne might have set up her own establishment and not been subject to her mother's whims. It wasn't unheard of for well-born single ladies to go their own ways and shock society — both of which Anne always loved to do. But she had too much regard for her family's consequence, or so she was fond of telling those friends who expressed surprise at her docility in this regard. Yes, despite her many other eccentricities, Lady Anne Hawley preferred to live with — and bedevil — her worthy mama, the dowager countess of Wormington.

Had she known that Mama had bestowed a toothache upon her to explain her absence from the picnic, Anne might not have been so unfilial as to display herself in Richmond Park on this lovely spring day. More likely, however, she would have gone right ahead, for not only did she have no patience with her mother's social stratagems, her mare was suffering for a good run.

The groom was mounted on a slug carefully chosen for the express purpose of allowing Lady Anne the illusion of solitude, and he lagged far behind. His mistress laughed aloud as she reached the foot of the hill and urged Dark Star on across a meadow.

"Hold tight, Lady Anne!" a deep voice called right in her ear. A strong hand suddenly seized hers, causing her to rein in sharply and her horse to rear.

"Good God, sir, you might have killed me!" Anne glared at the gentleman beside her. She recognized him as Phillip Renshaw, one of the shining lights of the Corinthian set, as well-known in society as anyone. Although she had met him once or twice over the years, she had never given him the least serious thought. He was handsome enough — with a fine, athletic figure and curling, dark hair in a Brutus crop — but this incident proved his manners abominable. She twitched her

8

hand away from his and eyed with misgiving the unfamiliar horseman who was only now approaching.

Larger and more substantially built than Renshaw, the second gentleman rode a sturdy bay that must be up to the weight of the Regent if Anne were any judge. Stroking Dark Star's heaving flank, she said, "I'll have you know my mare is unused to such dramatics. You've made her shiver. Good day." She turned her face away and clucked to the horse. The groom was only now arriving, and for the first time in her life, Anne was grateful for her servant's presence.

"But wasn't your horse running away with you, madam?" Mr. Renshaw called after her. When Anne paused and turned her eyes to him again in query, she was treated to a bright smile, a friendly smile which she chose to consider mocking. A pair of light blue eyes glinted at her from the cheerful, square-jawed face. "The rules of chivalry demanded that we follow after," the gentleman added.

Anne snapped, "Rules of chivalry, my—foot. My dear Mr. Renshaw, I never lose control of my horse."

Renshaw nodded. "Tell me, Lady Anne. Do you ever lose control?"

"It hasn't been necessary up to this time, sir. But I wouldn't push any further if I were you."

Renshaw's maddening smile was more intimate than ever. "Ah, wouldn't you, my lady? Perhaps I ought to take your advice, but it might be interesting to behold you in the full glory of your wrath."

Anne had the uncomfortable feeling that she was being teased, an odd sensation for one accustomed to having the upper hand whenever fashionable banter was the game. She decided to take the easy way out. "How droll you are, sir," she said with a well-bred smile.

Renshaw grinned. "Then I'm forgiven? Good for you, my lady. But I'm forgetting my manners." He motioned forward the gentleman at his side, who beamed all over his mustachioed face at being remembered at last. "Lady Anne, allow me to present Sir Stephen

9

Wrackham, baronet. Sir Stephen, Lady Anne Hawley."

Acknowledging the introduction with a queenly nod of her head, Anne noted that Sir Stephen's waving brown hair was longer than the current mode. And his clothes! Obviously not a Londoner. "Are you of the Surrey Wrackhams, sir?" she asked with a distant politeness. "I believe my mother has some acquaintance with that family."

"Quite so, quite so. I've a seat in Surrey," said Sir Stephen. "Lady Wormington, your ladyship's mother, Alicia Redding that was? Yes, m'mother knew her well. Schoolgirls together, seminary in Kensington, come-out same year, that sort of thing."

"Yes, I believe so."

"Mothers acquainted, eh?" said Renshaw. "If you don't mind my saying so, Lady Anne, the notion that you should have any connection at all with this rough diamond Wrackham is nothing short of amazing. Very good sort of fellow, make no mistake, but sadly countrified."

Anne brushed off this attempt at wit and kept her eyes on Sir Stephen in an attempt to take the overconfident Renshaw down a peg. "Is this your first visit to town, sir?"

"By no means, m'lady, but it's been nearly ten years. The war, y'know—regiment abroad, Waterloo, all that."

So he had been a military man, thought Anne in amusement. That would explain the astonishing mustachios.

Sir Stephen proceeded to tell a rambling tale of his father's death, his own subsequent selling out of the army, and his return to England. Then he'd had to put the estates in order—improvements and whatnot. In short, he hadn't found the time to come up to town. His old friend Renshaw's invitation, though . . .

Anne was surprised to hear such a detailed biography of the gentleman in response to a question which had needed no more than a civil "yes" or "no." "Then you'll certainly find much to amuse you here, Sir Stephen." She spoke more kindly than she had before. Although this country baronet had all the makings of a rattle, he was an amusing rattle, and it was so rare to meet anyone in society whose talk hadn't been corseted into the proper standard.

"No question, m'lady, no question," said Sir Stephen. "One of the great Corinthians, Renshaw here, to show a fellow about, just the thing for a sporting man like m'self. See all the sights, go a round with Jackson. And I mean to look out some new horseflesh, to be sure. Miss the hunting, though. Not the season for it, but miss it. A man can't ride in town."

"I hunt too, at home in Kent," said Anne. "But there is nothing like London during the season." One had to suppose that a newcomer would be excited by such a prospect, so she parroted the usual sentiments. In her secret opinion, however, this season was falling sadly flat.

"Remember it well," agreed the baronet. He seemed about to launch into a fresh torrent of prose when he was interrupted by his friend.

"To return to *your* exploits in the field, Lady Anne," said Renshaw quickly. "It's well known they have earned you the title of Diana the Huntress. I ought to have known that a horsewoman of your standing and evident skill wouldn't permit her horse to run away with her. Allow me to apologize."

Anne didn't allow herself to smile with the pleasure she felt at this compliment, but she did incline her head graciously. She enjoyed being known as Diana the Huntress, and gentlemen often wrote poems to her on that theme.

"Diana, eh?" Sir Stephen was saying. "Some Greek baggage, an' I remember from m'schooldays. Hunted, what? Can't say I recall. But still, Lady Anne, devilish spirited mount you've got there." Sir Stephen looked with masculine concern at the lady's thoroughbred.

"This mare of mine, Sir Stephen, is the pride of my

life," Anne uttered in frigid tones. "I should hope, in any case, that *I* wouldn't settle for a horse that was *not* spirited."

Sir Stephen's blundering apology was even more damning than his initial remark, involving as it did various clumsy allusions to the delicacy of females.

"You, my lady, would naturally settle for nothing but the very best," Renshaw attempted to save his friend.

"No, indeed," she agreed, turning from the unfortunate Sir Stephen to look right into Mr. Renshaw's eyes. "I never have."

"Nor will you in the future, I'm quite certain."

"By no means." A bit disturbed, Anne looked away from Renshaw. He was still baiting her, and she found it a little too pleasant. Signalling to her groom, she urged her horse forward. "I must go, gentlemen. Good day." She was gone before they could offer to escort her.

"Never saw such a seat," said Sir Stephen. "Left rather in a hurry. Suppose it's the usual way in the ton?"

Renshaw shrugged. "It's *her* way."

"Why did you quiz the woman like that? She didn't need rescuing any more than I do. The ordinary gallop, if you ask me."

Phillip Renshaw made his eyes go mockingly wide and innocent as he answered, "The *ordinary* gallop? My dear Wrackham, as the Lady Anne Hawley would be the first to tell you, *she* never does anything ordinary." He laughed as he set his chestnut off at a canter, and the two gentlemen rode in the direction opposite the one Lady Anne and her groom had taken. "That lady," Renshaw informed his friend as they moved along, "has refused more offers than most maidens ever get. Two dukes have asked for her since she came on the scene, and countless others. It does wonders for our consequence merely to be seen talking to her."

Wrackham nodded sagely.

Renshaw might have been flattered had he known that Lady Anne Hawley had paused in her haughty retreat to look back at him. "How strange," she murmured to herself as she paused under a tree. "Chivalry, indeed!" Rather than chance another gallop past Mama's picnic site, she decided to go tell Maria about this strange encounter.

Chapter Two

"Maria," urged a low, diffident voice. "I've loved you for years."

"Please—my dearest major, my very good friend— you know it won't do," returned the Comtesse de Beaulieu. "I never wanted you to love me. It makes for such uncomfortable scenes."

"But Maria, how could I not adore you?" Major George Harcourt, kneeling on the Aubusson carpet, gazed up into the lovely face he had worshipped for three years. In fact, he had been on the brink of an engagement to another woman when he first laid eyes on the beautiful young widow. But he had transferred his affections with a speed more befitting a schoolboy than a military man approaching forty. The comtesse's honey gold hair and soft green eyes enchanted him, and her platonic kindness, rather than putting him off, merely fanned the flame. The major knew there was no hope.

Maria de Beaulieu not only flirted with all and sundry, she freely admitted that she had no plans to remarry: she had worked hard to build the pleasant life she now enjoyed.

There were still those who remembered how Miss Maria Torrington, at the age of seventeen, had come from America set on making her fortune. Her scholarly father had left her penniless and saddled with a silly and equally penniless aunt (with no other kin in her native Philadelphia), Maria had chanced everything to come to London. Her father's birthplace had always fascinated her, and she believed that surely someone of her determination could make an advantageous match in that fabled land of dukes and earls.

Perhaps the most pragmatic seventeen-year-old to come on the London scene in years, Maria wedged herself and her aunt into the household of some Torrington relations, then set about meeting the eligibles. Her plans went awry, however. It seemed that even her blonde beauty and naturally flirtatious manner couldn't offset her lack of fortune in the minds of the wealthy bachelors she had set her sights upon.

Disillusioned, she was nearly ready to apply to an agency for work as a governess when she met Orphée de Beaulieu, an emigré who had managed to bring his fortune out of France intact. The Comte de Beaulieu, who reigned over a select circle of London scholars, was past sixty when he hit upon the idea of marrying the intelligent young Miss Torrington and molding her intellect.

Maria had never expected to find love and didn't at all mind the idea of furthering her education, which her father's death had cut short. She was flattered by the comte's interest in her mind, for she was fed to the teeth with empty compliments on her hair and eyes and figure from those bucks who scorned to consider her as a wife. After an ineffectual attempt to match the Comte de Beaulieu with her Aunt Kitty, Maria agreed to his proposal.

At the age of twenty, she found herself a widow with a goodly fortune and nothing to do but please herself. She had kept her place in literary circles and learned to refine the art of flirtation as she had earlier learned Greek and Latin. After seven years of widowhood, she had no desire to change her pleasant state. Never having been in love, she thought it unlikely that she ever would find a man original enough to touch her heart. And why should she give up her independence for less than love? Poor Major Harcourt thought he loved her (Maria doubted that he really did and hoped he would one day find the right woman), but she had no feelings for him except the most devoted of friendship — and so she told him whenever he asked.

As for the major, he had schooled himself to think of the comtesse as a friend only, for he delighted in obeying her commands. But every so often the old yearning would overtake him, and he would find himself in a position like this one, begging London's most self-acknowledged flirt to marry him. As always, speaking the words made it clear that his dream was not to be.

Major Harcourt was struggling to his feet when the door of Maria's drawing room swung open to reveal the sharp-nosed butler. "Lady Anne Hawley," announced this worthy, averting his disapproving eyes from madame's male guest.

"Thank you, Roy." Maria, lips twitching, rose from her chair just as the major made it to a standing position. The two glanced awkwardly at each other. Maria knew from experience that it would take a few days for her and her dear cavalier to regain their usual companionable footing.

Lady Anne breezed in. As the comtesse's closest friend, she ran tame in the household. She was dressed in her riding habit, a particularly dashing ensemble of claret-colored velvet which molded to her stately figure. Her train was looped over one arm, and she took off her hat as she entered. "Ah, I see I'm interrupting something. How do you do, Major?"

Harcourt made a stiff bow, and his face reddened to the ears. "Lady Anne! Your most obedient. Madame." He turned back to Maria for one last, regretful stare. "You will forgive me for leaving you now? An appointment . . ."

Maria understood his reluctance to engage in small talk after what had just happened. Reminding him not to forget her soirée the next evening, she let the major escape.

"I suppose he was proposing again," Anne said when the door had closed behind the man. She took her favorite seat by the lace-draped window. "Really, Maria, you shouldn't encourage him so."

Maria returned to the Louise Quinze chair, which, upholstered in deep green watered-silk, made a fitting frame for her white gown. "Encourage him!" she protested. "Anne, I never fail to tell him I will never, ever marry him. Poor, dear man."

"Hmph!" Anne's shrewd hazel eyes were doubtful. "It's your own fault all the same. You always do this. You're so determined to keep all these men around, as your friends or courtiers or what have you, that you don't give them the set-down they require to back out of your life."

"But Anne, why may I not keep my friends?" asked Maria. A hurt look appeared on her face.

A peal of laughter was her answer. "Because, you silly creature, in a few years' time, one won't be able to get in at your door — what with the crowds of young Werthers and their older cousins. Very well, I won't scold. I stopped by to get your opinion, not give my own."

"Oh?" Maria's ears pricked up. "What's happened? You've been riding, I see."

"Yes, and I must apologize for appearing here in all my dirt. But you should have been with me rather than lazing about, as I'm sure you've been doing."

"You're changing the subject, Anne, and as it happens, until Major Harcourt got here, I was working." Maria smoothed down the ribbons of her dress in quite a superior manner.

Her friend was immediately congratulatory. "On your novel? My dear creature, how admirable. In the middle of the season, too. I have never known you to do such a thing before. Why, I'd wager you'll finish it before the month is out."

For some time, Maria had been trying her hand at a work of fiction. She and Lady Anne judged it must be in the third volume by now, but somehow she hadn't managed to bring the story to an end. And in the face of Anne's enthusiasm, she had to be honest. "I wasn't exactly writing, but I was reading—well, I was reading this." She reached for a book on the table at her side and extended the slim, gilt-and-leather volume to her friend.

Anne opened the book to the title page and beheld a sentimental illustration of Love contemplating a burning heart. "Oh, Maria," she sighed. "Not *Glenarvon*."

Though she was already blushing, Maria rushed to defend herself. "I know you and I decided not to be a party to Caro's foolishness when it came out last year, but I—well, Anne, people have talked about it so much, I merely wanted to make sure I wasn't guilty of the same mistakes."

Anne laughed. "No danger of that, my dear. No one's ever accused you of having an affair with Byron, and in any case, I wouldn't expect you to fictionalize it to cause a sensation."

"It was more her writing style I was thinking of," Maria said.

"From what I've heard—mind you I haven't read this—she writes very badly indeed, pure melodrama at that, and you know Miss Ginevra Johnson herself praised those pages you let her read of yours."

Maria nodded. The famous bluestocking's good opinion meant everything to her. "Well, Caro Lamb does have it over me in one area. She finished this. Truly, Anne, reading only the first volume gave me a renewed desire to do better than she."

"I see no problem there, but first you must write."

"Yes, yes. Tomorrow at the latest. And now, my severe friend, what did you have to tell me? You're getting off the subject again, which makes me wonder if you aren't hiding something quite significant."

Lady Anne came to life. "Oh, my little adventure. I went out to Richmond today. My mare needed exercise."

"Anne!" cried Maria. "You didn't go near the duchess's picnic party?"

"As it happens, I *did* gallop right past the gimlet eyes of her grace and Mama, but that's not what I was going to tell you. I met two gentlemen whose behavior was so odd it quite infuriated me at the time, but now it merely seems amusing. The one was quite impossibly condescending in his manners. And to me!" Anne shook her head, remembering.

"Two gentlemen?" Maria fancied she detected more animation than usual in her friend's speech. Lady Anne Hawley normally took all dealings with gentlemen in her stride, to the dismay of the many females who wished to see her wed. Maria herself had been trying for years to arrange a suitable love match for her friend. "Who were they? And how, pray tell, did they manage to displease you?"

"It's a very foolish story. They were Phillip Renshaw and a country friend of his."

"Oh, the handsome Mr. Renshaw?"

"I wouldn't call him precisely handsome. He's tall enough, true, and those light blue eyes *are* rather attractive. But I can't say I like that sort of open, honest countenance in a man. His features are regular, but there isn't any mystery about him—no tortured brow, no scar on the cheek from a duel."

"My dear Anne, do be serious. Renshaw is a fine figure of a man."

"Yes, there is nothing at all amiss with his figure, but—"

"Don't keep me in suspense," interrupted Maria. "Who was with Renshaw?" Although she was already certain which gentleman had captured Anne's imagination, it never hurt to be curious.

"Oh, a harmless, jovial person," said Anne with a shrug. "A very large baronet who'll probably live all his days in Surrey and end up with a wife and ten children—if he doesn't have them now."

"Well, that disposes of him. What a terrifying picture you paint. Do I know the man?"

"I don't see how you could. He mentioned it's been

ten years since he was in town — his clothes certainly give that away — so he must have left London your first season. The army, you know."

"Then this gentleman and I have been ships that pass in the night. His name?"

"Wrackham. One Sir Stephen. Oh, his mother knew Mama, so I do have a sort of connection with him."

Maria, having made a mental note of the information, persisted in her interrogation. She soon had the full story of Phillip Renshaw's suspicious rescue of Anne, the fright to Dark Star (which appeared to be Anne's only real bone to pick with the gentleman), and the short conversation with the two chivalrous souls.

"Can you imagine?" Anne continued. "That bluff Sir Stephen had the gall to quiz me on my mount not being suitable for a lady! I suppose he's to be forgiven, though. Such a man is too simple to know that not all ladies are delicate as hothouse flowers. No offense meant to you, Maria. I know you are one such and proud of it. But Renshaw! I could swear he was laughing at me."

"He was flirting, and you know it, though he didn't hit upon the proper way to your heart." Maria held back a smile. "You can't permit it. How do you plan to even the score?"

Anne shook her head. "Their antics aren't worth dignifying with my attention. When next I chance to meet Mr. Renshaw — at Almack's, perhaps — I could be cold to him on purpose, but it isn't worth the trouble."

"Whatever you say. Now let's talk of something else. My soirée."

Maria was amused by her friend's reluctance to change the subject. "It's going to be a raging success, isn't it? Your evenings always are." Anne sounded almost regretful, as though she would have enjoyed abusing Mr. Renshaw and his graceless friend for a longer time.

"Yes," answered Maria. "We have done well, haven't we, for a pair of bluestockings?" Maria loved her literary parties and was proud that she had been able to keep them up after her husband's death, but she didn't hesitate to give Anne due credit for attracting some of the aristocratic names which gave the Comtesse de Beaulieu's soirées their special cachet.

Anne was quick to disclaim any influence in the management of Maria's parties. "It's true," she said. "I'd never miss one."

The two smiled at each other. Theirs was a lucky friendship which could be traced back to an evening years ago when Lady Anne, in the ladies' retiring room at Almack's, had made an obscure literary allusion. The frivolous Comtesse de Beaulieu had shocked Lady Anne to the tips of her slippers by understanding the reference, and their friendship had blossomed from that moment on.

The ladies were discussing the details of the next evening's plans when the door opened. Maria's head snapped up. Roy knew he was never to interrupt a *tête-à-tête,* and this was the second time today he had done it. "Well?" she demanded.

The butler's expression was distinctly pained. "It's Miss Torrington, Madame."

Had his eyes rolled heavenward? How dare he make fun of poor Aunt Kitty! "Well? What about Miss Torrington, Roy?" Maria asked coldly. She knew she had no talent for managing servants, but instinct told her that sternness was necessary in the case of her sometimes insolent butler.

"An altercation on the pavement outside, Madame. I believe your presence would facilitate matters."

Maria and Anne looked at each other. "Oh, heavens," said Maria. "Don't tell me it's another of Auntie's scrapes." She and Lady Anne jumped up and left the room.

On the pavement of Curzon Street, a strange sight met their eyes. A small, narrow-faced man dressed in a shopkeeper's apron was struggling to remove a package from the hands of a slender woman in dove-gray walking clothes. From the front door, Maria cried out in her most dramatic tones, "You fiend, unhand that lady!" Lady Anne, a woman of action, swept down the steps and administered a cut to the little man's shoulders with her riding crop.

He sprang away from his victim, cursing.

"Oh, Maria!" sobbed the lady in grey. She ran up the steps and dissolved into tears on Maria's shoulder.

As she patted her aunt's back, Maria cast a look of definite disapproval at her butler, who was standing to one side with a hint of amusement on his face. "Why, Roy, did you not rescue Miss Torrington yourself? It's obviously a simple case of theft."

"Aye, it is that!" cried the small shopkeeper. Careful to keep out of range of the tall lady's whip, he stormed up the stairs. "This old mort lifted a card of black lace from my shop, and I mean to 'ave it back!" He wagged his finger in Maria's face.

Miss Torrington looked up. "Old?" she wailed. "Oh, Maria." She dissolved in tears again.

"There, Aunt, calm yourself," whispered Maria. Aunt Kitty was over fifty, but she took a justifiable pride in her charming looks. Her figure was still excellent, and her hair, though it had gone white early, was abundant and wavy. And her large violet eyes still played havoc with the superannuated beaux of the ton. How typical of Aunt to take no notice of the charge of thievery in the traumatic aftermath of such an insult. Stroking Aunt Kitty's shaking back, Maria wondered, not for the first time, precisely who was chaperoning whom in this household.

While Maria soothed Aunt Kitty, Anne climbed the steps and touched the shopkeeper very lightly with her crop. He spun around and started back. Pleased at the devastating effect she was having, Anne said, in her most regal tones, "How dare you make such an accusation against this lady, you — you worm. You could never hope to prove such an absurd thing. This is Miss Katherine Torrington, and she is not without friends."

The man's little eyes glinted. "Friends? She'll need 'em. 'And over that package and we'll see who can't prove what."

Miss Torrington still clutched the package in her gloved hands. Anne gently withdrew it and started to untie the string.

"I bought two cards of white lace and a yard of co-quelicot ribbon at this monster's counter," cried Aunt Kitty, her face still buried in Maria's comforting shoulder. "And he knows I paid him for them." She shuddered. "Oh, Maria, he must have followed me all the way home."

" 'Ad to 'ire a hack, I did, to keep up with 'er," affirmed the shopkeeper, looking more and more like a sly fox.

"And waited until my carriage had gone round to the mews to make your assault, no doubt, so you wouldn't have to deal with my coachman," added Maria.

Anne had undone the package. "Well, man, do you accuse this lady of not paying for these purchases? Here we have the ribbon, and the two cards of white, and—" Her fingers closed around a card of black lace. She said nothing.

"What'd I tell you?" insisted the shopkeeper. "Slipped that into the packet while I wasn't looking."

"I never did!" cried Aunt Kitty. "Maria, I swear to you—"

"No need to swear,, Auntie, this is an old trick," said Maria calmly. She favored the shopkeeper with her most haughty stare. "No doubt this person thought you would be happy to pay him a gratuity to see he takes the charge no further."

The man nodded. "Naturally I wouldn't like to be troubling a genteel household with a court case. Not much in the fashion, is it, that sort of thing."

"Good lord!" cried Anne. "You can't think your empty threats could induce us to grease your palm?"

"Oh, no, ma'am," agreed the shopkeeper. He swept a very insincere bow. "I'll just be toddling along now to

Bow Street. The runners have ways of dealing. The old thief'll spend this night in gaol, for I've a witness. My clerk saw 'er sneak the lace into her parcel."

Miss Torrington's tears had worsened to the point where she was in the midst of an attack of ragged sobs.

Maria sighed. She knew her aunt was no thief, but she could also see how the innocent lady had been an easy target for this oily shopkeeper's wiles. Maria didn't doubt that the man would go to Bow Street, and the runners would have to take Aunt Kitty into custody if, as the shopkeeper claimed, he had a "witness" to the supposed theft. Maria could not risk Aunt Kitty being upset a moment longer, let alone facing a charge of thievery.

"My butler will pay you for that ugly black lace, you horrid creature," said Maria. "And you may take it back to your shop with you, for we don't want anything so vulgar. Roy, come indoors with us and get my purse."

Roy ran his sharp eyes over the shopkeeper and gave a tight nod.

"But, Maria," sniffed Aunt Kitty. "I didn't do it!"

"Of course you didn't, Aunt, but you wouldn't care to deal with all the indignities of proving you didn't."

"I suppose not." Aunt Kitty blew her nose into her handkerchief. Her sobs had wound down, and she was back to quiet weeping.

Anne was exasperated. "You're only encouraging this despicable man to try the same trick on others," she told her friend.

Maria said nothing. In her own way, she was as disappointed in herself as her friend was. Inside the house, she gave Roy the purse and told him to limit the amount to ten guineas if he could. Then the three ladies went into the drawing room, and Maria rang the bell. Aunt Kitty needed tea and a sip of brandy, and Maria was feeling in want of refreshment herself after the energetic scene. "Aunt, do tell me which is the horrid man's shop," she said. "Anne and I will want to set the wheels in motion to take him quite out of fashion."

Anne, still disgusted with Maria, had flung herself into a chair. Now her expression brightened. "That *would* be amusing," she said. "Though I still can't like the creature's getting away with blackmail."

Aunt Kitty also smiled. "Oh, Maria! What a lovely idea."

"I can't risk your going to gaol, Aunt, but we must see that that wretch is punished. I hear of such tricks being played on shoppers all the time." On naïve-looking female shoppers, Maria added silently. "Aunt, please don't go out shopping alone anymore. If your maid had been with you, the rascal couldn't have scared us with talk of witnesses, for you would have one too."

The clock on the mantelpiece chimed the hour. "I must be going," said Anne. "The least I can do for Mama, after my terrible prank, is not be late for dinner."

"What terrible prank?" asked Aunt Kitty after Lady Anne had taken her leave. She was sipping at a glass of brandy a solicitous housemaid had delivered into her hand and appeared to have forgotten her traumatic experience already. "Has dear Lady Anne been causing talk again?"

"It's merely something that happened to her at Richmond," said Maria. She smiled as she recalled Anne's encounter with the two gentlemen. Renshaw . . . a very handsome man indeed. Didn't he live in Mount Street? "Now do let me tell you about two fascinating men I've decided to invite to tomorrow's soirée," Maria said to her aunt.

Chapter Three

Breakfast was served late the following morning at the Renshaw house in Mount Street. The gentlemen had, after all, not returned home until dawn.

"Famous run of luck, what?" commented Sir Stephen Wrackham as he tore into a well-filled plate.

Renshaw, who was attacking his own victuals with less enthusiasm, eyed his large friend with a grin. "It isn't unusual, Wrackham, for one who has just come on the town to have the devil's own luck. Of course, the phenomenon is more noticeable in boys just down from university. But a novice is a novice, and an old country stick like yourself is no exception, it would seem, to that old rule. Don't count on it continuing."

Sir Stephen bristled. "Not a novice, y'know. Not at all. Just not done it at White's these ten years. Army man. D'you take it I've never played?"

"Only quizzing you, Wrackham," laughed Renshaw. "Jealousy on my part, I assure you, nothing more. God knows I didn't mean to lose what I did."

"Not short of funds?" Sir Stephen steeled himself to make the offer of a loan if necessary. He couldn't feature Renshaw, one of the wealthiest men of his acquaintance, standing in financial need no matter how much he dropped at the tables, but it wouldn't do to be behindhand should that be the case.

"Short of funds?" repeated a puzzled Renshaw. "By no means."

"Glad of it," said Sir Stephen in relief.

The men applied themselves in good earnest to their

meal. Renshaw, in keeping with his usual custom, was wearing a silk dressing gown in a paisley pattern. With his ruffled shirt peeking out from the heavy quilted collar and no starched cravat yet marring the muscular brown column of his throat, he was the picture of a fashionable gentleman at leisure.

Wrackham had elected to join his friend *en deshabille*. His goal of refurbishing his seedy wardrobe while in town had not yet been attended to, and his own ancient Banyan had seen him through the wars and looked it. Moreover, he appeared to be wearing nothing under it. The sight of a burly bare chest and a pair of strong legs adorned only with rundown slippers had already caused one housemaid to shriek when she had observed her master's guest in the corridor earlier.

Once he had finished off two helpings of beefsteak, kidneys, and eggs, Renshaw began to sort through the stack of mail at the side of his plate. While he did so, Sir Stephen stolidly carved his way through a third slab of beef.

The post was somewhat out of the ordinary this morning. There was a note from the foreign office asking Renshaw to help entertain an emissary from the court of Ispahan who was momentarily to arrive in town. The summons made Renshaw's eyes light up. Though he was no longer in the diplomatic service, he did miss the life on occasion. Sometimes, in the rush of activities which made up a London life of pleasure, Renshaw thought wistfully of the exotic experiences in his past. He presented such an ordinary and unexotic appearance to the world that one might guess he had spent his early youth on the playing-fields of Eton. In actuality, he had traveled with his father to this and that capital of the Ottoman empire — and even farther afield — on missions for His Majesty.

Eventually young Renshaw had begun his own diplomatic career — something he had put aside on his parent's death and somehow never picked up again. This unexpected call back to the diplomatic fold, doubtless

27

due to the fact that he had once spent time in Persia and knew the emissary's language, made Renshaw toy with the idea of requesting a foreign post. Acting as guide to this Persian would help him decide if he wanted such a radical change in his circumstances, though, according to the note from Castlereagh, the dignitary's visit was to be largely of a social nature. Mirza Ali Abdul Khan, read the letter, was a cosmopolitan gentleman, well-traveled and conversant in English customs, who would expect to see London life after completing his unofficial and very private mission to the Regent.

Renshaw put the letter from Castlereagh aside and opened the next one, addressed in a flowing, feminine hand. "Well!" he exclaimed. "This comes as a surprise."

Sir Stephen looked up from his plate to find his friend staring in amazement at a small, gilt-edged note. "Invitation, I take it?" he asked.

"Yes," answered Renshaw. "But not one I expected to get." He tossed something across the table to Wrackham. "One for you came under cover of mine," he said. "Prepare to enter literary circles, man."

Sir Stephen started. "Lit'ry circles?" He turned the card over in his large hand. "No, b'gad! Not a lit'ry man." He scrutinized the tastefully done script. "Who's that? Bow-loo? Foreign name. Met a Countess Bow-loo and forgotten it, have I? Must have been foxed."

Renshaw chuckled and studied his own card. "Maria, the Comtesse de Beaulieu, holds the most exclusive literary salon in town, Wrackham. I've never before been so distinguished by the good widow. I wonder why it should be now, and why you, of all people, should be invited along with me. Means to have us there as a team, it would seem. Oh—no offense meant by my incredulity, dear fellow. It's simply that what you said is true. You aren't a literary man, and neither am I."

"No trouble about it," Sir Stephen said. "Regrets. Go to White's." He beamed at Renshaw, quite pleased at his effortless solution to a dismaying problem.

Renshaw, frowning in thought, paid his friend no heed. "Lord Elliot, of course, goes there regularly, and he's a representative of our set of sporting blockheads. Could be that the lady asks us in compliment to him, though he told me he wangled his way in merely to dance attendance on Lady Anne Hawley—" He suddenly stopped speaking, and his well-molded lips curved upward.

"What's that you say? Lady Anne, the Greek what's-it from Richmond?" put in Sir Stephen. "She has to do with this bookish foreigner?"

Renshaw nodded. "The two ladies are bosom-bows, no doubt about it. Lady Anne, in addition to her sporting exploits, is quite a bluestocking, and Madame la Comtesse de Beaulieu considers herself a leader of the literary set in town. She gathers the haut ton into her drawing room with the lifting of a little finger, quite as her husband used to do. It wouldn't do to miss this occasion to further your education and our consequence, Wrackham, though the reason for this honor is a mystery." Renshaw's frank blue eyes were dancing. The Comtesse de Beaulieu and Lady Anne Hawley *were* the best of friends. Might not the latter lady have persuaded the comtesse to invite Renshaw to this soirée? And Wrackham? Perhaps his inclusion was a feminine ruse, meant to avoid singling out Renshaw. It was gratifying to have awakened Lady Anne's interest.

"Met the countess when I was foxed, did I?" asked Sir Stephen doggedly.

"No, you haven't met her," Renshaw assured the singleminded baronet. "The comtesse writes me a word here, very prettily asking me to bring you along, as she's heard you've but lately come to town."

"The devil you say!" Sir Stephen's eyes widened. "Heard of me?"

"It would seem so."

Sir Stephen frowned. "Not a famous character as yet," he murmured to himself. "Arrived but last week, devil take it all! How come foreign lit'ry widows to be

29

looking me out? Good God, man, a fellow's not safe!"

"London's a perilous place, Wrackham, full of unforeseen dangers. You'd best go along with me. I've an idea it wouldn't do for me to show my face without you. The Beaulieu woman has some wish to get us there together."

"Send regrets, old fellow," exclaimed Sir Stephen. "Go out to get some amusement. Not spend the evening talking a lot of books." He gave his friend a shrewd glance. "You can see Lady Anne somewhere else. Bound to be out riding again. Opera, rout — that sort of thing. No need to go fastening yourself to her old widow friends."

Renshaw let out a laugh. "Old? My dear good fellow, it's plain you haven't been long in town. Maria de Beaulieu can't be much above twenty-five. And a lovelier woman, Wrackham, you'd be hard put to find. A diamond of the first water, make no mistake. A lush honey-blonde with a very engaging manner." He chose to ignore Sir Stephen's remark regarding Lady Anne Hawley.

"Trying to catch me, Renshaw," said the baronet. "You know I've an eye for a pretty woman. Well, damme, it won't work. Send regrets." He nodded his head in emphasis, and the subject was closed.

Chapter Four

Mr. Renshaw's encounter with Anne Hawley at Richmond Park had not gone unnoticed. While he and his guest breakfasted in Mount Street, two of the most diligent young gossips in town were talking over his affairs and those of dear Lady Anne.

"You really should have seen her mother's face, Nell, when Anne flew past the picnic on that black charger," said Lady Juliana Bickerstaff with evident relish. "One of the gentlemen told me Phillip Renshaw went speeding after her. The talk's already going about that she was scheming to get Renshaw's attention, but I can't believe that of dear Anne." There was a slight pause. "Can you?"

"Where Lady Anne Hawley is concerned . . ." Miss Eleanor Tabor, Juliana's hostess, was at a momentary loss for words. "Well, not to be rude — you know I hate that — but she never does let anyone else initiate anything, does she?" A note of well-bred disdain was clear in Nell Tabor's voice. "It was ever so, wasn't it, Juliana? We've both been acquainted with Anne Hawley since schooldays, and she's never been one to remain in the background."

"No, she's a fine, spirited girl, and always has been," said Lady Juliana. She herself had never been a retiring sort, and though she might gossip about her schoolfellow Anne, she was nearly always disposed to defend her.

"Well," returned Nell with a sniff. "Lady Anne may be very lively, but it hasn't got her married." She poked rather fiercely at the embroidery in her hands. She was an excellent needlewoman as well as being pretty and well-bred, so why *she* wasn't married at the age of twenty-six was a complete mystery. Well, not a complete mystery . . . But one small indiscretion in her past shouldn't make a difference after all these years. It was a comfort that Lady Anne, not much younger than Nell, was also on the shelf (although in Anne's case that term hardly seemed an apt description).

"She hasn't stayed single for lack of offers," put in Lady Juliana. Then she checked herself in some chagrin. Nell Tabor had never to anyone's knowledge received a suitable offer since that unfortunate business eight years ago. If she had, she would surely be married. "Dear Anne is quite an original," Juliana added in an attempt to soften the unintentional blow to Nell's self-esteem. Why not imply that the eccentric Anne Hawley scared away more men than she attracted? It wasn't true by any means.

"Original indeed," replied Nell. Her blue eyes had narrowed at her visitor's first suggestion that Lady Anne had had her chances, but the thought that the Earl of Wormington's sister was too much out of the common way to attract a man was much more pleasant. Nell was quite ordinary in her behavior—her one shocking lapse had taught her that lesson—and becomingly modest about her wealth of attractions. She hardly ever mentioned that her family was one of the oldest in England. Nor was she vain about her looks. Her flaxen hair was always arranged simply and in perfect taste, and she dressed with a quiet elegance quite absent from the striking costumes affected by Lady Anne. Not that Mama would ever permit such display. Mrs. Tabor had often wondered aloud to Nell what the dowager Lady Wormington could be thinking of to let her daughter go to such extremes in dress. "And her intimacy with Maria de Beaulieu," added Nell, "is one of the most *original* things about her. Really, that little upstart—foreigner."

"Now, now, my dear, I know what you think of Maria." And I know why, Lady Juliana added silently. Maria and Nell were old enemies. Once, as young girls, the two had been friends, but all that had changed. "There is nothing wrong with Maria's English relations," Juliana put in. Much as Juliana loved a good gossip, she drew the line at hearing her friends' origins questioned.

"But Juliana, she's an American!" cried Nell. "Certainly that she even got into society is an odd quirk of fate."

"She got into it as you and I did, presented by her family," returned Lady Juliana. "The Torringtons were her sponsors, and she is one of them. And you can't call the Comte de Beaulieu an upstart—old French aristocracy, some connection of my own mother's on the maternal side—"

"Oh, yes, you're related to half of Europe, I know that," sighed Nell. "It's only that the Beaulieu woman is so—so notorious. One is always hearing some story about her. Take her behavior at Morland House the other night, with both the duke and the duke's brother. One can only suspect the worst."

"Maria is a flirt, make no mistake," said Lady Juliana, laughing. "But she makes no secret of the fact that she is, *and* that she means nothing by it. You can't blame a widow as young as she for not wanting to live in seclusion."

"There's a difference between not living in seclusion and behaving with complete abandon," said Nell severely.

Juliana shook her head and smiled. "How Maria would laugh to hear you speak so serious. There will be stories about any widow, and Maria isn't by nature one to remain in the background."

"We've already discussed *that* as a failing of Lady Anne Hawley's," retorted Nell. "How sad that her friends should be afflicted with it as well."

Juliana was about to say something very sharp in

33

defense of the absent ladies when she recognized that poor Nell's acid words were probably provoked by envy. And who could blame her? Anne and Maria enjoyed a prominent place in the social scene. Eleanor Tabor, with that scandal in her past, must never aspire to more than genteel obscurity.

The two ladies were frowning, Juliana in sympathy and Nell in irritation, when the Tabors' ancient butler flung open the door and announced Lady Wormington. A muffled peal of laughter escaped Juliana. Lady Anne's mother! How very amusing that Nell had been raking the dowager's daughter over the coals but a moment before.

Nell jumped up in anxious politeness. How lucky that she had broken her appointment at the modiste's and was here to receive, for Mama was abed with the headache. The dowager Countess of Wormington was indeed a rare visitor in Albermarle Street, one to whom every mark of respect was due.

Lady Wormington, a small woman with graying red hair, had been hoping to see Mrs. Tabor about a charitable matter. Learning that her hostess was unwell, the dowager seemed openly resentful that civility now demanded she pay a call upon a little blonde spinster. But Nell took no notice of her ladyship's brusque behavior: it would have been an honor to have a countess in the house had she started to throw the china.

"I must say, Miss Tabor, it's a shame your mother is having another of her migraines," said Lady Wormington. "If her health won't permit it, she ought not to embroil herself in these woefully demanding charities. And I wouldn't blame her if she didn't, for it's all I can manage to exert myself in this cause, and I won't do it again except by proxy. The Duchess of Morland tricked me into this, and I let her as usual."

"Mama will be grateful for your concern, my lady," responded Nell. Her deference to rank always amused Lady Juliana.

"Yes, and you tell her what I say, Miss," snapped the

dowager. "No more attempting what she can't do. Is that clear?"

"Yes, my lady," said Nell respectfully.

Juliana, eyes sparkling with mischief, ventured to inquire after Lady Wormington's daughter.

"Oh, Anne is somewhere out and about as usual," said Lady Wormington with a casual wave of a small gloved hand. "The child is nothing if not independent. I suppose you've already heard how she was galloping her horse yesterday out at Richmond, right in front of the Morland party. Oh, yes, you were right there, gel." She nodded to Lady Juliana. "The duchess had something to say to me, you may be sure, and I gave Anne the sharp edge of my tongue. Not that it does any good. Ah, that child is one of my greatest trials. She can't be bothered to join her mother in paying calls of this sort. In this case, I can't say I blame her."

Nell's eyes narrowed at this slight, but she was ever sensible of the privilege of rank and said nothing.

Lady Juliana's friends often described her as irrepressibly wicked, and now she gave proof of this by saying in a casual tone, "What do you think, my lady, of Anne's new conquest? Mr. Renshaw is one of the handsomest men in town."

Lady Wormington's hazel eyes were cold as ice as they regarded the younger lady. "*Mr.* Renshaw? I don't believe I've heard the name, but then I rarely hear names of that sort. You must be mistaken, child. My Anne would never make a flirt of a *Mr.* anyone." By her furrowed brow, the dowager betrayed her knowledge that Anne would do just as she pleased, especially if the doing would irritate her mama.

"Oh, but Mr. Renshaw isn't just anyone," Lady Juliana said. "He was with Lord Castlereagh in Vienna, you know. And though he hasn't done much with himself in late years, the foreign office still sometimes makes use of him. I hear there's an envoy from Persia arriving soon, and Mr. Renshaw is to take the man about." Juliana casually let drop her intimate connection to the highest circles in government. She had known about Mr. Renshaw's recent appointment before he had himself—not that such knowledge was of any use to her except as fodder for gossip.

"Hmph!" Lady Wormington tossed her head, setting the purple plumes of her bonnet to waving. "Persia, of all the out of the way places. This Renbird person may be attracted to Anne as you say—she's a most lovely girl—but he won't get far, mark my words."

The younger ladies were both guilty of wishing Mr. Renshaw *would* captivate Lady Anne—Nell because a *Mr.* would be no brilliant match for her rival, and Juliana because it would be such fun to see Lady Wormington disconcerted.

When Lady Wormington firmly changed the subject to the orphans' fund she and Mrs. Tabor were concerned with, the lively Lady Juliana began to droop with boredom. She was relieved when her husband burst into the room in his usual brusque fashion. He had dispensed with the services of the butler, who peeked in at the door after the young man to say shakily, "Mr. Bickerstaff."

Roger Bickerstaff was a large, raw-boned individual who seldom said a word except in agreement to some comment of his wife's. He was "something in the foreign office," and some said that it was precisely his bumbling, unintelligent appearance that made him most useful in that capacity. (Others, it was true, said he really *was* bumbling and rather thick.) He strode to Juliana's side, clapped his hand on her shoulder, and administered curt greetings to all the females. "We're late," he then announced.

"Great heaven, so we are," cried Lady Juliana. She smiled to herself at the success of their husband-and-wife code as she cast about for her reticule. Whenever she favored Roger with a certain pleading look, he was signalled to offer any excuse to release her from company as soon as could be. He had the same signal for her, in his case involving a raised eyebrow, and she often managed to extricate her husband from unpleasant society with a trumped-up excuse of her own. It was a lovely system, and she wondered that all married couples didn't make use of it. Perhaps they did.

"Good God, what a strange young man!" exclaimed the dowager the moment the door closed behind the couple. "I never cease to wonder why the Marquis of Carrborough allowed his daughter to choose such a one. Not even a title!"

Nell shrugged. She supposed Lady Juliana had married for the usual reason: because she had been asked. And there was nothing wrong with the Bickerstaff family. That "strange young man" owned half of Staffordshire. The foreign office business, however, Nell tended to discount. Any post of employment was dangerously close, in her mind, to ungenteel labor.

"Miss Tabor, are you not attending?" A sharp voice broke into Nell's roving thoughts.

"Good gracious! Lady Wormington! Wasn't I?" asked Nell in confusion. "I was worrying, I suppose, over my dear mama."

"I said, Miss, are you going tonight to this literary soirée thing of Maria de Beaulieu's?"

"Not this time," replied Nell vaguely.

Did Lady Wormington know that she never went to those exclusive parties? Maria de Beaulieu never invited her, which was hardly surprising. Nell and Maria had been only distantly civil to each other since their falling-out years ago. Though Nell was well-schooled in the principles of Christian forgiveness, she also knew that, if it were not for the comtesse, she would be married today. The very correct Miss Tabor nearly ground her teeth as she thought of how much she hated Maria de Beaulieu.

Chapter Five

"More champagne, Madame?" murmured a low voice in Maria's ear. She looked up to smile into the sad, dark eyes of Major George Harcourt. The poor dear! He was especially mournful the evening after a proposal. At times like this—when that pale, brooding face stirred tremors of guilt in her bosom—it helped Maria to remember that Harcourt's continually morose bearing was much imitated by certain young tulips of the ton. She didn't doubt that his was a melancholy nature, but there *was* the consolation that he might possibly enjoy his pose a little.

"Thank you, Major, I'd love some," she answered, and he crossed the room to fetch her a glass. Maria, alone for the moment, was free to observe her guests, who swirled and eddied around her like a school of brightly colored fish. But fish, Maria reflected with a smile, wouldn't talk nearly so much. It was gratifying to realize that this evening, like all her literary evenings during the season, would be a success. The musicians in the group had just performed to loud acclaim, and now the evening was given up to conversation. Maria had managed to secure some of the most sought-after names in the literary firmament. Even now, she could see Mr. Coleridge holding forth on the lectures he'd been giving on literature and philosophy, Tom Moore discussing the latest on his noble correspondent Lord Byron, and her own dear friend Miss Ginevra Johnson expounding upon the Rights of Woman with her usual didactic air to an awed circle of females.

Maria sighed. On nights like this she almost believed that—if her eyes were but a little sharper—she might see dear Beaulieu holding forth in one of these clusters of the literati. Though never the center of her life, he had always been a comfortable, fatherly presence. How very much he had taught her, and how sad it had been to lose him after only three years of marriage. The seven years that had since passed had done little to dim his memory. Even now, she would sometimes walk into one of the rooms in this elegant house and be surprised when he was not there.

When the door of the salon opened, Maria snapped out of her melancholy. Heavens, she mustn't let Major Harcourt's gloom influence her. Enjoying the swirling effect of her new gown of silk gauze, she moved across the floor to greet her late-arriving guests. Phillip Renshaw. Excellent! Anne would be so surprised and, Maria dearly hoped, pleased. The figure hovering behind the handsome Mr. Renshaw had to be the country baronet. He was gigantic and mustachioed, with light grey eyes peering in the manner of a startled bird from beneath heavy, dark brows.

"Mr. Renshaw," Maria held out her hand. "How kind of you and your friend to accept my invitation on such short notice."

Renshaw smiled. "Madame, the pleasure is ours. I'm overcome by the honor you do me—and my friend—by asking us here tonight."

His artless smile was most attractive, Maria remarked, as were his blue eyes and his strikingly athletic figure. Maria withdrew her hand from Renshaw's—she must remember not to flirt with this one—and directed her attention to his companion.

"Madame," Renshaw said with another bow. "Do allow me to present my friend, Sir Stephen Wrackham."

Maria's hand was seized by a very large one, and she had to smile at the ticklish sensation of mustachios as the baronet saluted her. "Madame, most happy to make your acquaintance," said Sir Stephen, and he

39

heartily shook the hand he had just kissed.

Maria extricated herself with some difficulty. "*Enchantée,* Sir Stephen. I heard you've but recently come to town. I hope you don't think me overbold to invite you here, but I knew you to be Mr. Renshaw's friend, and I was afraid he might not venture into such dangerous territory as my drawing room without a companion." She smiled up at Sir Stephen, hoping her friendliest manner would put him at ease.

"Not bold. Delightful," cried Sir Stephen. "Most happy. Lit'ry circles, what? An honor."

Renshaw had to smile at his friend's *volte-face.* Wrackham's adamant declaration that he would not be caught in bluestocking company had been hard to overset. It wasn't until Renshaw promised a visit to Watier's after the soirée in Curzon Street that Sir Stephen had assented. Even at the Comtesse de Beaulieu's door, the baronet had continued to be skittish, grabbing Renshaw by the arm and suggesting a detour to White's. The instant he was confronted by what he would no doubt later refer to as a "demmed fine woman," however, Sir Stephen didn't look to be regretting his situation.

It passed through Maria's mind that this oversized baronet definitely had some allure, although she could not think what. Now, how could one unfasten him from Renshaw so that the latter might seek out Anne? Maria's sharp eyes noticed that Renshaw's own had begun to wander, quite as if he were expecting to see someone in particular. How charmingly blatant he was being—but then, his "rescue" of Anne at Richmond hadn't been exactly subtle.

Renshaw took matters into his own hands. "I believe I see some acquaintance over the way," he said brightly. "Will you excuse my leaving Wrackham with you, Madame? I assure you he's a very good sort of fellow, if a bit countrified." With those words and a mischievous look at Sir Stephen, Renshaw moved off in the general direction of Lady Anne.

"Abandoned you to my company, M'dame, what?" Sir Stephen cast a look of frank admiration at Maria. "Talk books now, I expect. Lead the way."

Maria's warm laugh rang out. She suspected his staccato way of speaking was not an affectation as it was among the dandies, but rather due to genuine nervousness. "Oh, my dear Sir Stephen, you mustn't be afraid that this is some sort of schoolroom. It's merely that some of my friends happen to be scholarly. Miss Ginevra Johnson, for instance, whom you must perceive over in that corner, the lady in pearl gray poplin? She is said to have more education in her little finger than all the dons of Oxford rolled together."

"The devil you say!" exclaimed Sir Stephen.

"I'll introduce you later," promised Maria, enjoying the look of alarm that crossed the rugged, good-natured face. Why, he was even rather handsome, and his inability to dissemble gave him charm. "And there are others as well. We can't have you disappointed in your introduction to literary circles."

"Not take the trouble, M'dame, beg you," cried Sir Stephen.

"Oh, it's no trouble," said Maria. Then, having had her joke, she decided to be kind. "But that can wait. For now, sir, tell me what are your impressions of London? Are you being sufficiently amused?"

These words were enough to launch Sir Stephen into a detailed discussion of his favorite subject, himself. For a while, his artless observations of society entertained his hostess, but as the moments passed and he showed no sign of slowing down, she began to cast about in her mind for a change of subject. Sir Stephen was describing, seemingly card by card, his recent run of luck at White's, when Maria noticed Major Harcourt drawing near with two champagne glasses.

Sir Stephen, who had been reveling in the fact that he had the full attention of the loveliest woman he had yet met in London, felt something very like a jealous rage when he realized that this *tête-à-tête* was being interrupted by a pale, medium-sized fellow who came up to them and quite boldly cleared his throat. Then Sir Stephen took a closer look at the intruder.

"Harcourt, b'gad!" he exclaimed. Seizing one of the champagne glasses, he drained it and set it on a table, then pumped the hand he had freed.

"Wrackham, by all that's holy!" said Major Harcourt.

Maria merely stared and sipped at the champagne Harcourt managed to pass to her.

"Same regiment, M'dame," Sir Stephen explained excitedly. His countenance was wreathed in smiles. "Waterloo — not seen each other since — two years. Great chance meeting you like this, Harcourt."

Major Harcourt was quick to agree, but he kept his eye on Maria, sensing that tales of army life were better confined within the walls of one of the clubs.

Maria, realizing that Sir Stephen wouldn't be easily dissuaded from discoursing on that theme, shook her head and smiled indulgently. "You gentlemen must have a thousand things to say to one another," she stated, knowing that, in at least Sir Stephen's case, she wasn't exaggerating. "I must attend to some of my other guests. If you'll excuse me?"

"Madame!" cried Sir Stephen, torn between his desire for feminine company and his overpowering urge to talk of the old days with a long-lost comrade. "Not meaning to drive you off — speak with Harcourt later — club."

"My dear sir, not for worlds would I keep you from doing it now," Maria insisted. She moved swiftly across the room.

"Lovely little lady, that," remarked Sir Stephen when Maria was out of earshot.

"The loveliest one I know," said Harcourt. He sighed in the romantic manner so widely imitated by the younger set.

Sir Stephen was too excited to notice such things. "Now about that little Belgian filly —" he began.

Harcourt interrupted, suggesting that his friend try to hold his voice down, but then he readily entered into the spirit of reminiscence.

Phillip Renshaw, who had never been a soldier, was trying to bring military tactics to bear on the problem at hand. What was the correct approach to Lady Anne Hawley? He could see her well enough, sitting at the center of a group of gentlemen. When he noticed his fellow sportsman Lord Elliot sulking in a corner, Renshaw delayed the issue by going to say a word to his friend.

"My boy, what ails you?" was Renshaw's greeting, delivered with a companionable clap on the back.

Startled out of his brown study, the muscular blond youth glared at the other man. "*She* ails me," he said through his teeth.

Renshaw followed Elliot's gaze. "The Lady Anne? Gave you a set-down, did she?"

"She made some pleasantry at my expense," said Elliot. "Didn't choose to act the lapdog—came away. Damn it, Renshaw, she's playing with me."

Renshaw nodded in sympathy. He knew of the lady's biting wit first hand, and the stolid Elliot could be no match for her there. "I hope it didn't seriously offend you, though. Lady Anne would be sorry to lose your admiration."

"I won't be angry with her more than a minute," said Lord Elliot. "It's that infernal charm of hers, devil take it! But you might let me enjoy myself, Renshaw, while my rage holds." He peered more closely at his friend. "Renshaw! You don't usually attend these bluestocking things, do you?"

Renshaw admitted he did not, wondering what Elliot would say if he knew that Renshaw, too, was there for the purpose of pursuing Lady Anne.

"Well, dashed odd way to spend one's time, ain't it?" replied the young baron, knotting his brows. "She's driving me mad, Renshaw! First I tried to make her jealous by joining forces with Miss Johnson over there—didn't serve. You might leave a fellow."

Renshaw held back a snicker. The formidable Miss Ginevra Johnson, a spinster who valued men solely for their intellects, wasn't the most believable rival to Lady Anne. Renshaw took his leave of Elliot, reasoning that the pangs of thwarted love were best suffered in solitude. If Lady Anne had captivated the young man to such an extent, she must be making enemies right and left among the matchmaking mamas of the ton. Every season has its catch, and this year the popular imagination had lit upon the handsome, blond Baron Elliot.

Renshaw edged his way nearer to Lady Anne, who looked as fine tonight in a low-cut gown of white sarcenet as she had the other day in her riding habit. Her dark curls were bound up by a silver-embroidered white bandeau, lending her a more regal appearance than ever. The place of honor by her side was occupied by none other than that most precious pink of society, Viscount Westhill, who was in the middle of a story that was making the lady and her court laugh.

Fighting down a rush of jealousy, Renshaw reminded himself that there was no harm in Westhill. The slight, light-haired youth—with his extravagant tailoring and affected mannerisms—was *not* in the petticoat line. He was a pet of Lady Anne's, a childhood friend as well as a singing partner.

"Man-milliner," Renshaw murmured under his breath, running his eye over the tulip's garish striped waistcoat, barely visible behind its load of fobs and seals. And pale lavender breeches! Was this young exquisite responsible for the current sickening vogue for lavender breeches, or was he simply following the crowd?

Westhill, sensing Renshaw's hard blue stare, stopped speaking to turn his dead-pale face in indignation upon the interloper, and Lady Anne followed his friend's gaze. "What, my lady," Renshaw greeted his quarry in a friendly, teasing tone, "recovered so soon from your near escape at Richmond?"

"Mr. Renshaw!" exclaimed the lady. "How do you happen to be here, sir?"

"Madame de Beaulieu was good enough to request my presence," answered Renshaw in surprise. He had obviously been vain in assuming that Lady Anne had asked the comtesse to invite himself and Wrackham.

Anne shrugged. So Maria was taking a hand in one's affairs? Well, that was nothing new, for the comtesse was a notorious matchmaker. And was that country squire person here as well? Casting her eyes about, Anne soon made out the large figure of Sir Stephen. Maria must think herself very clever.

"Dear Maria is certainly democratic in her ideas," she said on a sudden devilish impulse. "But then she *is* from America and must be excused."

Renshaw realized that he, like Lord Elliot before him, had been made the subject of one of Lady Anne's pleasantries. The surrounding gentlemen, including that fop Westhill, would use the incident to his cost unless something were done immediately. "I'm sure Madame la Comtesse de Beaulieu need not be excused for any of her behavior," said the gentleman calmly. "But I can hold no grudge against any of her friends whose words might require my forgiveness."

Anne's eyes brightened with the light of battle. Was the man daring to call her ill-mannered? Here was Westhill, already sniggering beside her, and at least two of the other gentlemen were regarding Renshaw in visible admiration. No one got the better of Lady Anne Hawley in the delicate art of raillery. Something must be done, and at once. "Sir, your leniency is wonderful," she said in her coldest tone. "If only your gallantry didn't suffer by comparison."

Her dignity had been salvaged along with her reputation at repartée. Lord Westhill was soon delivering another clever quip, but Anne had to struggle to laugh along with the others. Why should she care that Renshaw, evidently not of a mind to stay and become one of her côterie, had turned on his heel and was crossing the room?

"I swear to you, Aunt Kitty," Maria was saying in another part of the room, "if you and Sir William don't join me at supper, I won't know what to do. I'm to partner Lord James, you know, and he . . ." Maria dropped her eyes and willed herself to blush.

"Heavens, child," gasped Miss Katherine Torrington, "has Lord James been taking liberties? You know I prefer not to deal with Sir William, but in this case nothing could be more necessary. Your own family shall stand by and protect you from that rake. He takes after his brother the duke, I hear."

Maria felt just a bit guilty. It was true that Lord James Lofts had been known to take the slightest of liberties, but not without her permission. He and Maria understood each other and enjoyed a flirtation without a hint of anything serious. Under ordinary circumstances, she wouldn't give up a comfortable interlude with Lord James, but she had promised her kinsman, Sir William Torrington, that he would sup with Aunt Kitty this evening. Sir William, like many another sixty-year-old swain, adored Aunt Kitty, and Maria was ruthless in beating down her aunt's protests that she and Sir William did not see eye to eye. Maria was determined that Aunt Kitty find true love (and, incidentally, an establishment separate from Maria's). Miss Torrington's recent scrape with the shopkeeper had made Maria realize anew that she wasn't up to dealing with her aunt and would rather give over the office to a suitably protective gentleman of a certain age. Sir William met all the requirements.

Aunt Kitty bustled away in a fever of maidenly indignation to find Sir William and lay plans for their rescue of Maria from that dreadful Lord James. As Maria wondered what detail to see to next, two young women rushed up to her.

"Madame, we're so grateful to you for asking us here," exclaimed the younger lady, a small, brown-haired beauty in demure white muslin. "Only think! Tonight I've seen Mr. Coleridge and Mr. Moore and Mr. Luttrell and so many others!"

"Georgina, don't be overly effusive," said the elder, whose more buxom figure was shown to almost too much advantage by a low-cut gown of light blue satin. "Madame, it's a lovely gathering."

"My dears, I'm only sorry Miss Georgina came out too late for the greatest thrill of all," said Maria. "Had she been here last year, she might have seen Lord Byron, but now, with him gone off abroad, I fear she never will." The Miller girls were not favorites of Maria's, but they were closely connected with the Wormington family, and Maria was willing to overlook for Anne's sake such shortcomings of the Millers as their Russell Square direction and their little vulgarities.

Their sister's marriage had caused a stir, to be sure! Young Lord Wormington, Lady Anne's brother, had gone to the Lord Mayor's Ball on a lark, met Miss Pamela Miller, a daughter of the solid merchant class, and, heedless of his mother's vapors, married the girl of his choice. Miss Constance and Miss Georgina Miller had climbed on their sister's shoulders into such inner circles of the ton as Maria's drawing room, and everyone but the highest sticklers had shrugged, muttered a phrase about new blood, and made room for the two attractive girls. For it was evident that they were rich — too evident, in fact, to one of Maria's fastidious taste. Had no one told Miss Miller that it wasn't the thing to wear one's fortune around the neck? Maria surveyed the profusion of large sapphires that decked Constance's bosom, ears, hair, and arms tonight. Even more shocking was the set of emeralds with which Miss Georgina — a young girl just out — was adorned. Their City papa must have paid a king's ransom.

"How exciting to be a young lady in her first season."

47

Maria smiled warmly at Georgina.

"Lord, it's been years since we were in her situation, hasn't it, Madame," said Constance Miller in her frank way. Constance wasn't one to be sensitive about her age or ashamed at having attained it still unmarried. Yes, she informed her lower-born suitors when they accused her so, she was holding out for a title. And why not? Papa said that his money must be good for something. Constance meant to catch a title for herself and a higher one for Georgina, and thanks to the Wormington connection, she now had the means to meet the right men. What a change from her younger days, which had been spent in the fringes of City society where hardly a knight or an honorable had crossed her path. She was past her early twenties, but what did that matter? An heiress such as she would not be put out of the running by a minor thing like age.

"Miss Miller, please don't talk as if we were absolutely ancient," Maria laughed.

"Not at all, Madame," Constance returned in good humor. "We're at our prime, I'm convinced — you, myself, and my sister, Lady Anne Hawley. All of us a cut above the schoolroom chit." She made a face at her sister.

"It's no use trying to set my back up, Constance," said Georgina in a cheerful tone. "You know I was never any use in the schoolroom, so I know you can't mean me."

The sisters laughed heartily together while Maria looked on. When they had recovered their seriousness, Miss Georgina nudged Constance. "Let's not forget the reason we wanted to speak to Madame."

"To be sure not," agreed Constance. She turned to Maria. "We wanted to ask you about two of your guests. Major Harcourt I'm acquainted with, but the tall gentleman is a newcomer to your salon, I think." Miss Miller's honest gaze riveted on Sir Stephen Wrackham, who was deeply engrossed in rough-sounding conversation with Major George Harcourt.

Though the ladies were many feet removed from the baronet, and there were any number of people chattering in between, once in a while some snatch of talk involving "Waterloo," "famous snuff," or "demmed fine women" was audible.

"That is Sir Stephen Wrackham," replied Maria, wondering at her reluctance to impart the information. "He's just come to town from Surrey." She cast a look of indulgent amusement at the baronet. He was a most endearing gentleman, and she somehow felt protective of him. Did she want him for her own court? Surely not.

"*Sir* Stephen?" asked Constance. "Baronet?"

"So I believe. I can't remember," returned Maria coolly. Really! Miss Miller might as well have a pad and pencil, she was so businesslike about the matter.

"Well, I'll soon find out. He seems a sensible man," said Constance decidedly. "And built on a fine, large scale."

Georgina giggled. "Come, Constance, how can you know the gentleman to be sensible? You haven't even met him."

"Well, child, perhaps the comtesse will remedy that for us," her sister retorted.

Maria couldn't refuse the introduction. She had known Constance Miller long enough to be familiar with her blatant huntress's view of the marriage mart, and a part of her—the French, pragmatic part which Beaulieu had schooled into her—agreed with those who called Miss Miller's honesty a breath of fresh air. "You haven't even asked me if Sir Stephen is a married man," she admonished the lady with a little smile.

Constance took no offense. "I vow, Madame, sometimes I am a scatterbrain. Is he?"

Maria was not sure, but she had to offer as her opinion that a gentleman on an extended visit to town, staying with one of London's noted eligibles, must surely be single.

Constance sighed in relief. "I'd lay a wager you're

49

right there. And now, Madame, would you present me to this gentleman? And little Georgina has a fancy to meet your Major Harcourt — if you aren't afraid of having one of your beaux stolen, of course."

Maria beamed at the two Miss Millers. "Major Harcourt is no property of mine, and as for Sir Stephen, I'll be happy to present both of you to him." If these vulgar City girls chose to entrap either gentleman, it was none of Maria's affair. Miss Georgina was probably indulging in a bit of hero worship for an older man, for Major Harcourt had to be twenty years the young girl's senior. And might not Sir Stephen Wrackham be an altogether suitable match for Constance?

A break in the surrounding company brought Major Harcourt into view. He was facing Maria, and she managed to catch his eye. By the language they had developed over years of eye contact at parties, she let him know that she wished his presence and his companion's. He said something to Sir Stephen, and in the distance Maria heard, "What? Says she wants us? B'gad, man, where is she, then?"

As the two men approached, the Miller ladies settled their jewels more firmly on neck and hair. "My dear Major," said Maria as that gentleman arrived, followed by a puzzled Sir Stephen. "How clever of you to understand my silent summons. I wish to make you gentlemen known to two ladies of my acquaintance."

Sir Stephen was soon bending over Miss Constance Miller's hand with a startled air, blinking in the glare of her sapphires. His manner was much the same when he was introduced to Miss Georgina and her emeralds. He was not at all used to such a display of gems. Not that the sight was by any means unpleasant, and after the initial shock wore off, his manner toward both Miss Millers was easy and gallant.

Major Harcourt, after rousing himself to make the acquaintance of the pretty and openly admiring young Georgina, withdrew into his habitual gloomy silence, his eyes on the comtesse. Sir Stephen thus found himself in the enviable position of talking to three ladies at once. Wishing Renshaw could see him, he glanced about until he located his friend in a corner with that excellent young pugilist, Lord Elliot, whom Sir Stephen had met at Jackson's Boxing Saloon. But Renshaw's eye wouldn't be caught, devil take him! Sir Stephen had expected his friend to be near Lady Anne Hawley, and he wondered briefly why that was not the case. Then he turned his full attention back to the women, and began to regale them with his impressions of town life, the fires of his monologue fed by their polite questions. Damned if that buxom woman in the sapphires wasn't a fetching piece! Must be wealthy, too, and M'dame la Countess had definitely said "Miss." The child in white with the emeralds, now, was a bit too young for Sir Stephen's taste. And as for Maria de Beaulieu—But here the baronet's thoughts halted in respect. It did pass through his mind that these blue-stocking affairs weren't so bad after all.

Maria, watching Constance Miller begin her campaign on Sir Stephen Wrackham, suddenly felt depressed. Why was she so terribly fagged? It must be the exertion of the soirée. And her plans for Anne and Mr. Renshaw beginning a flirtation seemed to have gone completely awry. Sighing, she forced herself to concentrate on her guests. For once it was an effort.

By the time she allowed Lord James to partner her in the delicate supper of lobster and cold chicken that she had ordered in such happy expectation of this deadly dull party, she was absolutely listless.

Chapter Six

Maria slept late the morning after her soirée. The servants were used to her habits and took care not to tread a step which might disturb Madame. The day was well advanced when Miss Torrington, no early riser herself, braved her niece's sanctuary.

"Maria, you must get up. It's a lovely spring afternoon," she said in a cheerful, chirping tone.

Maria, struggling to consciousness, took aim with a lace pillow and managed to wing her aunt's cap. "Next you'll be pulling open the curtains to let in the sun, Aunt Kitty, and that I can't permit," she murmured with a resigned, sleepy smile.

"No, dear, I promise I won't," giggled Miss Torrington, carefully replacing the pillow on the bed. But I must tell you that Lady Anne has called and would like most particularly to see you. All the servants were afraid to beard you in your den, but I took courage."

"Oh! Well, of course I'll see Anne." Maria got up, threw on a dressing gown, then surveyed her pale face and tumbled hair in the nearest mirror. Shrugging, she moved to a long chair and gratefully sank down.

Miss Torrington bustled away, and in a matter of minutes Lady Anne appeared in the bedroom. Her gown of striped muslin, with a spencer of cherry red velvet and a high-crowned bonnet, made her look wide awake and cheerful—dismayingly so to Maria's mind.

"Not yet up and about, I see," was Anne's wry comment as she sat down in a wingchair near the fireplace.

52

"It was very late when I got to bed," Maria excused herself.

"Well, my dear, everyone goes to bed late in the season. But I was up with the birds for a brisk canter through the Park on Dark Star."

"Don't quiz me. You went to bed when the birds were getting up, as did I."

"Well, I was up by noon in any case, and that was hours ago. Now I'm going to force you to bestir yourself for a drive in the Park."

"The Park?" Maria's tired eyes revealed puzzlement.

"Yes, you may have heard tell of it. Many people drive there in the fashionable hour, and today we'll join them. Hurry into your best driving costume." Anne rose from her chair and pulled the bellrope.

"Anne, how dare you ring for my maid!"

"Don't scold. I'm going to be insistent, Maria, so you had better give in with a good grace."

Maria knew when she was defeated. She rose from the long chair and crossed the room to examine the cards on three bouquets of flowers which the maids had brought in while she slept. "Have you a particular reason for wanting to drive in the Park today?" she asked, glancing at Anne out of the corner of her eye. "Haven't we agreed that it's too boring to parade there?"

"Well, it is a terrific bore, but one does like to meet with one's acquaintances from time to time." Anne's voice was casual. "Who sent your flowers?"

"The red are from Major Harcourt, of course," said Maria with a shrug. "Always so kind."

"You know my opinion of *that*." Anne shook her head. "Someone should set that poor man free."

Maria ignored this remark. "The pink ones are from Lord James Lofts, with a new poem written in French in compliment to me." With a marked lack of interest, she dropped the poem next to the major's card. "And the third bouquet," she continued, examining two dozen white roses in a lovely oriental vase, "seems to be from a secret admirer. There isn't a card."

Anne, her interest piqued, came over and searched through these flowers in her turn. There was indeed no identification of the giver. "Who do you suppose sent them?"

"Maybe it was Sir William Torrington," Maria said. "He came to my soirée for the first time last night. I've been teasing him to do so for years, for it did seem hard that the head of my English family wouldn't come to my parties simply because he disapproves of women having thoughts in their heads. I'll have to laugh at him for this. He makes such a show of his attachment to Aunt Kitty that he should more properly have sent flowers to her."

The ladies, forgetting for the moment that the flowers were not actually known to be from Maria's kinsman, laughed over Sir William's plight. "I've tried to match those two since Aunt Kitty and I came to England," Maria said. "They quarrel so much that I simply know they're meant for each other."

Anne shook her head at this. "If they really don't see eye to eye —"

At this point Hester, the abigail, entered the room. While Maria began to dress, Anne left to seek out Miss Torrington in the morning room. There she and Maria's aunt spent some comfortable moments discussing the previous night's party. After she had finished pouring into Lady Anne's ears complaints about the difficult Sir William, Miss Torrington remarked, "I'm so glad you're taking Maria out today. I could have sworn she was out of spirits last night at supper."

"She needs more fresh air," said Anne. "Won't you come with us, ma'am? I have Mama's landau, and it can easily seat three."

"No, no, dear Lady Anne, you children go along by yourselves," returned Miss Torrington. "How could you flirt with the gentlemen with an old duenna sitting by?"

Anne argued that Mistress Kitty was *not* an old duenna, courtesy she knew the elder lady expected, and then added with some force that they did not go to the

Park to flirt.

"Well, I know *you* don't, my dear," said Miss Torrington. "But I assure you my niece will have that in her mind. Dear Maria, of course, means nothing by it." She sighed. "Poor thing. So young a widow, and never to have known love. Beaulieu was a fine man, Lady Anne, but their affection for each other wasn't what I would call love."

"Maria was devoted to the comte," said Anne. Maria did not hold such romantic views, Anne knew, and she didn't for a moment regret her marriage—though, as far as Anne could tell, the union had been based solely on Maria's gratitude for an establishment and Beaulieu's wish to educate a young girl. Maria had perfected her French and Latin under her husband's tutelage, but had she been schooled in matters more intimate? That question still plagued society. Anne had never been able to pry the answer out of her friend, but she was fairly certain the Beaulieus' marriage had been platonic.

"And have you, Mistress Kitty, ever been in love?" she asked. For it had always seemed odd that Miss Torrington, such a romantic lady who was a beauty in her middle years (and who must have been dazzling in her youth) should have spent her life a spinster. Even her refusal to countenance Sir William's suit was a mystery when viewed in practical terms.

"No, Lady Anne, I haven't," replied the elder lady with a smile. "Should I find the right man, I will marry. And not before."

So that was it, Anne thought. Miss Katherine Torrington, for all her fifty years, was still looking for her prince. Anne could only respect the older woman's high standards, for something of the same kind was responsible for her own single state at the age of five-and-twenty. She would scorn for herself such a sentimental reason as Mistress Kitty's search for true love, but a certain fastidiousness had definitely held her back from accepting the most eligible offers.

Whatever that sentiment was, it certainly hadn't operated in Maria's case, thought Anne. But then the French were notedly cynical about matters such as marriage, and Maria was very French, by attitude if not by blood: the influence of her emigré husband stretched much further than the occasional use of a French phrase. Anne had often wondered at her friend's lack of sentiment. In a certain way she envied it — unlike Miss Torrington, who was sure that her niece had tragically let a whole dimension of life pass her by.

Maria now entered the room, attired in an almond green pelisse and a frivolous bonnet. She appeared quite wide awake and didn't at all look the part of a tragic heroine. "Well, Anne, let's be off. It's barbarous to drag me out of bed this early, but what's done is done."

The two were soon settled in Lady Wormington's lozenge-emblazoned landau and on the way to Hyde Park. Despite Maria's insistence on the earliness of the hour, it was already five, when the fashionable world of London was wont to display itself in the alleys and drives. As the warm air caressed her skin and fluffy, white clouds moved lazily across the blue spring sky, Maria felt her spirits lifting. She smiled and bowed to the various acquaintances they passed. Lady Juliana Bickerstaff waved from the seat of a daring new high-perch phaeton, and the Duchess of Morland gave the distant nod which was all she ever granted anybody.

"There is Lord Westhill," Maria said, spotting the slight, exquisitely turned-out figure on a nearby walk. "We must stop and speak, so I can thank him again for singing last night."

"He ought to thank *you* for the opportunity of display," laughed Anne, but she managed to hail her young favorite and beckon him to the side of the vehicle, where Maria warmly thanked him for the song — no, it was three songs — that he had consented to perform.

"A mere bagatelle, Madame, assure you," he an-

56

swered modestly with a sweeping bow. "And I will be happy to oblige you at any other time."

"I'm sure the occasion will arise," said Maria graciously.

"And should it not, his lordship will invent one," put in Anne, her eyes twinkling.

Lord Westhill, in high good humor thanks to the perfectly sleek fit of his new coat from Nugee, chose not to be insulted. "Lady Anne, you can only be speaking as one musician to another," he cried. "We both of us must be honest and admit that we owe it to our public to perform as often as possible."

Anne had indeed sung the night before and hadn't been hard to persuade. She was forming a suitably clever reply when she felt a discreet nudge in her ribs.

"Isn't that Mr. Renshaw over the way, my dear?" asked Maria, with an odd note of excitement in her voice. "With his large baronet friend, and—another gentleman?"

Anne let her eyes follow Maria's across a stretch of crowded parkland to where Phillip Renshaw and Sir Stephen Wrackham stood in conversation with a swarthy, unfamiliar man. "I *think* that is Mr. Renshaw," she replied, hiding her own pleasure and nervousness. "But I don't know the darker gentleman. Oh, Robert, who is that with Mr. Renshaw and Sir Stephen Wrackham?" she addressed the young viscount.

Lord Westhill leveled his quizzing glass and peered at the three under discussion. "Good God!" he exclaimed. "That Wrackham fellow is impossible. He calls that a coat?"

"The gentleman with him and Renshaw, my lord," repeated Maria. "Do you know him?"

"Don't believe I do," answered Lord Westhill. "Foreign, from the look of him. No other excuse for that dark a skin. And a beard, of all things. Must be from the back of beyond."

Maria noted in annoyance that Anne had modestly averted her eyes from Renshaw. If anything were to be done, Maria must do it herself. She stared at Sir Stephen Wrackham until she caught his eye, whereupon she gave a pleasant nod.

"I say, Renshaw! There's M'dame la Countess with your Diana," she heard Sir Stephen's booming voice. "Pay respects." Then Maria had the pleasure of seeing him stride across the grass toward her, necessarily followed by Renshaw and the intriguing, dark gentleman. She stole a glance at Anne and thought she detected the ghost of a smile. If she had overheard the last remark, Anne must be flattered, for it was proof that Renshaw had been talking of her.

As soon as Sir Stephen Wrackham reached the side of the carriage, he seized the comtesse's hand and saluted it warmly. "M'dame! Delightful soirée. Pleasure to meet you here, Lady Anne." He bowed to the regal figure beside Maria. "A pleasure. Not riding?"

"Obviously. And neither are you, Sir Stephen," said Anne. She tried to hide her distraction. Mr. Renshaw and his unknown friend, who hadn't chosen to follow Rackham's breakneck pace across the green, were only now approaching the landau.

"No, not riding," agreed Sir Stephen genially. "Rode earlier. M'self and Renshaw saw you — from afar, y'know."

Anne nearly blushed.

Lord Westhill was inspecting Sir Stephen at close quarters. The young exquisite, raising his darkened brows in consternation, blanched as he scrutinized the larger gentleman's deplorable coat.

"Lord Westhill, Sir Stephen Wrackham," said Maria. "I don't recall if you met last night."

"We've met," said Sir Stephen. "White's. Eh, Westhill?"

"Sir Stephen and I are indeed acquainted," admitted Westhill with a delicate shudder.

Renshaw and his other friend were now beside the carriage. "Madame!" Renshaw's greeting was jovial. "And Lady Anne. What a delight to encounter two

58

such charming ladies." Having saluted Maria's hand, he let his eyes meet Anne's. He was nervous, that lady noted—as unsure as she was. She suddenly relaxed.

"I'm so happy to see you, Mr. Renshaw," she said in an attempt at reconciliation. She had gotten the best of him last night in their verbal sparring, but it was social folly to make enemies among the Corinthian set. Making up with him was the wise thing to do.

"Your happiness couldn't equal mine, Lady Anne," returned Mr. Renshaw with a smile. The cordiality between them fully restored, Renshaw commenced to introduce his foreign-appearing companion to the ladies. "Madame la Comtesse de Beaulieu, Lady Anne Hawley, give me leave to present Mirza Ali Abdul Khan, newly arrived in town as an emissary from the court of Ispahan. My lord, the two most charming women in London."

Maria had felt the foreign gentleman's eyes upon her ever since he and Mr. Renshaw had come up to the carriage, but she had chosen not to stare back, however much she might wish to. Now the introduction compelled her to look into the pair of fine, brown eyes which gazed at her in evident admiration from a darkly handsome face. Maria had hardly ever seen a man with a beard before, and it occurred to her to wonder how that neatly trimmed oddity would feel beneath one's fingers. The thought made her blush.

Lord Abdul was hardly taller than Viscount Westhill, but with an athletic figure shown to much advantage in a flawlessly cut coat and snug-fitting pantaloons in the first stare of Continental fashion. Only an extremely large ruby in the intricate folds of his cravat betrayed that his origins were far more exotic than those of his male companions. It made one long to see him in the costume he must wear in Persia. And perhaps he had a harem at home! Maria found herself fascinated, not disgusted, by the thought. Never in her life had she met a man who was so much out of the common way.

She held out her hand.

"Madame." Lord Abdul's deep voice revealed only a slight foreign accent. "I am overwhelmed."

"How do you do, milord," Maria replied. He seemed to have to tear his eyes away to pay his compliments to Lady Anne, whom he nevertheless favored with an admiring look. Maria experienced an irrational flash of jealousy on seeing her friend so honored.

After Westhill had been presented to the eastern gentleman and had eyed the ruby suspiciously through his quizzing glass, Renshaw asked Lady Anne for the pleasure of her company on a ride the next morning. She agreed. This meeting with the Persian emissary reminded her that Renshaw had been involved in politics now and again. Yes, he had been one of Lord Castlereagh's equerries at the Vienna Congress a few years before. And his acquaintance with Lord Abdul proved that he was still connected, however casually, with the foreign office. Renshaw rose up a notch in Lady Anne's estimation, for she had been thinking of him as a useless, albeit intriguing, sportsman.

When the conversation lagged to the point of leering glances and blank or flirtatious looks, Sir Stephen took it upon himself to break the spell. "Excellent weather, what?" he said loudly. "You agree, M'dame?" He smiled up at Maria.

She had begun to feel too warm under the eyes of Lord Abdul, and she was grateful for even so commonplace an interruption. "Very fine for this time of year," she answered, struck by the fact that Sir Stephen Wrackham did, at least, try his best in a social situation. What a wonderful man he was, so amusing.

"Wrackham, your perception is exceptional. The weather is indeed fine, and I'm sure we all agree," put in Renshaw with a laugh. "Milord Abdul is, I'm certain, used to a far different climate, but luckily he's been spared our English rain for the moment."

Here Lord Abdul joined in. "Everything in England—the weather included—is a delight to me." His eyes were still on Maria.

"Then you, milord, are just the same as I," said that lady, "for I was also delighted with everything here when I came from Philadelphia ten years ago."

"America, b'gad!" exclaimed Sir Stephen. "Renshaw mentioned—I'd forgotten. Find England to your taste, M'dame?"

Maria nearly laughed. It had been at least nine years since anyone had asked her that. "I like it very much, sir."

"And you, m'lord?" Sir Stephen bowed to the other foreigner in the company.

"It is much to my taste," responded the gentleman from Ispahan. He returned the bow, but his liquid, dark eyes did not leave Maria.

"Famous." Sir Stephen beamed upon everyone in simple pleasure, his pride as an Englishman satisfied as well as his ability to maintain a good conversation. The subject of foreign parts having been alluded to, he next saw fit to regale the company with tales of his own adventures during the late war.

"Good heavens," said Lady Anne before many minutes of this had been allowed to go by. "You will excuse us, gentlemen, but the horses mustn't be left standing any longer." She gave a signal to her driver. It was perfectly true that the team had been restless for some time and must move on, but Anne could have sworn that Maria gave her an annoyed look.

"Lady Anne, you cannot abandon us," cried Westhill.

"No, indeed," added Renshaw with a charming smile.

"Gentlemen, we must. Good day."

"Good day, gentlemen," Maria was forced to add. Her eyes lingered for an instant on Lord Abdul. She would have to make some enquiries.

To her shock, Maria found that Sir Stephen was grasping her hand. "Famous soirée, M'dame—must thank you again," the baronet said eagerly. "Lovely ladies there—yourself most lovely, and Lady Anne—

and Miss Miller."

"Miss Miller? She would be charmed, sir," said Maria, a bit confused. "Is there some message you would send her?" It seemed strange that the baronet should pull the name of Constance Miller out of the air for no reason. The City heiress had already captured him, then.

Sir Stephen looked alarmed. "No, M'dame, many thanks. Greetings if you see the lady, no question. I only meant to compliment the ladies present — all the ladies."

"How gallant, sir," said Maria, still a bit hard put to follow the circumlocutions of Sir Stephen's mind. "My guests — my female ones — would be flattered." The landau began to move. "Good day," she added with a little wave of her hand and a special smile for Sir Stephen.

Wrackham didn't know any more than Maria why he had mentioned Miss Miller. He had hoped to praise the comtesse's looks without seeming particular in his attentions and felt that he had pulled it off rather well. She had seemed pleased with his general compliment to the ladies at her party. But why the devil he had chosen to single out Miss Miller he couldn't say. "Snuff?" he said with a shrug, taking an enamelled box out of his pocket. "You won't find this sort amiss. M'lord?"

Each gentleman accepted a pinch. When the operation was complete, and the box returned to the pocket of the coat which so alarmed Lord Westhill, they all stared after the landau.

"Artemis and Aphrodite out driving together," remarked Renshaw. "A sight you won't see anywhere but in London, my lord," he told the foreign gentleman with a smile.

The diplomat appeared somewhat confused, as did Sir Stephen, but neither man demanded an explanation.

"Latin names," Wrackham muttered. "Town's an odd place. Get Latin at school."

Westhill sniggered at this, and the quizzing glass

came into play. "One must return to classical times," he informed Sir Stephen in a nasal drawl, "to find terms adequate to praise such ladies as the Comtesse and Lady Anne. Unfortunate you don't approve."

"Do approve," cried Sir Stephen. "Never said I didn't."

"Who could not approve any compliment made to two such beauties, whatever its source?" put in Renshaw, still looking after the carriage.

"There is indeed much beauty in your London, Renshaw," added Abdul. His eyes were thoughtful. "A widow, did you say?"

Chapter Seven

The Bruton Street establishment of Madame Hélène was one of the most discreetly elegant houses of fashion in Mayfair. Madame, a rare talent in her chosen *métier*—which she had elevated to an art—dressed the most beautiful and original women in town. Maria de Beaulieu, Lady Anne Hawley, and Lady Juliana Bickerstaff all frequented her rooms. She had become, in fact, the rage of the ton.

Today the modiste was giving her personal attention to two of her richest customers, the Miss Millers. Though the papa of these ladies did engage in trade, it was Madame's opinion that his money was as good as many another's, and his daughters were certainly a pleasure to dress: both of them were extremely attractive. The elder sister was a handsome, well-developed creature whose taste was for the very best. Little Georgina did not care what she had on, true, but her sister saw to it that no expense was spared. In any case, Madame Hélène preferred that very young girls defer to the modiste in matters of dress. With Georgina it was easy. There was never any argument, never any insistence on a costume too *soignée* or too ornate for one of her pristine youth. She accepted the best willingly and showed every costume to advantage with her slight, pretty figure and soft brown hair. Her little face always held an animated expression which proved that her enthusiasm for areas other than fashion was real indeed. Her elder sister's eyes revealed that same wholehearted enjoyment of life—a quality which was, Madame ad-

64

mitted in secret, more becoming to a lady's appearance than any garment the canniest Frenchwoman could supply. If only the Millers wouldn't insist on ruining the elegance of their costumes by the addition of inappropriate quantities of *bijoux!*

Constance Miller was being fitted for a yellow satin ballgown overlaid with spangled gauze, a dress she had ordered to accompany the necklace of yellow diamonds Papa had just given her. She had brought the necklace with her today, and the sight was, Madame Hélène assented, most striking.

"Now if Mademoiselle will but limit her jewels to this lovely *parure*," said Madame in a pleading tone. A sharp-featured, auburn-haired little woman in a severe dark gown, she was supervising the hemming of the gown by one of her seamstresses. Constance regarded herself in a large gilt mirror, and Georgina looked on from a nearby armchair.

"Nonsense, Madame. I have some perfectly lovely gold and diamond bracelets in my jewel case which would suit to perfection," laughed Constance. "You can't expect me to let them sit gathering dust because of your ideas of simplicity. No, you needn't lecture me, my mind is made up. And would you have me forget the yellow diamond earrings Papa bought me to go with the necklace?"

"Papa says we must display our most valuable assets to a censorious world now that we find ourselves in the first circles," put in Georgina as she thumbed listlessly through a copy of *La Belle Assemblée*.

Papa Miller could be in the right, thought Madame Hélène in her shrewd way. If the beauty and noble connections of these City girls didn't get them husbands, a pointed display of their wealth would surely turn the trick. But how regrettable from the modiste's point of view!

"Yes, Georgina," Constance said. "I've been in the world some eight years longer than you, and I can tell you that Papa is right. Of course one is beset by every kind of fortune hunter, as I've warned you, but among those unprincipled rakes are some respectable noblemen who will quite naturally be impressed by wealth. Indeed, what gentleman isn't? Lord, when I think of the dozens of vulgar cits who used to offer for me, it makes my head spin. And to think I nearly gave up on a title and settled for that rich Mr. Carter, Papa's friend. It was a very near thing, I assure you. Then sister Pamela caught Lord Wormington and I took heart again. What can be done once—and by Pamela, of all people—can be done again." She gave her reflection a determined look.

"But, Constance," said Georgina, "must it be a title?"

Her elder sister laughed at the young girl's sudden seriousness. "Lord no, child, but we hope it will be in your case. You've been presented to any number of eligible peers already, and you've only just come out. Should you set your heart on a man without a title, only see to it that his background is unimpeachable, and Papa is sure to give his consent. But, my dear, no one from the City."

"I wasn't thinking of anyone in the City," said Georgina.

"La, you aren't really in love with Major Harcourt, child? That was surely only a whim on your part, wanting to meet him the other night? He's deep in the toils of Maria de Beaulieu." Constance gave her sister a piercing look.

Georgina shrugged, trying her best to appear unconcerned. "Are they engaged?"

"No. Maria isn't one to marry, but to keep gentlemen dangling for years at a time. So she's done with the poor major. I warn you, sister," said Constance as casually as she could. "Don't be so foolish as to think of him. He's years too old for you, and what do we know of his family?"

"We might inquire?" suggested Georgina.

"Sister! Show me some encouragement from this man first, and then we'll make our inquiries. Or, rather, Papa's man of business will." Constance decided she would put Major Harcourt out of Georgina's mind by seeing to it that the young girl met more eligible nobles nearer her own age. Pity it was that Lord Elliot hadn't seemed to notice Georgina when they had met at Almack's, or again the other night. Now *there* was a fine figure of a man.

"Ah, the miseries of *l'amour!*" cried Madame Hélène, whose sharp ears had missed none of this exchange. She had often remarked that her clientèle didn't consider her presence to be a hindrance when confessing their innermost secrets. True, she didn't move in the social circles of any of them, but information gleaned this way had been useful to her more times than she could count. "But Mademoiselle Georgina is very young," she added with a smile at both ladies. "Now. If she would care to try the blossom pink muslin? We have only the hem left to do, as on Mademoiselle Miller's gown."

Georgina gave a small groan—fittings bored her so much—but she followed Madame Hélène without further protest into the other room.

A commotion in the outer salon indicated that another client had arrived. "Ah, that will be Mademoiselle Tabor, to be fitted for the sky blue crêpe," announced Madame Hélène, and she bustled away. "You will excuse me?"

Constance nodded absently, her eyes on her own reflection. This gown should be perfect for the coming ball at Morland House. Now her only question was whether Sir Stephen Wrackham would be there. If he should be, she meant to dazzle him.

Madame Hélène fluttered back into the room followed by Miss Eleanor Tabor, the latter clad in a deep blue pelisse and blue-lined straw bonnet that was almost severe in its quiet elegance. "Miss Miller," the young woman greeted Constance with the slightest of nods.

"Miss Tabor, how do you do?" replied Constance

heartily. She had never chosen to respond in kind to Miss Tabor's coolness. She knew of Eleanor Tabor's distinguished lineage and was thus aware of the reasoning behind her frozen manner. Besides, she could not recall seeing Nell Tabor behave warmly toward anyone, be they noble or common.

"How do *you* do?" countered Nell with a distant little smile.

"Very well indeed, Miss Tabor. My little sister and I are just seeing to our newest ball dresses—for the coming affair at Morland House, of course." Constance wanted to make sure that Nell Tabor knew she and Georgina had every entrée to the magic circle of the ton.

Miss Tabor gave another tight nod of her head before passing on into the inner room.

Constance continued to be absorbed in her own reflection until Georgina came in with Madame Hélène and a subordinate seamstress, who was directed in pinning up the hem of the blossom pink muslin. The gown was altogether charming—elegant in its lines, trimmed richly about the hem with rouleaux and ribbon knots—yet still demure enough for one of Georgina's tender years.

"My love, that costume will be ravishing with your diamonds—and perhaps the ruby pendant Papa gave you for your eighteenth birthday," said Constance in admiration.

Madame Hélène shuddered at the idea of such a quantity of jewels on a young girl just out, but she had given up advising Miss Miller for the day and said nothing aloud.

"I daresay," shrugged Georgina. "It doesn't much signify what one wears. Do you know that Miss Tabor was abominably rude to me just now, Constance?" she added in a lowered voice. "She positively looked *through* me instead of returning my greeting." Her voice grew even softer. "Is it only our unfortunate connection with trade?"

"Probably, dear, but you mustn't mind it," said Constance in an offhand manner. "Nell Tabor has very high standards."

Georgina made a face. "They must be high," she said. "Lady Anne Hawley is our sister, and Lord Wormington our brother."

"Mademoiselle Tabor is perhaps — how you say — absentminded *ce matin*," suggested Madame Hélène, who had been discreetly all ears as usual.

"It could well be," agreed Constance.

Georgina gave another shrug — which was most disconcerting to the busy seamstress — then stared into space.

"Mademoiselle Georgina! *Ne bougez pas!*" admonished Madame Hélène before rushing back to the other room.

Georgina was no scholar of French, but she had heard that identical phrase from Madame's lips often enough to understand that she was being desired not to move.

The modiste returned to the room behind Miss Tabor, who was wearing a sky blue gown which was most effective with Eleanor's blue eyes and flaxen hair. The elegantly draped overskirt of crêpe suited her slight figure to perfection.

"Now I pray you, Mademoiselle, observe the effect of the drapery in this large mirror," said Madame Hélène. She stationed her client before the most imposing of the many gilt-framed looking glasses which decked the walls of the salon. "You perceive that it is as you asked. Not at all *décolleté*, a sweeping line, *mais très feminine.*"

"You've done well as usual, Madame," admitted Nell, peering at her reflection.

"I must say how much I admire you in that color, Miss Tabor," put in Constance.

When favored with such an obviously genuine compliment, even Eleanor Tabor had difficulty maintaining the proper coldness towards these impossible City people. She allowed herself to smile at Constance.

"Why, thank you. Light blue was always my color," she said with a touch of smugness. "And that gown you're wearing is most striking," she added with particular leniency. Though the golden gown might be becoming to Miss Miller, Nell couldn't approve of such *décolletage*. It was quite shocking, in fact.

After exchanging compliments, the ladies warmed a little toward each other. Georgina looked on silently while Miss Miller and Miss Tabor held a superficial conversation about their mutual acquaintance. Miss Miller was certain that Miss Tabor had heard thus-and-such of Lady Juliana Bickerstaff's recent purchase of a high-perch phaeton. Miss Tabor wished Miss Miller to know that the dowager Countess of Wormington had lately paid a visit to herself. She also took the opportunity to convey her regards to Miss Miller's sister, the young countess.

"I'll remember to do so when I next write to Pamela," said Constance. "She is increasing, you know, and inclined to be bored. I write her every week with all the latest London gossip. They are quite buried in Kent."

"But Castle Wormington is surely one of the finest seats in all England," Nell pointed out. She was fond of the country herself, had a special weakness for great country houses. On the rare occasion when she was invited to one, she amused herself no end.

"Much Pamela cares for that," laughed Constance. "She isn't much use in the country. Won't ride. She drives Lady Anne quite mad."

Nell Tabor smiled. "Pity," she said. "But speaking of Lady Anne, how does she do, pray? I hear Mr. Phillip Renshaw is her latest conquest."

"Is he?" asked Constance in surprise.

"I have my information from Juliana Bickerstaff, who has it on the best authority," said Nell. "But perhaps it's all exaggeration. Heaven knows I mean your sister-in-law no ill in speaking of it. Poor Lady Anne is constantly in the company of Maria de Beaulieu, and *she* is the greatest flirt in London. Her reputation might

70

be rubbing off on Lady Anne." Nell ⸱

"The Comtesse isn't in *your* good boo⸱
remarked Constance.

"Let's just say that I find much of the behavi⸱
exhibits to be in atrocious taste," amended Miss Tabo⸱
with a sly smile.

"Is the Comtesse quite wild, then?" asked the wide-eyed Georgina.

"Miss Georgina, you are much too young to know about such things," said Nell in the tone of a stern governess. These were the first words she had addressed to the young girl.

"Come now, Miss Tabor," said Constance. "Maria de Beaulieu might be a flirt, but she means nothing by it."

"*That* is the worst kind of flirt," sniffed Miss Tabor. "She'll find herself in trouble over it, mark my words."

Constance, sensing that the conversation was on very thin ice, deftly turned the subject. It was not until the Miller girls were in the carriage and on their way home that Georgina brought up the topic again.

"Why is Miss Tabor so horrid rude when speaking of our friend?"

"Which friend?" inquired Constance, for several different people had been mentioned by Nell Tabor, and none had appeared to much advantage.

"The Comtesse de Beaulieu, of course," elaborated Georgina. "She abused her quite roundly."

Constance sighed. She didn't like to gossip, and certainly Georgina didn't require a direct answer to this question. On the other hand, her young sister might derive some benefit from hearing the tale. "Well, sister, there is a reason for her abuse," she began. "If I should tell you the story, it mustn't go beyond this carriage, for it's long ago and all but forgotten. Have I your promise?"

"Yes. Do tell me," urged Georgina.

"My dear, it involves a scandal," said Constance, "and it might not do you any harm to be warned against the kind of rash behavior that ruined Miss Tabor's life."

... her life?" Georgina began to
... everything. She was an avid
... ...al novels, and the heroines' lives
... ...ed by appalling and shocking circum-

... her chances of making a good marriage,
... *is* a young lady's life," continued Constance.
... child, here is the tale. When Miss Tabor was just
out, about your own age, she quite foolishly eloped.
And as if that in itself weren't bad enough, it was with
her dancing master that she ran off to Gretna. It was
said she was in love, and that she honestly intended
marriage — *that* sort of a marriage would have been the
wreck of her life, to be sure — but they never made it to
Scotland. They were found out, and Mr. Tabor
brought his daughter back home, but not before she'd
been out all night with her intended bridegroom."

Georgina stared. "All night?"

"Yes, and to her cost, the story leaked out. Her reputation was ruined." Constance paused for effect. "And
that, child, could well be the reason for Miss Tabor's
overly formal ways today. She's making up for that one
indiscretion — eight years ago it must be."

Georgina looked puzzled. "But what has the Comtesse de Beaulieu to do with all this?"

"It's a bit tangled. There are two things really," said
Constance. "To begin with, Nell Tabor and Maria were
great friends at that time. Nell confided to Maria her
tendre for the dancing master, and the Comtesse mentioned the matter to her husband — whether in confidence or no, who can tell? The Comte de Beaulieu
belonged to the same club as Nell's father and warned
him of the attachment, so Nell's plans were foiled.
Then Mr. Tabor had the bad taste to bruit about his
gratitude to the Beaulieus and thus bring the matter to
Nell's ears. It's never pleasant to have a confidence broken."

Georgina nodded. "But that's so many years ago.
Can't she forgive the comtesse?"

"She did forgive her, for Maria de Beaulieu begged her to," said Constance. But there's something else that Miss Tabor has against the comtesse." She frowned. "I don't know if *you* need to hear this part, though."

"Oh, you can't leave me hanging," urged Georgina.

Constance had to agree. "Very well. As you might imagine, Miss Tabor has hardly received an eligible offer since that elopement of hers, for her fortune isn't large, my dear, and the scandal was. Her manner, too, is at fault. She doesn't know how to behave with gentlemen. She's too openly on the catch for them. There's nothing of the actress in her. In any case, several years ago she met a gentleman who seemed to be growing fond of her."

"And he was?"

"Major George Harcourt," intoned Constance.

"*My* Major Harcourt?"

"Indeed. And they might have made a match of it — Lady Juliana Bickerstaff, a close friend of Nell's, says it was a very near thing — had not Maria de Beaulieu come into the picture."

Georgina looked down. "So Major Harcourt turned from Miss Tabor to the comtesse."

"He did," said Constance. "And Nell has never forgiven Maria. Oh, they meet in company and are civil, but there is nothing like friendship between them now. And there you have the explanation of Miss Tabor's words today."

"Thank you, Constance, for telling me. I needed to know," said Georgina. Then she added in a small voice, "He must be very much in love."

"Major Harcourt? Of course. You mustn't think of him, dear," Constance said. She reasoned that the story of Nell Tabor's failed romance with the major might be very useful in making Georgina give up such a futile chase before it had really begun.

"Still, he hasn't offered marriage," Georgina considered aloud.

"Or she hasn't accepted. Remember, Maria is one to

keep them dangling. And why should she marry? She's a titled widow — a French title only, but still given to her by courtesy — and she has a substantial fortune. She has no need to be in a hurry."

Georgina frowned in thought. "Major Harcourt changed his mind once. He could change it again."

"Georgina, I beg you not to have your head in the clouds over Major Harcourt. Oh, a handsome, brooding face has its attractions, I know. And the major is a famous character — what with all the young bucks who imitate his listless ways. But he has no title, and very likely no fortune to speak of." Constance frowned.

Georgina said no more, but she gave a small sigh and turned her head to look out the window. She had a lot of thinking to do.

Chapter Eight

Lady Anne made it a point when in town to attend the Opera as often as she could. Two nights following the afternoon she and Maria had met with Renshaw and his diplomat friend in Hyde Park, she was engaged to do just that.

Lady Juliana Bickerstaff kept a box at the Opera and had invited Anne and Maria to join her and her husband, and the young women were to bring escorts of their choice. Anne and Maria, though known widely as originals, showed no imagination at all in their selection of the favored gentlemen. They simply did the usual and sought the protection of Lord Westhill and Major Harcourt. Lord Westhill was always eager to hear the opera, and Major Harcourt was not far behind in his eagerness to be with Maria. So it was that the ladies found themselves in the Bickerstaff box, accompanied by their most favored old friends. Both Lady Anne and the comtesse were somewhat on edge about the evening's possible outcome. The same question was in both their minds: would Mr. Phillip Renshaw be there with his friend the eastern gentleman?

"Dear heaven, what a delicious squeeze," cried Lady Juliana as the group made itself comfortable. As the female of rank and nominal chaperone, she quite naturally settled into the chair with the best view of both stage and pit and let her gaze rove over the tiers of boxes. "The Regent is to be here tonight. Perhaps that's the reason for the crowd. I swear I see everyone I've ever met." She began her favorite occupation of waving and smiling at those closest to her.

Major Harcourt, clearing his throat, leaned towards Maria. "You are looking lovely tonight, Madame," he ventured.

"Thank you, Major," replied Maria with a smile, her eyes

75

scanning the house. She knew she did indeed look well in her gauzy blue gown, with the diamond necklace Beaulieu had given her on their last Christmas together twinkling at her bosom. She had dressed herself thinking that she might possibly encounter Lord Abdul.

Lord Elliot and a clutch of his large-boned sporting friends were jostling each other in a box across the way, but Renshaw and Lord Abdul weren't with them, Maria noted. Why did such young men attend the opera? And if they must, why did they not stay in the pit where they belonged? Feeling suddenly cross, she pointed Elliot's party out to her companions.

Lord Westhill drawled, "So, Lady Anne, I won't have to compete with Elliot tonight for your attention."

"You never do, you know," laughed the lady. Her eyes, like Maria's, were busy darting here and there in the crowd.

"Oh!" Maria let out a little gasp. "Anne! Isn't that Mr. Renshaw there in the corner box? With Lord—Lord Abdul, wasn't that the name? The gentleman we met the other day?"

Anne turned slowly and deliberately in the direction indicated by her friend. Her eyes immediately met those of Mr. Renshaw. Confused, she smiled briefly and looked away.

"I believe they've seen us," said Maria. She started to blush, for she didn't doubt that those intense dark eyes which had so disconcerted her in the Park were regarding her fixedly.

"Hmph," said Mr. Roger Bickerstaff, looking as though he would rather be anywhere else on the planet. "So that's the Persian fellow. Wondered what he looked like."

"Quite an exotic person, upon my word," contributed Lady Juliana. "I hear he was quite attentive to you in the park the other day," she said to Maria.

Maria shrugged, wondering if Lady Juliana's spies were behind every blade of grass. Her friend's powers of tattle-mongering—or would that be tattle-gathering?—never ceased to amaze her.

The appearance of the foreign gentleman was causing a

great sensation. The whispers from other boxes seemed all to concern him, and Maria noted with something very like jealousy the languishing looks which several beauties of the ton were directing at the swarthily handsome foreigner.

"Wears a ruby in the daytime," was young Westhill's comment. His quizzing glass quivered ominously. "I believe that ill-dressed baronet is in back of the box as well," he added with a well-bred shiver. If Sir Stephen's morning coat had been so upsetting to the discriminating mind, his evening dress would surely be frightful. Lord Westhill could only hope that he would not be called upon to view such a horror at close quarters in the course of the evening.

Maria's eyes also picked out the mustachioed countenance of Wrackham. She bowed pleasantly, and a frank smile from the baronet was her reward. Then she returned to the dangerous pastime of gazing surreptitiously at Lord Abdul, an exercise interrupted only briefly by the flamboyant entrance of the Regent in the company of Lady Hertford.

Neither Anne nor Maria was sure what went on during the performance, but both ladies came suddenly to life during the intermission. "Perhaps Renshaw and his friends will visit our box," remarked Maria casually.

"Would you care to walk up and down the hall, Madame?" asked Major Harcourt, quite as if he hadn't heard the lady's remark. Throughout the whole performance thus far, his eye had seldom been on the singers.

"Why, no, thank you, Major," replied Maria. "But should you and Lord Westhill wish to do so, please feel free to leave Lady Anne and me alone." Mr. Bickerstaff had already escorted his lady out for some refreshment. "I'm quite a capable chaperone for Anne, and perhaps Mr. Renshaw's party will come to see us." She smiled innocently at Major Harcourt, who responded with one of his more morose glances and kept his seat.

Westhill and Lady Anne were enjoying themselves quizzing the company. If Anne's attention span was shorter than normal, Westhill either did not notice or was too courteous to mention the fact. The young tulip was in the middle of critiquing the headdress of a dowager sitting opposite when the curtains in back of the box parted, and Renshaw came in. He was followed, as expected, by his two friends. Lord Abdul wore flawlessly sober evening dress, the severity of his black costume set off by the large jewel in his cravat and a wonderfully ornate brocade waistcoat. And Sir Stephen Wrackham had on a loosely cut coat worse than anything Westhill could have imagined in his wildest nightmares.

"Good evening, Mr. Renshaw," said Anne as the gentleman made his bow before her.

"Lady Anne, your servant," murmured Renshaw, taking her hand. His friendly eyes glittered.

Wrackham, seeing Renshaw engaged with his Greek heroine, hastened to the side of the comtesse and grasped her small hand with his usual heartiness. "M'dame!" he cried in high spirits. "Saw you across the way — your most obedient — lovely gown, M'dame." Quite pleased with himself for turning such a pretty compliment, he gazed down at Maria with open admiration.

Maria blushed, but not on account of Sir Stephen. She greeted the baronet politely, half-wishing that she and he might have a chance sometime to further their friendship. She tried to indicate that he might now feel free to speak with Major Harcourt, but Sir Stephen showed no inclination to move from in front of her. He left her no choice but to stretch out her hand to the foreign gentleman and call his name. "So kind of you to pay us your respects, milord," she added with a smile.

Sir Stephen was shifted to Major Harcourt's vicinity as Lord Abdul bumped against him in his haste to greet Maria. Her green eyes didn't leave the Persian's dark ones as he kissed her hand. "Madame," said his lordship in that intriguing voice. "I am most pleased to do so."

Major Harcourt cleared his throat, reminding Maria that one introduction had not yet been made. She speedily presented Lord Abdul to her escort. To her dismay, the major then engaged the diplomat in a masculine conversation which seemed chiefly to turn upon horseflesh. Sir Stephen, rather than join them, took this opportunity to return to Maria's side.

"Opera," he said, surveying the house.

Maria had to smile.

"My first time," added the gentleman in a confiding manner. "Famous sport."

Maria decided to be philosophical: although she might really wish to speak with Lord Abdul, Sir Stephen was also intriguing in his way. She tried to draw him out on his musical interests and was surprised to find herself laughing at his ingenuous description of a concert of Ancient Music he had recently blundered his way into. Only once or twice did Maria's eyes slide to Lord Abdul, so tantalizingly near, so different from any man she had ever known. . . .

Anne and Renshaw were having difficulties, as Lord Westhill seemed determined to provide the whole of their entertainment himself. He had begun by voicing his approval of Renshaw's coat and was now elaborating on the theme of haberdashery, the merits of Weston versus those of Nugee being brought forth for the entertainment of his audience.

Renshaw watched Lady Anne covertly as he murmured monosyllabic replies to the frivolous remarks of a man he considered a useless tulip. Good God! She seemed to be enthralled by the conversation of this man-milliner. They were constantly together, Westhill and she. It couldn't be possible that she had a genuine interest in the boy, could it?

"Westhill, enough of your frippery talk," said Lady Anne. This unexpected voicing of his own thoughts relieved Renshaw for a moment. Then he considered that such free speech was certainly a sign of an intimacy.

"Let's return to quizzing our neighbors. It's vastly more amusing and our duty as operagoers," said the lady with a satirical smile.

Westhill's laugh—a very affected laugh, to Mr. Renshaw's way of thinking—rang out. "Ah, yes, it's too true, Lady Anne," he said in mock sadness. He shrugged his exquisitely clothed shoulders and raised his brows. "You and I are in the minority. Who else but the two of us came here tonight for the purpose of hearing the opera? We are, perhaps, the only ones in the polite world who can claim that. Unless," he turned towards Renshaw with a bow, "our companion Renshaw is also one such?"

"I enjoy the music," said Renshaw shortly, returning the young viscount's bow. So Westhill and Lady Anne met on common ground in their interest in music!

The intermission soon drew to a close, and people began returning to their seats. When Renshaw, Wrackham, and Abdul were forced to take their leave, all did so with every sign of reluctance.

Maria, in the act of offering Lord Abdul her hand in parting, suddenly felt a piercing gaze upon her — a gaze other than the burning one of the Persian gentleman. There was nothing odd about such a feeling, for everyone went to the opera to ogle everyone else, but Maria felt compelled to turn and see who it was regarding her. She started upon realizing that his royal highness the Prince Regent, leaning back in his ease in the royal box, was nodding at her as if in approval. He raised his hand in a brief gesture of greeting.

How odd! She had never been associated with the Carlton House set, would be surprised if the prince remembered her name from her court presentation, and was certainly not the type of woman to attract him. She lowered her eyes in respect, not knowing what response to make to such an intimate-seeming salute.

"That Lord Abdul you were talking to is a dashing fellow, Madame." It was Roger Bickerstaff, of all unlikely people, claiming Maria's attention, and all thought of the Regent flew from her mind. She and Lady Juliana's stolid husband had never exchanged two words. "Bound to be a devil with the ladies," continued Bickerstaff. "Women like that sort of thing."

"You don't mean it," put in Lord Westhill. "A dark fellow from who knows what odd corner of the world? Impossible, Bickerstaff!" Not for the first time, Westhill privately thanked the stars that his own skin possessed the dead-white pallor affected by the dandy set and achieved by hardly ever going out-of-doors in daylight. What appeared to be the natural shade of Abdul's skin was, to be sure, no darker than the roughened, sun-bronzed hide of that sartorial disaster, Wrackham, but it was still nothing in the fashion.

"Women are taken in by all sorts of things, and the exotic is quite in vogue," said Lady Juliana.

"Not in the petticoat line myself," shrugged Westhill, which remark effectively brought the subject to a close.

"Did you and Lord Abdul have an enjoyable discussion, Major?" Maria found time to ask her escort before the music struck up.

"Enjoyable? Yes," said Major Harcourt, careful not to meet the lady's flashing eyes.

Hiding her annoyance with difficulty, Maria turned her eyes to the stage. She *had* enjoyed speaking to Sir Stephen Wrackham, but it had been too bad of the major to monopolize Lord Abdul the way he had! She could even swear that her old friend Harcourt harbored some sinister motive — was it jealousy? — for keeping her from the company of the foreign gentleman. Save for two brief words of leavetaking, Abdul had been unable to exchange one syllable with her after his capture by the major. Maria had held the secret hope that he might ask to call, but Harcourt had managed to render that wish an impossibility.

She could not but ponder the horrid luck both she and Lady Anne were having. Glancing sideways at her friend, she thought she detected a slight expression of dissatisfaction on Anne's classic features. Anne and Mr. Renshaw hadn't found it possible to begin anything like a flirtation either, beset as they had been by Westhill's chattering. Her matchmaking energies as unsettled as her personal ones, the Comtessse de Beaulieu ended the evening in an odd mood. Two questions troubled her mind, neither of which had to do with Lord Abdul. Why had the Regent honored her with his notice? And would she one day have to shatter the romantic dreams of Sir Stephen Wrackham? He seemed to be growing fond of her, and for some reason the thought of hurting him made her wince.

Chapter Nine

The morning after the opera, Major George Harcourt sent his usual bouquet of red roses to the Comtesse de Beaulieu, accompanying them with a typically diffident note conveying his hopes that Madame had slept well. Then, perceiving his supply of personal snuff to be rather low, he proceeded to stroll with some languor from his rooms in Bond Street to the Old Snuff House in the Haymarket. After taking his way down King Street and through St. James's Square, he soon found himself entering the establishment where "Major Harcourt's Sort" was stocked on the shelves along with the blends of other London notables. His personal blend was much effected by those young and imitative bucks of the ton who were also wont to display a morose bearing and a marked lack of enthusiasm for life in general.

The Old Snuff House was quite a meeting place, so the major wasn't surprised to find himself hailed by sundry of his acquaintance. However, he didn't single anyone out for particular conversation, and he was ready to leave as quietly as he had come in when a genial, booming voice reached his ears.

"Harcourt!" cried Sir Stephen Wrackham. "Just been buying some of your sort. Famous snuff. It's the best I've had. Enjoy the opera last night?"

Major Harcourt nodded dismally.

"Lucky devil, by jove! The Countess Bow-loo at your side, eh? Lovely woman!" Sir Stephen smiled.

"A very lovely woman," Major Harcourt agreed.

"You seem quite taken with her, Wrackham."

"Taken," repeated Sir Stephen. "Above m'touch. Still, her devoted admirer, Harcourt, I must say."

"Then you have much in common with many another," said Harcourt. His voice was grim. "Both Englishmen and others."

Sir Stephen glanced at his old comrade-at-arms. "M'lord Abdul, you mean? Jealous, what, Harcourt? Your property?" he asked in his blunt way.

Major Harcourt looked his shock at such language and said stiffly, "The Comtesse de Beaulieu is the property of no man. I'm her devoted friend and—champion, should she need one."

"Didn't mean anything by it," cried Sir Stephen, aghast at his blunder. "I call myself M'dame's champion as well."

The major's rare smile came into evidence, and he shook Sir Stephen's hand warmly. "Fellow knights, are we, Wrackham?" He laughed.

"Yes, b'gad," said Wrackham. "I mean to say, baronet. M'lord Abdul's another one," he told the major, and they walked out of the shop together. "Talked of nothing but her. Odd sort of fellow, what?"

"A bit exotic," nodded Major Harcourt. "Some ladies may find that attractive. I would say your Lord Abdul could do well for himself if he has female conquests in mind." The major had not failed to notice the frankly inviting looks the foreign diplomat had provoked from among some of the female haut monde. Not to mention the interest Harcourt thought he had perceived—and had tried to check—in the comtesse.

"Females are an odd lot," agreed Sir Stephen thoughtfully. He stopped suddenly in his tracks and stared off down the street. "Harcourt! Look there, coming at us."

Harcourt's slightly nearsighted eyes followed the direction indicated by his friend. "Damned if I'm not dreaming," he gasped in his turn. "Old Gerry!"

General Cumberland Gerard, a stocky, barrel-chested, grizzled man approaching fifty, continued his martial tread up the Haymarket, oblivious as usual to all that was not in his direct line of vision. He took note of two gentlemen ahead, one extremely large and bearlike, the other tallish and aristocratically slight, who seemed to have lost the power of locomotion. Sensing some slight familiarity, General Gerard gave the two men a second look from under beetling brows. "What the devil!" he roared. "Major Harcourt and Captain Wrackham! Two years if it's a day."

"Nearly that, I believe," agreed Major Harcourt as the general, no stickler for military etiquette in men not serving under him at present, initiated a pumping of hands all round.

"Waterloo," added Sir Stephen.

"Wrackham, you haven't lost your memory," declared the general. "Come to the club, what? A bumper all round."

"Famous!" cried Sir Stephen, and he and a somewhat less enthusiastic Major Harcourt marched down the street with their old commanding officer.

Over quantities of port, the gentlemen renewed their acquaintance, Wrackham and Harcourt feeling at first a certain diffidence which was soon dispelled by the jovial, easy manner of the general. Harcourt, who never liked to dwell on his military past, but had gotten more in the way of it since encountering Sir Stephen, found he was actually enjoying himself.

In any case, the talk didn't turn long upon past battles. General Gerard, a bluff man of few words, was not one to boast of his military victories nor to mention his failures. The gentlemen were soon deeply involved in reminiscing about the Brussels society of 'fifteen and the sundry adventures they'd had, mostly involving what Sir Stephen and the general referred to as "Belgian fillies."

"Your personal life, now, my lads," roared the general when this subject had been exhausted. "Either of you married?"

Both of his former subordinates got across the impression that they, in common with Shakespeare's Juliet, dreamed not of that honor.

Gerard nodded in understanding. "Not a marrying man myself. Wouldn't have done to be leg-shackled with the career. I've been abroad two years with the Army of Occupation, lads. But — well — I retired at last, and I mean to settle. Buy a country estate and marry some lass of good family. Get an heir." He gave a ribald chuckle.

"Most happy to hear it," said Sir Stephen heartily. "You've picked the lady out, sir?"

General Gerard's rugged face softened. "I've been hanging about a young woman here in town," he confided. "One Eleanor Tabor."

Major Harcourt choked on his port, and Sir Stephen gave his friend some healthy thumps on the back while the general continued. "Not a schoolroom miss by any means y'know. Wouldn't do at all at my age. She's below thirty, though, and pretty as they come. Wouldn't do to be riveted to one of those old hags of spinsters that are flitting about. Good family, goes back to the Conqueror. Not a large fortune, but a competence. Wouldn't do to take a gal without a penny to bless herself with, when plenty of rich-uns are roaming about the town free as birds." Gerard was silent for a moment, thinking over the excellencies of his proposed bride. "Either of you know her?" he asked as an afterthought.

While Sir Stephen denied acquaintance with any such paragon as Old Gerry had described, Major Harcourt was considering whether he, too, ought to disclaim all knowledge of the lady. Three years ago, he and Nell Tabor had been very close. Indeed, it would certainly have come to an engagement had he not changed his mind about the lady. It was truly not that unfortunate scandal in Nell's past involving the dancing master of which Harcourt had been thinking when he'd broken it off with her. Quite simply, it had been brought to his attention, during one of their not infrequent quarrels, that Nell had a domineering streak which wouldn't suit his retiring personality in the least. And then, of course, he had met Maria de Beaulieu and soon forgot that such a person as Eleanor Tabor existed. He was thankful that the matter hadn't reached the point of a declaration, but it might as well have. There had been much talk about his attachment to Miss Tabor, talk which had since died down. Still, it was well known in society that Nell, who had once been the friend of the Comtesse de Beaulieu, was barely civil to her now.

"I once knew the lady," the major at last responded to his general's question.

"Devilish pretty girl, what?"

"A lovely young woman," agreed Harcourt honestly.

"I haven't met her, Harcourt?" asked Sir Stephen, his eyes lighting up at the mention of Miss Tabor's good looks.

"I don't think so, but you surely will. You and Renshaw go everywhere, and Miss Tabor is much in society," said Major Harcourt.

"Not a lit'ry woman?" queried Sir Stephen, his mind harking back to the salon of the Comtesse de Beaulieu.

"No," replied the major. He believed he followed the baronet's train of thought, and he wondered what Sir Stephen would say if he knew the real reason Maria didn't invite Miss Tabor to her soirées. "I wouldn't call her so."

"Can't abide bookishness in a woman," put in the general at this point.

Sir Stephen regarded Old Gerry with something like hostility. "Some fine women're bookish," he said with a strange light in his eyes.

"Lot of squinty-eyed old frights," scoffed Gerard,

and he tossed off some more port. "Wouldn't marry one."

Wrackham's black brows furrowed dangerously. He had opened his mouth to speak, but he was forestalled by Major Harcourt, who, sensing the outraged chivalry at work in the breast of the baronet, hoped to avoid the sight of Old Gerry planted with a facer in the middle of his own club.

"It's plain the general hasn't been long in town, Wrackham," he said smoothly. "For if he had met the Comtesse de Beaulieu or Lady Anne Hawley, he wouldn't retain such ideas on intellectual women. Have you met either lady, sir?"

"No," answered Gerard, who was a bit puzzled both by Sir Stephen's black looks and Major Harcourt's air of having averted danger. "Can't say I have. A pair of bluestockings?"

"Extremely beautiful ones," amended the major.

"Demmed fine women, both of them," added Wrackham through tightly gritted teeth.

Gerard was beginning to look belligerent himself. "I say, Wrackham, what's got into you?" Sold-out commissions or no, the general knew insubordination when he saw it.

Sir Stephen, a bit the worse for his port, was slurring his words ever so slightly. "Not squinty-eyed frights," he insisted. "Demmed fine women." He rose from his chair.

Major Harcourt deftly grabbed his coat and pulled him down again. "Easy, Wrackham," he muttered. By this time, the general was glowering.

"Not one to bear an insult to a lady," said Wrackham in a low, dangerous voice. "Call him out." Luckily, this last was said in a tone so low that Harcourt barely heard it himself, and there was no chance that Old Gerry had done so. That the old military man was extremely suspicious, and not a little drunk himself, was sickeningly apparent to the major.

"Nonsense, Wrackham," said the general under his

breath. "You're foxed!"

"Not so foxed I'll bear an insult to a lady!" Wrackham roared. He stood up again, and before Harcourt could stop him, he had grasped the coat front of his old commanding officer. "Demand satisfaction!" he growled.

"Good God, Captain, for what?" bellowed the general, and he freed himself with difficulty from the baronet's grip.

Major Harcourt let out a sickly laugh and made a last-ditch effort to save the situation. "Devil take it, Wrackham, don't you know a joke when you hear one?" he said in a deliberately slow voice. Once more he forced his large friend back into his seat. "Call out our old general? Have a little sense, man!" The major forced himself to smile at General Gerard, then gave Sir Stephen a conspiratorial wink.

"What's this about calling a man out?" demanded Old Gerry. He wasn't one to be fobbed off with that fool Harcourt's lame excuses. "He wants to call me out?"

Summoning up all of his dignity, Major Harcourt executed a short bow in the direction of the general. "Sir Stephen," he said, "had some idea, sir, that by your remark on the—er, the apperance of intelligent women, you were insulting two friends of ours who happen, as we have said, to be extremely beautiful—and intelligent as well." He paused to see if the calmness of his words would have any effect on the still-fuming Sir Stephen and the incredulous Old Gerry.

"Demmed fine women," Sir Stephen muttered again, but he seemed to have regained his senses.

General Gerard still didn't comprehend the details of the situation, but he realized the chief things: his old captain was dangerous when crossed, as well as extremely large and broad-shouldered. He had no wish to go feet-first out of his club that day. "Fine women, I'm sure," said the general.

"Let's drink to them," suggested Major Harcourt brightly. "What say, Wrackham? The general will drink to the comtesse and Lady Anne Hawley, and we will drink to Miss Eleanor Tabor." He sat back down, amazed at his own genius, and signalled to the waiter for another bottle of wine.

"Miss Eleanor Tabor," said the general, happy to return from the puzzling, dangerous subject of blue-stockings to familiar ground. "A woman after my own heart, gentlemen. Beauty, breeding, fit to bear sons — doesn't do, you know, not to check that angle — and a reputation spotless as the Beau's neck-cloth." He sighed. "Caesar's wife, in fact."

"Greek again," murmured Sir Stephen. "Never will understand town."

As Major Harcourt nudged Wrackham warningly, he had a disturbing thought: perhaps the general hadn't heard of that long-ago scandal involving Nell's elopement.

"I'm going into politics once I'm settled," the general informed his companions. "Get into the House. Having a wife whose relations go back to the Conqueror won't hurt a bit, what?"

Major Harcourt was suddenly very uncomfortable indeed.

Chapter Ten

The night Constance Miller and countless other young ladies had been so diligently planning for arrived at last. Morland House in Berkeley Square was ready to receive the glittering throngs of London society for the event of the season. The grand ballroom was lit to perfection, flowers were placed on every available surface, a full orchestra played from a discreet gallery, and — under the eye of the most famous French chef in town — an opulent supper was readying in the kitchens.

Beneath the glittering chandelier on the main landing of a sweeping, red-carpeted staircase stood the Duke and Duchess of Morland. She was an elegant white-haired lady who had been dismissed as a gawky Maypole in her youth, but whom time and elevation to the rank of duchess had endowed with a surfeit of regal dignity. And he, also handsome and white-haired, was a "wicked duke" in the style of the prior century, whose libertine ways did not irritate his duchess any more than the buzzing of a particularly large fly.

To such a formal affair as the Morland ball, it was best that a lady arrive in the most sedate fashion possible. Thus, Lady Anne Hawley arrived with her mama, the dowager countess of Wormington, as her sole companion. Even Maria de Beaulieu, who ordinarily could count on any number of gentlemen as escorts, was chaperoned only by her Aunt Kitty. The four ladies met just inside the ballroom.

"I vow, we four are the handsomest women in the room!" declared Lady Wormington in her usual blunt way. She always spoke her mind and didn't stick at the fact that at least a dozen people might overhear such a remark and interpret it as sure conceit. The dowager countess had not at all given over thinking with complacency of her own beauty, and she was honest enough to acknowledge that opinion aloud. Neither was she behindhand in admitting that her daughter Anne, though technically a spinster, was a magnificent creature whose influence with the gentlemen hadn't diminished at all. As for Maria de Beaulieu, she was a silly, feather-headed ninny for all her reputed bookishness, but she *was* very pretty in a vague, blonde sort of way. And Miss Katherine Torrington, even sillier than her niece, was in very good looks. Lady Wormington supposed that time had left Miss Torrington largely unravaged because that good lady hadn't had the cares of a family. Children *did* age one.

The ladies had just found chairs within view of the dance floor when Lady Wormington said in resignation, "Well, here come the Miller sisters to put themselves under my wing. Alfred was such a fool."

The others understood the reference to the marriage of Lady Wormington's son and remained politely silent.

"Lady Wormington, it's so good to be able to find you in this squeeze!" Constance greeted Pamela's mother-in-law with the cheerful familiarity she used with everyone.

"The duchess's gatherings have never been thin of company," replied her ladyship coolly. "How are you young ladies tonight?"

"Quite well, my lady," said Constance. "This is Georgina's first Morland House ball, you know, and I'm determined she shall dance every dance."

"And as I'm just as determined, we have only the gentlemen to wait for," added Georgina with a little laugh and a diffident curtsy in the direction of Lady Wormington. The circle widened to take in the Miller girls, and Miss Torrington engaged them in bantering conversation about their *beaux*. Lady Wormington, hailed by a friend, turned away, leaving Maria and Anne to shift for themselves.

"It's still very early, isn't it?" faltered Maria. Her eyes were engaged in a never-ending sweep of the crowded room.

"Very," agreed Anne, who was looking about as blatantly as Maria. "Pray, what did his grace of Morland say to you as we were coming in? I saw him take you to one side."

Maria smiled indulgently. "He made the usual improper advance. The dear man means nothing by it."

"Maria, you shouldn't be so naïve. The duke *never* means *nothing*," admonished Anne with the wisdom of one who had herself fought off several lewd invitations from his grace.

Maria shrugged. "Since I don't mean anything, it follows that *he* can't."

Anne was getting ready to offer her friend some sage advice about taking care how she behaved with the duke (for Maria, quite unintentionally, sometimes went too far) when Lord Westhill suddenly appeared.

"Ah, Lady Anne," said the young man, rising from his bow. "You are looking extremely well. And Madame. Both of you so elegant, it does one's heart good." Westhill saluted both their hands and ran an appreciative eye over their costumes. For one unlucky moment, his glance strayed to the less tasteful attire of the nearby Miss Millers. "Now, Lady Anne," he continued, "may I solicit the pleasure of a dance with you this evening?"

Anne laughed merrily. "Westhill, I beg you not to mention it. You know we should cut a ridiculous figure." She turned to Maria. "He never fails to ask for a dance, you know, though the very thought of standing up with a lady near a head taller than he must offend his delicate sensibilities. He's lucky I refuse him."

Lord Westhill let out a laugh of his own. "My lady, you've caught me in my own game. I mean but to do my honors to the ladies in the most painless fashion possible. I'm not fond of dancing, but I won't be condemned among the dowagers for not doing my duty. Though I must say, Lady Anne, that to dance with you would be a rare pleasure — one I still urge you to allow me."

"A pretty compliment, Westhill," retorted Anne. "And I must continue to refuse you, as you know I will."

His lordship bowed. "Then I'm off to nurse my disappointment with a fit of the sulks that may last the rest of the evening. Thank you, Lady Anne." With a charming smile, the viscount took leave of the ladies to join some friends who were engaged in quizzing the company from a spot near the fireplace.

"Impossible young man," said Anne, shaking her head.

"*Incroyable*, as my late husband would have said," agreed Maria. Her eyes, still roaming the room, were at last partially rewarded. "Look, Anne," she said, "Mr. Renshaw and Sir Stephen are coming over here, but — they seem to be alone." A worried frown flashed momentarily across Maria's face. Wouldn't Lord Abdul be with Renshaw if he were coming to the ball?

In an instant, Sir Stephen Wrackham was before her, bowing with what seemed to Maria an incongruous grace. Perhaps a ballroom brought out the best in the man. "M'dame!" he cried in simple happiness. "Lovely as ever—wonderful evening, what? Morland House—first time for me, y'know. Can't say I deserve the honor, but, mean to say, can't help asking . . ."

While Sir Stephen struggled with what Maria assumed was an invitation to join the first dance of the evening, Lord James Lofts rushed up and bowed over her head. "I must carry you off, Madame," said the duke's handsome brother in a persuasive tone. "Sir, forgive us," he added to the baronet, "but Madame la Comtesse is being abducted. I must have the first dance with her." With this flattering speech, Lord James took Maria by the hand and quickly swept her onto the floor.

"Arrogance of rank," muttered Sir Stephen darkly. "Not at all the thing." He turned from the sight of the Comtesse de Beaulieu taking her position at the head of the set with Lord James. She must, of course, be accorded the honor of opening the ball, thought the baronet. It was no more than she deserved. Still, the manner of the duke's brother in going off with her couldn't seem courteous to one of Sir Stephen's simple code of ethics.

Wrackham looked around and found that Miss Constance Miller was suddenly very much in evidence. She looked extremely fetching this evening, in a shiny sort of gown with a damned fortune round her neck. Sir Stephen approached her.

"Miss Miller," he said with his best bow. "Met at the house of M'dame la Countess—most respectfully, ma'am—join the set?" Constance was pleased to accept the offer, and the two joined the other dancers.

The lady was in a good humor, for she had just brought off what she considered a lucky *coup:* she had managed to push Georgina into dancing with an innocuous young tulip of the ton before the child could notice that Major George Harcourt was in the room. Constance's sharp eyes had not missed the exchange Sir Stephen had been having with the comtesse when Lord James Lofts rushed in. She considered it great good luck that the baronet's eye had fallen on her as his second choice without having to go to the trouble of outright flirtation.

Now that she was safely paired with her quarry, she could stop thinking about herself and return to the problem of Georgina. Young Daniels, the girl's present partner, was all very well for a dance, but he was not in the least an eligible *parti*. If only Lord Elliot would succumb! Constance hadn't seen the young baron yet this evening, but she was determined to capture him when she did. Meanwhile, she would enjoy the company of this large, pleasant baronet who was an unexpectedly graceful dancer.

No, it shouldn't be any trouble to bring him to a declaration. Constance wasn't yet certain she wanted such a thing to happen, but it did no harm to be thinking of one's own future as well as Georgina's. Sir Stephen did not thrill her, but he was a pleasant man, and it was high time to be settling down.

Constance would have been thrilled had she known that much the same thoughts were passing through Sir Stephen's mind. He was not hanging out for a wife — no, not the marrying kind. But Miss Miller was beyond a doubt pretty — famous frontal development, too — and her good-humored honesty was refreshing. She was no penniless miss, either, that was sure, and if she was a Cit, well, where was the harm? Deal extremely together, rich wife, children running about Snowfield Hall down in Surrey . . . Not a thing to rush into, certainly, but worthy of thought. Sir Stephen took Miss Miller's hand in the movement of the dance and favored her with his most jovial smile.

Maria wasn't having a pleasant time. Of course she was honored, and her vanity was gratified, by being chosen as Lord James's partner. Too many women coveted that distinction for her to be displeased by it. But she did think it a pity that Lord Abdul was not at the ball. He would have surely asked her to dance. It was rather a shame, too, that dear Sir Stephen Wrackham had been overset by Lord James in *his* effort to ask for the first dance. She was fond of the man, and for some reason it made her uneasy to see how perfectly contented he was in the company of Miss Miller.

Maria had to smile at her own folly. She had no serious thoughts of any man, and did she really want every gentleman she knew to be as unhappy as poor Major Harcourt? She could see that unfortunate now, giving way to gloom in a corner. No, she was pleased that Sir Stephen Wrackham wasn't one to fall into her net unasked, as had so many others. It would be a very good match for Constance, Maria thought resolutely, ignoring the little pang she felt at the thought.

When the dance was over, Maria refused Lord James's invitation to step out into the conservatory. Instead, she asked that he lead her back to Aunt Kitty, which he did with a tiny frown of surprise — the comtesse was never hard to persuade into a small indiscretion. He left with a hint that he would return to claim her for a waltz later on. Maria chose to be noncommittal and waved him away in haste.

"Child, you're as popular as ever," said Miss Torrington with a pleased nod of her turbaned head. "Half the gentlemen in the room are after you, I vow, and the other half are mad for Lady Anne. I was amused to see Mr. Renshaw beat Lord Elliot to her side and take her to the set, for I had just seen the same sort of thing happen with you, Sir

Stephen, and Lord James. And you were no sooner gone to the floor than poor Major Harcourt came up and asked me to tell you he'd look for you later." She paused. "Well, here comes Lady Anne again."

Anne was indeed returning, escorted by Mr. Renshaw. Her eyes were a bit brighter than usual, Maria noted, and she was smiling. Well, why shouldn't she be? She had danced with the man of her choice. Renshaw looked happy too, and it was truly a pleasing sight. But why must one feel so envious?

"Thank you, Mr. Renshaw," said Anne.

Renshaw bowed. "I think you know what a pleasure it was to dance with you at last. Now may I beg you to save me the first waltz as well?" He bent down to speak the next words in a lower voice, for Lady Wormington, though deep in conversation with one of her cronies, was near enough for extreme caution to be warranted. "It's so hard to say anything to one's partner when the movements of the dance are constantly interfering. Perhaps the waltz will afford us more opportunity for conversation."

"It ought to, Mr. Renshaw," Anne replied. As he moved away, she forced herself not to follow him with her eyes to see whom else he danced with — why should she care? — and turned to Maria, her face alight.

"You seem to have been satisfied with your partner, my dear," was Maria's comment as she watched Renshaw herself. "He seems to be heading for the cardroom," she added with a twinkle in her eye.

"That is none of my concern," said Anne offhandedly, but she was sensible of a great feeling of relief.

"Did you have a good time dancing with him?" Maria asked.

"He's a charming man when he's not insulting one's equestrian abilities," responded her friend. "We didn't have much chance to speak."

"Oh, Mr. Renshaw is a fine-looking young man, and so tall," put in Miss Torrington, her eyes aglint with matchmaking.

Anne was astonished to feel herself blush.

Maria let a small sigh escape. "Isn't it strange that one of Lord Abdul's standing didn't come tonight? I thought to see him here with Renshaw. I've seen every other diplomat in London but him."

"Is that the foreign gentleman you mentioned?" asked Miss Torrington.

"Yes, Aunt Kitty. His conversation was quite intriguing. I had hoped to see him to—to ask him questions about his homeland," Maria said.

"Yes, he's from very far away indeed, isn't he?" queried her aunt. She had a weakness for the exotic not uncommon in sedate maiden ladies.

"From Persia, Aunt."

"Well, that does sound quite far away. Perhaps dancing is not the custom in his country."

"Oh, I'm sure that's not it," said Maria. "He has spent many years on the Continent, you know, on one mission or another, and has grown quite conversant in Western ways." Maria intercepted a sharp glance from Anne. "Or so I would imagine."

"You seem to be quite well-informed about the man, Maria," remarked Anne.

"Well, you know how Maria loves politics," said Miss Torrington. "The man sounds interesting, and he may still come tonight. I imagine him as very handsome and exotic-looking. Something like that dark gentleman talking to Major Harcourt."

Maria immediately turned her eyes to the spot her aunt had indicated and beheld Lord Abdul, not ten feet from her chair, held fast in a discussion with Major Harcourt. Abdul looked directly at her. He said something to Harcourt, then the two men made their way through the crowd.

The Major arrived first and presented his diffident compliments to the comtesse. "I was desolated to miss you earlier," he said with his sad smile, and he released her hand with reluctance.

He had no sooner dropped it than Lord Abdul was standing before Maria. "Madame, I will not lose time in empty gallantries. This dance?"

Maria held out her hand.

Major Harcourt grew even more morose as he watched the Comtesse de Beaulieu and Lord Abdul make their way to the dance floor. To his jealous eye, they seemed absolutely besotted by one another. Lord Abdul could mean nothing honorable by his interest in the widow. The major had just asked the diplomat if he were married and had been told that, yes, his lordship did have that honor thrice over in his own country, so it followed that Maria was in some danger. Harcourt was not inexperienced in matters of the heart — did not his own hopeless love give him that distinction? — and he could see that this was not Maria's simple, light flirtatiousness. He had never seen her take such an interest in a man.

The major said a few words to Miss Torrington, paid his respects to Lady Anne's formidable mama, and was about to make his way back to a corner when he felt someone's eyes upon him. It was little Miss Georgina Miller, a shy smile upon her lips. She regarded him in frank admiration while trying at the same time to pay attention to the foppish young Mr. Daniels who had just brought her back to her chair from the last dance. She was a pretty little thing, and the major had noticed lately that she was always looking at him in that moonstruck way. Undoubtedly a case of mistaken hero worship, thought Harcourt. Personally experienced in the matter of unrequited love, he knew the signs. The child did deserve at least some small return for her attempt to cast out lures to him, though it wouldn't do to lead her on, of course.

"Good evening, Miss Georgina," he said with all the gallantry he could summon up in his depressed state. "May I have the pleasure?"

"Oh! Major Harcourt, you may," cried Georgina at once. She forgot all about Mr. Daniels and was truly thankful that Sir Stephen Wrackham and the censorious Constance hadn't come back. "Do let us hurry," she added, giving him her hand.

The major let himself be dragged out to the floor, reasoning that it didn't cost much to make a young girl happy in these troubled times.

Lady Anne had observed this little drama with an amused eye while she herself was accepting Lord Elliot's invitation for the next dance. Would Maria be annoyed, Anne wondered, that one of the Millers was blatantly trying to steal her most convenient suitor?

At the moment, nothing could have annoyed Maria. Though it was only a country-dance, and their hands met but rarely, she was carried away by the sensation of being with Lord Abdul at last. His dark eyes never left her and when he met her in the movements of the dance, he addressed compliments to her with a boldness she would never have excused had he not been a foreigner. When the set ended, she was beginning to feel comfortable in his society and wished that it wouldn't be unseemly for them to continue dancing.

Abdul actually voiced her wish. "Madame," he murmured as they started for the sidelines. "Why shouldn't we dance again? It is a waltz. Give me that happiness."

Maria returned his burning gaze with one quite as bold. "Why not?" she said, and she let him lead her back onto the floor. Even in her bemused state, she had the wit to look about and see that Mr. Renshaw had indeed sought out Anne for the waltz. Maria caught Anne's eye and smiled before Lord Abdul grasped her in his arms—a bit closer than was quite the thing—and she found herself whirled away across the floor, lost to all thought.

"You dance with passion," remarked Lord Abdul as they executed a difficult turn with precision. His smile gleamed "I wonder."

Maria found herself quite unable to ask him what he did wonder. He certainly danced "with passion" himself, but she could hardly return the compliment. Her face grew a little wistful even as her eyes smiled into Lord Abdul's. All her life she had wondered about love—tried to force it on her friends by her matchmaking, and despaired of finding it for herself. Passion, she supposed, was different from love. Well, it made no matter. To her, both were merely words.

"Sad, Madame?" Lord Abdul's charming voice broke into her thoughts.

"Oh, no," said Maria, continuing to look straight at him. His eyes were so strange—shining with sympathy, not kind exactly, but questing. She had seen something of that expression on the faces of men who made improper advances, and there had been plenty of those in her life. Lord Abdul looked somehow more intense, more dangerous, than the other men she had known. And he would almost certainly take liberties. What did she think about that?

"Madame," said Lord Abdul, "this is a ballroom. You must not be sad." He clasped her even tighter.

"I've told you already I am not," returned Maria, a little breathlessly. "I am merely thoughtful."

"And you are thinking that you have committed an unpardonable social sin by dancing twice in a row with me?"

"Hardly that, sir. There's nothing out of the way in two dances. In any case, I am a widow, not a young miss who must be careful not to raise any eyebrows. I do what I like."

"Ah! I am counting upon that, Madame."

Maria dropped her eyes. Discomfort warred with fascination as her exotic partner swept her about the sparkling room.

"Good God," said Lady Wormington to Miss Katherine Torrington at that very moment. "Isn't your niece dancing for the second time in a row with that foreign man?"

"I'm sure he simply doesn't know the customs here, and she was too shy to refuse him," said Miss Torrington, kindly endowing her niece with what would have been her own behavior. "Besides, as a widow, she has more license than a young girl." This was the excuse she nearly always made to herself for Maria's behavior. But an uneasy idea troubled her: perhaps dear Maria *was* going a bit too far with this particular flirtation.

"She ought to have taken the opportunity to school him in English ways rather than show herself a fool," insisted the dowager countess with a disapproving shake of her head. "But then I forget you ladies are Americans."

"In America, one is quite as formal," said Miss Torrington. She chose not to take offense at her ladyship's remark, knowing it would do no good. She would have liked to have told the dowager that one who has not seen America in ten years grows to feel positively English in that time, but there was no call to cause a scene. "Dear Maria was thoughtless," she said a little defensively, "but she means no harm."

"You may know that, Miss Torrington," said Lady

Wormington ominously, "but does Lord Abdul?"

Miss Torrington gave a worried little sigh.

The dowager countess was sorry she'd been unkind, and she had the grace to try and seek some diversion for the unhappy maiden aunt. After all, that silly Maria de Beaulieu was already dancing with the foreign gentleman, and there was no stopping her. Lady Wormington surveyed the immediate vicinity and perceived a familiar slight, fashionable figure lounging by. "Westhill!" she called imperiously. "Come talk to us."

Lord Westhill was quick to obey the dowager's summons. She knew his mama—they were neighbors in Kent—and it didn't do to displease either lady. Besides, he was fond of Lady Wormington and knew just how to amuse her. "At your service, my ladies," he said courteously, bowing also to Miss Katherine Torrington. "How may I serve you best? Would you care to abuse the company? Or is there some new scandal you'd like me to repeat to you in detail?"

He was unfortunate in his last remark. If ever there were a scandal brewing, it was out on the floor right at that moment. There might be nothing to signify in two dances, but two dances with an exotic diplomat . . . Both Lady Wormington and Miss Torrington remained silent.

"Good lord," exclaimed Westhill. "Have I failed so soon to entertain you? Come, ladies, don't be cast down into the blue megrims. This is a ball at Morland House, a grand occasion. The event of the Season, some say. Now I, for one, have taken care to come dressed in my best so as to honor the duke and his duchess, but certain others I could name seem to think her grace was meaning to give a masquerade, for nothing else could excuse such things as the hamhanded way that *that* gentleman"—and he indicated with a small whipping motion of his quizzing-glass Sir Stephen Wrackham—"has chosen to tie his cravat."

The ladies brightened immediately at this light-hearted malice, and Westhill continued to give his opinion of the costumes of many other guests. Soon the waltz ended, and Renshaw led Lady Anne back to the little group.

Anne was feeling somewhat flushed—the effect of the dancing, no doubt—and was rather glad that Westhill was with her mama. That way, Lady Wormington wouldn't be at liberty to notice any possible change in her daughter's manner. For Anne was feeling a bit oddly, to say the least. She'd had any number of men's arms about her in the years since the patronesses of Almack's decreed she might dance the waltz, and men other than Renshaw had murmured discreet compliments into her ear, but there was a difference. . . .

"Anne," her mother greeted her. "Here is Westhill come to give us his impressions of the company, and very entertaining impressions they are, too. Here, Westhill," she added, rapping the young man on the knuckles with her fan in a manner popular thirty years before. "My daughter is back, and I suppose you'll want to go off together as usual."

"Far be it from me to steal Lady Anne away from her cavalier," said Westhill in all honesty, with a bow towards Renshaw. He saw his opportunity for escape and, after favoring all the ladies in the group with his most skillful compliments, he headed back to his friends.

"Lord Westhill saw my reluctance to let you go, Lady Anne," said Renshaw boldly, for Lady Wormington was privy to every word he said. "I'm very grateful to him."

Anne, as sorry as she had ever been for her Mama's presence, didn't give in to the temptation to say that she, too, was grateful.

104

"Westhill is a fine young lad," said Lady Wormington directly to Renshaw. "Excellent fellow. Titled, witty, intelligent, a family that hasn't one mark against it, and a pretty fortune. His lands in Kent march with ours, and I am great friends with his mama."

Anne laughed uncomfortably. "I'm sure Mr. Renshaw doesn't care to hear Lord Westhill's history, Mama."

"And why shouldn't he, Anne?" asked Lady Wormington. "Lord Westhill would be glad to hear me praise him so. He's such a great friend of yours—has been from childhood, Mr. Renshaw—that you shouldn't be unwilling to hear good of him."

Anne was confused and not a little angry. She dimly perceived that, for some reason, her mother was wishing Mr. Renshaw to think that Lord Westhill was a suitor. It could be merely a motherly way of trying to arouse jealousy in the male breast of Mr. Renshaw so that his own interest would be heightened, but Anne didn't think so. No, Mama must disapprove of Renshaw in some way. Surely she couldn't still entertain those insane hopes of hers that the Marquis of Hamber would make another offer! For the moment, Lady Anne, proud and imperious from her birth, absolutely hated titles. "I'll always be fond of young Westhill," she said in what she hoped was a patronizing tone, hoping to repair any damages.

The music was striking up again, and the sets were forming for the next dance. "Gracious heaven!" said Miss Katherine Torrington in a kind of squeak, her violet eyes mesmerized by something she saw out on the floor.

Anne followed Mistress Kitty's gaze and was, for the moment, rendered incapable of all speech. For she perceived that Maria was staying with the foreign gentleman with the apparent intention of giving him a third dance in a row.

"The comtesse would appear to be hastening to her own ruin," said the dowager countess in a dry tone.

"Oh!" exclaimed Miss Torrington weakly. "I'm sure she means nothing by it."

"Of course she doesn't, Mistress Kitty," soothed Anne with an assurance she didn't feel. Really— Maria might flirt, but until tonight she had yet to make a public spectacle of herself. Anne could only resolve to take her friend to task at the earliest opportunity. She wondered how soon the gossips would begin to make use of this information.

As if in answer to Anne's thought, Lady Juliana Bickerstaff rushed up in a rustle of silk. "Do you see Maria?" she said in a whisper. "A third dance, I vow! Nell Tabor will love this."

"And I imagine Nell is here tonight," replied Anne with a sigh.

"Oh, yes," said Juliana. "I saw her earlier with that crusty old general she's been casting out lures to. It seems to be working at last, but enough of that. What *shall* we do about this horrid third dance? It wouldn't be so bad, but three in a row, and with such a visible gentleman . . ."

"I don't know," replied Anne.

"There won't be much hope for the dear creature's reputation if we don't think of something," Juliana went on.

"I suppose not." Out of the corner of her eye, Anne perceived that her mother was engaging Renshaw in conversation and wished that she might hear what was passing.

"What shall we, as her loyal friends, do about Maria?" persisted Lady Juliana.

"I don't know," said Anne for the second time. "She seems to have put something else ahead of decorum. And you know she has never been one to keep a tight rein on her flirting."

Juliana shrugged and moved swiftly on. Anne watched her go with a mixture of indulgence and impatience. The true gossip could not, after all, remain long in one place.

Anne became aware that her mama had finished with Renshaw and that he was turning back to herself. She looked into his eyes, anticipating another pleasant smile, and was surprised to discover that his face was more serious than she had ever seen it. Before she could comment on this development, a booming voice assailed her ears.

"Renshaw!" cried Sir Stephen Wrackham. A worried frown bedecked his craggy face. "Lady Anne! Came to ask Countess Bow-loo for the next dance, but I must have miscounted. Still on the floor with that foreign chap, what?" He was looking out at the dancers with honest misapprehension. "Could have sworn — but no, must still be the second dance. Foreign. Can't know what's the thing." His frown deepened.

Anne's heart sank. If such a simple, uncalculating brain as that of Sir Stephen had noticed something out of the way, then Maria's reputation was as good as gone. It wasn't that the Comtesse de Beaulieu had to maintain the image of a prudish, proper widow lady — far from it — But neither had she ever been involved in outright scandal. Anne knew that Maria wouldn't care a pin for such a small thing as a reputation, or so she would think until it was irretrievably lost.

While Anne and Sir Stephen watched Maria and worried in their different ways, Renshaw was called off to join an argument that several of his fellow sportsmen were having on the time it would take a curricle to race to Paddington from Hyde Park Corner. From the vehemence with which the gentlemen were discussing this problem, it seemed to Anne that Renshaw would be occupied with them for some time. Therefore, fearing that Sir Stephen might ask her to dance, and not wanting to observe Maria's indecorum any further, she excused herself to her mother and moved away with some idea of refreshing her toilette upstairs. However, just outside the ballroom door, she passed by the conservatory and couldn't resist stepping in to be alone with her thoughts.

Several daring couples had chosen the spot for rendezvous, including the duke of Morland and an easy-mannered viscountess whose husband was on a diplomatic mission to China. Still, Anne was able to find a quiet bench in the shelter of some tall palms, and here she sat down in private. Her head was whirling. She'd wanted to flirt with Renshaw, of course, but she hadn't meant for his manner and mere presence to turn her into a giddy schoolgirl, which they most certainly had. The cool and haughty Lady Anne wasn't sure she welcomed such a feeling. Her confusion on her own account was great, and added to it was the disturbing fact that her dearest friend was throwing all caution to the wind in her dealings with the Persian gentleman. Were both she and her friend under some spell? The evening's happenings deserved serious thought.

Anne hadn't even begun to do that thinking when a pair of well-shod feet were presented to her view. She looked up to see Mr. Renshaw staring down at her, and her heart leaped momentarily. Then she saw that his face was dark with what looked very like rage.

"Escaping me, Lady Anne?" he asked in a tone harsher than any she had yet heard from him.

"Of course not, Mr. Renshaw, why should I?" she asked, mystified by his ironic look. "You were talking with your friends, so I came out for a breath of air. Do sit down now," she suggested with what she

108

hoped was a casual air.

He accepted her invitation. "I'm surprised to find you alone," he remarked.

"Why? With whom did you expect to find me?"

Renshaw laughed bitterly. "Why, with Westhill, to be sure. He, or—let me see, I mustn't forget anyone—he or Elliot, or one or two marquises. I believe even one of the Royal Dukes was hinted at."

Anne saw it all. "Sir, you've been talking to Lady Wormington," she said with a teasing smile. She resolved to take Mama to task as soon as she returned to her side.

Renshaw's cynical expression looked odd on his usually open and honest face. "Your mother has seen fit to warn me off," he said. "I must be grateful to the lady."

Anne's eyes opened wide. "Grateful, sir?" she asked in disbelief.

"For showing me where your true interest lies," elaborated Renshaw. "No, don't take my words amiss, my lady, there's nothing wrong with hanging out for a title. Ladies higher-born than you have been known to do it."

Anne couldn't believe what she was hearing. Surely the man must be foxed. "Sir, I must ask you to apologize for making such allegations against my honor as a woman," she said in a frigid tone. "Hang out for a title, I? I have one already, if you please. And to accuse me of such behavior is infamous." Her hazel eyes flashed fire, and she rose from the bench, no longer able to bear such close proximity to the blackguard.

He rose with her. "Lady Anne, I can only wish you well," he said. "Lord Westhill and Lord Elliot are both quite attentive. And if, as your mother says, so many gentlemen of higher rank are also at the point of declarations, then you have only to take your pick."

"Sir, leave me at once!" cried Anne.

Instead, he gripped her shoulders in his strong hands. His light blue eyes stared deeply into her own, as close as they had been when he was waltzing with her. For one intense, frightening moment she believed that he was going to kiss her—and she halfway wished he would. But he merely muttered, "With pleasure." He released her with a wrenching movement and stalked away without looking back.

Anne, her shoulders smarting from the force of his grip, was left staring after him. She had never been so angry in her life, but she couldn't determine whether the fury coursing through her veins was directed more at Mr. Renshaw's credulity and insolence, her mama's insupportable meddling, or her own accursed pride. One more word from her might have cleared up his misunderstanding. In total confusion, Lady Anne Hawley sank back down on the bench and burst into uncharacteristic tears.

Chapter Eleven

Miss Ginevra Johnson, the famous bluestocking, didn't ordinarily go out in the evening except to attend some literary soirée or concert of Ancient Music. She hadn't attended the ball at Morland House, couldn't conceive in her purely intellectual mind that others in the world might have, and had no qualms about paying a morning call the day after the social event of the London season. A little before noon, she was sitting in the drawing room of the Comtesse de Beaulieu, confidently awaiting the servants' message that Madame would be down instantly. Although Miss Johnson had some idea of the hours Maria was in the habit of keeping, she saw no reason to sanction them. She also knew that the comtesse wouldn't wish to displease anyone of her own power in the literary world.

Miss Johnson was a thin, intense, dark-haired woman in her mid-thirties with what unkind souls were wont to describe as a squint, but which was really only a very direct way of eyeing the rest of the world. Her society was much sought after for its own sake, quite apart from her frightening intellectualism. When all was said and done, she and Maria were firm friends, though her austere way of life had little in common with the languid, luxurious existence of the widow. Each lady was, in her way, intrigued by the other.

Miss Johnson hadn't called alone this morning. She was accompanied by her cousin, a clergyman from Hampshire whom she wished to make known to the comtesse. The young man needed a patron, for he hadn't yet been able to procure a living. And Maria de Beaulieu had a certain influence with those in power whom Miss Ginevra Johnson recognized, admired, and couldn't claim for herself. Maria could charm; Miss Johnson could only discourse. Rich men, men with livings in their gift, might be swayed by a tinkling laugh and a charming smile where rational conversation wouldn't even be noticed. Miss Johnson was nothing if not practical, and her family was important to her. Dear Barrett must have the best chance he could, and meeting the Comtesse de Beaulieu would gain him a rare entrée into society.

As the country clergyman eyed the elegance of the drawing room furnishings with something like suspicion, the door opened and Miss Katherine Torrington entered, her face wreathed in smiles. "Miss Johnson!" the older lady cried happily. "So glad to see you. Maria will be down directly."

Miss Ginevra Johnson inclined her head graciously. Miss Torrington was one of the more ardent worshippers at her shrine, and it was always a bit wearing to be confronted by her enthusiasm, though of course one could not but be fond of the well-meaning lady. "My dear Miss Torrington," said the bluestocking in her dignified way. "Please allow me to present my cousin, Mr. Barrett Johnson."

Johnson made a smooth enough bow. "Charmed, Miss Torrington." His grave voice was a deeper version of his cousin's. He was a thin, black-haired young man in his mid-twenties, with sober clothing not at all in the fashion. His dark eyes held the same forbidding intelligence as those of his cousin Ginevra.

"Sir, it is a pleasure," fluttered Miss Torrington

in answer. She sat down at a respectful distance from Miss Johnson and added a bit apologetically, "You must forgive dear Maria her tardiness. She was out rather late last night."

"It is we who are at fault for calling at this early hour," protested Miss Johnson. Her expression betrayed a faint disapproval, however, and Miss Torrington fluttered more nervously as a result.

Luckily, the comtesse entered the room almost immediately, looking fresh and rested in a modish morning gown. A velvet ribbon bound her fair hair in a more demure style than the tumbled mass of curls she usually affected. "Miss Johnson," she exclaimed. "How kind of you to visit us." Her manner was all sincerity, and when the young clergyman was introduced to her, she was kindness itself. Aunt Kitty breathed a sigh of relief, for she had been terribly afraid that Maria would be out of sorts this morning. Hester, the abigail, had been adamant in her refusal to brave Madame's chamber, and Miss Torrington herself had had to go in to tell Maria of the Johnsons' arrival. Maria hadn't appeared pleased to be awakened before noon.

It was perfectly true that Maria, though gracious as ever and meaning every mark of respect towards Miss Johnson, *had* been annoyed to be routed out of her bed. Not that she had been asleep. On the contrary, she had never spent such a restless night in her life, for never had a man affected her the way Lord Abdul had. When Aunt Kitty had so timidly interrupted her solitary reflections, Maria's first thought had been to have the post brought in at once, before she made any move to dress. But there had been no note from *him*. And of her flowers, the only ones out of the ordinary were the two dozen white roses which she had been receiving from time to time from her unknown admirer.

They couldn't be from Lord Abdul (though she imagined he might do that sort of thing), for she had received the first of the mysterious bouquets before her first meeting with the exotic foreigner. The white roses were a great puzzle. Sir William Torrington had denied all knowledge of them, and Maria's other admirers were in the habit of identifying themselves. Of course, it could be someone she knew only slightly, or by sight only—men were so much more romantic than women. As to Lord Abdul, though disappointed in his silence, Maria was certain that she would hear from him in some way, and soon.

Barrett Johnson, upon finding himself face to face with the lovely lady his cousin had warned him he must impress, was somewhat at a loss. Maria, sensing his shyness, took care to draw him out and to question him about his background, which seemed to be very scholarly. He had taken a confusing number of honors at Oxford, and on his own had published several interpretations of medieval Italian texts. He assured the comtesse, however, that his true interest did not lie in dry scholarship. "I took orders for one reason only," the young man declared. "To exercise my true vocation to help others. I see my future in a country parish somewhere, madame. My scholarship will fall by the wayside, true, but my happiness will be made complete by the people I am allowed to guide spiritually and to serve."

"Such an ambition is truly noble," put in the romantic Miss Torrington.

"Very," agreed Maria. "And has no one, sir, put you in the way of getting a living?" Maria had her shrewd side, and it occurred to her that Miss Johnson might have a reason other than mere sociability for introducing her cousin.

"No, Madame. There are hardly any family ex-pectations, and that's as far as the matter has gone," admitted the young man.

"There must be someone," said Maria. "I'll think about it." She smiled at Miss Johnson. The Com-tesse de Beaulieu was not unused to petitions of this sort, but she had never before received one from her bluestocking friend. It pleased her to think that she might be of use to Ginevra Johnson.

Aunt Kitty, intrigued by the self-sacrificing young clergyman, engaged him in conversation. She was always too diffident to talk much to Miss Johnson.

That lady was thus free to have a word with Maria. "It's very important to me that I do some-thing for Barrett," she began. She had never been subtle and saw no reason to start now. "It wouldn't be a thing to be ashamed of, putting my cousin in the way of a living. He is an excellent clergyman, and while hardly Evangelical, he has a sincere de-votion to religion which is rare in these times."

"I can see that," said Maria. "He ought to suc-ceed." This was as far as she was prepared to go in encouraging Miss Johnson, for she hadn't yet had time to think which, if any, of her male friends might be the young man's benefactor. It wouldn't do to promise what one couldn't deliver.

Such vagueness was, however, quite enough for Ginevra Johnson. "I know we understand each other, Madame," she said with a pleased expression. "Now let us turn the subject to our own affairs. Pray tell me, are you continuing with your novel?"

Maria stared blankly. Since meeting Lord Abdul, she had not only neglected to write at her novel, she hadn't even picked up a book or a periodical. She had the grace to blush, for she felt her stand-ing in the literary world slipping, and she wasn't really certain that she cared. "I must admit I haven't had a moment to write recently," she was forced to say. "But it was more than half-finished when I last put it down."

"Splendid," said Miss Johnson. "With the season in full swing, there isn't much time for one of your social standing to write. Even I, with my quieter habits, have been making less progress than usual on my own work."

"Isn't it dreadful," said Maria.

"Indeed it's distressing," answered the bluestocking. "But in the summer we'll be diligent again. I tend to look on the spring in London as an opportunity to gather material, as it were. So many noted scholars are in town for one reason or another."

"To be sure," said Maria, wondering if she would ever touch her novel again. She must force herself to do so, of course, and not waste time in idle dreaming.

The Johnsons' visit was nearing an end when Lady Juliana Bickerstaff was announced. She came breezily into the room, attired in a dashing walking costume that exhibited Madame Hélène's genius to a fault. Greetings were exchanged all round, and Miss Johnson was particularly pleased by the opportunity to make Barrett known to a second great lady of the ton. When the Johnsons took their leave, Miss Torrington announced that she, too, had to be off, for she had promised to call on a friend. "It's Lady Wormington," confessed Miss Torrington with a smile. "And she isn't one to enjoy being neglected, so you must understand my going to her, dear Lady Juliana."

"Miss Torrington, don't be distressed," said her ladyship. "Your niece and I will have a comfortable coze."

Indeed, Lady Juliana appeared not at all reluctant to be left alone with her hostess, Maria noted. The instant the door closed behind Miss Torrington, Juliana regarded the comtesse with a shrewd blue eye and said, "My dear, what were you about?"

Maria's eyes widened. "What? I don't understand."

"Those three dances, Maria. It was quite ridiculous." Lady Juliana shook her head. "I wanted to confer first with Lady Anne regarding this affair," she went on in a businesslike way, "to see if she would rather have been the one to mention the matter to you, but she's indisposed this morning. So, as there is no time to be lost, I came direct to you. Three dances in a row! How could you?"

"Which three dances?" asked Maria coolly.

Juliana stared. "Why, the three you gave to that diplomat fellow, to be sure."

Maria smiled. So it had been as she had thought. In spite of the care she had taken to repair her foolish behavior of the night before (for she had known while in the act of doing it how ruinous dancing three times with the same gentleman could be to one's reputation), no one had noticed anything but her dances with the exotic Lord Abdul. Well, she could begin to remedy that at once, and it was great good luck that Lady Juliana Bickerstaff, more noted for her kind heart than her discretion, would be the one to help her. "I also danced three times with Lord James Lofts," she said.

"You didn't!" cried Juliana.

Maria shrugged. "Perhaps no one noticed. But I danced once with him to open the ball, and then twice in a row after my—interlude—with Lord Abdul. Three dances with the same gentleman must not really be so remarkable."

117

Juliana frowned in thought. "I vow I didn't notice at the time. But when I think of it—why, this is worse, my dearest creature. A double indiscretion!"

Feeling as sly as she ever had, Maria responded, "Lord Abdul didn't seem familiar with our customs, and it would have caused quite a scene to have put him off. But I knew that people would talk, and to my cost. So I thought to render my sins less exclusive by committing the same ones with my host's brother." She gave Lady Juliana a smile that begged for understanding. Her story was the truth. She was only leaving out her own attraction to Abdul, without which she never would have exposed herself in such a public manner.

Juliana nodded easily, but it was impossible to tell whether it was in relief or conspiracy. "My dear, you were in a difficult position," she said. "And to think that I, as your friend, came to call on you this morning precisely to think of some story like that, which we could give out to the world as the reason for your behavior."

"So kind of you," said Maria with another smile.

"Lord Abdul was difficult to put off, was he?" asked her ladyship. "I know he appeared to be quite taken with you." She shook her head in feminine sympathy at the vagaries of gentlemen. "Men are ridiculous creatures," she added reminiscently. "I wasn't out a year when those two junior officers in Papa's regiment threatened to fight a duel over me. Do you remember the case, Maria? It wasn't my fault, you know, I barely knew the two of them by sight."

Maria did remember this adventure and shook her head ruefully. "What can one do?"

At this moment, the butler entered. "Madame, a package has just arrived by special messenger," the

118

man said in tones that conveyed a parody of respect. He deposited a small, silver-wrapped box on a table near his mistress and bowed out of the room.

"Thank you, Roy." Maria picked up the box at once.

"I must say I don't like that fellow's manner," said Juliana with the aristocratic frankness she was famous for. "Looks positively sinister, with that dark hair and those beetle-brows. And a shade too oily. Have you thought to count the silver lately? Now if you're thinking of making a change in your staff, my dear, Lady Chester's butler's brother—"

Maria, who never took an interest in servant problems, did not admit that Mr. Roy sometimes gave her an uneasy feeling. "Roy is the soul of Puritan respectability," she said with a merry laugh. "Much more so than am I. He quite disapproves of my wild life, you know. And my abigail is moonstruck over the man, so he stays in any case. Now what could this be?"

"You must open it now so I may see, too," stated Juliana. All thoughts of domestic matters left her head as her curious eyes focused on the silver box. "I suppose it's from Lord James Lofts."

"Perhaps I ought to open it later," considered Maria mischievously.

"And perhaps not. Do go on," insisted her companion.

Maria eagerly tore the silver paper from the box, and she wasn't shocked to discover that under it was a case from a well-known jeweler. It happened occasionally that some one of her côterie would send her a trinket. She opened the lid.

"Good Lord!" cried Juliana in amazement.

Maria's hand shook so that the box nearly dropped. There, on a bed of black velvet, lay a magnificent diamond pendant on a chain of gold set with brilliants. She had never seen anything like it.

"Is there a card?" asked Juliana breathlessly. She had never seen a diamond so large.

"Here it is," said Maria, separating a white card from a fold of silver wrapping. She read it quickly and blushed. Written in French in an unfamiliar hand was the message, *To a dance filled with passion.* Maria nearly gasped at the audacity of the words. The double meaning, the gift itself—the man's purpose was clear as day.

"Well, who is it from?" asked Lady Juliana. "Is his grace of Morland trying to bribe you with diamonds, having failed in his direct approach?"

"It's from Lord Abdul," said Maria as tonelessly as she could. "You were right, Juliana. He refined more upon those dances than I realized he would. This must, of course, be returned, but without my seeming rude. No doubt in his country it isn't uncommon for a gentleman to present a lady with such a treasure as this on short acquaintance." She sighed a little as she looked at the pendant. "Wouldn't it have been glorious to own? Vulgar, of course, but magnificent."

"Try it on, my dear," suggested Lady Juliana with feminine zeal. "No one will ever know."

There was really no resisting. Carefully, Maria took the necklace from its box and went to the nearest mirror, where she tested the jewel's effect at the square neckline of her morning gown.

"Ravishing," said Juliana. "What a pity."

"Pity indeed. Well, Juliana, it will be hard to compose a note of rejection that is firm enough and friendly at the same time, for it wouldn't do to anger a foreign visitor." Maria sighed as though the weight of international diplomacy were on her shoulders.

Juliana nodded, all sympathy at her friend's plight. "What trials we women do have, to be sure. But you're a writer, luckily, and it comes easier for you. Well, I imagine I ought to leave you to compose that letter. Do you know the man's direction?"

"Oh, no," lied Maria smoothly. She was, in truth, perfectly cognizant of the fact that his lordship was in residence at Fenton's Hotel in St. James's Street. "I'll send a man out to get it." No need to mention the discreet questioning that had already obtained the information for her.

Lady Juliana took herself off rather quickly—in a hurry, no doubt, to spread the tale of all she had seen and heard that morning at the Comtesse de Beaulieu's. Maria, left to herself, fell into a dreamy state, the diamond in her hand. She was no innocent. She knew that, in sending the necklace, Lord Abdul was not following any custom of his country, but rather telling her in the common English manner of his wish to proceed further with their flirtation—much further. She only needed to know now whether she wished the same thing. A "dance filled with passion" might not be love, but it would certainly be more than she had ever known, and almost surely more than she could ever expect to know in the future.

For some reason, Maria's thoughts leaped to Aunt Kitty, still searching for true love at the age of fifty. Did Maria want to find herself at that age, still rejecting every man because he wasn't the perfect one of her dreams?

She hadn't lied to Juliana about how hard it would be to compose a letter to Abdul. It was the most difficult thing she had ever done. Summoning up all of her creativity, she tried to convey that she wasn't insulted, but that convention simply wouldn't

121

allow her to accept such a precious jewel. It was impossible to hold out more encouragement than that before she knew her own mind, and the note seemed cold and flat no matter what she wrote.

Finally it was sealed and ready, and Maria had only to wait for Aunt Kitty's return before sending the necklace back to her new admirer. For she was only human, and she must certainly see her aunt's reaction to the wonderful present before she said farewell to it forever.

When Miss Torrington did come in, her cheeks were very pink, and her violet eyes were flashing. "Maria, it's the most infamous thing!" she cried. "I've been sitting with Lady Wormington." She paused for breath.

"That's not infamous, Auntie," said Maria with a little grin. "Silly of you, perhaps, but not infamous."

"My dear, do listen," said Aunt Kitty seriously, placing herself on the sofa next to Maria. "You must know I've been busily speaking in your defense, for Lady Wormington has taken it into her head that you meant something quite sinful in dancing thrice with Lord Abdul last night. That *was* a foolish thing to do, child."

Maria sighed. "I know, Aunt Kitty, but I couldn't help myself. He was insistent." She left out the fact that she had been far from objecting to the gentleman's insistence. "But Lady Wormington shouldn't speak to you about my affairs," she added in some heat. "I'll tell her so myself."

"Maria, she spoke only for your good. She's fond of you, and you're her daughter's closest friend, so she feels a special interest," said Miss Torrington. "She was quite sympathetic, in fact, when I told her you'd no doubt been coerced by the gentleman and didn't know how to refuse without being rude."

122

Maria, recollecting that Lady Wormington's sharp eyes were very like Anne's in their seeming ability to see all, couldn't believe that the dowager had really been taken in by such a tale. But Aunt Kitty might as well think so. "I'm glad to have retained Lady Wormington's good opinion, Aunt, and thank you for defending me. But you're right. It was infamous for her to mention the matter."

Aunt Kitty laughed. "But, dear, I haven't come to the part I referred to as infamous." Her smile faded. "I know you will be shocked. Major Harcourt, you see, was talking to Lord Abdul last night, and asked him about his family. My dear child, the man has *three wives* at home! Lady Wormington tells me she nearly fainted when the major told her. And I myself was hard put not to show my surprise. Three!"

Maria stared into space for a moment, her green eyes wide with shock. Married? But of course a man in his mid-thirties would be married. She forced herself to smile at her aunt. "In his society, he would still be considered eligible, for I believe his religion would allow him four wives. But think of the confusion at the tea table!" She laughed, a little stiffly.

Miss Torrington was quite taken in by her niece's manner and delighted to find her so unconcerned with Milord Abdul's marital status. It was definitely a relief that Maria wasn't falling into a hopeless passion for the devilishly handsome foreigner.

Maria's emotions were in a considerable state of conflict, and she was glad that etiquette demanded she send back the diamond. She was even pleased that her note sounded stiff and unfriendly. The horrid man! He might have mentioned last night that he was married. In order to distract herself from these thoughts, she showed the pendant to

Aunt Kitty, enjoying the older woman's awe at the jewel and pretending to enter fully into her aunt's shock at a married man's having sent such a thing.

When at last the giant diamond was entrusted to the footman and sent on its way to St. James's Street, Maria found herself able to converse with Aunt Kitty in a normal way. She asked first after Lady Anne. Was she really indisposed, as Lady Juliana had said? How strange that was — Anne was so healthy. And had Lady Wormington truly seemed to forgive the shocking lapse of last night's dances?

"Oh, most decidedly," said Miss Torrington. "And, do you know, Maria, the fact that Lord Abdul is married may do you some good there. A married man can surely mean nothing evil by dancing with a lady in a public place."

How little Aunt Kitty knew of the ways of the world, thought her niece with something like envy.

Chapter Twelve

Lord Abdul had expressed an interest in observing at first hand that great marketplace of English horseflesh, Tattersall's, so there Phillip Renshaw conducted his noble charge. Renshaw happened to be hunting out a new team for his yellow curricle and would have been delighted in any case to display this wonder of the English equestrian world to a visitor. Sir Stephen Wrackham, always in the market for a riding horse that was up to his weight, went along as a matter of course.

Among the crowds of talkative gentlemen at the auction, they made a thoughtful trio. Abdul had received on the previous afternoon a certain valuable parcel, accompanied by a cold and courteous note, and didn't know what to make of the situation or of English women. Renshaw, his conscience at war with his hurt pride in the matter of his scene with Lady Anne at the ball, felt guilty, ungallant, and at a loss to mend matters. And Sir Stephen Wrackham, though at peace with his own personal life (he'd danced twice with Constance Miller at Morland House and had since spoken to her in the Park), was still a bit uneasy about the Comtesse de Beaulieu's good name and uncomfortable about being in the society of the exotic gentleman who was causing him that uneasiness. All three men were so preoccupied that Renshaw nearly missed his chance on the pair of matched chestnuts he had had his eye on, and the others

125

didn't even think to remind him.

When Renshaw remembered at the last minute to bid on the pair, he nearly lost them to Lord Elliot, who was notorious for picking up anything thoroughbred that might pull a sporting vehicle. The young blond baron finally gave in to Renshaw's superior wealth and determination and withdrew from the bidding. But he elected to accompany the group into White's for a companionable bumper.

"Renshaw, how's a man to compete with another Golden Ball?" Elliot exclaimed good-naturedly when the four men were settled. "But I was looking out for blacks, not chestnuts, as it happens, so no harm done."

"Glad to hear it, my boy," replied Renshaw. His purchase hadn't had the usual effect of putting him in high spirits, he noticed. It was the devil of a thing to be in the toils of a woman.

"There was more worth looking at last week," put in Sir Stephen Wrackham reflectively, and he proceeded to tell Lord Abdul in detail all about the team of grays and the sturdy black stallion he himself had found at Tattersall's the week before.

The foreign gentleman was compelled to listen, enthralled by the sheer length of Wrackham's speech if nothing else. While he did so, Lord Elliot and Renshaw eyed each other with suspicion.

"Have you seen Lady Anne since the Morland ball, Renshaw?" enquired Elliot at last. It was only on that night that he realized Renshaw was among his rivals for the lady's favor.

"No, I haven't," replied Renshaw. "She hasn't been out riding in the last couple of days."

"No," agreed Elliot with another suspicious glance. "She hasn't."

126

Sir Stephen's ears were as sharp as his tongue was overactive, and he turned momentarily from his conversation with Lord Abdul. "Lady Anne? Indisposed ever since the ball. I saw Miss Miller in the Park, and she told me so." He then turned back to Abdul.

Elliot and Renshaw had to smile at each other warily, partly in mutual understanding of their situation, partly in amusement at Sir Stephen's manner. "Miss Miller," Elliot said. "Lady Anne's sister-in-law. She's the one who keeps throwing her little sister at my head. Damned annoying."

Renshaw shrugged. "Both of them are pretty enough, as I recall. Not poor, either, from the looks of them."

"The City," said Elliot with a raised eyebrow. It was lucky that Sir Stephen happened to miss this comment, or his chivalry might have been aroused on behalf of Miss Constance Miller.

"They have high connections," Renshaw pointed out. "Much might be overlooked in the sisters of Lord Wormington."

Elliot laughed. "You're in league with Miss Miller, you devil. Have me riveted to that little chit, will you? And leave yourself a clear field with a certain lady." His tone was bitter under his joviality.

Renshaw laughed back, forcing himself to maintain a good humor. Elliot was younger and more impulsive than he. No need to take offense and cause a scene. "No such thing," he replied calmly. "The lady you're referring to won't speak to me soon again, clear field or no. I'm simply trying to give you friendly advice. And by fastening on that little miss, you'd gain Wrackham here for a brother." He laughed and slapped Sir Stephen on the back as he spoke, glad of his large friend's use as a diversion.

The baronet had long since ended his conversation with Lord Abdul and was regarding his friends with interest. "Brother?" he asked in puzzlement.

Renshaw smiled. "Never say you aren't dangling after Miss Constance Miller since the other night at the ball, old fellow. You could do a lot worse. A lovely creature. And should she favor your suit, then Elliot here, by marrying her sister, would have the pleasure of calling you brother." He paused for effect.

"Not precisely dangling," considered Sir Stephen seriously. "Thinking of it—you going after her sister, Elliot?"

The baron denied any such plan. "Renshaw's having his joke," he explained, staring moodily off into space.

Sir Stephen nodded in complete sympathy. "Often does, you know. Have his joke. Usually at my expense, but you've come in for your share, Elliot."

Renshaw turned to his large friend in alarm. "Old fellow, don't hold my jokes against me," he begged. "I never mean anything by them."

Sir Stephen gave his gruff assurance that of course no offense had ever been taken. "Lady Anne," he said out of the blue. "There's the trouble."

Renshaw and Elliot both jumped, and even Lord Abdul looked up with interest.

Pleased at having got the group's attention, Wrackham beamed. "Both dangling after the lady," he announced. "Why not? The best man will win."

Renshaw laughed, and his eyes met Elliot's. "He's right, you know."

128

"Damned if he isn't," agreed the younger man, extending a large hand across the table. "Out and out war, man. But no hard feelings. It's *her* decision."

"As you say," Renshaw agreed.

"Famous," said Sir Stephen with the air of Solomon sitting in judgment. "Now what comes to mind? The lady's indisposed."

Both young men looked curiously at the baronet.

At this point, Lord Abdul saw his chance to make a contribution to the conversation. "Gifts," he suggested with the assurance of one who'd had many dealings with women. He could only hope that these two young men would have better luck with their lady than he had had with the Comtesse de Beaulieu.

"Quite right, m'lord," cried Sir Stephen, pleased at the foreign gentleman's quick understanding.

Renshaw and Elliot looked at each other, and a slow smile broke out first on the face of the dark-haired gentleman, then on the younger features of the light-haired baron. "Flowers," they said in unison, and they were across the room in an instant, arm in arm.

Sir Stephen and Abdul were left alone.

"My dear sir," said the diplomat, "you seem to have solved our friends' dilemma with a rare tact."

Sir Stephen started. Many qualities had been attributed to him in his thirty-odd years, but tact had never been one of them. "Not difficult," he demurred. "Easy. No question."

"Still, good sir, you are to be congratulated for turning the young men's quarrel into a friendly rivalry," insisted the other, a smile transforming his darkly handsome face. "This Lady Anne is much sought after?"

"No question," said Sir Stephen. "She and M'dame la Countess, her friend. Give 'em Greek names, trail after 'em, all that. You know, m'lord. You're taken with the countess yourself, what?"

Lord Abdul bowed. "I am an admirer of beauty."

Sir Stephen knew he would do better to leave the subject, but in the interest of the Comtesse de Beaulieu's reputation, he felt constrained to mention the matter which had been preying on his mind since the night of the ball. "M'lord," he began in a familiar, man-to-man tone. "Those three dances weren't the thing. You'll know next time. Causes talk. Best for the lady not to."

The other nodded gravely. Did this large, lumbering fool think Abdul, familiar with every court in Europe, was ignorant of local custom? His three dances with the comtesse had been entirely deliberate on his part, an attempt to see how far she would go. "I thank you for your information," he said in a tone which did not quite hide his irony.

It was safe from Sir Stephen, however. He nodded, satisfied, and considered the matter quite at an end. It was with great pleasure that he styled himself Madame's champion, and he was delighted to have been of use.

The rival Corinthians had parted company just outside the door of White's and gone off in separate directions. Renshaw wandered down St. James's Street in a preoccupied manner which nearly caused him to crash head-on into more than one passerby.

It was all very well to establish a good-natured rivalry with Elliot, he thought, and to send Lady Anne flowers. But dash it all, what was the use?

Lady Wormington had made it quite clear that her daughter was destined for greater things than he could offer, and Lady Anne had not precisely denied that such was the cause. However, one thing stood out in Renshaw's mind regarding his recent interview with Lady Anne in the conservatory at Morland House: he had been abominably rude, and to a lady. He must make amends to Lady Anne Hawley. But as for setting up as her suitor? Jostling with Elliot to claim her for the dance? Struggling to come up to her in the Park before the odious Lord Westhill could reach her side? No, he wasn't the man for that sort of empty game, not when there was no hope of victory. Wrackham was a good-natured fellow, but he had been dead wrong in his estimation of the situation. Both Mr. Renshaw and Lord Elliot might be smitten by Lady Anne, but the former held no hope of winning her.

Having thus convinced himself of the hopelessness of his case, Renshaw proceeded to look for the largest, most original bouquet of flowers in London.

Chapter Thirteen

If Lady Anne Hawley had one quality which stood out, it was her bursting health and vitality. Not for her the idle hours spent on the sofa with lavender water or vinaigrette. Neither was she in the habit of sleeping late for any reason save extreme fatigue. Thus it was a shock to many of her friends to hear that she had succumbed to a slight indisposition.

Perhaps the most incredulous was Maria, who was used to being the lazy and languid target of Anne's barbarous beliefs on rising early, going out-of-doors, riding, and such. It was curiosity as much as concern which brought Maria to the door of Wormington House two days after the Morland ball, to request admittance to the sick chamber of her unfortunate friend. Attired in her newest walking costume and clutching a copy of Thomas Peacock's clever *Melincourt,* she thought she would amuse the invalid by reading aloud.

The Comtesse was shown up to the elegantly appointed chamber which served as Lady Anne's sitting room. Anne favored an austere neoclassicism in her furnishings, and the room had always reminded Maria of something one might find in ancient Rome or Greece. On a severely styled sofa with an elegantly curved back, a pale and languid lady reclined.

Maria tried hard to conceal her amusement as she cried, "Good heavens! It's as if an enchantress

132

had waved a wand and changed our places. But you're really ill, then, Anne? How sad."

Anne sighed deeply. "I'm just not feeling quite the thing, Maria," she said in quiet acceptance of her fate. "Nothing serious. Only a persistent headache that came on me the other night at Morland House." She cast a baleful eye on her friend. "*You* are looking well."

"Oh, well enough," shrugged Maria. Actually, she wasn't in the most excellent of spirits, for reasons having to do with a large diamond, a handsome foreigner, and her own confused mind.

"At least you have some color. I'm pale as a ghost," replied Anne. "But for the moment, it doesn't matter." She sighed again.

"Your usual remedy for me at these times is to drag me out-of-doors," considered Maria, her hand perilously near the bell rope. "Shall I ring for your maid, my dear, to get you out of that robe and into your smartest carriage dress?" She smiled maliciously.

Anne roused herself to give something like a shriek. "Don't you dare," she cried, breaking into a smile.

"No, I agree. We're much better off indoors today," said Maria. "Let the ton promenade through the Park at will. We won't care for any of them." She gave a determined little nod of her head.

"Are you thinking of anyone in particular, dear?" asked Anne from among the pillows.

Maria's large green eyes were suddenly furtive. She said nothing.

Anne decided to be stern. "You might as well out with it, you know. Juliana Bickerstaff has acted as your herald angel. She was here yesterday directly after seeing you receive a diamond big as an egg from Lord Abdul, and having swallowed

133

some hum about you dancing with him three times so as not to cause an international incident."

Maria shrugged. "I sent it back."

"Of course you did. You aren't a complete ninnyhammer, I would hope, especially with Juliana Bickerstaff standing by. What I want to know is what your own thoughts are on the subject."

"The subject, Anne?"

"Lord Abdul, Maria," elaborated Anne. "You took a risk to dance with him, and you're lucky to have come through unscathed. But why? Are you in love with the man?"

Maria stared. "In love? I?"

"It's been known to happen to women from time to time," said Anne. "Or so I collect from my reading."

"It doesn't happen to me," said Maria. "And my life is much easier because of it."

"At least it's easier to say so."

The ladies fell silent, each uncomfortable in her way. Maria wasn't in the habit of confessing the innermost secrets of her heart to another, and Lady Anne Hawley would certainly never be caught doing so. Up to now, such considerations had never entered into their friendship, for in the years they had known each other, both their hearts had remained untouched.

Maria was settled, or so she thought, regarding Lord Abdul. If she met him again in company, she would be cold and somehow make known her displeasure that he had not told her he was married. After that, a light flirtation might still be possible — she would have to see. She hadn't glimpsed the man for two days, and already she felt his influence fading.

As for Anne, after two days to think over her sentiments regarding Renshaw, she was still completely unsettled. To avoid coming to daggers drawn with her mama, as well as to have some logical reason for reddened eyes and a wan face, she had feigned indisposition since the night of the ball. It was safest to steer clear of Mama until such time as her own anger cooled, for Lady Wormington might be ignorant and officious in her behavior, but she hadn't intentionally ruined her daughter's life. That her life was ruined, at least for a time, Anne had no doubt. Renshaw was a credulous, rude, arrogant fool, but it was her misfortune to spend every waking hour thinking of him. In time, when Renshaw observed in the ordinary course of events that Anne didn't marry Elliot or (good God!) Westhill, he might come to see that he had been wrong. But a tender reconciliation scene ten years down the road didn't appeal to the dawning sentimentality of Lady Anne Hawley. She was too impatient for that. For the moment, she preferred a darkened room and gloomy forebodings of a solitary future.

Maria broke the silence by picking up the book she had brought with her. She began to read. Both she and Anne had enjoyed *Headlong Hall*, and Mr. Peacock's second effort was, at least initially, quite as amusing. But neither lady really had her mind on the reading, and it was a relief when a maid peeked in at the door to announce that the two Miss Millers were downstairs.

"Send them up," said Anne at once, straightening up and pinching her cheeks in an effort to give herself a glow of health.

Constance and Georgina, in much-trimmed pelisses and dashing bonnets, were shown in. "I heard from Lady Juliana that you weren't well, but I didn't like to disturb you before today," Constance began, eyeing her sister-in-law with concern. "Are you at all recovered, my dear?"

"I'm practically my old self," said Anne with more conviction than she felt.

"Splendid!" said Constance heartily. "No good giving in to such things. Madame," she added, turning to Maria, "how do you do?"

"Quite well. And you, Miss Miller?"

This was a lucky question—but then, anything would have been, Constance's spirits were so high. "I'm very well indeed, Madame, and I thank you for asking," she said with a broad smile. "By the way, Lady Anne, Sir Stephen Wrackham sends his regards and hopes you're feeling better." She paused significantly.

"We met him in the Park," put in Georgina. "He was with Major Harcourt."

Constance laughed. "Georgina, child, don't be referring to Major Harcourt in that proprietary fashion. The Comtesse will think you're trying to steal him away from her."

Georgina flashed her sister a murderous look. "I wasn't referring to the gentleman in any particular fashion, Constance, and it's unkind of you to say so," she said.

"My dears, the good major isn't my property in any case," Maria said in an attempt to soothe. It was apparent that all was not well between the Miller sisters.

"Yes, yes, we know that," said Constance. "But to return to Sir Stephen—"

"Oh," said Anne. "Were we discussing him?" Her eyes regained some of their sparkle as she considered that perhaps Constance had at last found a titled cavalier.

Maria looked up sharply at the matchmaking note in her friend's voice and wondered, not for the first time, why she should care if Sir Stephen

136

Wrackham, in whom she had no interest at all, were entrapped by Miss Miller. It was selfish contrariness, she thought with a sigh. Perhaps it was inevitable, when one's own heart was never touched, to expect every man in the world to follow in one's wake. Maria wondered why she felt none of the same contrary emotion at the thought that Georgina Miller might capture Major Harcourt's heart. Perhaps she was so used to worrying over Harcourt's unhappiness that the idea of anyone else taking over the duty had its appeal. Pity Miss Georgina was just out of the schoolroom and unlikely to hold any attraction for a mature military man.

Maria snapped out of her dreamy state when Anne's dresser entered the room and asked respectfully if her ladyship would like to see the flowers that had just been delivered.

"The very thing to cheer an invalid," said Maria. "Do bring them in, don't you think, Anne?"

"At once, please." Ann sat up straight.

A chambermaid then staggered in under the weight of a large porcelain vase which contained a superfluity of red and yellow roses.

"A pretty thought," said Constance, clasping her hands. "They're from that handsome Mr. Renshaw, I'll be bound. He was quite attentive at the ball the other night, my dear."

Anne's slender white fingers were seen to tremble ever so slightly as she tore open the accompanying note, and the observant eyes of both Maria and Constance noted a slight color in her pale cheek. Anne read the paper quickly and looked up in something like vexation.

"They're from Elliot," she said flatly.

"How kind," cried Georgina with a triumphant look at her sister. "I had no idea he was so attentive to you, Lady Anne. I suppose he's heard you're ill?"

"Yes, he writes a few very pretty lines hoping I'm on the way to recovery." Anne set the message down on a nearby table.

Constance was by no means pleased that Elliot was in the habit of sending flowers to Lady Anne, for how then could he marry Georgina? But it was encouraging at the same time, for Georgina's sake, that their sister-in-law didn't seem over-pleased with the young baron's attentions. Now, if only Georgina would cease her ridiculous pining over George Harcourt! The silly chit had been in raptures over his dancing a mere once with her at the ball, and when they had met him in the Park, in the company of Sir Stephen Wrackham, Georgina had taken the entire encounter in compliment to herself. As far as Constance could see, the pale, brooding major was paying her sister no more than the ordinary civilities.

"It was a lovely gesture on Lord Elliot's part," said Maria. She rose from her chair to go and sniff the flowers. "Roses are my favorites, though I must say I prefer them white."

"Oh, I think red and yellow is a lovely choice," said Georgina. "And I'm sure Lord Elliot meant for the bright colors to cheer Lady Anne. Such a romantic thing to do."

Constance shook her head over her little sister's inept attempt at recommending Lord Elliot to Lady Anne. She was about to comment sharply on it when the door opened again to disclose the maid, absolutely hidden behind a large, gracefully curved basket filled to the brim with wonderful spring lilacs. Their heady fragrance instantly filled the room, overpowering the perfume of the roses.

"My word," said Anne, a deep blush mounting

138

to her cheek. "Is there a card?"

"The gentleman came himself, my lady," replied the maid. "He left this." She handed her mistress a calling card as she bobbed a neat curtsy.

"The gentleman came himself!" gasped Constance.

"How vastly romantic," sighed Georgina, wondering if anything of the like would ever happen to her.

"Lilacs," was Maria's thoughtful comment. "Original."

There was no mistaking the glow in Anne's eyes as she surveyed her gift. "Original indeed," she remarked, touching the blooms. "Out of the common way to deliver them in person, wouldn't you say, Maria?"

"I've certainly never heard of the like before," agreed her friend. "May we ask, my dear, the identity of this gentleman who made such a figure of himself carrying this thing through the streets?"

"Renshaw," responded Anne, and she tucked the card in question carefully into her pocket.

Chapter Fourteen

Miss Eleanor Tabor descended the steps of Hookham's Library into Bond Street, followed at a discreet distance by her maid. She had found several novels today. No great reader, Miss Tabor was yet careful to scan, from time to time, those works she heard mentioned at parties. It didn't do to be bookish, of course. Gentlemen didn't like that, as Mama often pointed out. Where, for instance, had bookishness gotten Lady Anne Hawley? Not to the altar. On the other hand, one mustn't be abysmally ignorant when a new title was discussed at a social gathering, and thus Nell had picked up the author of *Waverly's* two latest — *Old Mortality* and *The Antiquary* — as well as Miss Edgeworth's newest work, *Ormond*.

She hadn't gone two steps towards her carriage when she saw Major George Harcourt approaching down the street, accompanied by a very large gentleman whom Nell thought she had seen before but couldn't place. She sighed in vexation. She didn't often meet Major Harcourt, and since their falling-out three years ago, it had never been pleasant to do so, bringing to mind as it did thoughts of past failures.

Major Harcourt seemed to suffer from a like emotion. His eyes were slightly averted from Nell's sharp ones as he bowed to her. "Miss Tabor," he said, discomfort evident in his low, well-modulated voice. "I believe you haven't met Sir Stephen

140

Wrackham? Please allow me to present him."

At that, the large, mustachioed gentleman who had been standing by with an expectant smile bowed at once. "Pleased, Miss Tabor," Sir Stephen said enthusiastically. "A rare pleasure, b'gad! I've heard much of you."

Nell found herself feeling a kind of triumph, for who but Major Harcourt could have mentioned her to this baronet? Perhaps Harcourt regretted his defection to that impossible Maria de Beaulieu. She smiled more kindly on the major and answered Sir Stephen Wrackham in her most pleasant manner. "How good of you to say so, sir. I trust you've not heard anything to my disadvantage?" These flirtatious words out, she suddenly remembered that there was, indeed, something to her definite disadvantage that the man might have heard. She blushed deeper at the idea, but Sir Stephen's manner didn't indicate that any story of a long-ago elopement was in his mind. One mustn't be so oversensitive. No one Nell met now seemed to have heard of it, and those old acquaintances who had, such as Major Harcourt, had the grace not to mention it.

Sir Stephen lost no time in elaborating on his statement. "Greatly to your advantage, Miss Tabor, no question. General Cumberland Gerard — served under him, Harcourt and I — is warm in your praise. Glad to meet a young lady m'old general thinks so highly of." As Sir Stephen spoke, his eyes strayed to the books held by Eleanor Tabor's maid, and he couldn't reconcile their presence with Old Gerry's offensive attitude on the subject of bookish women. His brow furrowed. "Books?" he said in frank puzzlement.

"Oh, yes," said Miss Tabor quickly, thinking that she recognized the normal masculine aversion to

141

anything blue. "Just a little light reading. I hardly ever find the time to pick them up, you know, but then one meets with so many pleasant people in Hookham's." She gave her most engaging smile.

"No question," responded Sir Stephen heartily, the mystery explained. Still, how he would like to quiz Old Gerry that his perfect and unbookish Miss Tabor exhibited in public her ability to read!

Major Harcourt cleared his throat and regarded his former love with a meaningful expression. "General Gerard does indeed speak highly of you, Miss Tabor."

"Thank you, sir," replied Nell. She cast a sly look up at him. "It's gratifying to hear that *some* gentleman thinks highly of one."

His ears reddening ever so slightly, the major returned, "What gentleman wouldn't, to be sure? There was never a question of that, Nell—" He stopped, realizing too late that he had used Miss Tabor's Christian name for the first time in three years.

She, too, seemed to have noticed, but her eyes were unfriendly as she replied, "Surely the question of a certain lady's reputation must have been in—someone's—mind."

While this barbed exchange was going on, Sir Stephen looked from gentleman to lady with interest. There was surely some mystery here. Affair of the heart, no doubt.

"The past is past," said Major Harcourt, a statement which was perfectly clear to one of his auditors if totally confusing to the other. "And no gentleman would think it otherwise than forgotten. No, Miss Tabor, no gentleman worthy of the name would do so." He lowered his eyes. He meant only good to Eleanor Tabor and thought by his words to convey a hint to her which she might

142

possibly — perhaps not, but possibly — need to remember as regarded Old Gerry. For Major Harcourt wouldn't care to wager that General Gerard would continue to pursue Nell should he hear of her long-ago attempt at elopement. "Caesar's wife" had certainly never contemplated such a thing, even as a giddy young girl.

Nell acknowledged the major's words with a distant little bow. "You are correct, sir," she said icily. "The man who wouldn't let the past die a natural death couldn't be called a gentleman."

"Surely not — miserable thing to do — past is past," put in Sir Stephen, thinking that he should contribute to what was probably a philosophical discussion whose finer points had escaped him.

Major Harcourt nodded. "Yes, the past is past," he repeated.

Nell's expression grew colder than ever. "And now good day to you, gentlemen," she said in a tone of dismissal. "If one of you would be so good as to attend me to my carriage, I have to be on my way."

Both gentlemen jumped to see her and her maid into the sober, elegant town coach of the Tabor family.

"Good day to you, ma'am," said Sir Stephen as he handed her in. An honor to have met you. Great pleasure. A great one."

Nell smiled with just the suggestion of warmth and wondered in passing if Sir Stephen were a married man.

"Pretty girl," remarked Sir Stephen to the major as the carriage moved away. "Old Gerry's taste ain't amiss. Demmed odd, the way she talks. An old entanglement of yours, man?"

The major wondered, not for the first time, at the mixture of shrewdness and simplicity that made up Sir Stephen's character. "Something of the sort. I prefer not to discuss it. The past, as we've all been noting, is past."

In her carriage, Nell Tabor was fuming. What horrid luck it always was to meet the man who had jilted her for the Comtesse de Beaulieu, an ill-bred American nobody. It was infamous! Nell believed sincerely that Maria had turned Major Harcourt against her out of pure spite and entrapped him herself for the same reason. For she hadn't married him, had she? Nell found such dog-in-the-manger practices concerning eligible men to be nothing short of vile. If a lady were not going to marry a gentleman, why not let him go free? A marriageable man held fast in the toils of a flirtatious, horrid little—person was a tragic case. At least General Gerard was wonderfully attentive. Even Mama, who had begun to be so unhopeful, could see that he was hovering on the point of a declaration. Nell didn't know when she had last known a man to be as impressed by those qualities of hers which most impressed herself—namely, her excellent family background and her undoubted domestic skills. If he were a bit older than she, well, that couldn't be helped. She was twenty-six and must be practical. With the one exception of Lady Anne Hawley, all her old schoolfellows had married, and most had set up their nurseries.

At the ribbon counter where Miss Tabor stopped to match some puce-colored silk for her mama, she had her second unpleasant encounter of the day. Nell sighed at meeting Miss Katherine Torrington face-to-face. It was impossible to pretend not to see the woman, but it was really too

144

bad to have to be civil to the aunt of that immoral widow.

"Why, Miss Tabor, how pleasant," Miss Torrington said with her usual simple friendliness. She knew, of course, of the coolness which existed between Eleanor and her niece—and of its causes. But such knowledge would not stop her from being polite to one who had been, in the past, such a good friend to Maria and herself. Years ago, when Maria had been married to Beaulieu, Miss Torrington had been very glad that a young girl like Nell Tabor had frequented the house and brought a companionship to Maria that she couldn't get from older people. Even knowing that Miss Tabor had chosen to end that intimacy due to quite mistaken ideas about poor Maria couldn't make Aunt Kitty forget the girl's past kindness.

"How do you do, Miss Torrington," responded Nell with the distant air she always affected before the older lady.

"I'm extremely well, thank you," twittered Miss Torrington.

"And your niece?"

"Very well, also," said Miss Torrington brightly. She didn't notice the icy tone of Miss Tabor's voice. It wasn't often that Nell asked after Maria.

"How unfortunate that the dear comtesse should remain ignorant of English customs after so many years here," remarked Nell.

Miss Torrington's smile faded. "I presume you're referring to the three dances that poor Maria gave to the foreign gentleman," she said frankly. "Really, it wasn't my niece's fault. He wouldn't be put off, and you know how difficult it is to deal with gentlemen, especially foreign ones."

Nell smiled slyly. Poor Maria, indeed! "I heard that from Juliana Bickerstaff," she had to admit.

145

"But really, dear Miss Torrington, you and I know the Comtesse, and often her behavior with gentlemen does serve to lead them on. It's evident that this particular gentleman thought that she wasn't averse to his attentions."

Miss Torrington put her head to one side. "How so?"

"The diamond," said Nell, laughing. "Such a mark of ardor, to be given on such short acquaintance—"

"It was sent back with all speed," interrupted Miss Torrington. Her clear violet eyes held a worried expression which hadn't been there a minute before. "He misunderstood our customs."

Nell smiled again, more slyly than before. "No doubt. Well, good day, Miss Torrington. Remember me to your niece."

Miss Katherine Torrington left the ribbon counter with no very good opinion of Eleanor Tabor. The girl was an incorrigible gossip. She, with her superior airs of virtue! The disturbing fact of the matter was that, if Nell were saying things like that about Maria, so derogatory to her reputation, perhaps others had also noted something amiss in Maria's behavior with Lord Abdul. Miss Torrington herself had no reason to doubt her niece's complete innocence. It was only the censorious world which was at fault. The three dances had apparently been understood, and forgiven, by everyone else with whom Miss Torrington had discussed the matter. Nell Tabor was such a spiteful little creature! But if *she* were spiteful, might not others turn so? It was a coil.

As the maiden lady wandered down the busy shopping street deep in thought, trailed by the abigail she was never free of since her unfortunate encounter with that blackmailing shopkeeper, her

146

reverie was interrupted by a familiar voice. "Katherine! My dear! What, not recognize your own cousin?"

"Oh, Sir William," said Miss Torrington in distraction. She looked up into the bright dark eyes of her relative. "Do forgive me. I was thinking of something else." So preoccupied was she with Maria that she forgot how irritating it was to meet Sir William Torrington.

The distinguished, white-haired gentleman regarded his lovely cousin in concern and undisguised affection. "My dear Katherine, what is the trouble? Might I help?"

Miss Torrington sighed. "No," she said. "That is, yes. I — I sometimes wonder if I'm doing my best to fulfill the place of chaperone to Maria," she confessed miserably and cast down her eyes.

Sir William made so bold as to pat Miss Torrington's arm. "My dear cousin, how much chaperoning can a widow of seven-and-twenty need? Maria is a mature and sensible woman. You don't have the charge of a little girl just out of the schoolroom."

"Sometimes," said Miss Torrington, "I wish I did."

"Is something wrong with our Maria?" queried Sir William.

"Oh, cousin, I don't know," sighed Miss Torrington. "I don't think so. That is, I didn't until just now, when a young lady of my acquaintance brought to my attention the idea that some people might, quite unjustly, be thinking that Maria is — is fast." She reddened slightly.

Sir William started. "Of course my young cousin is considered rather dashing. She mixes with a varied group, and all kinds of people attend her salons. But her good name is surely not

147

in question?"

"Sir William," said Miss Torrington, "you weren't at the ball at Morland House a few evenings ago?"

The baronet shook his head. He never went to dancing parties.

"Had you been there," his cousin continued, "you would have seen with your own eyes what I was unhappy enough to see with mine."

"And very lovely eyes they are, too," put in Sir William, unable to resist the opportunity to turn a neat compliment.

"Pray let me continue," pleaded Miss Torrington. "The thing is, Maria danced thrice — three times in a row, Sir William — with a certain gentleman who comes from some strange eastern land. It was quite the *on-dit* of the evening."

"That would be Lord Abdul from Persia," said Sir William with a nod. "Met him at the club. He seems to have an eye for a pretty woman. It's evident he doesn't know the customs."

Miss Katherine Torrington smiled. "Oh, was that your first thought, sir? Not that dear Maria was being scandalously flirtatious and leading the gentleman on?" She sighed in relief.

"Was she?" asked Sir William.

"Oh, by no means, cousin, so she assures me. The gentleman insisted, and she didn't know how to refuse without offending him. But you haven't heard the worst of it."

"And that is?" prodded Sir William.

"He sent her a diamond the next morning," whispered Miss Torrington with a furtive look around, quite as if the story of the necklace weren't all over London by this time thanks to Juliana Bickerstaff.

"Did he? But she would return it. Maria is a

well-brought-up young woman, and she has your counsel," said Sir William.

"Indeed she sent it right back. So, cousin, do you think that this whole unfortunate story would warrant my speaking to Maria more strongly than I have? I told her she was foolish, and applauded her sending the diamond back with all speed. I don't know what else to do, as chaperone and adviser." She sighed again.

"I fail to see the problem," said Sir William. "This Lord Abdul was struck by the beauty of our Maria, made advances she had to repel, and was given a needed set-down. How could that work to Maria's discredit?"

"This young lady I mentioned, whom I was speaking with today, seems to think that the whole thing was Maria's doing," said Miss Torrington fiercely. She wished she could shake Nell Tabor!

"Then the young lady is wrong," said Sir William. "No Torrington would act in an unseemly manner."

Miss Torrington shook her head. "Neither would a Tabor, sir, and this young lady is of that family. You know what they are, near puritanical. If such talk of Maria is going around town —"

Sir William laughed. "Do you mean that the young lady who defamed Maria's character is the Tabor girl, the one who ran off with the dancing master? She doesn't have room to talk, my dearest Katherine."

Blushing at the unwanted endearment, Miss Torrington said, "That was eight years ago, and Miss Tabor has been all circumspection since. Except, of course, that she's a spiteful little gossip."

Sir William shook his head, took his cousin's arm, and tucked it under his own. "A girl who tried to run off to Scotland, and a gossip at that!

149

If it is the opinion of such a person that is worrying a woman of your intelligence, my dear cousin, you surprise me."

Much soothed by his air of calm, Miss Torrington leaned ever so slightly on the gentleman's arm. Really, at times Sir William was quite a comfortable sort of man. If only he wouldn't be so disagreeable to one at other times. "Sometimes, cousin," she said in gratitude, "you surprise *me*."

"Surprise you, do I?" cried Sir William in high good humor. "There! More encouraging than ennui any day. Progress, to be sure."

Miss Torrington's beautiful violet eyes betrayed a complete lack of understanding at her kinsman's remark.

Chapter Fifteen

Mr. Phillip Renshaw was not by nature diffident, but in the case of Lady Anne Hawley, he
was inclined to be extremely careful. He had sent
her the basket of lilacs as a peace-making offer
and trusted that she would be generous enough to
accept them in the spirit in which they were
given. He was certainly resolved against beginning
to court her in earnest. He had more sense than
that. Nevertheless, he went to call on her the day
after delivering the flowers, taking Sir Stephen
Wrackham with him to underline the fact that he
was merely paying a friendly call on a lady with
whom he was casually acquainted.

To Renshaw's distress, he and his friend were
shown into a large salon seemingly filled with
people — a far cry from the small morning room
he had envisaged, where a solitary Lady Anne
would recline invalid-like upon a sofa. The lady in
question was the picture of health this morning in
her becoming morning dress, and she was sitting
with her Mama, Lord Elliot, Miss Ginevra Johnson, and a dark, earnest-looking young man who
was unknown to Renshaw. At sight of Lady Wormington, the normally fearless young man, who
had had no trouble in facing down roomsful of
the most daunting diplomats on the Continent,
was ready to retreat into the hall.

"My dear Mr. Renshaw," said the dowager.
"How good of you to pay a brief call. And Sir

151

Stephen Wrackham. I never look at you, sir, without recalling my schooldays with poor Charlotte. What a wonderful woman your mother was."

"No question, m'lady, most kind of you," said Sir Stephen with a reminiscent smile. After greetings to the others, he seemed perfectly content to enlarge upon the theme of his mother's youth with the dowager countess. This left Renshaw unmolested by the astringent comments of Lady Wormington and at liberty to join the others.

Miss Ginevra Johnson was extremely pleased at her luck in having chosen this morning to present Barrett to Lady Wormington. At one fell swoop, her cousin had met three men of property who might be able to do something for him: Sir Stephen Wrackham, Baron Elliot, and Mr. Renshaw. Any or all might have a living falling vacant or know of someone who did. The Renshaw property was very extensive, Lord Elliot had his seat in Shropshire, and didn't the baronet have some land in Surrey? Wrackham . . . surely that was the family . . .

"Your pardon, Lady Wormington, Sir Stephen," said Miss Johnson at the first hint of a lull in the pair's conversation. "I have a question to put to the baronet. Tell me, Sir Stephen, isn't yours the estate which is fortunate enough to shelter the ruins of Snowfield Abbey?"

Sir Stephen beamed. "Quite so, ma'am, quite so. Abbey. Falling down around itself. No question, quite a ruin. I'm trying to salvage it, you know. M'house, now, Snowfield Hall, didn't need much work." With Miss Johnson's slight encouragement, the baronet began a rambling discourse on the condition of his family seat. The main house was a Tudor manor, and the adjacent abbey had been acquired around the time Henry VIII had shut the religious houses. . . .

Miss Johnson, who was quite an authority on history, wasn't one to let Sir Stephen keep the floor even when his own property was in question. When he paused for breath, she broke in with a brief, concise, and knowledgeable account of Snowfield Abbey and its environs. "The old religious houses of England are a particular study of mine, aren't they, Barrett?" she said, turning towards her cousin.

"Indeed, yes," the young man answered. "I remember that paper you published two years ago on that nunnery in Hampshire."

"The research is fascinating," said Miss Johnson, her dark eyes alight.

"Must make free of m'place when you're in Surrey, ma'am," put in Sir Stephen, overawed by the fact that the tumbling-down pile of stones on his estate might become the subject of a study by a bluestocking, and a well-known bluestocking at that. His words became even more disjointed than usual in his excitement. "Most happy — show you around myself — no question."

"How kind you are, sir," said Miss Johnson with the friendly look of scholarly pleasure which was the nearest approximation she ever made to the flirting that went on between men and women of more frivolous natures. "I might one day have the occasion to avail myself of your invitation."

"Pleased — anytime — great example of a medieval house of religion, as you say. A great one," said Sir Stephen.

"What's that, Wrackham The old abbey?" Renshaw, who had been sparring with Elliot for the privilege of addressing polite commonplaces to

153

Lady Anne, turned to his friend with interest. "It is a fascinating old place, Miss Johnson."

"So I was informing Sir Stephen," said the bluestocking with a bow.

"Lucky the family place should have such a feature," elaborated Sir Stephen.

"Very lucky," agreed Renshaw thoughtfully.

Lady Wormington, so rudely robbed by that extraordinary Miss Johnson of her private conversation with the son of an old friend, chose to recapture Sir Stephen with a reference to yet another member of his family of whom she wished news.

The room remained too crowded for Renshaw's taste, and he had no chance to exchange a word with Lady Anne in private. The conversation which Miss Johnson, her cousin, and Lady Anne were having on the subject of the latest developments in literature left him and Elliot quite out in the cold. They stared at each other from chairs on either side of the lady each had hoped to impress. When Elliot made a move to go, Renshaw did likewise.

"Lady Wormington, good day. Kind of you to receive us," said Renshaw in parting. "Your servant, Lady Anne," he added with what he hoped was a look full of meaning. "Coming, Wrackham? We're to meet Harcourt at the club."

Anne gazed deeply into Renshaw's eyes as she acknowledged his farewell, then she lowered her eyes to her lap in the style of a green young chit rather than the sophisticated lady she considered herself. She was terribly confused by this visit, and no one, not even Renshaw, could have been more wishful than she that the room hadn't been so full of people.

Her mother's eyes, meantime, were flashing in irritation. "Well, Sir Stephen, Mr. Renshaw is meaning to take you away upon some ridiculous masculine errand which is no more, I'll be bound, than placing another bet at White's or some similar locality. You had as well go with the men, Mr. Johnson, and leave us females to our own devices."

Lady Wormington's words were satirical, but that tone in her voice quite escaped Sir Stephen. "Capital, Johnson. Join us," he suggested warmly. "Not seen much of town? Your cousin can't take you to White's."

The young clergyman started. "Accompany you, sir? Why —"

"Do go, Barrett," urged Ginevra. There was no telling what powerful men her protegé might meet if he went on a ramble with two of the most famous Corinthians in town.

"Come along, man," Elliot put in with his boyish smile. Though they had not exchanged two words, the young baron had taken a fancy to the impecunious clergyman.

"But Ginevra, I meant to escort you home," said Mr. Johnson conscientiously. He looked a little alarmed but was not really reluctant to go racketing off on some masculine adventure with Sir Stephen and the two sportsmen, both of whose athletic exploits even a recluse such as Barrett Johnson had heard lauded.

"No trouble about that, cousin," Miss Johnson insisted. "I have the carriage. Go along." Her voice had enough command to it to compel Barrett to give in with a good grace.

"It will be a pleasure, gentlemen," he said at last.

The four men were soon strolling leisurely

through the spring sunshine towards St. James's Street and their goal of White's, for Lady Wormington had guessed right at their intention: not only was White's their goal, but they meant to place wagers when they got there. Mr. Johnson walked beside Sir Stephen diffidently, awed by the company into which he had suddenly been thrust.

"Enjoying town life, Johnson?" Sir Stephen asked.

"Beyond a doubt, sir," answered the young man with a shy smile.

"Recently come up m'self, after an absence of ten years," confided Sir Stephen. "War, y'know. Famous sport, town. Society and all that."

"Indeed, sir. And the sights are all I had hoped. Have you visited the Tower as yet? I found it fascinating."

"Tower?" Sir Stephen frowned in thought. "Might not remember."

Mr. Barrett Johnson was perplexed, but he reasoned that the profusion of sights in London might well confound one of Sir Stephen's unscholarly bent, especially if visited in quick succession, as he himself had had to do in order to leave most of his time free for the people Ginevra was forever wanting him to meet. "It is a lot to take in," the young man said in sympathy. "Why, in the same day, I saw St. Paul's, the Abbey, the Tower, and even had a quick look-in at the British Museum, though of course I've spent several whole mornings there since."

Sir Stephen Wrackham didn't even bother to respond to such an admission. He merely stared.

Renshaw's ears had pricked up at this exchange. "Sights, eh, Johnson? No lack of them, is there? London is a fine place. But tell me, do you get much amusement?" Remembering the young man's ordained state, he added quickly, "Not that you'd want to be frivolous. But the opera is worthwhile."

"Oh, yes," said Mr. Johnson. "Cousin Ginevra is seeing to the finer points of my education in those areas. But the best thing she is doing for me is gaining me introductions to the best people of what I think is referred to as the ton — people such as yourselves, gentlemen."

"Pleasure," said Sir Stephen happily, charmed to hear himself included as a matter of course in the London haut monde. "Let us do something for your cousin, too. You bring her down to Snowfield, I'll show you around."

An idea which had been forming in the calculating mind of Phillip Renshaw needed only this opening. "Capital idea, Wrackham," he said. "Snowfield's a fine sight, and why shouldn't you make up a party to go and see it? It would be a rare scholarly outing, and it's just what people need at the height of the Season — an excursion out of town. Your place can't be more than an hour away."

"Hour and a half in a coach," amended Sir Stephen, his gray eyes thoughtful. "Excursion?"

Renshaw nodded. "The very thing, Wrackham. We'll make up a party from among our friends, go down and tour the abbey on some warm spring day. An abbey is precisely the sort of thing ladies adore, you know, with all that romantic reading they do, and then that about Byron and his goings-on at Newstead. Any young lady would be charmed to be included in your party." As Renshaw noted slyly the effect of these particular words on his friend, he added, "And there might be some lady whom you wish to show the house

157

and estate as well as the ruin."

Sir Stephen frowned and nodded his head, his eyes on the ground. Miss Miller! Of course, a great chance for her to see the old pile. He'd invite her, and her little chit of a sister, and of course Renshaw would have him ask Lady Anne. . . .

"Miss Johnson'd go, no question," considered the baronet aloud.

"Naturally," said Renshaw, "as she's responsible for putting the idea into my — your head. And Lady Anne Hawley."

"Naturally," repeated Sir Stephen with a shrewd look at Renshaw. His eyes brightened. "Countess Bow-loo?"

"To be sure, old fellow," agreed Renshaw, who knew Wrackham was a disinterested admirer of the comtesse.

Sir Stephen gave a pleased smile but then became thoughtful all of a sudden. "Can't," he said bleakly. "Can't have ladies down. No hostess."

Elliot, who had been listening and hoped to be included in an outing which would feature the presence of Lady Anne, took it upon himself to offer a suggestion. "No trouble about that, Wrackham. Ask some old harridan of your acquaintance to come along and lend countenance to the affair. You must know a dowager or two."

"The very thing!" cried Sir Stephen. "Lady Wormington. Knew m'mother, mother of Lady Anne, the very lady."

Renshaw's jaw dropped visibly. "Now let's think, old man," he said in a pleading tone. "Already we have the comtesse in the party. She is a widow. And Miss Ginevra Johnson is of a very upstanding reputation, and not exactly a young girl."

158

"No older than m'self," protested Sir Stephen. "Must have a dowager."

Renshaw desperately cast about in his mind for some other dowager whose presence would be less reprehensible to himself than that of Lady Wormington, but he could think of no one who was also acquainted with Sir Stephen. It was an unlucky thing that the deceased Lady Wrackham had gone to that dashed school in Kensington those years ago. Was there nobody else?

"I have it!" Renshaw finally cried. "Miss Katherine Torrington is no dowager, but she would be eminently suitable, and you know her, Wrackham."

Sir Stephen nodded. "Charming woman. But Lady Wormington—"

"Her ladyship doesn't go about much, you know," said Renshaw inventively. "I daresay she wouldn't care for a carriage ride she didn't have to take. But Miss Torrington is always eager for amusements, very much so for a lady of a certain age. Besides, she's a particular friend of Miss Johnson."

"Is she?" Sir Stephen frowned. "Of course she's the aunt of M'dame la Countess. Met her. Nice woman. But she doesn't know me well. M'lady Wormington—"

"Take it from me, Wrackham, Lady Wormington doesn't play chaperone," said Renshaw in a tone of finality. "Whereas Miss Torrington would be charmed to do you this favor."

"Think so?" Sir Stephen put his head to one side.

"Why not, man? She looked quite like the sort of lady who must long to see an abbey. All those maiden ladies read novels of the hair raising sort."

"Miss Katherine Torrington is a very good sort of woman," put in Elliot, who, along with Renshaw, had a certain dislike of Lady Wormington. Oh, she was all kindness to him, but there was an abrasiveness in her manner that daunted the young baron and made it difficult for him to approach Lady Anne with anything like a courting demeanor. "And she's always delighted to do a favor to the friends of her niece."

Sir Stephen smiled broadly at hearing himself termed a friend of the Comtesse de Beaulieu. "You men could be right. Never see Lady Wormington go about much—doesn't appear to enjoy it from the way she talks. Likes town life, where everything's close together. Told me so. I'll ask Miss Torrington. She'd do it for me, Renshaw?"

"Mark my words," said Phillip Renshaw with a sigh of relief. "And do you know, Wrackham," he added, "if you'd care to invite Lord Abdul along, this could be an opportunity for him to see more of the English countryside, as he's told me he'd like to do. Wouldn't come amiss, eh? The comtesse likes him."

Sir Stephen looked sharply at his friend. "Didn't know it wasn't the thing, three dances," he said earnestly. "I pointed it out to him m'self. As for M'dame, she couldn't refuse. Would have been rude. She sent back the diamond." His black brows came together dangerously.

Renshaw saw his mistake and was quick to correct it. "I didn't mean that the comtesse was at all improper in her preference, if she has one, which I'd say you're right in assuming she does not."

"Didn't want to be rude," repeated Sir Stephen.

Mr. Barrett Johnson, who had been listening respectfully, said with innocence, "You are speaking

160

of the Comtesse de Beaulieu, I take it? She's very gracious and charming. I met her the other day."

"Lucky man," said Renshaw with a smile. "She'll be inviting you to her literary soirées, and that will be a great thing for a scholar such as yourself."

"Lit'ry circles," said Sir Stephen. "Wonderful woman."

The four continued on their way, their minds on the coming excursion. Elliot and Renshaw thought only of Lady Anne. The baronet's thoughts tumbled between Maria de Beaulieu and Miss Miller. And Mr. Barrett Johnson was wondering just what connection the gracious and elegant Comtesse de Beaulieu had with such an unlikely person as Sir Stephen Wrackham; for that gentleman was certainly very protective of the lady.

Chapter Sixteen

Viscount Westhill leveled his quizzing glass and stared incredulously across the Park. "Good God, Michaels," he exclaimed to his companion. "Are the members of the Corinthian set thinking to set a distressing fashion of originality in the company they keep? First it was Renshaw, going about with that rumpled bear of a Wrackham and that eastern potentate person with the quite ostentatious ruby cravat-pin and such deplorable taste in waistcoats. And now whom do I see but my Lord Elliot, riding in company with a gentleman — ought I to dignify him by that name? — who is not only wearing the most horrifying coat I have seen in a week, but would appear to be mounted on nothing more than a hack from some such place as Tilbury's." Lord Westhill shook his carefully coiffed blond head. "As if these weary old eyes hadn't seen enough today to distress them, what with that dowager we just passed in the emerald green plumes." And his light eyes, which had been critically observing the world for nearly one-and-twenty years, rolled heavenward under their gray-black brows.

Mr. Michaels, a young pink of the ton who quite matched his noble friend in dandyism, said simply, "Pity."

"Elliot is showing round a country cousin, I'll be bound," added Westhill with disdain. "Wouldn't do it myself. Dead bore."

* * *

While these two young exquisites discussed the sartorial ineptitude of the friends of the Corinthians, Mr. Barrett Johnson, unaware that such vanity existed in the world, was quite enjoying his ride through Hyde Park with Lord Elliot. He felt lucky that Elliot had taken a fancy to him. Barrett and the Baron Elliot were the same age, and had been at Oxford—different colleges—in the same years. Although the paths of a wealthy young peer and an impecunious, country-bred scholar had quite naturally never crossed, their common attendance at that famed institution of learning had given them an opening for conversation. It soon became apparent to each gentleman that the other was a good, simple, well-meaning sort of fellow—not at all in one's own style, to be sure, but still a promising comrade.

Elliot had been genuinely shocked at the harrowing tale Mr. Johnson had told him of his cousin Ginevra's direction of the way he passed his days. Not that Johnson was finding fault. The introductions to his cousin's friends at select gatherings of the most erudite members of the London world of scholarship were of absorbing interest to him. But Barrett was used to a rural life, something his London-born female cousin didn't understand. Elliot's sympathetic invitation to ride in the Park at the fashionable hour had been jumped at by both Johnsons—by Ginevra in view of the people her protegé might meet in such company, and by Barrett, to whom the exercise seemed a true blessing. He cantered happily on his hired hack, wearing riding clothes that had been perfectly all right in Hampshire, beside the impeccably clothed and splendidly mounted young aristocrat he had met only the day before.

"Get you out in the world again, what, Johnson?" Lord Elliot said as they urged their mounts forward. "Not meaning to disparage your cousin, of course. Excellent woman. But it must be deuced uncomfortable, sometimes, spending all one's time with her."

"Ginevra means extremely well," said the young clergyman, "and her zeal for my betterment is all I could ask. She has a great family feeling. But yes, my lord, it's a bit difficult to break away for any outside activities. This is the first time I've been riding since I came to town."

"Call me Elliot," the young peer instructed his new friend. "Dash it all, titles are a lot of blasted trouble. Say Johnson, does your cousin mean to catch you a rich wife?"

Mr. Johnson started. "Why, no. Why do you ask?"

Elliot shrugged. "She's been introducing you round. Thought she might have an eligible connection in her mind. Family feeling, as you say." He paused. "Women often meddle in that way."

Johnson was quite at a loss for words. He was well aware that the honest reason his cousin was taking care to introduce him to the ton was so that he might meet a patron able to give him a living. It would be impossible to confess such a thing to Elliot, whom Ginevra considered in the light of a possible one such. Young Johnson had no personal ambition beyond a desire to use his ordination. He had always assumed that, when a parish had need of him, it would be thrown in his way. Even a curacy would start him out, and there was a distant Johnson cousin who might be able to provide him with that much, so he didn't consider his situ-

164

ation desperate. In any case, it would be unforgivable to hint of his need for a living to an honest, unthinking sort like Elliot. "Women often do meddle," he said finally. "But while I can't swear to Ginevra's innocence, I can't feature her even thinking of such a thing as finding me a wife."

"Lucky man," replied Elliot. "But I'd watch her. Could be she's slyer than you think. I never yet met the woman who didn't have it in her mind to marry a fellow off." His was the voice of bitter experience. As a young, unattached peer with a substantial estate (though his pockets were at present to let, pending his next run of luck at the tables) and a noted Corinthian to boot, he was the target of every careful mama who ever shepherded a marriageable daughter to Almack's in this unfortunate season. He was not precisely distressed by the number of young ladies whose eyes followed his undeniably tall and athletic figure, or who likened his blond hair and aristocratic profile to those of a Greek god. It never hurt a man's feelings to be thought desirable. But it was the devil of a thing never to be able to dance with a girl without it becoming the *on-dit* of the evening and giving rise to wagers on when a fellow would make the chit an offer. It was devilish hard, anyway, to be enamoured of the lovely Lady Anne Hawley and to receive no encouragement at all. Her thanks on receiving his recent gift of flowers had been distinctly cool. A man couldn't win.

"Your care when it comes to marriage is, of course, far different from mine," said Johnson. "While I, should I marry, must be on the lookout to form an eligible connection, you, Elliot, *are* a connection of that kind."

"To my cost, Johnson, to my cost," sighed Lord

Elliot. He enjoyed the honest note of sympathy in his new friend's voice. "I was hoping, you know," he added, "to give you something to go on if you're on the lookout for an heiress. I know several young ladies who would do."

"Do you?" Johnson was noncommittal. He was honestly not hanging out for a wife.

"Miss Georgina Miller, for one," elaborated the baron. "It might get her matchmaking sister off my trail if the chit were to marry elsewhere."

"I should hope so," said Johnson. Even the most ruthlessly title-seeking sister could hardly throw a married lady in Elliot's way. "Does Miss Georgina Miller want to marry you, then?"

"Can't tell," said Elliot flatly. "Don't care. The way her elder sister keeps flinging her at my head, she probably hasn't even had time to ask if the chit has a preference for me." He was being overmodest by this statement. He had no real doubt that Miss Georgina must have formed a tendre for him. He was eminently eligible, if he did say so himself, and eighteen-year-old misses were usually the ones to fall victim to his charm.

"I haven't met those ladies," remarked Johnson. "They are the usual run of plain heiresses, then?" He tried to sound as if it were nothing out of the common way for him to discuss women's looks.

"Good God, man, they're both pretty as one could wish," exclaimed Elliot with a laugh. "The elder, Constance, outshines Georgina, but both are uncommon fine-looking women. Unfortunate they should be from the City."

"I see," said Johnson with a sage nod of his head.

"Impossible background," continued Elliot. "But their sister married Wormington and that gives

166

them standing enough, so don't let that put you off if you've a mind to try for one of them."

"No such thing," protested the clergyman, reddening.

"An idea merely," said Elliot. He was quite prepared to leave it at that. In the ordinary course of events, perhaps at this excursion into Surrey that Sir Stephen Wrackham was putting on, Barrett Johnson might meet Georgina Miller and think better of his scruples. She was a dashed pretty girl. Of course, her sister was by far the more striking.

The young men continued their ride through the Park, Elliot pointing out various notables of the ton and stopping once in a great while to speak to someone. Not a few mamas prodded their daughters into more becoming poses at the approach of Baron Elliot. But Elliot had no thought of the female world at present, and he busily described to Johnson the variety of sporting events to be met with in the season. "Next month, I'm having a race with Lord Wormington to Brighton," he said. "Did it last year, and he beat me at it. Curricles, you know. The boy — earl, I should say, though the puppy must be at least two years younger than we are — had the devil's own luck. I've been trying to get him to go it again ever since. Now he says he will, though he wouldn't have it at first with his wife increasing. She fears his overturning and making her a widow, but I saw to it that he didn't let himself be ruled by the petticoat contingent. Shamed him into it, in fact."

"But if the race would truly upset Lady Wormington . . ." protested the conscientious young clergyman.

"Never say it," laughed Elliot. "Pamela Wormington was born a Miller, you'll recall, and nothing oversets those City people. Thick hides. Comes of dealing in trade."

Mr. Barrett Johnson wasn't in agreement with this harsh assessment, but he reasoned that Lord Elliot would no doubt learn tolerance in the course of time. Like himself, Elliot was only four-and-twenty, thought Johnson as he urged his hired mount to keep pace with the showy thoroughbred his new friend was riding.

Chapter Seventeen

Sir Stephen Wrackham had watched the sky from the time he set the date of his party until that day actually dawned. He was in England, and it was spring. One couldn't be sure that the fine weather would hold in order to give a lot of ladies a pleasant ride down into Surrey, but still one could hope. To everyone's delight and Sir Stephen's relief, the morning of the educational excursion dawned cool and fair. The pleasant group set off from the Renshaw house in Mount Street, the gentlemen on horseback and the ladies dispersed in two comfortable traveling coaches.

The ensuing day did justice to Renshaw's oft-voiced confidence in Sir Stephen as a host, an opinion which the good-natured former diplomat had been constrained to offer at least five times a day to encourage a worried Wrackham. It had been the baronet's opinion that anything might go wrong, if only to make him cut a sad figure in front of the Comtesse de Beaulieu and the other ladies. But everything was proceeding well. The invitations had all been accepted, and Miss Katherine Torrington had readily agreed to act as hostess. Besides that lady and her niece, the baronet had invited Renshaw, Lord Elliot, Lord Abdul, Lady Anne Hawley, the Miller girls, Miss Eleanor Tabor, General Cumberland Gerard, and Major George Harcourt. In addition, there was the nominal guest of honor, Miss Ginevra Johnson,

and that cousin of hers who had done so dashed
much studying at Oxford and whose interest in
medieval houses of religion was as great as Miss
Johnson's own.

Thus it was an evenly divided party of seven
ladies and seven gentlemen who lightheartedly
made the journey through the blooming countryside
into Surrey, to be rewarded at trip's end by the
sight of Snowfield Hall. A pleasant Tudor mansion
of aged pink brick, Snowfield Hall was set in a
small, tastefully laid-out park and surrounded by a
charmingly eerie wood, down one of whose path-
ways lay the mysterious ruin of Snowfield Abbey.

After an ample luncheon of cold meats, Sir
Stephen declared it time to visit the ruin. His
house, which he would also be charmed to show
anyone who might have an interest (this last was
said with a boyishly sly look at Miss Miller) must
wait until the scholarly zeal of all had been satisfied by a tour of the noted medieval structure. Sir
Stephen begged Miss Johnson, as the ranking
medieval scholar among the party, to accept his
arm for the short walk into the woods.

"Miss Torrington, other arm," he added with a
look of gratitude at his nominal hostess. "Do me
the honor?"

"Oh, Maria and I will manage perfectly," protested Miss Torrington. She shook her head with a
smile and grasped the arm of her niece.

Maria, who had been half hopeful, half afraid
that Lord Abdul would attach himself to her during the proposed walk, was relieved by this development. The other members of the party followed
haphazardly behind them. Miss Torrington's chap-
eronage was more effective than she knew. By taking charge of Maria (she had seen how the foreign

gentleman was ogling her niece), she had brought an end to any conspicuous male-female pairing and to the hopes of nearly every soul present. Renshaw, in mid-stride as he started for Lady Anne, was detained when a gloomy Lord Abdul joined him. Anne noted this and quickly approached the Millers, determined to walk arm in arm with both sisters. Miss Tabor was shrewd enough to contrive that she and the general should stroll together after the three ladies. Elliot, Major Harcourt, and young Mr. Johnson brought up the rear.

"Wonderful day, isn't it, gentlemen?" remarked Mr. Johnson, for he'd had no lady in mind to escort to the romantic and many-cornered ruin of the abbey.

"Why the devil did she fasten herself to the Millers?" Elliot muttered through clenched teeth. Major Harcourt merely cleared his throat, pulled an even longer face than usual, and was silent.

Mr. Johnson was a complete neophyte in matters of the heart, but he realized that both gentlemen must be in the throes of unrequited love and in no mood for casual conversation. He discerned from the direction of the major's downcast glances that that gentleman's quarry must be the Comtesse de Beaulieu.

It was but a short walk to the ruin, first across the small expanse of lawn which bordered the warm bricks of Snowfield Hall, then through a mossy wood of delightful gloom, the trees newly in leaf. The brick walkway was well kept and had obviously been recently refurbished. A turning of that path brought the group within sight of a tumbling-down pile of ancient stone which rambled hither and yon in a most romantic and provocative manner.

171

"Oh, how splendid!" cried Miss Georgina fervently. "It's just like *The Recess* and *The Romance of the Forest*." She turned to Lady Anne, remembering that her sister-in-law was bookish. "Have you read them, ma'am?"

"I may have, years ago," answered Lady Anne indefinitely. She smiled at the memory of how she had picked up all the romantic novels she could find when she was Georgina's age, including those of Mrs. Radcliffe and Mrs. Lee.

"Georgina," put in Constance. "Of course Lady Anne doesn't read such things, and you shouldn't either, so do be quiet." Constance was annoyed with her sister for stubbornly refusing to seat herself beside Lord Elliot at the informal meal which had just taken place. Georgina had chosen instead to cling to Major Harcourt, even though the brooding military man had done nothing but moon in the direction of Maria de Beaulieu.

"Constance, please let me be," said Georgina with a catch in her voice. She ran ahead of her sister and Lady Anne to the rest of the party, who were clustered round Sir Stephen and Miss Ginevra Johnson at the entrance to the ruins.

"Not safe at all beyond this one hall," Sir Stephen informed the others. "Had it propped up with stout beams here. Mean to do the same down that one gallery you see leading off just there. It goes to a row of cells, interesting to view if it weren't for the danger to the ladies. Another time. Let's step into the hall, though, what, Miss Johnson? There're the remains of a what'd-you'-call-it over to the side—place where they did some dashed thing, can't remember what."

Miss Johnson saw her cue and was pleased to take over the leadership of the group. Sir Stephen, whose knowledge of his abbey was limited to its refurbishing, sprang to the side of Maria de Beaulieu. He had seen the foreign gentleman also making his way in the direction of that lady, and he was ever conscious of the care which must be taken of Madame's reputation.

"M'dame," he said heartily. "Miss Torrington." He took a lady by either arm.

"A wonderful place, Sir Stephen," remarked Maria.

"Nothing—fortunate to have it on the property— history," said Sir Stephen modestly. As the three turned to listen to Miss Johnson's speech on the earlier days of the abbey, Lord Abdul stepped unobtrusively to Maria's side.

"Madame, your servant," said the foreign gentleman softly. He, too, made a show of listening to Miss Johnson's discourse, for he felt the annoyingly piercing eyes of his host upon him. It would seem, thought Lord Abdul in amusement, that the baronet had set himself up as Madame's watchdog, possibly in league with her aunt.

All Maria could do in response to Abdul was to gaze at him in her most frigid manner. This was the first time she and Abdul had been in company since she had learned he was a married man. It would be no bad thing to provoke questions from him on what he had done to vex her. He might then apologize and be graciously forgiven, after which they might proceed with their interrupted light flirtation.

Constance Miller tried to listen to Miss Johnson's history of the monks who had inhabited the place long ago, but her jealous eye had seen that Sir Stephen was in the clutches of Maria and Miss Torrington. She wasn't a bookish woman—she didn't even read light novels like that ninnyhammer Georgina—and Miss Johnson's speech meant little to her. She looked about. Where *was* Georgina? As Constance cast her eye about the ancient, tumbling-down stone room, overgrown with ivy, she identified every lady of the party except her sister.

"Good lord," she muttered half to herself. "Where *is* she?"

"What did you say?" whispered Anne.

"It's Georgina," Constance whispered back. "Did you see her leave?"

Anne's eyes swept the room and returned to her friend. "No, I didn't. Where would she be?"

"The Lord only knows," said Constance. "She was angry with me and must be having one of her fits of the sulks."

Anne nodded without much interest. Then she remembered where they were. This unsafe old building, and Georgina such a romantic little thing . . . "Heavens," said Anne aloud. "You don't think she's gone further inside?"

Constance gasped. "Oh, no. She heard Sir Stephen say it wasn't safe." But her blue eyes were suddenly alive with worry, and the note of fear in her voice was unmistakable as she envisaged Georgina lying unconscious where a falling rock had struck her.

The others turned to the two ladies. "Is something wrong, Miss Miller?" asked Miss Johnson, perceptibly annoyed at the interruption of her discourse.

Constance sighed. "It's Georgina. She's gone, and I can only hope she wasn't so foolish as to hide herself in this crumbling hulk of a place. I must go find her." She made a nervous movement forward

174

...nd felt a strong hand grasp her arm. Looking up, an... ...astonished to see Lord Elliot.

she was a...

"I'll accompany y...you," he said. "Mustn't go off by yourself in this place. We'll find her. Renshaw, you go outside—she's probably th...here."

"I do so hope so," fretted Constance, "but she was so taken with this abbey . . ."

Sir Stephen bustled up with assurances that the ...lace wasn't treacherous. He'd only meant by his ...ive an extra warning to would-be explor- ...organized for a search. It was de- ...ould look down the gallery ...cells, in case Georgina ...head to examine rapidly hastening into folly, and it was all her fault. "What should we do, Sir Stephen?" she asked. She was referring as much to the improperly dispersed guests as to Miss Georgina. She wished that Sir William Torrington were of the party. Maddening as the man could be at times, he always knew what to do in a delicate situation.

"Not to worry—not at all unsafe—find her immediately," said Sir Stephen. "Wait for the others outside, ma'am? We can look about the w——

"Oh, yes, that would be best." rington. "Didn't Maria go off some about the dear fided, feeling trust baron ning, for though Anne was with Renshaw and Maria with Lord Abdul, they had started off by walking all together on a path leading to the back of the abbey which seemed the most likely for Georgina to have taken. Renshaw's long legs soon managed to outdistance Maria and her companion, however, and even Anne, who was tall for a woman, was hard put to keep pace with him.

"Tell me, my lady," said Renshaw quietly, with a glance back at the other couple, "is there some reason you hesitate to walk with me in private? When Abdul suggested a moment ago that he and the comtesse might search another path, you were most insistent that they stay with us." He paused. "The flowers, then, weren't an adequate peace offering?"

Anne said as softly, "Your peace offering was all one could wish. It isn't that, sir."

"Your notions of propriety, then, make you reluctant to walk with me?" asked the gentleman, his eyes ironic. A glance behind had informed him that the other pair was far enough away for him to speak in a normal voice.

"I've never been one to conform to the puritanical notions of which you speak," said Anne. "At least not overly."

These words had the odd effect of making Renshaw stop dead in his tracks and turn to face the lady. "Is it that you sense some special danger?", asked earnestly.

Anne's clear hazel eyes met his. "I danger but what we make ourselves," s

Renshaw looked about him. Lord doubt for his own purposes, had slackened his pace to the point that he and the comtesse were quite out of sight behind a turning in the path. They would no doubt appear in a moment, so there was

177

no time for Renshaw to consider anything beyond the fact that his lady was for once not attended by her mama, or Lord Elliot, or that fop Westhill. His instinct telling him to choose action rather than words, Renshaw stepped forward, took Lady Anne in his arms, and kissed her fiercely.

Anne was not very surprised to find herself responding eagerly to something which should have shocked her more. After a very interesting moment, she extricated herself from her escort's embrace and said in a shaking voice, "Mr. Renshaw, there *is* danger."

As if to confirm these words, at that moment they heard Miss Georgina's scream, faint and far off. "Good God!" exclaimed Lady Anne, recalled to her duty. "Where is she?"

She and Renshaw hurried to an aperture in the crumbling wall of the abbey. Lady Anne, blushing hotly, wondered what might have happened had not that silly Georgina Miller chosen that precise moment to scream. Very likely nothing, Anne thought philosophically, with Maria and Lord Abdul so close behind. They *were* close behind, weren't they? She turned and saw them hastening out of the woods. They had clearly heard the scream, too.

Abdul and Maria had definitely heard Miss Georgina's cry. The foreign gentleman had just kissed Maria's hand with a shocking violence, raised his dark eyes to hers, and was reaching out to take her face between his powerful hands. At sound of the scream, Maria stepped out of his grasp automatically. "It's Georgina!" she gasped. "We're forgetting that we're on a search. Come, she'll be hurt or frightened." She followed the way

Renshaw and Lady Anne had taken with a quickness she hadn't thought of a moment before. Her head was spinning. He had been about to kiss her, but had *she* been about to let him? No one knew better than she what a kiss would promise in these circumstances.

Abdul, with his hand barely touching the back of her waist and his eyes gleaming strangely, had the look of a successful seducer. To Maria, his thoughts on the matter were clear. Her dignity resurfacing, she removed his hand from her person as they came in sight of the others. "Milord," she said, "we'll forget what just happened."

"Not likely, Madame," her companion contradicted her and shot a burning look into her eyes. They caught up with Renshaw and Lady Anne at the wall of the abbey. Some moments were passed in a discussion over whether the opening in the wall would allow them to pass through in safety and arrive at Georgina's side. The scream had not been repeated, and they didn't know what to make of that fact. The gentlemen were reluctant to endanger the ladies in their charge, and others were already combing the interior of the building.

As they stood in indecision, Sir Stephen Wrackham and Miss Torrington appeared at the opening in the wall. "Renshaw!" cried the baronet. "Heard the girl scream? Likely she's down this corridor, the back way to the cells. Don't come in, ladies. There could be some small danger." With chivalrous attention, he handed Miss Torrington out into the sunshine. "Madame, Lady Anne, chaperone to attend you." Sir Stephen glanced around at the quartet he had surprised. "Best to remain outside, ladies. No question it's safer. Gentlemen, join me, be so good. Screamed, you know."

"Gentlemen, do go at once," put in Miss Torrington. "The poor little thing, she must have seen something that frightened her. A—a mouse, perhaps." She shuddered at the thought.

Renshaw and Lord Abdul disappeared after their host into the old building and left the ladies to find their way back alone. Both men's faces betrayed a certain irritation at this interruption.

"Do let's hurry, girls," said Aunt Kitty. "Little Georgina may need our help."

Maria and Anne followed silently behind their chaperone. Each thought it best not to look at the other for the moment.

Constance Miller, hastening through the crumbling gallery with Elliot by her side, had also heard her sister's scream. It was very close to them, although it didn't seem to be rendered with much force. Still, Constance was aghast. "My God, that was Georgina!" she cried. "Let's run, my lord."

Elliot's expression was as grim and determined as it ever was on the hunting field or in the ring. "Step carefully, Miss Miller. There are fallen stones along this hallway," he said as he steered Constance away from a huge chunk of rock directly in her path.

The two turned a corner and came upon a startling sight. Miss Georgina Miller, blushing deeply and with an indefinable mixture of pain and happiness warring in her young face, was seated on a rotted wooden bench just outside one of the famous cells. But this in itself wasn't remarkable. What was singular about the sight was the fact that Major George Harcourt was kneeling beside her, her right foot in its pink silk stocking cradled in his hands.

Her neat kid shoe had been cast to one side.

"Georgina!" Constance ran forward. "Major, what is the meaning of this?" she demanded. As she neared the guilty-looking pair, she noted that blood was flowing from a scratch on her sister's foot. The stocking was ripped, and the major was attempting to bind the wound with a handkerchief. "Good God!" Constance knelt beside her sister. "What happened? Major, let me. Georgina, do you need the salts in my reticule?"

"No, thank you, Constance," replied the younger girl meekly. She stole a look of gratitude at Harcourt, whose eyes seemed to be avoiding her all of a sudden. What a pity, when only a moment or two before they had been staring so deeply into her own. She presumed that his detached manner was on account of her sister's presence.

"There, my dear," said Constance in a soothing tone. "The bleeding has stopped. Can you walk?"

"If someone gives an arm. It's the top of the foot," said Georgina. She tested her words by placing her foot gingerly on the ground. "It seems to be fine."

"However did you come to do such a thing?" her sister asked. "And what, in the name of heaven, did you mean by stealing off here in such a rude and capricious manner? After Sir Stephen warned us that the gallery was dangerous."

"I merely wanted to explore," said Georgina with a toss of her head.

"And the cut?"

"I tripped over a stone, and it had quite a sharp edge. But luckily"—and at this point Georgina gazed adoringly at Major Harcourt—"the major heard me scream and came to my rescue."

The major cleared his throat nervously. He felt

the gazes of both Miller sisters, one loving and one suspicious, as well as the amused eyes of Lord Elliot.

"Major Harcourt," said Miss Miller coldly. "How did you happen to be with my sister?"

"I'd stepped aside to light a cheroot," the major replied with a shrug, "when I noticed that Miss Georgina was taking off down this gallery. Thought I should follow to make sure nothing happened to her. The place isn't safe."

"Yes, Sir Stephen made that clear," said Elliot in good humor. "Lucky thing you were here, Harcourt."

"But most unfortunate that the headstrong behavior of a child should have made your heroics necessary," added Constance, and she fixed her eyes grimly on Georgina.

The younger lady chose this moment to burst into tears.

"My dear Miss Miller, the girl is overwrought," said Major Harcourt. He approached the weeping young lady. "Miss Georgina, do lean on my arm. It's high time we returned to the others."

Constance's eyes widened. Though she wouldn't have believed such a tale had it been told her, she could swear on hearing him with her own ears that Major Harcourt's tone toward her sister was other than avuncular.

"Lord Elliot, couldn't you—?" Constance made a gesture toward her sister.

But the major had already offered his arm to Georgina, had seen to it her tears were dried, and was urging her to lean heavily upon him.

"You'd best let it be, ma'am," was Lord Elliot's advice. The encounter had cheered the young baron to no end. So Harcourt was developing an

182

interest in the Miller chit, was he? Best of luck to him! Perhaps the elder Miss Miller would stop flinging Miss Georgina at one's own head. He offered his arm to Constance with a flourish.

"Thank you, sir," said Constance as she accepted the young man's escort. There was nothing more to be done at the moment about Georgina. A major! A simple half-pay officer with very likely little or no property and no prospect of a title!

Elliot was speaking to her, she realized. "Dashed brave of you, Miss Miller, rushing to your sister's aid like that—no fainting at sight of the blood or anything of that sort. Pluck, that's what it is," the young peer said with approval.

"I've never been one to shy away from such little injuries," said Constance in distraction.

Lord Elliot patted Miss Miller's arm. A bit upset over her sister, but spirited! Quite a spirited young woman. Just the sort of girl a fellow would wish to find, in fact, if one weren't already cherishing a hopeless passion for Lady Anne Hawley.

In the main room, the injured young lady and her party were greeted in a confusion of concern and questions by the rest of the guests, including Miss Eleanor Tabor. This lady approached Constance and said in a low tone, "Do you have a vinaigrette, ma'am? Lady Anne doesn't carry one, and I seem to feel a bit faint. The sun, perhaps."

Constance, wondering if her nursing capabilities should be called into action by the whole world, supplied Miss Tabor with the requested article.

As the two had moved out of earshot of the group, Nell chose this moment to cast a conspiratorial look, first at Lord Elliot's handsome profile, then at Constance. "My dear, I've tried, but I fail to understand it," she said with a sly smile.

183

"What's that, ma'am?" asked Constance without interest. She was busily worrying over the unfortunate intimacy of Major Harcourt and her sister, wondering what Papa would say if he found out.

"It's fascinating, this display of sisterly unselfishness," Nell elaborated. "But Miss Georgina is young, my dearest creature. Isn't this her first season? She has years to catch a husband."

"I fail to see what you're referring to," said Constance in wonder.

"Why, dear Miss Miller, what should I be referring to but the absurd way you are throwing away a perfectly eligible — and noble — catch. Lord Elliot is far too big a prize to go to your little sister."

"Good heavens!" cried Constance in shock. Then, lowering her voice to match Nell's confidential tones, she said, "It's absurd, Miss Tabor. Lord Elliot must be at least two years younger than myself. Such a thing is unthinkable."

But for the first time her eyes strayed to the manly form of Baron Elliot with something more in them than mere calculation.

Chapter Eighteen

Renshaw lost no time when his mind was made up. The very morning after Sir Stephen's party (the remainder of which passed without incident or opportunity for private conversation), the intrepid young man was knocking on the door of Wormington House, a gigantic sapphire ring in his pocket and a grim look on his face. If Lady Anne didn't accept his heart and fortune as repayment for that stolen kiss, he didn't know what he'd do, but it would be dramatic.

The servant informed him that the dowager Lady Wormington was receiving callers in the morning room. The man didn't know if Lady Anne Hawley was with her mother. There was no acceptable way to ask the butler to ascertain the younger lady's presence, so Renshaw had no choice but to take his chances with Lady Wormington in the morning room. If her daughter shouldn't be there, he would murmur one or two civilities and leave.

To his dismay, Lady Wormington was sitting quite alone. She looked imperious, and disapproval flashed from her sharp hazel eyes. "Mr. Renshaw," she said in a voice full of disdain. "You are my first caller today."

"Lady Wormington. Your most obedient," said Renshaw. "I hope I'm not too early for your convenience, but I wished to pay you my respects, and I also hoped to have a word with Lady Anne."

"My daughter isn't at home," replied her ladyship. "But do sit for a moment, Mr. Renshaw." With an air of command, she indicated a very uncomfortable-looking brocade chair.

Renshaw reluctantly accepted the seat. "My lady, I hope I find you well."

"Most kind of you to inquire, sir," the lady replied icily. "And I hope you're well?"

Fighting back the temptation to say, *I will be when I see your daughter, you old fright,* Renshaw responded, "Quite well, Lady Wormington."

"As I mentioned before, my daughter is not at home," said the dowager. Renshaw started, wondering if he had voiced his thought aloud. "And perhaps that's lucky, for I'd like to exchange a word with you in private." She smiled, but her eyes were unfriendly.

Renshaw forced himself to smile back. "You and I have talked before, my lady," he said, referring to the night at the Morland House ball.

"To little effect, it would seem," responded the lady in stern tones. "Mr. Renshaw, haven't I made myself clear? Anne is as good as promised—"

"To Elliot and Westhill, and perhaps one or more of the royal dukes, if I remember correctly," said Renshaw. A cynical smile gave his face an unaccustomed slyness. "Bigamy or worse, upon my word. Would your daughter really consent to such a thing?"

"Renshaw, do be serious," snapped Lady Wormington. "My daughter, Lady Anne, is to marry well. I won't have you coming round to confuse her. She isn't for you, young man."

This was plain language indeed. Renshaw stared. "Your daughter is of age, I believe?" he asked quietly.

"What, pray tell, has that got to do with it?"

"And there aren't any legal entanglements that would compel her to marry only with your consent?" Renshaw's tone was calm.

"My dear sir, you're talking nonsense," her lady-ship said even more snappishly. "My daughter Anne, I tell you, isn't to throw herself away, *Mr.* Renshaw."

It was not that Renshaw didn't understand. He knew by now that he was contending, not with Lady Anne's ambition spoken through her mother, but with the elder lady's lust for a titled marriage for her child. After all, this unfortunate dowager's only son had thrown himself away on Miss Pamela Miller, an heiress of City origin. That marriage had been a severe shock to the earl's mama, a shock she still did not hesitate to voice. Now Lady Wormington was clutching at her remaining single child as at a last straw. Hadn't Lady Anne already vexed her mother by turning down two dukes and a marquis, if gossip were to be believed?

"Lady Wormington," said Renshaw in a kind tone. "Let Lady Anne follow her own heart."

Lady Wormington's eyes flashed. "Sir, I tell you, her heart isn't with you. There are any number of titled men clamoring for her attentions, not least among whom is Viscount Westhill. His lordship's lands march with ours, and his mother—"

"Is your great friend. Yes, I've heard that," said Renshaw. "But isn't he a little young for your daughter?"

"A matter of a few years. Nothing!" cried her ladyship.

"And his grace the Marquis of Hamber, whom I've heard you mention as a candidate," continued Renshaw imperturbably. "Rumor has it he doesn't think to marry again."

"The man is a fool, and so I've told him, if he doesn't," returned Lady Wormington. "He is just of a proper age to make a spirited girl like Anne a good husband."

"He's nearer the age to make her a good father, I'd say," remarked Renshaw.

"And Elliot, a fine young man if only a baron, he's all attention," said the implacable mother.

To this statement, Renshaw could only agree, but he didn't choose to do so aloud. It was his private opinion that Lady Anne preferred himself to Elliot and that she thought of young Westhill only as a friend. He couldn't be sure, of course, but why else would she have responded as she had to that kiss he had stolen yesterday? He must speak to the lady herself. He rose.

"Lady Wormington, you say your daughter isn't at home, but she will be sooner or later. I wish to consult with her on this matter. It would be a pity should her true inclinations be different from your own." He bowed, turned on his heel, and left the room.

"Anne will never be at home to you!" cried Lady Wormington at his retreating back, the rage in her voice clear.

Her ladyship's temper matched her hair, Renshaw was thinking as he left the house. So Lady Anne was to be denied him in her own home, was she? As Renshaw descended the steps of Wormington House, he noticed that Lord Westhill was ascending them.

The young nobleman, exquisitely dressed, was quite blithely running up the stairs with a roll of music in his hand. He and Lady Anne were to practice a new song which they meant to offer in duet at the next musical evening at Morland House.

The sight of Westhill was too much for the impassioned and unsatisfied Renshaw. He had managed to keep calm before a woman, but this young pink wouldn't get by as easily as Lady Wormington had.

"Good day, Renshaw." Lord Westhill nodded pleasantly enough as they passed on the steps. The younger man was relieved that the other had concluded his visit. Renshaw was always making sheep's eyes at Lady Anne, and such behavior was reprehensible to one of Westhill's fastidious nature.

Renshaw, for the second time in as many days, didn't stop to think. He seized the young viscount by his faultless shirtpoints and glowered down at him. "Tell me, Westhill," he demanded in dangerous tones. "When am I to wish you happy?"

"Renshaw, you've run mad," gasped his lordship, and he struggled to free his crumpled linen from the taller man's rough grasp.

"I'll have a straight answer from you, you man-milliner," said Renshaw. With icy calm, he retained his hold. "When, I ask, are you and Lady Anne to announce your happiness to the world?"

With a superhuman wrench, the young dandy freed himself and stroked his injured shirtpoints. "Sir, you are obviously foxed, or I would demand satisfaction for this outrage," he said with dignity. "Good day." He turned and continued on his way up the steps.

"Not one step more, Westhill, or you'll find yourself needing a surgeon," cried Renshaw, grabbing the young man's arm. "I asked you a question, and I'll be damned if you're going anywhere till it's answered."

The viscount paused, gingerly removed the sleeve of his new coat from the other man's wrinkle-provoking hold, and said, "I don't believe you asked me a question at all, sir. You merely muttered some drivel about announcing one's happiness with Lady Anne, by which I must conclude that you are in your cups at this hour of the morning." He sniffed.

"Then you aren't planning to make an offer to

189

the lady?" asked Renshaw, amusement dawning in his eyes.

"An offer — to Lady Anne — I!" gasped Westhill in genuine disbelief. "Not in the petticoat line, sir."

Renshaw smiled. "I thought as much. Forgive me, old fellow. I had to be sure." He started down the steps, chuckling to himself. He'd just thought of someone else he might apply to for permission (nominal though it was) to marry Lady Anne. He'd go see her brother, the Earl of Wormington, at once. "Bespeak a new coat of me at Weston's, my boy," Renshaw called over his shoulder to Westhill. He touched his hat. "I'll leave word with them. Good day."

"Good day, sir," replied Lord Westhill, wondering why the world had suddenly gone mad. "I'm buying most of my things of Nugee these days," he put in. "Still, Weston can cut a coat. Pleased to accept your offer." He glanced ruefully at his own rumpled appearance. "A morning's work ruined," he muttered.

"Fortunes of war, Westhill," replied Renshaw jovially.

The young viscount looked after the enigmatic Renshaw. A mixture of incredulity and repugnance was evident in the languid eyes which were discernable through a disdainfully lifted quizzing glass.

Chapter Nineteen

Alfred Hawley, the young earl of Wormington, had no reason to be dissatisfied with life. At the age of twenty-two, he was master of an earldom with everything a man could ask for: extensive estates, a country seat where he was free to spend each day in hunting field and stable, and a rich wife increasing. His only possible complaint lay in the scarcity of company in his Kentish neighborhood. In these parts, estates were few and far between. The next place, the house of Viscount Westhill, lay ten miles distant from Castle Wormington. Not that Westhill, even had he chosen to reside in the country, would be a congenial companion. No, for that Lord Wormington had only two choices. He could pay a visit to town, or he could entice some of his more sporting male friends to visit him in Kent.

As the shadows fell on a fine spring evening, the earl rode up to the main entrance of his castle. It was an imposing old pile, the castle, the remains of the Norman keep limited to one ancient and well-preserved side wall. The place had been rebuilt under Charles II in the severe classical mode of Inigo Jones, and it presented a satisfyingly simple aspect which its young master didn't find amiss. He was a simple man. The park whose green lawns circled the castle was full fifteen miles round, and the formal gardens, set out in the Italian style, (though a bit ornate for his lordship's unassuming

191

taste) were admired by many. The entire place had been refurbished in his father's time, leaving the new earl nothing to do but see that things were kept up and allow his wife to take a hand in interior decoration.

Lord Wormington, a handsome young man with light, ruddy hair and an aristocratic, sun-bronzed face, took after his mother's family. He was diminutive in stature — no taller, and somewhat slighter in bone structure, than his sister Anne. It caused young Alfred no little chagrin to think that he, the son of a large, imposing father, should have to resemble his mother. But lightness had its uses, and he sometimes wondered if his ability to win every race he entered had as much to do with his weight as his whip hand.

As he swung down from his thoroughbred and threw the reins to a waiting lackey, the earl noticed a smart curricle with a pair of blown post horses on the front sweep. A visitor, and a male one! Lord Wormington ran up the steps of his castle in pleased anticipation.

The butler informed him that a Mr. Phillip Renshaw had called and was presently sitting with the mistress in the Yellow Saloon.

"Renshaw! Capital!" cried his lordship, striding towards the room. The Yellow Saloon was one of Pamela's recent attempts at decoration, and Wormington was sensible of a slight pang that Renshaw should have occasion to view it. Oh, Pamela had assured him that her saloon was all the crack, but such a profusion of gilt furniture and yellow brocade was sometimes blinding to a fellow's eye.

Young Lady Wormington, a buxom, pretty girl of twenty who looked very much like her sister Constance Miller, was indeed sitting with Renshaw. Though she had met her husband's friend only once or twice before, she suffered from her husband's loneliness for new society. The fact that she had no amusements but needlework and letters now that the dowager and Lady Anne had gone to town made Lady Wormington more eager than usual to talk with someone who had just come from that enchanted metropolis. Her delicate situation had lately been making Pamela feel nervous, stupid, and a bit shut in on herself, so anyone who could break up the monotony of her day was welcome. Since Renshaw's unexpected appearance, she had held him captive at her side and made him tell her all the news.

"How *are* Anne and my dear mother-in-law?" she asked. She gave a pettish sigh. "It was so comfortable when they were just across the Park in the Dower House and I could run over to visit them every day. Now that they're so far off, all I get of their society is the occasional letter."

"As it happens, I saw Lady Anne yesterday and left her well," said Renshaw. "And I had the—the happiness of seeing the dowager Lady Wormington this very morning, ma'am. She is also well."

"This very morning!" gasped Pamela. "Then you've come sixty miles since morning?" As accustomed as she was to her husband's constant racing, she didn't think that such speed would be adhered to by an ordinary gentleman traveler. "Do you have some reason for this haste?" she asked curiously. "A race, perhaps?"

"No race, my lady, but I am a man in a hurry," said Renshaw with a smile. "I have to speak to your husband on a most particular matter and then start back to London this very night."

"I can't allow that, old fellow," said Wormington, who all of a sudden burst into the room and rushed up to pump his friend's hand with youthful enthusiasm. Lord Wormington wasn't one to stand upon ceremony. "Now that we have you captive, you'll stay to dinner, and you'll pass the night here, too. Lady Wormington agrees with me, I'm sure."

"I've already given the orders for Mr. Renshaw's room to be prepared," replied young Lady Wormington slyly. "You *will* stay, Mr. Renshaw, to please me?"

Renshaw smiled and shrugged. "When confronted by such hospitality, I can hardly refuse," he said, reasoning that he wanted to be on as good terms as possible with *some* of Lady Anne's relations. "But first thing in the morning, back to town I go."

"What the devil is the hurry, man?" queried Wormington with a slight furrowing of his brow. He flung himself onto a yellow-striped sofa.

"A matter of business, Wormington," replied Phillip Renshaw. "Let's discuss it after we dine." Then, seeing Wormington's frown deepen, he added, "It's not a matter of loaning me money, old fellow. I assure you."

"Shouldn't think so, with you swimming in lard," returned his host easily. "A mystery, Renshaw? I'll play along."

"And now what about my sisters, Mr. Renshaw?" broke in Pamela, returning to the agreeable subject of town gossip. "Constance writes me of a Sir Stephen Wrackham, a friend of yours who has a very pretty estate in Surrey. Do give me your opinion. Is there anything there?"

"In Surrey, Madam?" asked Renshaw, pretending innocence and trying to maintain a serious expression.

Pamela's pleasant, hearty laugh rang out. "Oh, Mr. Renshaw, you know I'm talking of there being a flirtation between Constance and the gentleman. Do tell me what you know," she demanded in her frank, easy way. What had seemed impertinence in Miss Pamela Miller was, she had discovered, nothing more than a becoming, regal air in Lady Wormington.

Renshaw didn't know much, he had to confess. Wrackham had danced with Miss Miller at a recent ball, he said, and was known to have called in Russell Square. The Miller sisters had been among the guests at an excursion which Sir Stephen had hosted to his seat in Surrey only the day before.

"Then there hasn't been a declaration?" asked Pamela, disappointed. "Since he's staying with you, sir, you'd be the first to know if he has marriage on his mind."

"Surely the second," amended Renshaw, smiling.

Pamela laughed in pure delight. How wonderful it was to have such an amusing guest! Whatever the gentleman's business with Alfred was, she meant to tease her lord to persuade Renshaw to stay at least an extra day to conduct it. She had no interest in what the business might be, reasoning that anything of the sort must lie outside her feminine scope of comprehension.

Renshaw could see the salutary effect his humorous speeches were having on the lady and did his best to continue his entertainment through dinner, which he was forced to attend in his driving clothes. It was only when he and Wormington were alone over their wine that he grew serious at last.

"Well, my dear fellow," he said, playing with the handle of his glass of Madeira, "may I mention that business now?"

"Mention away," said the young earl cheerfully.

Renshaw set the glass down on the table with a force that nearly shattered it. "Well, then, not to beat about the bush, Wormington, it's your sister Anne."

"Anne, is it? What's she done?" the brother of the most original lady in London asked in no great surprise. If Anne had embroiled Renshaw in one of her scrapes—such as the time she had driven her brother's own high-perch phaeton through the park quite unasked, or the bleak occasion when she had prevailed upon Elliot to race that same phaeton with his from one end of the Steyne to the other that summer at Brighton (Prinny looking on, too, devil take it!)—then Wormington was prepared to hear it with equanimity. "I'm getting used to Anne," he said. "Out with it. What's the trouble?"

Renshaw frowned. Apparently Wormington had no idea of what his business concerning Lady Anne was. Well, the boy *was* young. "The thing is, Wormington, I'm in love with her. Want to marry her." He swallowed hard. This was the first time he'd said the words to anyone.

Wormington's eyebrows flew up, and he ran around the table to clap his friend on the back. "Well, then, do so by all means," the young man cried. "Glad to get her off my hands. Not that she's precisely on them. A very pretty fortune comes with her from my grandmother's estate. Spirited girl—make an excellent wife. I take it she agrees?" The earl's face was suddenly serious.

"Well, I have every hope . . ." Renshaw's voice trailed away.

"It's *her* consent you have to worry about, Renshaw," warned his lordship. A severe nod of his head gave him a sudden and unsettling resemblance to his mother. "She's refused half the ton, you know. Drives m'mother mad. No, my man, Anne answers to no one but herself. M'mother knows that to her cost." He stared at Renshaw. "Good God!"

"What is it?" asked that gentleman curiously.

196

"Dash it all, I don't suppose you're a duke in disguise?" said Lord Wormington with a shrug. "Can't be helped. But if Anne takes you, the dowager'll have fits, I warn you."

"She already has," Renshaw informed his host with a shudder in remembrance of that morning's interview.

"Good lord, man, don't tell me you've applied to Mother for permission to marry Anne? Crack-brained thing to do. I'm surprised you're alive to tell the tale," cried the earl. "You should have heard her take on when I said I was to marry Pamela. Didn't leave her bed for a fortnight. Now, I'm not saying you ain't an excellent fellow, for you are. Birth and fortune. But without a title, that don't mean much to the dowager. Anne's her last hope of a great match." His lordship grinned at his friend. "But you'd know all that. So Mother talked to you."

"She did indeed," said Renshaw.

"Always been like that from the time we were children. The way she takes on, you'd think Grandfather Redding had been a king instead of a baronet. She married up to get m'father, come to think of it," the earl considered. "I was to do the same. Didn't. Pity, but as I say, it can't be helped. You say Anne's in love with you?"

"I can't be so conceited as to say so without first applying to the lady," said Renshaw.

"Do so, then, man," advised the lady's brother heartily. "Pleased to have you in the family. Take it as consent from the head of it. You don't need it, Anne being of age and more, but take it all the same. M'mother may squawk, but she can't do anything else. Might make for an unpleasant wedding." He laughed. "And don't expect her to pay you a visit too soon."

"That, Wormington, won't be in the question," said Renshaw, laughing in his turn. It was pleasant to talk in this way to *her* brother. It made one feel that all was indeed settled. Talking companionably of other things, the two men made their way to the drawing room to join the solitary young Lady Wormington. Renshaw found it no effort at all to be at his most witty and charming for the remainder of the evening.

The next morning, after an early breakfast in company with his prospective brother, Phillip Renshaw was on the road to town, whipping up in a pitiless manner the various hacks that chance provided him. It was early afternoon when his winded team made its way through heavy traffic to the Wormington town house.

Travel-stained though he was, Renshaw was also extremely invigorated by his journey, and by the pleasant dreams he had been spinning of his success at journey's end. He ran up the steps of Wormington House in a cheerful mood.

"I realize her ladyship is not at home to me, you fool, but I know she's in there all the same, and I will get past," he told the butler, summoning up all the dignity he could muster. "Is the dowager Lady Wormington in?"

"Also gone out, sir," responded the butler.

Renshaw paused for a moment, considering his next move. He glanced over the servant's shoulder. The butler wasn't nearly as tall as himself, and Renshaw could see clearly into the front hall. Surely that figure descending the stairs — "Lady Anne!" called Renshaw.

On hearing Renshaw's voice, the lady — for it was indeed she — hastened to the foot of the stairs. She immediately saw that the butler hadn't let him past and guessed at her Mama's hand in the situation. "Good God, Reynolds, what are you doing?" she said sternly. "Let the gentleman in."

Renshaw regarded her in fascination as the butler stepped aside. She was dressed for riding, in the velvet habit she had worn that day he'd pretended to rescue her at Richmond, and her manner was regal. She was really a fit bride for a duke, but, as her brother had said, that couldn't be helped.

"Will you marry me?" he asked.

"Yes," answered Lady Anne Hawley.

"You wretched girl, you'll do so over my grave!" shrieked a familiar voice. Renshaw and Anne looked up to see the dowager Lady Wormington descending the stairs. She had stopped on the last landing and was clutching at the bannister dramatically. "As for you, Renshaw, be gone from this house this instant. Reynolds, do something!"

"Reynolds, do nothing, unless you want to assist her ladyship to her chamber or bring her a fortifying drink," directed Anne. She turned her eyes from her mother back to Renshaw and returned his bright, happy gaze with one quite as intense. So happiness could come this instantly! How shocking it was that she didn't even want a moment to think things over. She knew somehow that she was embarking on a life of rare adventure, and Phillip Renshaw was the very man she wanted beside her.

Reynolds, a natural diplomat, chose not to move. The newly engaged couple stood near each other without touching. Renshaw reached into his pocket and drew forth a small box from which he plucked, almost casually, a gigantic sapphire set in a white gold band. "May I?" he asked with a boyish smile.

Anne let fall her riding crop, extended her hand

as one in a dream, and watched Renshaw fit the magnificent jewel onto her finger. At this point, she couldn't resist another glance up at her mama. The dowager was speechless with apparent horror.

Renshaw, too, cast a worried look at his future mother-in-law. "Sorry to propose with your mother standing by," he said with another grin.

"At least this proposal isn't in the common way," replied Anne, returning his smile. Their eyes met in mutual appreciation of the scene. Reynolds was standing dumbfounded to one side, a footman in full livery was also looking on from a corner, and Lady Wormington loomed above them like a malevolent fairy at a legendary christening.

In unison, Anne and Renshaw burst out laughing.

"I'll never see you again," cried Lady Wormington from the landing. "Neither one of you."

"Anne," said Renshaw intensely, "let's be married soon. As soon as may be." He hadn't let go of her hand after placing the ring on it, and he gave her palm a lingering kiss as he spoke.

"Do let's," said Anne.

"Break what little is left of my heart, then, with a runaway marriage," put in lady Wormington from the stairs. "It's nothing to me, to be shamed before all London."

"Please, Mama, you nearly ruined my life with your meddling. The very least you can do is let my proposal proceed without your aid," Anne said with a sigh. Originality, it would seem, must needs carry over into all facets of one's life.

"You ungrateful child," moaned her ladyship. "Reynolds, have my dresser sent to me, and quickly, with my salts. I feel an attack coming on."

The butler hurried off to do his mistress's bidding while Renshaw continued to hold his betrothed by the hand and look lovingly at her. "I'd kiss you," he said in a low voice, "but your Mama—and the footman—might not approve."

"I've never yet let Mama's disapproval stand in my way, and I see no reason to start now," responded Lady Anne, clasping her arms round Phillip Renshaw's neck.

The single shriek which Lady Wormington uttered before she fainted on the stairs was perhaps comprehensible under the circumstances.

Chapter Twenty

Major George Harcourt allowed himself to be steered out of St. James's Street and through the portals of Fenton's Hotel. "Have a drink with me," said Sir Stephen Wrackham, "and we'll go out to Jackson's. Young Elliot's having a bout with someone."

"I'm glad to have met you, old fellow," remarked Major Harcourt. "I haven't seen you since last week in Russell Square."

"Quite so, Harcourt, quite so," answered Wrackham. "Hanging about the Millers, are you?"

Harcourt cleared his throat and kept his eyes on the stairs they were ascending. "I go there merely to pay my respects," he said. He didn't really know why the opulent house in Russell Square should have become one of his haunts. Miss Georgina, of course, was a taking little thing, and after her unfortunate accident at Wrackham's abbey, Harcourt had felt bound to call on her once to see how her wound was healing. That once had turned to many times in the few weeks since the fatal party. It didn't do to lead such a young and innocent girl on, of course. Her adoration of him was evident, and gratifying, but he took care to keep his treatment of her on an almost fatherly level. He'd been telling himself lately that a sure way to cure a young chit's calf love was to quell it constantly with an unloverlike manner. This he did almost daily, even though the suspicious eye of Miss Georgina's elder sister was always upon him, and the senior Millers were too vulgar to be borne.

"Miss Miller's a fine young woman," Sir Stephen was saying. "The little girl's nice too, of course."

"Miss Georgina is not, at eighteen years of age, a little girl," considered Major Harcourt, frowning. He glanced up at his old comrade as they entered a comfortable sitting room. "Thinking of getting leg-shackled to Constance, Wrackham?"

"No, b'gad, it hasn't gone that far," answered Sir Stephen in alarm. "Don't want you to think so. A man could do worse, though—could do worse." He advanced with a masterful tread into the room and called out in his booming voice, "Walker!"

The baronet's valet, a small, wiry man whom Harcourt recognized as an old soldier under Wrackham's command in army days, hurried into the room and set out port and glasses at his master's instructions. The man was not the ordinary gentleman's gentleman, thought Harcourt in amusement. Walker's clothing was as rumpled and ill-fitting as Sir Stephen's. But it was kind of the former captain to give the man a place. There were few enough for peace-time soldiers.

"Are you settling in, then?" asked Harcourt, his eyes surveying the elegantly decorated room as he drank off his first glass.

"No question, old fellow," replied Sir Stephen, letting his own satisfied glance roam about the place. "Dashed comfortable, a hotel. Not quite the thing, but one mustn't care for that. With Renshaw married and gone into Sussex, and m'self going home at the end of June—it's already late May, Harcourt, looked at the calendar just the other day—no use to set up lodgings. I must stay in town, though. Season. Invitations." Sir Stephen shook his head in his own particular imitation of world-weariness.

"You were at Renshaw's wedding, weren't you, Wrackham?" asked Harcourt. He was as eager as anyone in town for first-hand details of the marriage that had been the talk of the ton. It wasn't unusual that Phillip Renshaw should have fallen in love with the beautiful Lady Anne Hawley. Many men did, every season. But it was nothing short of remarkable that the elusive lady, who had refused one man after another, should have accepted him. Even more shocking was the fact that the couple had announced their engagement, been married, and were now rusticating at Renshaw's place in Sussex — all in the space of two weeks.

"Yes, famous wedding, small family party," replied Sir Stephen with a smile. He and the Comtesse de Beaulieu had shared the honor of being the only outsiders to be invited down to the private ceremony which had taken place, at the insistence of the young earl and his countess, at Castle Wormington in Kent. The Miller sisters had been there, of course. To Sir Stephen's eye, the dowager Lady Wormington had seemed upset about something, probably the fact that Renshaw and Lady Anne were marrying quickly, in the country, without giving the lady's mama the usual opportunity to brag on the matter before her acquaintance, give a lot of parties, and that sort of thing. "Famous thing, a country wedding," Sir Stephen went on. "Chapel at the castle. No fuss, a honeymoon at Renshaw's seat in Sussex. Famous."

"Better, indeed, than those overdone affairs at St. George's, Hanover Square," said Harcourt in agreement. "And Renshaw's gone for how long? Three weeks? It'll be a bit lonely for you, Wrackham."

Sir Stephen shook his head. "No, there's plenty to do, no question. I'm going about with Elliot—

done up, poor young chap, by Renshaw's winning out with Lady Anne. The boy needs new interests. Took him to the Millers once. I'll take him back again."

Major Harcourt started. Could it be that Lord Elliot was finally taking the bait which Constance Miller had been holding out to him for months, and beginning to court her sister? The major's normally brooding countenance grew even more morose. Of course, he wasn't sorry to see that fine young girl being chased after by a handsome, athletic peer in his first youth. It would be a good thing for her to marry the young man. She'd be Lady Elliot, then, and would become the title greatly. Harcourt sighed and absently took a small silver box from his pocket.

"Snuff?" he asked.

Wrackham accepted a pinch with his usual enthusiasm, sneezed appreciatively, and continued with the conversation. "Yes, as I say, there's plenty to do in town, with Renshaw or without him." He paused. "Miss him, though."

Harcourt nodded. "And there must be another gentleman who'll feel the lack of Renshaw's society. Lord Abdul."

"He's feeling it already," Sir Stephen informed him. "With Renshaw busy the last couple of weeks, m'lord Abdul's been at loose ends. Saw him once at Countess Bow-loo's. She wasn't at home. She and the aunt have been out all the time, helping Lady Anne with the bride clothes or some other demmed frippery notions. You'd know that, though, Harcourt. Always visit the Countess yourself, don't you? Great admirer of hers."

It occurred to Major Harcourt in a flash that, for the first time in nearly three years, he had let a week go by without calling at the home of the

Comtesse de Beaulieu.

"I'm the lady's admirer and always will be," he said. "But it seems she hasn't had time for any of us, what with her preoccupation with her friend's wedding. The Comtesse always did have a match-making streak," he added, "and she might be thinking she arranged the whole thing."

"Ladies' notions," said Sir Stephen indulgently. "It was Renshaw's idea, the whole thing. Talking of Lord Abdul, though, Harcourt. He's staying at this very hotel. Wouldn't come amiss to have him in for a drink, now would it?"

"By all means," agreed Harcourt in no great enthusiasm. He didn't trust Abdul in the matter of the Comtesse de Beaulieu, though it did seem that the two couldn't have furthered their relationship — thanks to Lady Anne and her bride clothes. Maria would be back from Kent now, though, and doubtless Lord Abdul would seek her out. What Harcourt could do to keep Maria out of danger he didn't know, but it would behoove him to be watchful.

Sir Stephen was thinking much the same thing, and his wish to have the Persian gentleman into his rooms for a drink was partly inspired by a feeling that, as long as Abdul was in one's own sight, he couldn't very well be with M'dame. The foreigner meant to dazzle her. He spoke French with her, talking a lot of books, most likely. At least he hadn't had the chance to do so since the party down to Snowfield, with Lady Anne's engagement having come about only a day or so after. Now, though, Lady Anne was gone, M'dame back in town — "Walker!" called Sir Stephen.

The man looked into the room. "Cap'n, sir?"

Sir Stephen gave orders for an invitation to be sent to Lord Abdul to join the gentlemen. Walker left the room to execute these instructions with a military attitude it did Major Harcourt's heart good to see after two years. The old soldier was back shortly with the message that Abdul was in and would be pleased to wait on Sir Stephen. "Servants he's got, not English," Walker confided.

Major Harcourt struggled to keep from laughing aloud, and Sir Stephen nodded seriously, as if he were carefully digesting this information.

In a very brief time, Lord Abdul was announced. It seemed to Harcourt that he came into the room a bit warily, but his dark eyes were friendly enough, and he professed himself to be quite grateful for the invitation. Walker went off to fetch coffee for him and, supplied with snuff, Abdul was soon bowing politely to Sir Stephen's effusions.

"Renshaw's gone, y'know — we should hang together a bit more, what?" the baronet suggested in a friendly, open manner.

Abdul was taken aback by the overture, but his courtesy soon came to the fore. "With pleasure, sir," he said evenly.

"We're going over to Jackson's in a bit — see Lord Elliot in a bout," said Wrackham. "Join us?"

The diplomat bowed. "Nothing would please me more," he said with dignity. "It cannot be for long, however, for I am engaged this evening to dine with Miss Ginevra Johnson — an early dinner for London."

"She does keep vicarage hours," nodded Harcourt. "I didn't know you were intimate with her, sir." It was curious that Miss Johnson, a bluestocking uninterested in men but for their intellects, should have taken a fancy to an exotic gentleman whose chief allure, if one were to go by the reactions of the ladies of ton and demimonde, didn't lie in his scholarship.

"The lady and I find a common ground in our studies of religious philosophies, and a great source in each other for intelligent disagreement," explained the foreign gentleman with a smile.

Sir Stephen Wrackham stared hard at Abdul. So he *was* lit'ry! He'd bear watching. "Miss Johnson's a fine woman," the baronet put in.

"A true lady and a true scholar," added Major Harcourt.

There was some reason to believe that the minds of all three gentlemen in the room turned, on hearing Harcourt's description of Miss Johnson, to another woman of their acquaintance who had some claim to those qualities.

Chapter Twenty-one

"Maria, let's drive out in the Park," said Miss Katherine Torrington in her most persuasive tone. "It's a lovely day."

Maria looked up from her late husband's old copy of Voltaire. "But, Aunt, someone may call."

"My dear, you know this isn't one of our regular days at home. I believe you should get out and take the air," Aunt Kitty insisted.

"You're trying to take Anne's place, aren't you, Aunt Kitty?" said Maria with a laugh. "Well, you needn't. I want to get somewhere with my reading."

"But, child, you've been staring at that volume for half an hour and have yet to turn a page," persisted the aunt.

Maria sighed. It was true that her concentration had never been worse. She had a lot on her mind. Foremost among her thoughts was that, except for two brief meetings at parties, she hadn't seen Lord Abdul for two weeks. Anne's marriage plans had been taking up so much of her time! She had spent practically all those two weeks in Bruton Street at Madame Hélène's and the rest in the wedding party to Kent. Maria still had to smile at the memory of the dowager Lady Wormington's poorly hidden chagrin at the clever matchmaking of the Comtesse de Beaulieu. To think that her invitation to Renshaw for that quite recent soirée had initiated Anne's present happiness! It gave one a sense of power. And how enjoyable that quiet wedding down in Kent had been, with herself and Sir Stephen Wrackham the only guests outside the family. Maria frowned slightly as she remembered the baronet's attentions to Constance Miller. Now why, pray, did that make her unhappy? Constance would make Sir Stephen an admirable wife, and it was clear that matters were progressing in that direction. Why this sense of foreboding then?

As Maria pondered this, the door opened and Roy announced a visitor.

Miss Eleanor Tabor entered the room, causing Maria to start violently and Miss Torrington to drop her fringework. Nell hadn't set foot in Curzon Street in years, and it was evident that this was no simple social call, for Miss Tabor's light blue eyes were flashing and her color was extremely high.

"Do sit down, Miss Tabor," said Maria in her most gracious tone, putting aside her book and trying to keep her eyes from betraying her shock.

"I won't sit down," cried Nell, "I've merely come to say what must be said, and then I shall leave, never to return."

"We're surprised to see you, dear," put in Miss Torrington with an innocent air.

"Ma'am, I should think you would be surprised, for I find it extremely difficult to behave with the proper civility to your niece. And I've found it so for the past three years!" These words out, Nell burst into angry tears.

This was too much for the tenderhearted Miss Torrington. She fluttered from her chair to put an arm around the weeping girl and lead her to a sofa, where Miss Tabor sat down without protest and accepted a handkerchief. "My dear child, you're overly excited," said the maiden lady. "Try to be calm."

"H-how can I be calm," sobbed Nell, "when I find my prospects ruined once again? And due to *your* meddling!" The last words were directed to Maria, who had been wondering if she and her aunt were being treated to the spectacle of Nell Tabor running seriously mad.

"How have I meddled?" asked Maria. No one was more aware than she that Nell's grudge against her already had a good foundation. There had been an unpleasant scene like this one three years ago, when Nell had raged into Maria's drawing room to accuse her of stealing away George Harcourt's affections and, in addition, informing him of that long-ago elopement scheme in Nell's past. Of course, Nell had also justifiably blamed Maria, all those long years ago, for betraying her plans to marry the dancing master. Maria really had no idea that her husband's tongue was so loose that he would betray her bosom friend's secrets to none other than the father. She had spent days in icy silence before forgiving the comte's lapse. But what was she supposed to have done now?

"Don't insult me by asking, you know very well," retorted Nell, drying her eyes. "You, of all people, who are very likely no better than you should be, to be spreading the tale of my long-ago indiscretion even now."

Maria saw it all, or thought she did. "I take it that General Gerard has learned that you tried to run off to Gretna Green when you were eighteen?"

Nell's response was to burst loudly into fresh tears.

Miss Torrington's bright, innocent eyes had been moving from Maria to Nell and back again. "Miss Tabor," she said, "if the general would let such ancient history weigh with him — you were but a

211

child! — then he's not worthy of your devotion."

"I agree," said Maria.

Nell's eyes flashed. "You told him of it, then, to test your theory?"

"My dear, you're mistaken," replied Maria. "I haven't spoken two words to General Gerard since I met him, and I certainly haven't sought him out to tell stories about you. I assure you that, however he heard of the matter, it wasn't through me."

"Indeed," put in Miss Torrington with an unfortunate lack of tact, "everyone who was in town in those days knows about it."

"You needn't remind me," said Nell with a sniff. "But who else but your niece would want to hurt me? She makes a habit of blasting my hopes."

"But why should I want to?" said Maria. "If I'd known you thought I was so spiteful and malevolent, I could well have wanted to hurt you, but until this moment I hadn't realized the depth of your hatred." Her voice shook slightly, for she was more than half inclined to join her former friend in a bout of tears.

Miss Torrington, with a worried glance at her niece, went on trying to smooth the matter over. "Why, anyone at all, Miss Tabor, might quite innocently have mentioned your little story to the general, thinking he must know already. It was no great secret at the time."

"I asked you not to remind me of that," said Nell, her voice quavering.

Maria had recovered herself. "Miss Tabor, I must ask you in the future not to come to me when chance disrupts your life. Your problems are not my doing." She had a momentary pang as the clock seemed to turn back and she remembered the pleasant days of their girlhoods, when Miss Eleanor

Tabor and the newly married Comtesse de Beaulieu had been such friends. What a pity that friendship couldn't be mended.

"Chance!" cried Nell. "Was it chance that tore Major Harcourt from my side?"

"It must have been," said Maria with dignity.

"Girls, let's be calm. I'll ring for some tea. That ought to fortify us. And perhaps if we are silent for a moment—" Miss Torrington was pleading desperately when the door opened again to disclose the butler and another visitor.

"Madame, I am your slave," said Lord Abdul. His dark eyes were gleaming as he hurried across the room to salute Maria's hand. "At last I find you at home." He bowed toward the ever-present maiden aunt. "Miss Torrington, good day." He then gave a questioning look at Miss Tabor. "But I've surprised you with another visitor. Miss Tabor, I believe? Your servant. Would it be better for me to go away again?" Abdul's eyes were sharp, and it was evident to him that the interview in progress was anything but pleasant. The flaxen-haired woman's red eyes and the aunt's worried expression were testimony to that, though his lovely comtesse betrayed no emotion but graciousness and genuine pleasure.

"Don't go, Lord Abdul. I'm leaving now myself. I can see that *privacy* is wanted here," said Nell Tabor, rising and gathering up her reticule. "The comtesse and I have finished our conversation." She shot another angry look at Maria. "I doubt we'll have another." She left the room.

"What a strange young woman, Maria," said Miss Torrington softly as the door closed behind Miss Tabor. "Such intensity! I cannot like it. Maybe I should speak to her mama. A rest in the

213

country—"

"Don't trouble yourself about it, Aunt. She'll get over it. The disappointment was crushing to poor Nell, and she couldn't have meant what she said," replied Maria as lightly as she could. She had been trying to control her flush of embarrassment at Nell's spiteful remark regarding privacy when she tossed her head in sudden decision. Why not enjoy herself, if the tattlers were already busy? "You must excuse all this, sir. Mere feminine squabbles." She smiled at Lord Abdul. "Do be seated."

"Pleased," said the foreign gentleman, choosing a chair very near Maria's. His compelling eyes turned to Miss Torrington. "Are you both well, ladies?"

"Oh, yes, and being very quiet now after the excitement of dear Lady Anne's wedding," said Miss Torrington. She quite warmed to the gentleman, for although she didn't trust him, his manners were excellent "Of course the season is still going strong and we've seen from the stacked-up invitations that we are never to have an evening at home, but it isn't the same with Lady Anne gone off to Sussex."

Abdul smiled. "I, too, feel the lack of my friend Renshaw." He turned back to Maria and noticed the book on the table beside her. "Voltaire? Excellent, Madame. Might I not amuse you ladies by reading aloud?"

"How kind you are, sir," put in Miss Torrington. She might have made the suggestion herself, for what could be more harmless than reading? She wished suddenly that Sir William were on the scene to observe how well she was chaperoning Maria.

"Sir, I'd like that very much," agreed Maria. As

she handed the volume to Lord Abdul, their fingers touched slightly, and her nerves jumped.

The reading had barely gotten underway when Roy again entered the room. He murmured something discreetly to Miss Torrington.

That lady gave a little gasp. "Oh, dear me," she said in alarm. "Maria, excuse me for just a moment. There's something amiss in the kitchens. I must go to the housekeeper." She had risen at the butler's words, but hesitated. Should she leave Maria and that exotic gentleman *tête à tête*? She cast a worried look at her niece.

"Go ahead, Aunt Kitty," said Maria. She and her visitor were only reading, after all. There was no danger in such an innocuous pastime, and even had there been—"You'll be back in a moment, dear. Go along."

Miss Torrington nodded nervously and followed Roy out of the room with one backward glance. Innocent enough, to be sure. Maria in one chair, the diplomat reading French—he *was* a cultivated gentleman—in another chair. There was nothing to be concerned about.

When the door closed, Lord Abdul snapped the book shut and regarded Maria steadily.

"Madame," he said in a low voice, "would you hear more?"

Maria stared into the swarthy, handsome face. Had anyone ever looked at her with such blatant desire? She said nothing.

Abdul, his admittedly vast experience with women standing him in good stead, took Maria's silence as sufficient encouragement to rise from his chair, spring in one movement to her side and kiss her with a rough force she had never before experienced.

215

She put her hands on his shoulders and forced him away, her expression disbelieving and her face aflame. "Sir," she faltered. "My aunt—she'll be back—please read to me."

Lord Abdul's smile was knowing as he returned to his seat and picked up the book again. "Madame," he said in a casual tone as he searched for the place where he had left off, "we must drive together in the Park. Tomorrow? I have Renshaw's curricle at my disposal."

Maria lowered her eyes. "I should like that."

"And the rout at Lady Sefton's tomorrow? Are you going?"

"Yes, milord," she said in a tone as casual as he had made his own.

"Then we'll have the pleasure of each other's company twice tomorrow," stated the gentleman, his eyes more intense than ever. "And for the future?"

"The future, sir?" asked Maria. She hoped that her knowledge of his marital status, which they had never discussed, was apparent in her voice. For them there could be no future.

"We must simply let it unfold," replied Abdul. His provoking eyes returned at last to the book.

The moment he began to read, Aunt Kitty came back into the room. Maria struggled to maintain her calm. After all her years of pointless flirting, she was being swept into something very dangerous.

Aunt Kitty's chirping voice brought her back to reality. "You must speak to the staff yourself, Maria," she said with a shake of her curly white head. "They aren't at all clear on what they are all doing. That message that just took me to the kitchens was a complete waste of my time, for nothing was wrong after all, and Roy and the housekeeper were

216

near at daggers drawn over the origin of the message."

Neither Maria nor her aunt noticed the sly flash of triumph in the romantic dark eyes of their foreign visitor. These servants had been particularly easy to buy.

"I'll speak to them," said Maria vaguely. She had never had a talent for managing servants, and she was in no mood to think of domestic matters now.

"Now do go back to your reading, sir. My interruption was quite impolite," Miss Torrington urged.

Abdul bowed. "You, madam, could never be judged other than gracious," he said with an enigmatic smile.

When Abdul ended his visit, he made sure to remind Maria of her engagement to drive with him on the morrow, kissing her hand lingeringly as he did so.

When the gentleman was safely out of the room, Miss Torrington cried, "My dear! Driving out with that man in the Park, and at the fashionable hour! What will people say?"

"Why should they say anything? I often go driving with gentlemen — Major Harcourt, Lord James Lofts, lots of people," Maria responded with what she hoped was an offhand air. She was still trembling inside at the memory of that kiss. It had unnerved her so much that she couldn't remember if she had taken pleasure in it at all.

"But, child. There are already those three dances and that diamond," said her aunt.

"All that was ages ago, and I believe I was acquitted in any case."

"Oh, but Maria," sighed Miss Torrington. "What you do with gentlemen of our own kind and what you do with a gentleman from another land are

217

very different things in the eyes of society."

Maria nodded. "Yes, Aunt, you do show insight there," she said with some surprise. "But the engagement is made."

Aunt Kitty sighed again. "And besides going driving with him, there is the unfortunate fact that Nell Tabor saw him coming to visit you. She will not be still, you may depend upon it."

"If that's the case, Aunt Kitty, I might as well drive with him as not," said Maria reasonably. "People will be talking anyway."

"I cannot like it," warned Miss Torrington.

"Don't worry," advised Maria. "He's a very courteous gentleman—you can see that yourself—and it amuses me to talk French with him." She had to struggle once more to keep her voice on an even, matter-of-fact level.

"I'll trust to your discretion, Maria," said Aunt Kitty, but she privately resolved to consult Sir William Torrington on the matter. It was perfectly true that Maria often drove out with gentlemen, but there was the hint of something different, almost sinister, in this case.

"Thank you, Aunt," replied Maria. She didn't know if she would be worthy of that innocent trust. Indeed, she had never in her life felt her free will slipping from her as quickly as it had this morning. She had set the tongues of the ton wagging time and again in her years of widowhood—even during her marriage—but she had never yet purposely set out to do so. However, neither had she ever felt such a powerful attraction to any of her flirts. Was she at long last starting down the road to dalliance? Lord Abdul obviously thought so. Maria wasn't certain, but she suspected that she had already gone too far in this flirtation to draw

218

back when the crucial moment came and the gentleman demanded more. The idea was worrying, but it was also very exciting.

Chapter Twenty-two

Mr. Barrett Johnson turned the corner of a row of shelves in Hookham's Library and came upon a strange sight. A light-haired lady in a gray velvet pelisse and a fashionable bonnet of like color was sobbing quietly into a volume of Maria Edgeworth.

"Miss Tabor," he said quietly and stepped up to the young woman with chivalrous interest. "It *is* Miss Tabor, isn't it? Barrett Johnson at your service. We met at Sir Stephen Wrackham's party down to Surrey. May I help you in some way?"

Nell Tabor's blue eyes, brightened by tears, met a pair of sensitive, dark ones. "Sir, there is no help for me," she said dismally. "I'll try to control myself. Please let me be."

Not for nothing had Mr. Johnson been ordained as a clergyman. "Miss Tabor," he said sternly, "there is always help."

"I suppose you're talking of church and such things, for you're a clergyman, aren't you, sir? But no prayers can help me now," said Nell gloomily, and she dried her eyes.

"Perhaps—" Mr. Johnson glanced around the library. It wasn't crowded. Even so, there were people about who would soon notice the young lady's tears and make her sad situation food for gossip. "Perhaps if I were to see you home," he suggested.

Nell shook her head. "I have the carriage, and my maid is waiting." She wished most desperately to be left alone. Another tear rolled out of her eye, and she was obliged to retire into her handkerchief once more.

"Miss Tabor, this will never do," said Barrett Johnson with all he could muster of authority. "I'll walk with you down the street, your maid following behind, and you'll tell me what is troubling you. It will help you to talk about it." He looked warily around the room once more. "It would be unwise to let anyone notice your tears," he said.

Nell drew in her breath, and her wet eyes also darted round the room. "Sir, I—you don't think anyone has noticed? I was perfectly calm, then somehow when I came in here to peruse the shelves, I found myself thinking of—of *it* again, and I—" She gave a quiet sob, and the handkerchief came into play again.

"Be calm, Miss Tabor," urged Johnson. He had never dealt with women, but he suspected that they were only human. He patted the young lady's sleeve encouragingly and tucked her hand under his arm. "We'll go out into the street and take the air."

"Very well, sir," sniffed Nell Tabor. She was not in the habit of disagreeing with gentlemen.

The two young people waited a moment, Johnson's thin, dark-coated form shielding the lady from possibly curious onlookers. When Miss Tabor's eyes were finally dry, they left the library and descended into Bond Street. There Miss Tabor announced to her servants her intention of returning home afoot, in Mr. Johnson's company. The carriage went on its way, and Miss Tabor's maid fell discreetly into step a few paces behind the couple.

"Now, ma'am, isn't it better outside?" Mr. Johnson's intelligent face looked up into the bright spring sky. "A lovely day. Makes one long to be in the country, though."

"I wish I were in the country—far, far away," said Nell. "Yorkshire, perhaps, or—or anywhere. It's so miserable here, sir."

"Then you don't enjoy the empty amusements of town?" asked Johnson curiously. "It isn't often that I meet with a young woman of sober mind."

"Of course I am very sober, and I hate the frivolous life of London and the wicked people who make up society," stated Nell. It was perfectly true. She hated all the shocking goings-on in town. Balls were amusing, of course, and the opera—but it was no pleasure to be constantly thrown together with the likes of Maria de Beaulieu and the other fashionables whose behavior was absolutely vile. Nell's eyes filled again.

Barrett Johnson noted this development. In an attempt to draw his companion out, he said quietly, "It must continually overset one of your upstanding nature, Miss Tabor, to be obliged to mix with those whose manners are not as highly principled as your own." He had some vague idea that the lady's morose and tearful state must be due to an indecent comment from a gentleman or some other immoral circumstance.

Hearing her high principles lauded made Nell's tears flow faster, and she had a hard time avoiding another fit of sobbing. "Oh, sir, you aren't aware of my—my past, and you would very likely not choose to walk with me if you were," she cried.

"Calm yourself, ma'am, and remember we're in the public street," whispered Johnson. They had just passed several people of fashion whose looks had been curious, to put it mildly. Johnson hoped that none of the lady's acquaintance had been among them. He was well aware that tongues wagged on the least provocation. "Would it help you to think of me as a disinterested advisor, and to tell me of this past of yours?" He smiled gently. Surely this well-bred young lady could have committed nothing worse than a small social misdemeanor.

Nell caught her breath. She had never of her own free will let fall a word about her long-ago indiscretion, and it amazed her that the young man's suggestion was so tempting. He *was* very young, but there was something solid about him. Surely he wouldn't turn from her in disgust on hearing her poor little tale, and if she didn't tell him, he was bound to find it out from someone. Maria de Beaulieu and her ilk would see to that. "Sir, it's really none of your concern," she faltered.

Johnson smiled again. "Come, now, Miss Tabor. All of us are concerned with one another, and I, who have pledged my life to helping my fellow man, am certainly no exception. If you trust me, your trust will not be violated."

Nell sighed. "If that is true, Mr. Johnson, you would be the only person in my experience who hasn't violated a trust of mine."

"Surely not, Miss Tabor."

Shrugging, Nell said, "It's true that I'm thinking of one person in particular when I speak of a trust violated, but certainly no one in London has ever been behindhand in spreading gossip concerning my poor little adventure. Shall I really tell you?" she appealed to him.

His eyes were warm. "If you want to."

Nell felt her muscles go tense, and she glanced behind her to see that the maid wasn't following too closely. Not that the abigail didn't know all the details of her mistress's past follies. Nell began, "Mr. Johnson, you must promise not to be shocked with what I tell you." She managed a faint smile.

"You have my pledge," said the young man.

Nell nodded, satisfied. "Sir, it's a very simple story, and a foolish one — as I can see now that I'm older and wiser. But at the time it seemed the only thing to do, and I can't fault the fact that I followed the dictates of my young heart." Nell was never one to make light of her troubles, but somehow she was uneasy, knowing she was speaking in too dramatic a manner.

"It's always admirable to follow one's heart," said Mr. Johnson. He was struggling to maintain his equanimity for, by this time, he had imagined every sort of past adventure for Miss Tabor, foremost among his conjectures being a country inn seduction or even a bastard child hidden away.

"I was eighteen, and I was in love, Mr. Johnson," continued Nell more easily than before. Luckily she did not see the shock on the gentleman's face as he thought he heard his wild conjectures being confirmed. She noticed that his presence was truly comforting, but she didn't look at him. "The gentleman wasn't an eligible connection, and my family would never have approved." She took a deep breath, then brought out the horrid truth. "He was my dancing master!" There! Now let Barrett Johnson recoil if he would.

"A dancing master," the young clergyman repeated. He hid with difficulty his relief and his shame at having thought so badly of Miss Tabor. "No, not a fit mate for one of your standing, ma'am."

He didn't seem unduly shocked, Nell was relieved to see. "You may as well hear the worst, Mr. Johnson," she went on. "My father wouldn't countenance such a match, and so — in desperation as I thought — this man and I planned to elope to Gretna Green. I assure you, sir, that whatever my method, my thoughts were always of marriage. And, I must assure myself for my own comfort now, so were his." She cast down her eyes.

"I'm sure they were," said Mr. Johnson. "Your plan was surprised, then? By your father, I would guess?"

Nell's eyes narrowed in bitter remembrance. "Indirectly, sir, indirectly. I was foolish enough to confide my plan to someone, my closest friend at the time, and she was disloyal enough to betray my secret to her husband, who in turn told it to my father." Her face reddened angrily at the memory.

"And you can't forgive this friend?" Barrett Johnson asked, venturing a fairly safe guess.

Nell drew herself up with dignity. "Never think I'm such a monster. I did forgive her, ages ago. Sir, this regrettable incident took place eight years ago, and to think that I would bear such a grudge —"

"How could I? You must forgive me," said the young man quickly.

Nell granted him a gracious nod. "She begged me to forgive her, and I did. She swore that she'd repeated my tale to her husband only because he'd guessed the half of it. I was constantly at their house in those days, and the husband may well have remarked something odd in my manner. And she, this friend, swore further that she had told her husband the plan was to be kept in confidence. But he, as luck would have it, was a friend of my father's, and he lost no time in betraying the scheme. Papa caught us up and brought me back to London, but —" she paused and dropped her eyes again —"not before I had remained out the entire night. Of course word leaked out, and my reputation was ruined." She stopped speaking and ruefully dabbed at her eyes.

"The world is overcensorious, Miss Tabor. You must find it in your heart to forgive society as well as this friend of yours." Mr. Johnson's pleasant voice was firm. "But is this old story the reason for your tears today? You can't still be haunted by it."

"Yes and no," answered Nell. It was odd. Once she had confessed one thing to this young man, the desire to confess all seemed to mount in her. "Sir, I may as well tell you. But first let me mention that, after I was allowed to go back into society after my elopement scheme, my behavior was all circumspection. I have made sure I paid for that youthful lack of judgment by being very strict with myself."

"Admirable," put in the clergyman.

"Thank you," Nell said. She had known a clergyman would approve of her words. "Now I must go on. Because of my reputation, I haven't exactly been overwhelmed with eligible offers in the past few years."

"The world is censorious, as I said before," said Barrett Johnson in sympathy.

Nell nodded. "But twice in the past years gentlemen have become very fond of me, and each time the man has been made to—to cry off, in effect, through the evil machinations of that same horrid woman who ruined my elopement plans those years ago." She started to cry again, but very softly, remembering the presence of her maid behind them. "The last gentleman was on the point of a declaration—even Mama didn't doubt it—and this very morning he came round to tell me that—that—"

"Don't continue if it disturbs you," begged Mr. Johnson. He was not certain he wanted to hear the intimate details of the conversation between poor Miss Tabor and her unworthy suitor. "If he could let such a thing weigh with him, he is not deserving of your tears, and you have nothing to regret."

226

So lately had similar words been spoken by Maria de Beaulieu and her aunt that Miss Tabor stiffened with anger. "He's going into politics, sir, and can't afford to have his wife's past be anything other than spotless. I couldn't blame him, and he was all kindness." She flinched at the memory of General Cumberland Gerard's last words to her. *A fine girl you are, m'dear—always will say so,* he had muttered with his eyes to the ground. *But you must understand . . . going into the House . . . Otherwise, might have married you anyway.*

"He was kind enough," she amended, shuddering.

"And you say that the lady whom you forgave for her first indiscretion has purposely sought out this man to tell him your secret? And has done so before, in another case? Miss Tabor, I find that incredible."

"I wouldn't put anything past her," cried Nell in real anguish. "General Gerard would have married me, he said so himself, but for the knowledge coming to his ears. And who else has a motive to hurt me?"

Mr. Johnson stared. "Miss Tabor, my dear Miss Tabor, do you mean to say that the gentleman who nearly made you an offer was General Cumberland Gerard? My dear young lady, he must be above fifty years of age." The young man's face expressed true consternation.

"He is a very respectable man," said Nell.

Johnson shook his head. It seemed to him that Miss Tabor had experienced a narrow escape rather than a piece of ill luck. The bluff, aging military man whom Johnson had met recently was certainly no fit match for this pretty, gently bred young lady. "There is respectability, and there is suitability," he said gently. "Often they're very different things. But to return to your former friend. Did the general tell you it was she who informed him of your past?"

"Not precisely," Nell said. "He didn't say where he'd heard it. But no one else could have a motive to hurt my prospects, I tell you, and after what she did to me three years ago—"

"Ah!" Johnson detected the bitterness in his companion's tone. "I'd forgotten that other incident."

The image of George Harcourt was suddenly before Nell. "In that case, she stole away the gentleman's affections. She denies it, he denies it, but the fact remains that he fell madly in love with her and forgot me instantly."

"And did they marry?" asked Johnson.

"Marry? Maria de Beaulieu isn't one to marry. She hasn't a moral about her. It's her style to keep gentlemen dangling while she flirts unmercifully with them all." Nell was so upset that she didn't notice she'd mentioned the name of her sworn enemy.

But Mr. Johnson had noticed. "Ah, it's the Comtesse de Beaulieu whom you dislike so fervently."

Nell reddened. "It's no great secret."

"And none of my affair," Barrett Johnson added quickly.

"This very day," confided Nell, "I went to see her and told her what I think of her. I've wanted to do so for ages. Her behavior is always most shocking." She shook her head in outraged propriety.

"My dear Miss Tabor, you didn't!" said Mr. Johnson with a slight gasp.

She looked up at him, surprised at his sudden lack of sympathy. "Why, yes, I've just said I did."

"But what an uncharitable thing to do! Surely one of your high morals would go to such a person to forgive, not to condemn," her companion said with severity.

228

Nell was immediately on her high ropes at such insolent religious zeal on the part of this young man, but at the same time she felt a twinge of regret that she had disappointed him. "I rushed out of the house in anger," she said. Directly after General Gerard had left her, she had ordered up the coach, blood in her eye, and gone tearing off to Maria's house. It had been an impulsive action. Reason told her that the more ladylike thing would be simply to avoid Maria from this day forward, never giving the creature a hint that she had been found out in her latest foul deed. But, Nell considered in her own defense, she had only followed her heart's dictates. Had it really been uncharitable? Considering Maria's history, and her present scandalous behavior with the Persian gentleman, Nell thought not. The Comtesse de Beaulieu surely deserved any unpleasant thing she got.

"Miss Tabor, for your own peace of mind, I would have you go to the comtesse again, ask pardon for your hasty words, and begin your friendship anew," the young clergyman said.

Nell couldn't have been more shocked had he suggested she become a performer in Astley's circus. "My dear sir, I couldn't lower myself to do such a thing."

"You would, on the contrary, raise yourself," the gentleman said.

Nell sighed in vexation. "Sir, I can't do it. Anything else, but not speak to Maria gain. You don't know the woman. Besides doing me those wrongs, she is behaving in a most notorious manner with Lord Abdul, the emissary from Persia."

"Those words have the unpleasant sound of gossip, ma'am," said Mr. Johnson, his dark eyes more disappointed than ever.

They had long since turned the corner into Albermarle Street and were approaching the Tabor residence. Nell was relieved. It was suddenly very distressing to be questioned by this priggish young man. She didn't like him at all. "This is my house, Mr. Johnson," she said stiffly.

The young man's sad eyes swept over her. "I'm sorry to have made you angry. You're upset, and you don't mean the half of what you say. Think of your duty to your own conscience, and also ask yourself: are you quite certain it was the comtesse who did you this latest wrong? If, as you say, your elopement scheme is common knowledge, it could have been anybody."

Nell shook her head. "It was she. I'm sure."

Johnson smiled slightly and saluted her hand. "I won't argue with you when I don't know the facts myself. But tell me, Miss Tabor, may I call? Perhaps it would amuse you to walk in the Park tomorrow. And do you know my cousin Ginevra? She'd be happy to receive a visit from you. I know you're a young lady of scholarly interest." (This he assumed from her tendency to seek refuge in books when she was overset by her emotions.) "And I might take you to discuss literature over tea with my cousin." He would have to search his inexperienced brain for decorous ways to entertain the lady, but that she would need diversions in the coming days was clear to him.

Nell was struck by the kindness of the young clergyman's offer. "Sir, I'd be pleased to walk with you tomorrow. Shall we say five o'clock? I'll have to confirm it with my mama."

"Excellent. I'll call at that time," said Johnson, and he gave his best imitation of the bow with which Lord Elliot favored the ladies. He smiled once more and was gone down the street.

Nell looked in speculation at the retreating figure, so unfashionably clad and yet somehow so dignified and upstanding. How odd that, disapprove of her though he did, he should desire her company. He wasn't at all a man of consequence, but he was a friend of Lord Elliot, and that gave him automatic stature. And should General Gerard be in the Park next day, it would do him no harm to see that Miss Eleanor Tabor was not in the least suffering for lack of male company.

Chapter Twenty-three

"My dear good fellow, the Comtesse de Beaulieu has always been a flirt, and I daresay you are refining too much upon what is merely her usual behavior," said Viscount Westhill. He regarded the waistcoat of his companion, Roger Bickerstaff, with a gimlet eye to drive home the fact of his disapproval—both of such talk and such dress.

"Juliana has it from the best sources and the evidence of her own eyes," retorted Bickerstaff. "The widow's making free with her favors this time for sure. And why not? The Regent approves." He gave the other man a wink. "The foreigner drives her everywhere, every other dance at parties, exchanging knowing looks, all that. Things a fellow like m'self wouldn't notice, mind you, but m'wife has sharp eyes."

"Your wife, my dear Bickerstaff—and I mean this in all respect—is the worst gossip in London," exclaimed Lord Westhill. He was defending the good name of the comtesse both for her own sake and for that of Lady Anne, who was still in Sussex and not present to safeguard Maria's reputation. Chivalry of this sort wasn't in Westhill's line, but neither was it common for him to hear a lady of his acquaintance made the subject of a ribald remark by that fool, Roger Bickerstaff—and right in the morning room of White's! Westhill had really been left no alternative but to beckon Bickerstaff (and one couldn't but deplore his coat as well as waistcoat though heaven knew that stocky build must try the patience even of a Weston) into a small sidechamber and respectfully ask him to retract his words. Westhill's respect was not for the patently unintelligent Mr. Bickerstaff, himself, but for his superior strength and size—of which Westhill would be the first to admit he had a quaking fear. But what the devil did this large lump of a man mean by "the Regent approves"?

Lucky for the peace-loving viscount that Bickerstaff, who was always ready to repeat any sort of story he heard for its interest value alone, was just as ready to take back whatever he might say. "Don't mean the lady any disrespect by pointin' out her devotion to the crown, assure you, Westhill," said Bickerstaff. "Good day." He turned back to the other room. The very sight of that fop Westhill aroused the ire in him. He was better off making any interview with Westhill short and sweet.

Lord Westhill disdainfully lifted his quizzing glass to watch Bickerstaff leave. He then crossed to one of the only two easy chairs in the little room, flung himself into it with every attention to the welfare of his sleekly fitted coat, and sighed loudly. Suddenly he raised his eybrows and gasped, for sitting in the chair opposite him was Sir Stephen Wrackham.

"I didn't make m'self known," the baronet said with an apologetic smile. "Didn't want to interrupt you and Bickerstaff. What the devil does the man mean, Westhill? Devotion to the crown?"

Westhill glanced around, then leaned forward. "Bickerstaff tends to make much of the fact that his father-in-law obtained him a place in government, and at the oddest times he chooses to flaunt a supposed intimacy with affairs of state. In reality, I suspect our dear Bickerstaff occupies his time in the diplomatic equivalent of boot blacking. Apparently, he's picked up that our Prince smiles on this supposed liaison between the comtesse and the Persian, for whatever reason. But pay no attention, Wrackham. The man's a fool." He felt it didn't behoove him to mention that, at least in the areas of size and regrettable taste in dress, he considered Wrackham to be just one such as Bickerstaff.

"Have a mind to call him out m'self," said Sir Stephen. "I can't have the name of M'dame la Countess bandied about."

"He's simply repeating what he's heard, Wrackham, like many another parrot," shrugged Westhill. His eyes were darting towards the door of the room. It wasn't part of his day's plan to remain closeted with Sir Stephen. "No harm in the man really, or I assure you I would have demanded satisfaction myself. Any friend of Lady Anne Renshaw's is under my protection," he added in his most grandiose manner.

"I must have a word with m'lord Abdul," said the baronet. "Can't have *her* behavior questioned. I've noticed they have been much together—his doing. Going back to Persia soon, so he says. Didn't choose to meddle before, but must put a word in his ear and see he leaves her be."

"My dear Sir Stephen," said Westhill with raised brows, "before you do such a thing, are you quite certain that Maria de Beaulieu would welcome such interference on your part? Perhaps she enjoys the gentleman's company."

Sir Stephen's countenance darkened dangerously, and Westhill immediately regretted his words. "You defended her yourself!" exclaimed the baronet, very nearly roaring. "She likes his company. They speak

234

French. Her husband spoke French with her—told me so herself—and she misses it. Nothing wrong in it."

Westhill nodded sagely, privately wondering if Sir Stephen were really taken in to the point where he could believe that a woman's interest in Mirza Ali Abdul Khan could be limited entirely to the language arts. It was evident that the baronet admired the comtesse, but Westhill hadn't supposed him so blind in his admiration as not to see the quite extraordinary attention Maria had been paying the foreign gentleman in the last couple of weeks. Lord Westhill decided to be charitable and open the eyes of poor, besotted Sir Stephen. He was only a sort of *cavaliere servente*, to be sure, for the world knew him to be romantically in the toils of Miss Miller and her jewel-case. But if he intended to go about defending the Comtesse de Beaulieu, he might as well know what he was up against.

"You might not know, coming from the country as you do, my good sir, that widows are accorded a sight more freedom than the ordinary—er— young lady," Westhill began cautiously. "What I mean is, no one in the highest circles would condemn Madame de Beaulieu if she were to—that is—" Unable to find the words to go on, Westhill was sure of the one thing he should *not* say: that many who had scoffed at the young widow's flirting in the past would be glad to see her at last caught by cupid's darts and made unhappy—as she was destined to be when the foreigner left for home.

But he had said more than enough already. His light eyes bulging with rage, Sir Stephen made a lunging move toward the suddenly quivering Westhill before he remembered the man's inferior age and stature and resumed his seat. "Take it back,"

235

he said in what was perilously close to a growl.

"My dear sir, I'm only making you current with the prevailing mood of society. Who knows anything about the comtesse's actions but the lady herself? If the ton is saying certain things, though, you might as well know," said the young viscount, trying to keep his shuddering well hidden. "Only speaking as your friend, and hers, I assure you."

Wrackham relaxed and nodded, satisfied. "What else?" he asked.

"Sir, your powers of observation are as keen as my own. People will talk when they see a particular lady and gentleman together a good deal. Can't be helped. Wouldn't worry about it if I were you. You may speak in her defense, of course, as do I, but Abdul will be returning home before long, and the whole regrettable incident will be over. I daresay there's nothing to it. When has Maria de Beaulieu failed to pay attention to a handsome man who flattered her?" When he saw Sir Stephen begin to frown again, he added quickly, "But she means nothing by it. It isn't the lady's fault, to be sure. It's her enemies who are inclined to gossip, even more so than her friends." He was thinking specifically of the loose tongue of Lady Juliana Bickerstaff

"Enemies?" queried Sir Stephen. "She can't have enemies, wonderful little lady."

"Her good qualities don't preclude her having enemies," said Westhill, reminded of all the ill feelings rampant among the dandy set in light of his own superior taste and style. "Jealousy, my dear Wrackham." His was the voice of bitter experience. "Jealousy."

"Of course," said Wrackham. "Keep defending her, Westhill. We must do our best, no question."

236

He rose and took leave of the young exquisite, who, it must be said, wasn't sorry to see him go. Men such as Wrackham made Westhill very nervous.

The anxious baronet went straight from White's to a certain elegant house in Curzon Street, where the comtesse's butler informed him that the ladies were out. Damned if the butler didn't have a look of sly insolence on his ferret-like face as he said the words, too! His mind all worrying solicitude — for he had a great fondness for Madame, a great one — Sir Stephen turned his steps towards Russell Square.

The Miss Millers were already entertaining two male visitors. Constance had a welcoming light in her eyes as she greeted Sir Stephen, and he sat down to make five in a group that included Major George Harcourt and Baron Elliot. Even in his distraction, Sir Stephen noticed that Lord Elliot's face was as brooding as Harcourt's. The poor lad hadn't been the same since Lady Anne had married Renshaw.

"Seen the countess lately, Miss Miller?" Sir Stephen asked his hostess.

Constance started. Gentlemen didn't make a habit of beginning their conversations with her by a reference to another lady, and she couldn't say she liked the style. "The Comtesse de Beaulieu, you mean? Why, yes, last evening, at the opera."

"She was well?" persisted the baronet.

"She looked to be," replied Constance. This was extraordinary! "Do you have some fear for her health, sir?" she asked with a touch of sarcasm.

"Wondered. Merely wondered," said Sir Stephen in an offhand manner. He moved uncomfortably in the chair which had suited him very well only a moment before. "Not seen her the past few days. I mean to write Renshaw," he invented. "Message to Lady Anne saying her friends are well."

Constance laughed. "You may be sure that the Comtesse writes to dear Lady Anne herself, as do I, and there is no shortage of messages."

Sir Stephen, to Constance's surprise, frowned. "Not wanting to think you'd gossip."

"Whatever do you mean, sir?" asked Constance, turning towards Lord Elliot as if for protection. That gentleman shrugged.

"Sir Stephen is referring to the comtesse's entanglement with Lord Abdul, sister," put in Miss Georgina in her high, clear voice.

"Georgina!" gasped Constance. "Talking of gossip—"

"Excuse me," said Georgina demurely, casting down her eyes. She raised them after only a moment and added to the group at large, "You mustn't think I meant anything by the remark. I love the comtesse. She's only flirting, Lady Juliana says, though it does look bad—"

"Georgina!" repeated Constance in sisterly anguish. "To think that you should know about such things. Do hold your tongue before the gentlemen, at least."

"I may be young, but there are some things I know," said Georgina with dignity, giving Major Harcourt a sidelong look.

That gentleman, thinking he ought to help Miss Miller, engaged Miss Georgina in a conversation about that evening's proposed visit to Almack's and even went so far as to solicit the promise of a waltz—for the patronesses of that august institution had lately given the young lady permission to perform the dance.

238

Constance, while much soothed by the reference to Almack's—she and her sister had succeeded in storming the ramparts of that temple of exclusivity, thanks to Lady Wormington—still had cast a worried glance toward her sister and that impossible middle-aged nobody of a major before devoting herself to Sir Stephen and Lord Elliot. She was growing accustomed now to the latter gentleman's visits to Russell Square—in the beginning to talk of Lady Anne and his blasted hopes, but lately to discuss things in general, especially the sporting life he loved. Constance could never discover in him any marked preference for Georgina and assumed that Elliot saw in herself merely a sympathetic ear for his troubles.

Recently, though . . . Well, one couldn't refine too much upon one remark of Nell Tabor's. And it was clearly unsuitable to be thinking romantic thoughts of a man younger than oneself, a man moreover who might marry where he chose and wasn't hanging out for a fortune. Sometimes Constance had to remind herself sternly that Sir Stephen Wrackham was undoubtedly more suitable to her purposes, in age and situation. Georgina must make the great match, and so she would as soon as she recovered from her absurd attack of calf love for Major Harcourt. A baronet was quite good enough for the elder Miss Milller. Let Pamela and Georgina play the Miss Gunnings and marry high. Yet it was a gratifying notion that Lord Elliot was beginning to cast what might be jealous looks at Sir Stephen Wrackham. Constance felt her heart flutter momentarily, then chided herself for a romantic fool. Lord, she was growing just as silly as that widgeon Georgina.

Sir Stephen held the floor for the length of his

call, discussing the wedded bliss of Renshaw and looking forward to the time, very shortly now, when the newlyweds would arrive back in town. "Great thing to have them back. A great one, no question," he said heartily.

Constance smiled. "It was all so highly original of Lady Anne, being married in the middle of the season and then returning to town before the end of it. I even believe she means to give an entertainment in her new home before we are all quite dispersed to the shore and the country. And it's extraordinary for a bride to open her husband's home to guests before she's had an opportunity to redecorate."

"Renshaw's house is fine as it is," put in Sir Stephen in loyalty to his friend. "Lacked only a hostess." He smiled at Miss Miller with a meaningful gleam in his eye, then lowered his gaze quickly. What the devil! It was dashed uncomfortable flirting with the woman. He'd meant to marry this time, no question—never meant to play fast and loose with the lady. But dash it all, best hold off. This didn't seem to be such a good idea after all. Sir Stephen felt a moment's pang of guilt at his disloyal thoughts of Miss Miller, but a surreptitious glance at the watchful Lord Elliot gave him a hint that she might have another string to her bow than his worthy self.

When Sir Stephen ended his visit with the Millers, he declined to accompany Elliot and Harcourt to Tattersall's. Instead, he turned once more in the direction of Curzon Street. In a remarkably short time, he was knocking again at the door of the Beaulieu residence.

This time, his luck was better. The butler, still with that odd look of insolent slyness on his sharp face, informed the baronet that Madame was indeed receiving callers. Sir Stephen strode into the drawing room with a sense of foreboding.

"Why, dear Sir Stephen. How kind," said Miss Torrington in greeting. She cast aside her knitting to extend her hand. Wrackham saluted it good-humoredly, but his mustachioed countenance was seeking the face of Maria. *She* was on the sofa, smiling at him in a friendly way, and Lord Abdul sat close beside her.

The only other visitor in the room was Sir William Torrington. "Wrackham, sit down," said this gentleman, his handsome face truly welcoming under his fine head of white hair. "Been trying to entertain Miss Torrington myself and making a mull of it. Only your entrance made her drop that deuced needlework. Devil with the ladies, what, Wrackham?"

"Yes—mean to say—" Sir Stephen found himself confused and unable to make a clever answering quip. He sat down as near to Maria and her foreign guest as he could. "Fine weather, what?" he said brightly when he was settled. "Nearly summer."

"A lovely day," agreed Maria with a smile. She was glad to see Sir Stephen. With her relations right in the room, the intense looks and murmured compliments of Lord Abdul had been making her very uncomfortable, and any interruption was welcome. Remembering the rumors she had lately been hearing, she wondered if she ought to ask after Miss Miller's health. Sir Stephen was said to be constantly at her side.

"Madame and I will be out to see the day first hand later," put in Lord Abdul. His glance at the comtesse was almost one of ownership. "We're driving in the Park."

241

"What, again?" remarked Miss Torrington, and she shot a worried look at her kinsman.

"Making that rather a habit, Maria?" offered Sir William when he saw Katherine's distress. "I'd hoped to persuade you to drive out with myself and your aunt. Family party."

Maria smiled slyly. "I know you two need a chaperone, Sir William, but today you must do without me. Aunt Kitty will take her maid for protection."

"Oh, Maria, as if that were necessary," put in Miss Torrington. "Sir William and I are friends and second cousins." She blushed prettily.

"The Park," Sir Stephen said. "I'll be there m'self. Hope to meet you all. A famous thing to go out and see friends, no question. An awful squeeze in the Park, y'know." That was true, wasn't it? Everyone was in the Park at the fashionable hour. What if a lady were driven there often by a gentleman? Not a lot could happen with the ton looking on. A lot of talk, but nothing else. No doubt M'dame knew that. Besides, the lady couldn't help it if the same gentleman always asked her. Sir Stephen made a mental note to put a word in Harcourt's ear and get him to drive out with the comtesse. The major had been seen only the day before squiring the Miller chit, but dash it all — something was due an old friend like M'dame. Sir Stephen couldn't be so bold himself. He looked surreptitiously at the comtesse, a frown of comradely concern fleeting across his face. A crying shame if her spotless reputation should be injured due to the unthinking foreign ways of Abdul. Wrackham would put a word in the man's ear. Fond of the comtesse as he was, the foreign gentleman would draw back once he heard that his actions were causing talk.

With all this in mind, Sir Stephen saw to it that he left the house with Lord Abdul. He suggested that, as St. James's Street was nearby and the hotel their mutual goal, they stroll back that way together.

"Is something wrong, Maria?" asked Aunt Kitty when the drawing room door had closed behind the two gentlemen. "You're being very quiet today."

"It's nothing, Aunt." Maria shook her head and lowered her eyes in consternation. Why should she be so weary today? She was growing tired of holding Abdul back, that must be it. His every glance said he was ready to progress beyond flirtation, but Maria hadn't yet convinced herself to take that fatal step. A powerful attraction was not love, but could a dashing widow expect any more? Sir Stephen and Constance Miller—*they* might have the good fortune to find love in the rigors of matrimony. But as the Comtesse de Beaulieu, condemned to one affair after another . . . Maria sighed and retreated to her chambers to lie down. She did not even notice Aunt Kitty's discomfort at being left alone with Sir William Torrington.

Out in the spring sunshine Sir Stephen was losing no time in coming to his point. "You're fond of M'dame la Countess, what, m'lord?"

Abdul's dark eyes were immediately furtive. Was this another instance of the baronet's absurd watchdog tactics? "I honor the lady greatly," said the Persian in an expressionless voice.

"Capital, m'dear fellow, capital," cried Sir

Stephen.

Abdul started visibly and returned the baronet's smile with caution. "It's not unusual, surely, to admire such a lady?"

"Everyone does, no question," agreed the baronet. "M'self, Harcourt, Lofts. A regiment of admirers. Knights."

Was this gentleman, this self-professed knight in ill-fitting armor, giving a warning that such a regiment might be dangerous to cross? "I count myself among your number," said Abdul.

"Great thing, to be sure," said Sir Stephen. "As M'dame's friend, I mean to give you a warning. Gossip, you know. Doesn't do. Go about with her a bit less. You're going back home soon, what? Talk can't hurt you. Can hurt *her.*" He looked earnestly at the other man.

Lord Abdul's eyes were thoughtful as he took this in. "Madame la Comtesse and I have found much common ground for discussion, and if it seems that I monopolize her time, then you must remember that I'm soon to return to my homeland. You must sympathize with me, sir."

"No question, m'lord," said Sir Stephen. "Painful separation leaving new friends. Returning to the family though, what?"

"To be sure," replied the foreign gentleman.

Sir Stephen noticed that his companion's manner had grown suddenly cold, and he wondered if he ought to have hazarded that last reference to the man's three wives. Well, what was the harm? Had 'em, didn't he?

The gentlemen's talk turned to more general matters, but there was a strain between the nominal friends. When they turned in to Fenton's Hotel, it was in relief that each parted from the other—

Abdul to prepare his most persuasive speeches for his drive with the comtesse, and Sir Stephen to order his horse so that he might also be in the Park and in a position to observe every minute of that drive.

Chapter Twenty-four

Lady Anne Renshaw's first appearance as a married woman was to take place at the Duchess of Morland's musical evening. As that fatal night approached, the polite world grew curious, and those who hadn't received an invitation to Morland House sought out ways to beg one. Her grace had never been applied to by so many people whom she could ordinarily neglect to invite due to their lack of interest in music. When all was said and done, the duchess was more delighted than not to find that what she had conceived as an intimate, select gathering was turning out to be the musical event of the season. Rumor had it that the Regent might look in. In preparation for this possibility, the duchess had caused a throne-like gilt chair to be placed in a prominent position, and she had seen to it that one of the musical groups performing was his royal highness's favorite wind band.

The rooms began to fill, and sooner than anyone could have expected, the place became—in the words of Lord Westhill—shocking tight. The Regent did arrive and, accompanied by his entourage, surged his way to the makeshift throne. To the astonishment of all, he seemed to be settling in for a long visit.

When the stir of this had died down, the music was at a momentary lull, and the company had not yet become too absorbed in its own conversation, the Renshaws were announced. Lady Anne came sweeping into the room on the arm of her husband. She was resplendent in a gown of pale lilac gauze, and he was as striking in his coat of purple-black superfine. The newlywed couple paused a moment, as if conscious of the sensation they were creating, and then Lady Anne whispered something to Renshaw. They headed in the direction of Maria de Beaulieu.

The comtesse, with her Aunt Kitty beside her, was sitting at the center of a group of admirers which included Lord Abdul and Sir Stephen Wrackham. Maria looked up happily at sight of her new-married friend. "Dear Anne, and Mr. Renshaw. You're causing quite a sensation."

Anne accepted the gilt chair which several gentlemen vied to place for her. "Maria, it seems an age since we really talked," she said with a smile. "I don't count that call you paid me. Too many others were there."

"Very true," remarked Maria. "It was hard to find a seat."

"Curious onlookers, Madame, wanting to observe our wedded bliss," put in Renshaw. He placed his hand on the back of Anne's chair, and they looked at each other for an instant before Anne's bright hazel eyes returned to her friend.

"In any case, Maria," she said with a serious look. "We must seize a moment this evening to talk."

"By all means." Maria put her head to one side. She knew this insistent manner of Anne's. There must be something very particular on her friend's mind if it couldn't wait until a morning call when they could be private.

"Oh, Lady Anne, you're looking so well," said Miss Torrington heartily. She had to rejoice to see such a happy bride and groom after all the empty marriages of convenience which distressed her year after year among the ton.

"I am remarkably well, Mistress Kitty."

"And are you singing tonight?" continued the maiden lady.

"Yes, Westhill and I are doing our new duet," said Anne with a mischievous glance up at Renshaw. "That is, if I can persuade Phillip to control his jealousy."

Renshaw smiled. "As this is such a public affair, I'll trust the two of you," he quipped in return. He then turned away when a member of his Highness's suite tapped him on the shoulder and murmured in his ear. With a bow to the ladies, he was gone to pay his respects to the Regent.

Anne, observing this, felt honorbound to be glad at her husband's prominent place in society, but she knew he was no intimate of Prinny's and could only hope he was not going to become one. She had turned her attention to the conversation in Maria's circle. Consisting as it did mainly of empty compliments, Anne wondered how she could ever have found such talk fascinating, for her own group of admirers used to behave the same way.

Lord Abdul was saying, "Allow me to make the observation, if you please, that Lady Anne Renshaw and Madame la Comtesse are, as always, the loveliest ladies in the room."

"No question," added Sir Stephen Wrackham wholeheartedly.

What must Constance Miller think of this development, wondered Anne. She was amused by the baronet's protective air and the obviously suspicious looks he was casting Lord Abdul. Sir Stephen's chivalry was very welcome, of course. Any help was gratifying at this point, for things between Maria and the Persian had evidently gotten out of hand. Even if Anne had not received news of Maria's behavior—in every letter sent down to Sussex and from every caller since her arrival back in London—she could have figured it out herself. The leonine expression of ownership in the eyes of Lord Abdul and the quiet air of acceptance with which Maria regarded him were obvious to all.

Just then, the dignified and stately figure of Sir William Torrington advanced upon the group. "Sir William!" exclaimed Anne. She extended her hand as the white-haired baronet made a courtly bow. "It's so unusual to see you out of an evening."

Sir William smiled. "I am a great lover of music, and I heard that you were to sing tonight, dear lady. Could I deny myself the happiness of hearing you? Not to mention that your first appearance since your marriage is an event not many have chosen to miss." He gestured to the crowded room. "Should I be behind all London in welcoming you back?"

"You are gallant as ever, sir."

"And of course his female relatives welcome Sir William's protection," put in Miss Katherine Torrington.

"Which I give with great pleasure," replied the baronet. He bowed again, favored his kinswoman with a warm, affectionate smile, then turned his eyes towards his other cousin. "I trust Maria is also glad to see the old boy?"

"Oh, Sir William, how could you doubt it?" said Maria.

"You are a delight, my dear," responded her cousin. He took a position of seeming permanence between Miss Torrington and her niece, put his

249

hand on the back of Katherine's chair, and began to discourse on the musical selections to be given that night.

"Old songs are my own favorites," remarked Sir Stephen Wrackham loudly after hearing Sir William express a preference for the airs and ballads of the past century. "No question."

"When Maria used to play the harp, she favored those old melodies," said Sir William. His manner toward Wrackham was most cordial. It both amused and delighted him that the gentleman, though reputedly a suitor for Miss Miller's hand, should have enough friendly admiration for Maria to wish to protect her from Lord Abdul's attentions. For that same reason, Sir William had bestirred himself from his comfortable fireside. Dear Katherine was extremely worried, and it was certainly no hardship for him to stay at both ladies' elbows nowadays. Extremely convenient in the matter of Katherine, in fact.

"Ah, Madame, you play the harp," said Lord Abdul with a tender look. "You must do so for me."

"Delighted, sir, but I haven't touched the instrument for months. It would be laughable, I'm sure," said Maria. She felt her cheeks grow warm under his intimate gaze.

"Famous instrument, the harp," put in Sir Stephen. "Most happy to hear it m'self, M'dame."

Maria started visibly. This was the first time that Sir Stephen Wrackham had expressed a particular desire for her company. "As I told Lord Abdul, sir, any performance which I could give now wouldn't be worth hearing. Give me time to practice, and I'd be glad to favor you both with a song or two."

"See that you do practice, Maria," put in Anne.

"It's time you got back to your old interests."

"My life is quite hectic during the season, but perhaps in the summer—"

"It would be an excellent change for you to do so now," said Anne. "I keep up my music, you know."

"But Anne," returned Maria with a smile, "you are well known for your energy."

"You're becoming well known yourself, my dear," said Anne in a low tone. She watched Maria's eyes widen in surprise, then she dropped the subject.

Anne was soon obliged to leave the group to find Westhill and arrange the details of their upcoming performance. "I pray the boy has remembered the music," she said with a sigh. "I see him over there with Mr. Michaels and Mr. Denny, and I mean to accost him." As she left the party of friends, she had to accept again the many wishes for good luck in her performance and the happiness everyone felt at her return to town and their midst. She was more and more glad that she and Renshaw had decided things as they had. What could be more original, indeed sensational, than a short honeymoon and a return to London at season's height?

Maria, returned to the center stage of her little group, smiled at Sir Stephen Wrackham and opened her mouth to speak, but Lord Abdul forestalled this attempt by addressing a comment to her in low, intimate French. Maria wondered, as she gave Sir Stephen an apologetic smile, why her foreign friend had to be so possessive. She was beginning to find his manner annoying. He was not a husband, after all, at least not to her. She thought wistfully of the truly intimate bantering Anne and Renshaw enjoyed and wished . . . she did not know what she wished.

251

"Do you see that dreadful woman across the room, my dear," Nell Tabor remarked in a spiteful tone to Lady Juliana Bickerstaff. "She seems to be on quite intimate terms with the diplomatic set." Her blue eyes glittered maliciously. "But that's nothing new."

Lady Juliana likewise directed her clear gaze across the crowded expanse of drawing room. "Does her behavior shock you, Nell? It's doubtless a harmless flirtation, as I tell everyone. I've never known Maria de Beaulieu to indulge in anything else, I must say."

"Dear Lady Juliana, you are too innocent and trusting where your friends are concerned," said Nell. Quite abruptly, she turned the subject to the Italian singer who was just getting into place beside the pianoforte.

"To be sure, she's had excellent reviews, Nell, but why are you so changeable tonight?" Lady Juliana was exasperated. Lately, Eleanor Tabor was not at all amusing to talk to. The girl had developed a disconcerting habit of beginning a good gossip and then quite suddenly turning the talk to something quite innocuous and unrelated to *on-dits*.

"Oh, no reason," said Nell Tabor demurely. She could discern Barrett Johnson approaching through the crowd.

"It wouldn't come at all amiss," said Constance Miller. "She seems bent on convincing everyone in town that she and that foreign man are—well, you know what people are saying."

"Yes, I think the time has come to put a word

in the silly thing's ear," Lady Anne answered in low tones. "I didn't want to do so without consulting you, my dear. I know I can trust your discretion. You've been in town lately and have observed her behavior at close hand, whereas I haven't. But I can't stand by silently and allow a friend to play the fool before the ton. And Maria is thoughtless. Possibly, she doesn't realize that the way she's acting now is being regarded in a more scandalous light than anything she's done before."

Constance was flattered that Lady Anne had chosen her to confide in. Though they were sisters-in-law, they had never been very intimate. She couldn't know that Anne had deliberately chosen Constance, with her solid middle-class respectability, as the most likely of her acquaintance to know—and care—what she was talking about in the matter of Maria's behavior.

"Suppose you contrive to bring her into that notorious little room next to the large Venetian glass on the far wall, the one where the duke always tries to get women alone," Anne said. "I'll be there. I mustn't be overly stern, but the situation does warrant words of some kind, and the sooner the better." Anne looked across the room at Maria and noticed that the comtesse was blithely ignoring a hovering Sir Stephen Wrackham. "So kind of you to contribute a beau to the cause of protecting our foolish friend, Constance," she added.

"You mean Sir Stephen, I suppose." Constance shrugged. "He's not my admirer, and besides he's such a kind man. He seems to regard Maria as quite the lady in distress." Constance had to admit to herself that she was slightly irritated that Sir Stephen had been living in Maria's pocket. Not that Constance retained any serious interest in the

253

man—at least not much of a one—but it wasn't terribly flattering to see one's professed admirer clinging to the side of another woman.

Constance knew, of course, that Wrackham's interest in the comtesse was pure chivalry. Hadn't he called Maria "above his touch" any number of times? She also knew that her own sensible feelings of friendliness towards Sir Stephen were very different from the flutterings she experienced in the presence of Lord Elliot. She sighed again. Elliot was becoming more and more attentive. However, attentions paid and proposals made were two different things, and Constance was well aware that she must keep more than one iron in the fire if she really wished to get herself off this season. And lately it had seemed very necessary to do so. If Georgina shouldn't meet the one of her choice this year, how much easier and more proper it would be to chaperone her when one was Lady Wrackham or Lady Elliot.

Constance felt her heart sink. Could there really be much pleasure in landing a baronet when the handsome Lord Elliot was in the world? Her eyes sought out the young blond baron and found him talking to Phillip Renshaw quite nearby. That such a man should condescend to a City heiress older than himself was ridiculous in the extreme. Constance told herself resolutely never to think of it again. She was being as silly as Georgina was over Major Harcourt.

But there was more pertinent business at hand to occupy her thoughts. She effectively forgot her own problems by concentrating on the Comtesse de Beaulieu's, and the next few minutes were spent collecting Maria by some ruse while Lady Anne made her own way to the chamber selected for the difficult interview. A very puzzled Comtesse de Beaulieu, who had been told mendaciously that the demitrain of her gown had started to tear, was led into the room.

"Anne, what is so important it can't wait for to-morrow?" asked Maria curiously, after examining her hem with care. She wasn't in the best of humors. Constance had interrupted her just as she was arranging the details of the private harp concert she had consented to give for Sir Stephen and Lord Abdul on the morrow.

Anne sat down beside her friend on the small room's only sofa, and Constance excused herself. "I need to speak to you for a moment, Maria," said Anne. "As your friend."

"And the subject of our talk?" Maria's voice was heavy with suspicion.

Anne sighed. "It's your flirting, Maria. It's come to the point where it must stop. You're cutting quite a ridiculous figure."

"My flirting," said Maria, incredulous that Anne should speak to her in such a manner. "My dear Anne, has marriage turned you prudish in less than a month? I always flirt."

"But never to this excess, and with one gentleman in particular," countered Anne. "Many have noticed, my dear, that your behavior with Lord Abdul is rather . . ." Her voice drifted away as she searched for the right word.

"Notorious?" suggested Maria with a bitter smile.

"Exactly," agreed Anne in her maddeningly frank way. "Dear, it has become quite the *on-dit*. Every letter sent me down in Sussex made mention of the fact that you and his lordship are constantly together and apparently on the most intimate of terms. You are no innocent. You know what

255

everyone must be thinking."

Maria flushed angrily. *"Honi soit qui mal y pense,* as Beaulieu used to say. And you think the same?"

Anne looked steadily at Maria. "I won't know," she said, "unless you tell me. There's no judging from your behavior."

"Well!" Maria felt her hackles rising by the minute.

"You might as well know that you're causing a scandal. Why, Lord James Lofts told me this very evening that it made him quite ill to see you fawning on that foreign gentleman. Granted that Lord James might be considered a rival of sorts, and he may have spoken from spite, but that he should have thought fit to mention the matter to me at all shows that things have gone far enough."

The flush had disappeared from Maria's cheeks. She was now white with fury. "Have you insulted me enough, or is there more?" she asked in an icy tone. "What the rakes of the world think is of no interest to me. Next you'll be warning me that Nell Tabor is talking, quite as if she doesn't ordinarily do so."

Anne made an unsuccessful attempt to smile. "Maria, I only speak for your good." She looked curiously at her friend. "Tell me, is it that you've formed a tendre for Lord Abdul? I would understand, my dear."

Maria remained silent, eyes lowered.

Anne was wild to be out of the room. Maria had been right: she *was* being prudish. "Please try not to think badly of me. I am only trying to help," she said in a tone much softer than she usually employed. Then she nearly bolted out of the room.

Maria kept her eyes on the floor until the door

had closed behind her abashed friend. It wouldn't do for Anne to see her crying.

She was wiping her eyes with a scrap of lace when the door opened. "Mr. Renshaw," she said in surprise. "Did Anne send you? I assure you I'm quite the thing."

Phillip Renshaw looked as sheepish as Anne had on her exit from the room, Maria noted. "Anne?" he said. "No. I haven't seen my wife in the last half hour. I've come, Madame, to deliver a message."

"A—a message? You look so serious, sir. Do sit down. Is it my Aunt Kitty? Has something happened?"

Renshaw placed himself in a spindly chair, the only seat in the room besides the sofa. "Oh, no, Madame, it's nothing like that. I must say that I am a most reluctant messenger, but I have received my orders. Orders, Madame."

Maria was by now so mystified that she knew not how to respond. She simply stared.

The regard of those clear green eyes seemed to be too much for Phillip Renshaw. He looked at the gilt cupids bedecking the mirror above Maria's head as he said, "Madame, the Regent spoke to me tonight, in my capacity as Lord Abdul's official—er—liaison, I suppose the term would be. His royal highness wished me to convey to you that— that—Madame, there is no easy way to say this."

"Apparently not," said Maria dryly. She wished with all her heart that she could ask him what, pray, she might have to do with Lord Abdul? Unfortunately, she had quite a bit to do with the man and couldn't deny it.

"You are my lady's dearest friend, and I have no wish to insult you," said Renshaw, the misery clear in his voice. "But I have been commanded, Madame, and it is simply this. The Regent would not be displeased should you give in to Lord Abdul. Far from it. His highness is most anxious that Abdul's visit to our shores be all that is pleasant, and—"

"You've said quite enough, Mr. Renshaw," Maria interrupted, her eyes flashing fire. "You may tell your precious prince—ah, I never have liked him!—that Maria de Beaulieu is neither an instrument of diplomacy nor a plaything to be passed about at his discretion."

Renshaw rose and bowed before Maria. His honest, open countenance radiated shame. "Madame, I must beg you to forgive me for saying these things to you. Can you understand, though, why I had to? A royal command."

Maria tossed her head and muttered something quite unladylike in French about the sort of royalty that could issue such commands. "And to think," she added in fury, "I was so happy to see Anne marry a man like you!" On this note, she ran from the room, her head spinning with all she had heard this evening. So the Regent *had* been watching her! She had never cared for the Prince of Wales, but she could never have imagined he would issue such blatant orders to a member of the fair sex.

Her cheeks, already red, grew hotter as she wondered whether Lord Abdul had had the impertinence to discuss her with the regent—complaining, perhaps, about his lack of progress? No, surely not. She had simply been flirting, and everyone must realize that, especially Lord Abdul, who was so expert in the art. But *had* she been merely flirting? Hadn't she been toying with the idea of fling-

258

ing caution to the wind, of becoming the fashionable, free-and-easy widow many thought she already was? Maria was certain that she would not sleep this night. She had too much thinking to do.

In the hall, she met Aunt Kitty and Sir William Torrington. "My child, we've been looking everywhere for you," said her aunt. "Why, what is wrong? You're so flushed."

Maria dropped her eyes. "It's nothing, dear aunt. I've had a bit of a shock, but nothing important."

"Good, because we wish to have a word with you, Maria," answered Aunt Kitty with a nervous little glance up at Sir William. "Perhaps it isn't the best time, here in front of everyone, but—"

Maria sighed. "May I guess, Aunt Kitty? You wish to tell me that my behavior has become shocking in the extreme, and to warn me to change my ways. Well, your point is taken." In dismay, she felt a tear roll out of her eye. "If you'll pardon me, my dears, I'll join you later." Without another word, she dashed away, taking no notice of the people she passed. Thus it was no surprise that she should run headlong into someone. Rebounding from this accident, Maria looked up into the kindly face of Sir Stephen Wrackham.

"M'dame!" the baronet exclaimed. "I've been looking for you—take you in to supper—not feeling the thing?" Concern was written all over his countenance, and Maria was accordingly quite touched.

"The headache," she whispered, staring into his sincere eyes. Here was one person who would always stand her friend.

"A bit to eat, just the thing for a headache," Sir Stephen remarked inventively, and he led her toward the supper room.

Maria remained silent as she struggled to regain

her calm. This was doubly difficult, for her happiness at being taken in to supper by this gentleman was quite out of proportion. Sir Stephen's friendship was no longer enough for her, but one of her dubious reputation could claim nothing more from this upstanding soul.

Chapter Twenty-five

In Maria's opinion, the flowers did little to cheer the room. She'd had the various bouquets brought down to the drawing room and placed about to give her courage for the interview she must face this day. The usual pink roses from Lord James Lofts had been accompanied by still another poem, and Lord Abdul had sent a dozen yellow roses with a brief wish, written in French, that they might speak privately soon. As Maria sat awaiting Abdul, however, it wasn't to his flowers that she reached out her hand. Rather, it was to the two dozen white roses, in their charming oriental vase, which had no card. The comtesse had long since given up asking her various gentleman friends if they anonymously sent the flowers to her. She now had the idea that they were the gift of some very young man too shy to step forward or to pay her any other attention. Such disinterested gallantry was comforting. She plucked a white rose from the vase and tucked it into the band which bound up her blond hair.

At that moment, Roy announced Lord Abdul.

The foreign gentleman's dark eyes took a quick survey of the place and smiled at Maria. "Where is your charming aunt today? And I see I've arrived before Sir Stephen Wrackham. How lucky."

Maria's cheeks grew warm. She had arranged it all. Aunt Kitty had gone visiting, but had she not, Maria would have asked her to perform some errand. As for Sir Stephen, the time she had given him to arrive was a half hour later than that which she had given Lord Abdul. "Milord, I arranged on purpose for us to have a moment alone. We must talk."

Lord Abdul said nothing. In one leonine movement, he was on the couch, his arms around Maria, and his lips wandering.

She pushed him away. "Sir, this is at an end," she said softly. "I saw to it that we were alone so I could tell you."

"At an end?" Abdul seemed disbelieving, even amused. "Madame — Maria, if I may be so bold. It is only just beginning." His arms circled round her again.

Maria held him off, wishing she had been shrewd enough to place herself in a chair rather than on a sofa where the gentleman could not confuse the issue with physical contact. "I've already gone too far, and I have no excuse for it," she said. "I've led you on shamelessly, but I mustn't allow myself, or you, to go further."

Abdul smiled, his expression still one of complete assurance. The lady was experiencing a natural trepidation when it came to the point, but no matter: this could be surmounted. "Maria, *ma chère*, we are not children," his charming voice coaxed. "We both know where we have been leading."

Maria tried to smile. "All London knows I'm a flirt. It never means anything with me. Every gentleman of my acquaintance understands that."

"Was there nothing between us just now?" murmured Abdul, touching her hair.

"There was something," she said. She couldn't deny that she was drawn to this man. But as she had tossed on her bed the night before, she had come to the conclusion that her feelings for him

262

were physical, nothing more. And she would be no better than a courtesan if she were to give herself without giving her heart.

"Of course there was something," said her companion. "Desire." He might have been reading her thoughts.

She shook her head. "You'll soon be gone. We'll forget each other. Why do something we'd regret?"

"Will we regret?" Doubt was evident in his voice.

She looked at him steadily and made her voice severe. "*I* would."

He was still smiling. "Your upbringing has been strict. I have read much about your America. The Puritan influence. You haven't lived in England many years. It can't be easy to go against your values, though both your head and your heart—"

"My background is not Puritan in the least," protested Maria. She drew back the hand he had taken in his grasp. "But—" She found it hard to explain. How much did he know about the Regent's "message" to her? She couldn't simply declare that, having been given the royal command to succumb to Lord Abdul, she had discovered she no longer wanted to in the least. "People are talking already," she said, though the prim words sounded terribly lame.

"Don't you enjoy a little notoriety?" asked Abdul.

"Yes, up to a point. But when—when my friends and even my relations give me warnings about my behavior, I must draw the line, sir."

"Let them talk. Haven't you told me time and again that in London one talks, with or without cause? It's too late to stop them."

"Very true," admitted Maria. "They are talking very hard."

"And you, a citizeness of this sophisticated capitol

and a lady of independent ways—or so I thought—
you mean to allow the narrow, provincial opinions
of a few busybodies to guide you?"

Maria flinched at the accusing words. "It's not a
question of giving in to my friends' opinions." It
occurred to her that there was *one* excuse Abdul
might very well believe, and it might even be true.
She lifted her chin in sudden decision. "Did it never
occur to you, sir, that I might have formed an attachment to someone else?"

"That can have no bearing on you and me,"
shrugged Abdul. Not for nothing was he a practiced
diplomat. Another man? That was a ridiculous
statement, given her behavior with himself. If he
would just allow her to talk, he thought, she would
retract this silly tale and be won back to his purpose within a very few minutes.

"No," said Maria in extreme agitation. She rose
from the sofa, crossed the room and stood behind a
table. "I can't." The moment had come for the
speech she had planned out in her mind as she had
lain awake the night before. She had to be far away
from the man when she gave it. "I've only just
found it out, but I can't behave in the way that
society most likely thinks I am behaving already. I
know my conduct has led you to expect more than
I can give, and I'm sorry, truly sorry. I haven't been
a lady."

He seemed to sense her desire to be physically
separate from him. Accordingly, he crossed the
room and braved her fortress. His arms about her,
he murmured into her ear, "You can give everything."

Maria tore herself away. "Lord Abdul, I can give
you but one thing, and I choose not to. I must ask
you to leave. I can never see you again." She felt

264

the tears forming and knew that, for her composure's sake, the scene must end quickly. "Please go, milord. Don't make it more difficult for us both."

A spark of anger dawned in his eyes. "Madame, you throw much away with your prudish words. And I must say that I do not understand. You are no maiden who must offer virginity as a marriage portion. You have even told me that you never wish to marry again. Tell me for my own information, that I might comprehend your culture, what is your true reason for refusing me?"

Maria lifted her chin. "Sir, I have asked you to go. Any gentleman worthy of the name would do so." She was suddenly angry with the man. How dare he cross-question her about her motives? Her favor was a gift which she would bestow as she thought fit.

There was true rage in his eyes now. "I go," he said coldly. "But I could have left you with a wonderful memory. Instead, you will find yourself with nothing, and it will be what you deserve." He turned on his heel and left the room without a backward glance.

Her knees weak, Maria sank into the nearest chair. She had done it! She was safe now, but she had never felt so lonely. Lord Abdul was special, her mind insisted. He amused her and excited her, and if he didn't touch her heart, who ever had in the seven years of her widowhood? He was right: she *had* been left with nothing.

She was grateful to have more than ten minutes to collect her thoughts before Sir Stephen Wrackham was announced. "Madame," the large baronet greeted her genially. "Before my time, what? Lord Abdul's not here yet." He observed her face as he made his best bow. "Not feeling the thing, M'dame?

Let's do the harp another time. Say the word, I'll go away."

Maria looked up into the kindly, mustachioed face. How comforting this man was! His solidity did her so much good. Constance Miller was a lucky woman. "My dear Sir Stephen, I'm quite well. Do sit down."

Sir Stephen accepted a chair and asked after Miss Torrington.

"Gone out on a visit," explained Maria. "She's due back at any moment."

"We'll wait for her," nodded Sir Stephen. "Wait for Lord Abdul. Not meaning to be early," he added with a worried frown. M'dame certainly had been perturbed about something a moment ago. Perhaps he'd mistaken the time entirely.

"Oh, Lord Abdul isn't coming," said Maria. It was an effort to speak lightly. "He was called away by an emergency of some kind. Business, I expect," she invented quickly. "Something only you gentlemen can understand. So if I am to play the harp, you must be my sole critic, Sir Stephen. Will you be severe enough?"

The baronet looked his incredulity. "Severe? Admire your performance, M'dame, no question. Only polite thing to do."

To her surprise, Maria was moved to laugh. "My dear sir, that's already a blow to my confidence as a performer."

"Didn't mean any disrespect, M'dame," said Sir Stephen. "Only mean to say I admire whatever you do. Bound to be excellent."

"You haven't heard me play," said Maria. "I assure you it's been a long while."

"Wait, then, if you like," suggested Sir Stephen. He was perfectly content to merely sit and visit with the comtesse for any length of time. In fact, the playing of a musical instrument would necessarily cut off all conversation, and he had quite a lot to tell her. There was the recent purchase he had made of a new thoroughbred, the dinner that Renshaw and Lady Anne were intending to give, and a dozen other items worthy of note. "Wait until Abdul can join us."

Maria colored. "We might as well do it, now you're here. I expect Lord Abdul will be very busy from now until he leaves the country, and who knows when he'd be able to find the time?" She gave the baronet a bright smile. "You *do* want to hear me, don't you?" She was very anxious to play. It would be a way of avoiding conversation until she could control herself better.

"Delighted, M'dame, no question." Sir Stephen looked at her keenly. Seemed upset about something. He'd lay odds it was to do with Lord Abdul. Disappointed he couldn't be present, probably. Well, there was no harm in that. It'd do M'dame good to get out of Abdul's clutches for once. The dashed foreigner had been taking up all of her time.

At that moment, the door burst open and Miss Katherine Torrington entered the room on the arm of Sir William. "My dear Maria," said the maiden lady. She directed a bright smile at their guest. "I had no idea you were expecting Sir Stephen. How pleasant, sir."

"An impromptu harp concert, Aunt," said Maria casually. "Do the two of you care to listen?"

"By all means, my dear, what a treat," said Sir William. "I remember how often you used to play. Wrackham! Pleased to see you, my boy. Rare to find a man such as myself with a genuine interest in music."

267

"Genuine interest," echoed Sir Stephen, beaming in the direction of Maria.

"Oh, Maria, so you've taken dear Lady Anne's advice about getting back to your music," said Miss Torrington, more fluttery than usual.

"Something of that sort, Aunt," replied her niece. She looked curiously at Aunt Kitty, who was really as jumpy as a cat. She wasn't even showing her ordinary distaste that Sir William had placed himself next to her on the sofa. Most unusual, thought Maria as she moved to the harp and busied herself in tuning the strings.

"Capital!" remarked Sir Stephen to the amusement of the others in the room.

Maria bent her head so that Sir Stephen wouldn't see her smile. How lucky she'd invited him! She hated to think what state she'd be in now if he hadn't come along to cheer her.

Aunt Kitty's voice suddenly interrupted Maria's preparations. "It will be impossible for me to sit through a performance, Maria, without first telling you something." Miss Torrington looked at Sir William with soft eyes as she spoke.

"But, my dear!" protested Sir William. "Sir Stephen is here, and our announcement is for family ears only."

"Why?" protested the lady. "I am sure Sir Stephen will find it out soon enough."

"My dears, what are you talking about?" broke in Maria, completely mystified.

Her aunt blushed. "We wanted to tell you last night at the party, Maria, but you were indisposed." She hesitated. "We didn't like to trouble you when we saw that you had the headache."

Maria's face had grown worried, and she knew she must be very pale. Memories of the previous evening's indignities came rushing back to her. Was it possible that her aunt and cousin were meaning to give her a scold in front of Sir Stephen regarding her loose behavior? It was unthinkable. "Surely any private message for me can wait," she begged.

"No, Maria, it can't," her aunt said firmly. "Sir William?" She looked up at the gentleman.

The white-haired baronet took Miss Torrington's hand and patted it gently, an act which caused the eyes of his younger cousin to widen considerably. When had Aunt Kitty ever countenanced such behavior? A slow suspicion began to dawn in Maria's mind, but the thought was too wild. . . . It couldn't be!

"Well then, Maria," began Sir William. "You and Sir Stephen may be the first to know. Your Aunt Katherine has consented—last night, in fact—to make me the happiest of men."

"Congratulations!" boomed Sir Stephen Wrackham, rising from his seat to pump Sir William's hand. "Best wishes, ma'am," he continued with a bow in Miss Torrington's direction. "You'll be happy together, no question—deal extremely—can see it myself!"

Miss Torrington demurely accepted the large gentleman's compliments and then looked anxiously at her niece. "And you, Maria? Do say you're pleased. I know this comes as a shock—to me as well as you—but Sir William and I have gotten to know each other quite well in the past weeks." She paused, painfully aware that the very thing which had brought her together with Sir William was her worry over Maria's shocking behavior. "Maria?" she repeated. The girl was very quiet, and her face was white behind the strings of the harp. It would be horrid if her niece didn't rejoice with her and the man she had so surprisingly come to love. Indeed, Miss Torrington had suspected more than once that Maria was trying to encourage a match in this very direction.

"M'dame!" Sir Stephen exclaimed. "Overwrought. Do let me help. Not unusual to be overset at happy news. Ladies such as yourself are too delicate to bear surprises—"

Miss Torrington gazed in amazement at Wrackham, who was now hurrying across the room in the direction of the harp. Then she took a closer look at Maria.

Her niece had quite suddenly burst into tears.

Chapter Twenty-six

Miss Ginevra Johnson addressed the gentleman who was her sole companion in the drawing room. "Major Harcourt, I don't believe I've had the pleasure of seeing you lately when I've called here?"

The major shifted uncomfortably in his seat. It was perfectly true that he hadn't called on the comtesse in a while. He had been busy, after all. He doubted very much if he would have called this morning, either, had he known that Miss Ginevra Johnson would be here, and that the late appearance of the comtesse would necessitate his remaining alone for any length of time with the formidable bluestocking. "I've had many matters of business to occupy my time, Miss Johnson," he said respectfully. Why the devil did he feel he had to excuse himself to this woman?

Miss Johnson nodded shortly. She wasn't fond of Major Harcourt, had no patience with his morose, brooding ways. Indeed, it wouldn't do Maria de Beaulieu any harm if he did visit her a bit less often, and she hadn't been able to resist the opportunity to take the major down a well-deserved peg. All men, with the rare exception such as Cousin Barrett, were too egotistical, and it was all the fault of women. She wouldn't add herself to the overfawning multitudes.

Maria entered the room before the strained silence between her visitors had grown unbearable. She was looking quite well, if a little tired, and greeted her visitors with genuine pleasure.

Major Harcourt cleared his throat. "And have you been well, Madame?" he asked. "It's been a while, to be sure, since I—"

Maria's airy laugh rang out. "Don't be absurd, sir. You can't be here and in Russell Square at the same time."

As the major lowered his eyes, Miss Johnson looked on in total ignorance of the comtesse's reference. Not for Ginevra Johnson the vain practice of repeating *on-dits*. Such behavior was quite beneath her. She thought a bit. Russell Square—that would be the Millers. Was the reason for Maria's raillery that Harcourt had developed a preference for one of those city-bred sisters?

While Miss Johnson puzzled over this, Major George Harcourt thought bleakly of his last interview at the house in Russell Square. There Mr. Miller and his man of business had informed the military man that, after an investigation of his finances and background, they were unable to approve him as a suitor for Miss Georgina. This was doubly distressing to the major. For one thing, he was perfectly respectable, if not rich and titled, and resented being told that he was unworthy to form an alliance with a family of cits. For another, he had never asked Miss Georgina or her father if his addresses would be welcome. Papa Miller's interview had been Harcourt's first inkling that his behavior was being interpreted in such a way. Having been so rudely awakened, he was not sure how to treat Georgina. Oddly he was more resentful than relieved to know that a marriage he hadn't even thought of, with a chit young enough to be his daughter, was impossible. Was he now to discontinue his visits to the Millers? *That* was not an option.

"Major Harcourt, I'm afraid I've angered you, and I beg pardon," the voice of the comtesse disrupted his gloomy thoughts.

Harcourt looked at her. A wonderful woman, and he had been at her feet for three years. In a flash, he realized that he was there no longer. His eyes were sadder than ever as he contemplated his disloyalty. "Madame, you could never do so," he replied.

"I won't tease you any more," promised Maria. She turned to her female guest. "Besides, I am sure our nonsense is boring Miss Johnson."

Ginevra Johnson gave the gracious, beneficent expression that passed with her for a smile. "I can't call anything boring that treats of the relationships between men and women, Madame, unaware though I am of anything Major Harcourt may be intending in the direction of Russell Square," she said earnestly. "For, do you know, I've been indirectly involved myself in an affair of the heart. My cousin Barrett, Madame, is paying particular attentions to a young lady, and I must say it's doing him good. I hadn't thought of marriage when I brought him to town, but he appears to have it on his mind."

"But Mr. Johnson surely isn't in a position to marry?" queried Maria. She wondered when such purely feminine talk had last passed from the lips of Miss Ginevra Johnson. The poor major was the one who must be bored now.

Miss Johnson's eyes lit up. "Oh, Barrett can afford to marry now. That is one of the things I called today to tell you, Madame. Baron Elliot has given my cousin a living in Shropshire—that of his major estate, in fact."

Maria clasped her hands. "But that's wonderful news! Then his visit to town has truly been a success. Who is the young lady who has fixed his interest?"

"Miss Eleanor Tabor," said Miss Johnson. Maria and Major Harcourt were strangely silent as Miss Johnson continued. "Miss Tabor is a sensible girl, though her learning is merely superficial. I vow she doesn't know Radcliffe from Johnson, and was quite astonished to learn from me some of the more basic philosophies of Mary Wollstonecraft. But she's quite willing. And Barrett has managed to improve her mind by directing her reading. She's already quite a different woman from the shallow creature I used to meet at parties. And she's from a good family. She is to show us the chart her father made, tracing the Tabor family back to the Conqueror. Though she's a year or two older than my cousin, he is the steadier of the two. And the great thing is, she shares his wish for a rural life engaged in helping others. Not ambitious, true, but they'll have quite a competence. Lord Elliot has been so very generous." She paused. "It won't be bad, either, for Eleanor to remove herself from town. People are inclined to gossip, so I hear, about some little mishap years ago when she tried to elope."

Maria had been staring incredulously since the moment the name of Miss Tabor was first mentioned. Had Nell really managed to hook that quiet young man? The miracle was that she would have wanted to: he was so obscure. On the other hand, at least he was young, a fact which must appear to advantage to one willing to settle for General Cumberland Gerard. And Mr. Johnson, aware of her past, was willing to discount it. What luck for her former friend!

"I'm so happy," Maria said in all sincerity. "It means a lot to me that Miss Tabor has found the right man."

"He is indeed a rare find," affirmed Miss Johnson with excusable family pride.

Major George Harcourt listened silently to the two women. He had been surprised to hear the name of his former love mentioned in conjunction with that of Barrett Johnson, surely the most unassuming, openhearted young chap to come on the scene in years. If he really married Nell, it wouldn't be a mistake, Harcourt was sure. He'd seen the young clergyman from time to time and sensed a core of strength in the youth's personality which he himself lacked. No, Barrett Johnson would have no trouble in handling Nell Tabor, and he was most welcome to do so.

"This is really a time for marriages," Maria exclaimed gaily, a wistful expression in her green eyes. "The two of you might not have read the *Gazette* yet this morning—"

"I never do," put in Miss Johnson with a disapproving frown.

"Should you do so, you'll find that my Aunt Kitty is soon to marry Sir William Torrington. My plans for those two have succeeded after ten long years."

"Miss Torrington and Sir William? You don't say so, Madame!" exclaimed Major Harcourt. "What a piece of good luck for the gentleman. Miss Torrington is surely the catch of this or any other season," he added, for he knew how Maria always appreciated compliments to her aunt

"And where is the lady today?" asked Miss Johnson. "I'm sure that the major as well as myself would like to express our best wishes. It is odd," she considered with a studious frown, "to think of those two marrying. Hasn't Miss Torrington mentioned to me more than once that Sir William disapproves of any talk concerning the Rights of Woman?"

"They've managed somehow to overcome their differences of opinion, or perhaps to disregard them," replied Maria. "In answer to your first question, my aunt has gone out to an early fitting. She tells me it's ridiculous to think of bride clothes at her age, but I'm determined she should be fitted out royally."

"And so she ought," said Ginevra Johnson. "It's her first time, no matter what her age. Fifty, isn't it?"

"And she looks no more than thirty," put in Major Harcourt.

The three might have continued complimenting the absent Miss Torrington indefinitely had Roy not entered the room to announce Lady Anne Renshaw.

Anne was stylish in a new walking costume of midnight blue, with a plumed bonnet in the first stare of fashion framing her classically lovely face. "My dear Maria, it's been an age," she said with an anxious look. She and her friend hadn't met since the musical evening at Morland House a week before.

"Anne, I'm delighted to see you," replied Maria with more than her usual friendliness, and all difficulty was at an end.

Miss Ginevra Johnson was delighted to see the other woman whom she considered to be, along with the Comtesse de Beaulieu, the most educated in the metropolis besides herself. After first asking after the health of Mr. Renshaw, she launched the group into a literary discussion. The conversation grew more and more erudite, and Major Harcourt began to exhibit definite signs of leavetaking.

Maria regarded the man with a kind of pity. He was at sea, poor gentleman, and obviously being made unhappy by something or someone. It was no longer herself, that was certain: the recent absence of his former offerings of flowers was testimony to that. It must be young Georgina Miller who was being unkind. Well, the major would always be one who must be *made* happy, as he couldn't be so by himself.

When the gentleman had bowed himself out of the room, Miss Johnson shook her head. "Not to take exception to any of your friends, Madame, but that major is so eternally depressed that it does one's spirits no good."

"Poor dear man," sighed Maria.

"Harcourt is a sad case," remarked Anne. "Do you suppose he's really after little Georgina, as Constance says?"

"Time will tell," said Maria with a shrug.

"Well, now that he's gone, we may talk more freely," said Ginevra Johnson. "I didn't know, Madame, if he was in on the secret of your novel. Tell me, have you worked on it lately?"

Maria smiled. "I thought you'd ask me that, Miss Johnson, and I'm happy to report that yes, in the past few days I've been making great strides. I'm quite pleased, in fact."

"How wonderful, Maria!" put in Anne. "So that's why I haven't seen you out."

"Yes, I'm making an effort to return to my scholarly pursuits," said Maria, her stern words contrasting oddly with the beribboned morning gown she was wearing.

"Admirable," said Miss Johnson.

"In the season, Maria?" asked Anne. Her eyes were suddenly very sharp.

Maria shrugged. "What better time? Town life is all frivolity anyhow." She glanced at Miss Johnson, who would certainly agree with such a sentiment.

"I haven't often heard *you* voice such a thought," said the bluestocking with enthusiasm. "But come to think of it, I heard something very like that recently from another unexpected source — the Persian gentleman, Lord Abdul."

"Lord Abdul?" asked Maria in a choked voice.

"Yes, he mentioned to one of my other guests, who was chiding him for not appearing more frequently the past few days in his usual haunts, that London was entirely frivolous and he wouldn't be altogether sorry to leave it. Quite a bold thing to say, by the way, in a roomful of English people."

"But Lord Abdul is always bold," said Anne with an eye on Maria. Her friend was calm now, thank heaven, but her face *had* whitened a shade at mention of the fatal name.

"Be that as it may, he's an intelligent man, and I'll miss arguing him into a corner," continued Miss Johnson. Blissfully unaware of anything so sordid as scandal, she talked in the same vein for the length of her visit, discussing Lord Abdul's opinions on this philosophy and that theory with no notion that her subject was at all worrying to her two listeners.

When she finally took her leave, Anne lost no time. "Well, Maria," she snapped, "what is all this?"

"All what?" Her companion fingered a curl at her temple.

Anne laughed. "It's all very well to speak of a return to scholarship, but to put the thing into practice during the season passes anything you've done before. And as to the reason I came to call in the first place, you haven't been out of doors this week, and you're too pale for words. You must come out with me this afternoon. If you dislike the Park, we'll think of somewhere else. But, in my opinion, this thing is best braved at once, not avoided."

"What thing is that?" asked Maria in a dignified manner.

"This sudden aversion you've taken to Abdul, my dear," said Anne. She remembered with some discomfort a certain conversation at Morland House. "It's good that you've stopped being seen with him, but you're bound to meet him sometime, just in passing. If I were you, I'd get it over quickly."

"Well," said Maria, "I must be thankful then that I am not you, for I never want to see the man again, and no power on earth could make me do so willingly." She found to her dismay that she was blushing deeply.

"And why not?" Anne asked in a tone that indicated she would not be put off.

Maria sighed, considering with a frown the advisability of letting Anne in on her secrets. She decided to give over — but without mentioning the treacherous part her dear friend's husband had played. "Abdul and I had a dreadful quarrel," she said quietly. "I told him I couldn't — well — that I couldn't continue to allow his attentions."

"And what reason did you give him?" Anne's eyes were especially keen.

"My reputation, of course. And I hinted that I might care for someone else. To a man of that stamp, a rival was the most believable reason I could come up with."

Anne nodded shrewdly and decided not to press further on this point. Had Maria really given Lord Abdul a false excuse? And what had made her change her mind? When Anne had left her in that room at Morland House, Maria's mood had been resentful, and Anne had been certain her warning had been wide of the mark. Somehow, though, Maria seemed to have had a change of heart.

"This seclusion of yours must end somehow," Anne said, frowning. "And if you don't want to be surprised by a view of Lord Abdul, we must contrive some other way for you to get back into society."

"Why?" Maria's tone was calm.

"Because it's where you belong, you widgeon," cried Anne in exasperation. "Now, I love a good book as well as you do, but never tell me that the Comtesse de Beaulieu, who has half London at her feet — I myself have the other half — is satisfied to sit and read, or even write, for the rest of her life with no sort of society at all. Next you'll be wearing a hair shirt and writing sonnets, and that I won't stand for."

Maria had to laugh at such an image of herself. "But Anne, I'm tired of society. I care nothing for these empty games."

Lady Anne sighed. Maria was prone to overdramatize. That lecture at Morland House must have initiated a reaction in Maria that, had she been catholic, very likely might include retirement to a convent. It would have to be stifled before Maria began to enjoy the role too much. "You care everything for these empty games," said Lady Anne roundly. "You had friends visiting you just now, and don't tell me you weren't glad to see them. You aren't a hermit, my dear."

"Perhaps I'm a little bit afraid?" ventured Maria.

"Without any reason at all."

Maria looked into the distance. "It's true that many people have been here to inquire after me," she said. "Sir Stephen Wrackham has been most kind, and you saw that Major Harcourt was just here, though I can't call him my cavalier any longer. And Lord James Lofts sent me two dozen roses this morning instead of the usual one."

"You see!" said Lady Anne triumphantly. "And do the anonymous white roses still come?"

Maria nodded, smiling at thought of the unknown young boy.

"So you have not only friends but admirers," returned Lady Anne. "Now there's only one thing to do to regain your spirits."

"And that is?"

Lady Anne's hands moved expressively, and she smiled. "You must give a soirée. The one sure way not to meet Lord Abdul at entertainments is to give parties yourself, and not invite him."

"A soirée?" Maria sounded doubtful.

"I'm sure Ginevra Johnson would be glad of one more of your parties before the season ends," coaxed Lady Anne. "As I would, and a score of others. Do say you will, and soon, before Phillip and I give our dinner."

"It would be a small, impromptu affair," said Maria slowly. She couldn't seem to help herself: she was already going over the guest list in her mind. And there happened to be a new gown readying at Madame Hélène's that would be perfect—

"My dear, you really have no choice," said Anne in a tone of finality. "You must give a party to regain your social standing. Anyone who sits at home in sackcloth and ashes, refusing all invitations, must do something to redeem herself."

Maria's eyes narrowed. "I'm not altogether sure the ton deserves that I should go to the trouble," she said with a toss of her head. "You say my flirting has become a byword. Would I not be giving people a chance to give me the cut direct? Why should I do that?"

Anne's vehement rebuttal to this piece of nonsense was very strict indeed. No one would cut the Comtesse de Beaulieu: how was it possible that a small flirtation could bring even the highest sticklers to that point? By the time Anne was ready to leave, she was out of patience with Maria, but she had accomplished her objectives. The wavering ninny-hammer was to give a soirée—practically on pain of death — and she was also to come driving with Anne in the Park that very afternoon, resolved to brave whomever she might see.

Anne's expression was speculative as she descended the steps of the Beaulieu house and began a brisk walk back to Mount Street, her maid scurrying to keep up with her. There was only one thing to be done about Maria. Somehow she must be married off. Oh, there *was* a candidate, but it would take a touch of magic to bring the thing off creditably, given Maria's birdwitted belief in her unsuitability and the gentleman's unknowing state. Luckily for all parties concerned, magic was one of Lady Anne Renshaw's specialities.

Chapter Twenty-seven

"Mademoiselle," moaned Madame Hélène. "*La petite* Georgina Miller is an easy task compared with you. *Ne bougez pas!*"

Miss Torrington, who was being fitted for a lace-trimmed gown of cornflower blue silk, obligingly tried not to move. She had always been a little afraid of Madame Hélène and preferred to have her gowns run up by a sewing woman she knew privately. Good fabrics could be bought quite cheaply at Layton and Shears' or Grafton House. Besides, the demure old lady who made the majority of Miss Torrington's wearing apparel was biddable as a lamb, in contrast to this small Frenchwoman who expected one to be guided by her own taste. "You're sure this style isn't too youthful for me?" faltered Miss Torrington as she looked down at herself. The blue gown was a quiet enough shade, true, and there was nothing undignified about the cut, but such a quantity of lace! She couldn't approve, though Madame Hélène had grudgingly given permission for a cap of matching lace. Sometimes Katherine Torrington definitely wished that her niece Maria had been a bit less insistent that one's bride clothes be of the very best.

"Mademoiselle, be but guided by me, and you will appear to advantage," said Madame Hélène a little testily. She was determined to override the questionable taste of this lovely *dame d'un certain age* and turn her out a true gem. It was a challenge, given the ridiculously cumbersome cut of the bombazine gown the lady had worn into the shop, but Madame Hélène liked a challenge. She was at her best when dressing originals, and a fifty-year-old bride was original indeed.

Miss Torrington sighed. It seemed to her that she had been coming to Madame Hélène's for these fittings all her life. Things had certainly been easier in the days before her engagement. If only Maria's absurdly lavish ideas on the clothes necessary to attend a middle-aged woman into married life could be satisfied, there was hope of her life becoming easy again. Maria was a problem, to be sure, in the Torringtons' future plans. Aunt Kitty could never leave her niece, and Sir William understood that. His opinion was that Maria herself must marry. It was dashed odd, he said, that a beautiful young woman like the Comtesse de Beaulieu hadn't been snapped up years ago, and now her choice must be either to say yes to one of her suitors or to make her home with her newlywed relations. If she refused to do either, then Sir William thought that some elderly Torrington female might be summoned as a chaperone for Maria. Miss Katherine Torrington had not yet mentioned anything about such arrangements to her niece. Her fond hope was that Maria would find the one of her choice now that she was out from under the grip of that disturbing foreign gentleman, Lord Abdul. And Aunt Kitty would not stand for Maria marrying again except for love, having already seen her niece through a marriage of convenience that had probably altered the girl's values for the worse. No, Maria must wait for love, and perhaps she would find, as Miss Torrington herself had, that the companionship of some valued old friend would ripen, quite naturally, into a deeper feeling. Aunt Kitty thought very hard as she tried to choose someone from among Maria's male acquaintance who might fit the role.

"*Alors, Mademoiselle, cela suffit pour aujourd'hui,*" said Madame Hélène airily.

"*Très bien,*" chirped Miss Torrington. She had picked up enough French from Maria and Beaulieu to realize that she was being set free. She hurried into the inner rooms to change, humming a little tune.

Madame Hélène looked after the lady, shaking her head. That figure was extraordinary in a woman of her age. One would give much to have the dressing of her entirely, and to consign the bombazine sacks to the rag bag. The niece would have to be spoken to. The Comtesse was coming in soon to collect her aunt and to check on the progress of a new gown she herself had had rushed that she might be able to wear it at her coming soirée.

There occurred at this time one of the unfortunate results of economic success. Had Madame Hélène not been all the rage among members of the ton, she wouldn't have had to leave the arranging of some of her appointments to her assistant, a featherheaded young person who had nothing of tact about her. For Madame Hélène, with all her knowledge of the small plots and counterplots of the polite world, would never have been stupid enough to schedule a fitting for Miss Eleanor Tabor on the same day that the Comtesse de Beaulieu was to visit the salon. When Miss Tabor walked into the room, Madame Hélène made a mental note to take her foolish subordinate to task. Then she greeted her client with her most charming, if wary, smile.

"Ah, Mademoiselle, you come to see the straw-colored gauze. Believe me, it is a lucky choice, though you are so insistent it will not become you," the couturière said with every appearance of serenity.

"Madame, I'll be glad to admit I was wrong, since the gown is already being made up," returned Miss Tabor with a smile. Actually, she was wondering not if a color such as straw would be becoming to her flaxen hair, but rather if the gauze ball gown would be of any use at all once she was settled in Shropshire. Well, there *must* be assemblies there. In any case, it was too late to change the gown for one of sober-colored silk more suited to a rector's wife. Nell made a mental note to wear the gown before the end of the present season—her last, thank God, as a single woman.

While Madame Hélène and Miss Tabor were absorbed in their discussion of color, an assistant hurried out from the back reaches of the establishment and informed Madame that Miss Torrington wished to make an impossible change in the neckline of the blue silk.

"*Dieu me preserve,* I have done with that lady's starched notions," said Madame Hélène with an anxious look at Nell. "I'm coming." The modiste hurried out of the room, promising to return in a nonce.

"Torrington!" Nell gasped audibly and changed color. She hadn't met Maria de Beaulieu's aunt since that horrid day when she had stormed into their house and made a scene, a scene which Barrett was slowly convincing her had been quite foolish. A little bit of Nell's heart still insisted that—as Maria had sinned by telling General Gerard about Nell's elopement—she deserved to bear the consequences of her victim's righteous anger.

Madame Hélène's visit to the other room was quite short. Miss Katherine Torrington had been easily returned to reason. She was quite a biddable lady, in fact, and it would be a pleasure to tyrannize over her more and more in the days to come.

"Madame," said Miss Tabor with a touch of severity, "did I hear the girl say that Miss Torrington was on the premises? I am not at all pleased that you should arrange things so. You know how matters stand between myself and that family."

The modiste sighed. This problem had momentarily slipped her mind. "As it happens, an error of one of my staff caused this discomfort, for which I beg pardon, Mademoiselle. But I, Madame Hélène, cannot be bothered to keep up with all the small wars which are taking place among my clientèle," she added with a proud lift of her sharp chin.

"Well, at least it's only the aunt, and not the niece," said Nell.

Madame Hélène decided to be bold. "Mademoiselle," she said. "It cannot be said that much passes by me. The ton is too constantly in and out of my rooms. It is *ridicule,* assuredly, not to forgive a little indiscretion made by the Comtesse de Beaulieu years ago, or even that more recent incident with the military man."

Nell flushed. Barrett might with all propriety tell her to forgive — after all, announcement of their engagement had been sent to the *Gazette* — but to let one's dressmaker dictate to one was impossible! "I forgive in time, Madame," she said with dignity, "and hold nothing against the comtesse for those two things you mentioned. She is in my bad books at present for an indiscretion of more recent date. It was through her machinations that word of my schoolgirl elopement came to the ears of a — a former admirer of mine."

Madame Hélène nodded. She had heard of the defection of General Gerard. But it was news to her that the Comtesse de Beaulieu was being held responsible for that defection which was, in the light of Miss Tabor's engagement, more to be congratulated than deplored. "But Mademoiselle," she felt bound to say, "surely you've been told that it was

287

through a remark of Monsieur Bickerstaff's that the general learned of your past. I thought all the world knew that."

Nell Tabor stared. "Mr. Bickerstaff?" Her schoolfellow's husband would indeed know everything about Nell's past, she had to concede, for Juliana Bickerstaff's tongue ran at both ends.

The modiste bowed. "It isn't a function of Madame Hélène's establishment to pass on gossip, but I cannot believe that no one has told you of this. I myself had the story from the gentleman's wife. Perhaps she didn't wish to cause you pain."

Nell was stunned into silence.

"Ah, the Lady Juliana, a very loose tongue has that one," Madame Hélène continued. "Unfortunate, is it not, that such talk gets about. But perhaps it is not so unfortunate this time, for Madame la Comtesse de Beaulieu is already held accountable for so much that it is surely unjust to fasten her with crimes she has *not* committed." The modiste made her tone casual. "Now would you care to step inside, Mademoiselle, to try on that straw-colored gown which has given us such quarrelling already?" Madame Hélène ushered Miss Tabor into the fitting room, aware that she had given her client muchneeded food for thought.

Miss Torrington was waiting in the outer salon when her niece, the picture of fashion in a violet carriage dress, walked into the establishment. "Oh, Maria," said Aunt Kitty and put aside the copy of the *Lady's Magazine* she had been perusing. "Do tell me that these tiresome fittings are drawing to an end."

"But, Aunt, in your position as the wife of a baronet, you'll need a very extensive wardrobe," returned Maria wickedly. She wondered if she would succeed in her latest plan to have Aunt Kitty's entire wardrobe made by Madame Hélène. "Fittings can be less frequent," she considered. She had been trying to think of ways to make the world of fashion more palatable to her aunt's retiring mind. "They have your measurements here, and we'll tell Madame Hélène that your health doesn't permit you to come as often as she might ordinarily demand."

"Yes, something of that sort," agreed Miss Torrington. "Shall I wait for you now, my dear, while *you* are poked and prodded by these sewingwomen?"

"Oh, no need for that. Why don't you take the carriage off for half an hour and meet me here?" suggested Maria.

"Well, there *is* a hat I have my eye on in Bond Street," said Miss Torrington. "It's the very thing for that silver-grey walking costume you made me order. Quite modest, really—trimmed with a lovely knot of silver ribbon and a bunch of violets. I did want to seize a moment to go and see it again."

"Aunt, go and buy it this very minute." Maria was pleased that her aunt was exhibiting of her own accord an interest in finery. Once again, one of her well-laid plans was succeeding. If only one could manage oneself with half as much success.

Miss Torrington promised to be back within half an hour, and her niece sat down in a rose and gilt chair to await the appearance of the modiste. After a brief moment alone, Maria began to worry: Madame Hélène was never behindhand in greeting her clients. Did this slight mean that the reputation of the Comtesse de Beaulieu had been ruined beyond repair? Lady Anne insisted that such was not the case, but Maria had these twinges of uneasiness whenever the least little thing went wrong. She had otherwise quite recovered her old spirits and meant to live out her days as a scholar and a hostess, making matches among those few of her friends who might be left single after this busy season. Lord Abdul and his strange hold on her had been but a brief and exciting aberration in a life which would henceforward be quite dull.

As the comtesse let such virtuous thoughts drift through her mind, Madame Hélène bustled into the room. *"Madame, votre pardon, je vous en prie,"* cried the modiste in real anguish. "I have had a small tragedy. One of my wretched women has trodden on Lady Juliana Bickerstaff's new riding habit as it stood on the model and twisted the train almost beyond repair. But forgive me — these matters are of no interest to you."

"No need to apologize, Madame," returned Maria, relieved at the honest regret in Madame Hélène's voice. Her own consequence had not suffered the ultimate lowering which offhand treatment by a dressmaker would denote. It was a lucky escape, and Maria was almost ashamed of her own pleasure that she didn't stand on the other side of the line which the ton sometimes quite arbitrarily drew. She might have given her reputation as an excuse for breaking with Lord Abdul, but she really cared nothing for it. Or did she? Apparently, she was a more conventional creature than she had always thought.

"Ah, you are not displeased? *Bon,*" said Madame Hélène. Her eyes darted now and then to the inner room where Miss Eleanor Tabor lurked. Was the comtesse as resentful of the Tabor girl's hatred as she had every right to be? And would she be angry at the young lady's presence? Madame Hélène pragmatically decided to meddle no further. The two ladies must take their chances. "I have the gown for the soirée nearly finished," the modiste went on. Her eyes gleamed as usual with the pleasure of creation. "A *tour de force,* to be sure. This pale shade of mauve will be a friend to you in the future, Madame, though you haven't used it before."

"I put myself in your hands, Madame. Shall I try it now? There was that question about the sleeve—"

It was at this stage in the proceedings that Miss Eleanor Tabor chose to walk into the room, dressed in her own things and ready to leave. She stared blankly at the Comtesse de Beaulieu, who looked back in silence.

"Good day, Madame," said Nell a little shakily.

"Good day to you, Miss Tabor," returned Maria, wondering what she had done to deserve such civility. Her last meeting with Nell had been that shrill scene in the drawing room in Curzon Street.

"Is yours the mauve muslin gown embroidered with seed pearls which they were just taking out when I came through?" Nell asked. "It's lovely," she then added, a little desperately. She knew how ashamed Barrett would be if she didn't make some attempt at reconciliation with Maria in light of what she had just learned.

"We had some words about the color," said Maria. "But as usual, Madame won out. She is always right."

"Yes," replied Nell. "She's put me, with this hair of mine, into a straw color that I never would have chosen, and it works admirably."

"It sounds very pretty," said Maria. "I ordered the gown you just saw for the soirée I'm giving shortly. Perhaps you'd do me the honor of attending, in company with the Johnsons?"

There was ever so slight a pause. "I'd be delighted, Madame," said Nell in a quiet voice.

The ladies' eyes met briefly, and they both blushed. Nell made her compliments as quickly as she could and hurried to her scheduled rendezvous with Barrett. She had so much to tell him!

Left alone with the comtesse, Madame Hélène remarked, "How fine to see you two ladies friends again. I suppose the softening of Mademoiselle's manner is due to the fact that she's soon to be a bride. Ah, these marriages, madame! They are all around us. Do *you* never think to marry again? It might be a very good thing, *n'est-ce pas?*"

Maria was taken aback. "Marry? I? Never, Madame Hélène. It's absurd to think that the question will arise. I'm past the age for such things."

The other laughed. "This you can say, madame, to one who has spent the morning fitting the wedding gown of Mademoiselle Katherine Torrington? We are finding in this season that age has little to do with eligibility."

"There are things other than age to think of," said Maria with a sigh. And being a dashing widow was one of them, she thought. She passed in front of Madame Hélène and proceeded into the fitting room. No, *she* would never marry.

"Ah, Madame, that remains to be seen," responded the modiste. She didn't like to see her client in low spirits but did not know how to raise them. Unfortunate. Still, considering the morning's work, Madame Hélène could not but feel a little smug.

Chapter Twenty-eight

"A lit'ry gathering's just the thing," said Sir Stephen Wrackham. He replaced his snuffbox in the pocket of a new coat which set on him remarkably well, considering the unholy fuss Weston's man had made during the measurement of the baronet's substantial proportions. "Glad to see M'dame in spirits," he added. "First time in a long while she's looked herself."

"To be sure, Wrackham," Major Harcourt replied. His languid eyes followed Sir Stephen's across the crowded drawing room to where the Comtesse de Beaulieu was laughing softly in response to some comment of Lord Westhill's. Yes, it did one's heart good to see Maria in her accustomed role of hostess, surrounded by well-wishers and admirers. But where the devil were the Miss Millers? It wasn't like them to be late to a party.

"Don't see M'lord Abdul," Sir Stephen said. "Litry fellow and a friend of M'dame's, but I don't see him. Odd. Not sorry, y'know, but it's odd he's not here."

Major Harcourt's finely etched eyebrows lifted in consternation. Did Wrackham know nothing? The falling-out between the Comtesse de Beaulieu and Lord Abdul, the details of which were unknown, had taken place at least two weeks before. The two had not been seen in each other's company in all that time and seemed to be avoiding each other. On the one occasion the comtesse had encountered the diplomat in the Park, nothing had passed between them but the coldest of bows. "I have a feeling his lordship won't be present tonight," the major said.

"Thought as much, Harcourt," replied the baronet in a hearty voice. "Not sorry," he repeated.

"No," said Harcourt. "No more am I." The two gentlemen stared silently across the floor at Maria.

"Let's join her," suggested Wrackham. "Not wanting to intrude, but there's room in her circle. Coming, Harcourt?"

"No, Wrackham, I must speak to Lady Anne," said the major with a bow. His eyes were brooding as he followed Sir Stephen's quick pace across the room to Madame's side, but he nearly smiled to see the horrified look young Westhill gave the large baronet. Wrackham was a good soul, and his disinterested kindness to Maria in the past difficult weeks put Major Harcourt's own conduct to shame.

Harcourt found Lady Anne Renshaw holding court over a group of admirers, foremost among whom was her husband. The major diffidently presented his compliments to her ladyship and stood back quietly to audit the conversation. It wouldn't be seemly to interrupt with his personal question. He would wait for a lull.

But Phillip Renshaw noticed something anxious in the military man's bearing and took him off to one side. "Well, Harcourt, why the long face? Something wrong?"

Harcourt cleared his throat. "I merely wanted to ask her ladyship if her sisters-in-law are to attend tonight. I notice they aren't here yet."

"Elliot is bringing them," replied Renshaw. His shrewd look bespoke a full knowledge of Harcourt's attachment to the younger of the sisters, and the major reddened in conscious embarrassment. "Talking of Elliot," continued Renshaw in a change of subject. "What do you say to the outcome of his proposed race with my brother Wormington? The route's been changed, you know. They mean to take the Dover road as far as Rochester, rather than race to Brighton. Something about young Lady Wormington's not wanting her husband to go as far away as the Brighton race would warrant. Breeding, you know. They get skittish."

"My money's on Elliot," said Harcourt with a gloomy look. He could never think of the young athlete without wondering how the boy stood with Miss Georgina.

"Mine's not," replied Renshaw in a fine show of family loyalty.

Further elaboration on the probable outcome of this race was cut short when Lord Elliot entered the room with a Miss Miller on each arm. The gentlemen watched Maria sail across the room, her mauve draperies floating becomingly, to greet her guests.

"So good of you to come, my dears," Maria greeted the Millers. As usual, her eyes were riveted by the blatant display of jewels. Heavens, it must be like living in Ali Baba's cave! "And my Lord Elliot, I am so glad," she added. She looked up at the gentleman with the same honest gratitude she had shown to every guest that night.

Maria soon made her excuses and returned to the group she had left, but her eyes narrowly observed the Millers and their tall escort from a distance. Constance, it would appear, was the sister to whom Elliot addressed most of his remarks, and to whom his honest blue eyes looked with the same worship with which he used to favor Lady Anne. It was a surprise, this development, what with Constance as good as married to dear Sir Stephen. And were Lord Elliot's intentions serious? These triangles were a problem, for it was unthinkable that poor Sir Stephen Wrackham, who had been so kind to one, should be made unhappy. Perhaps Constance could be warned — Maria laughed to herself. How could she, of all people, put a word in Constance's ear not to play the flirt?

When Major Harcourt made his bow before Constance Miller, he had to hide a quiet shudder as her suddenly cold blue eyes regarded him with blatant anger. Dash it all, a man couldn't get used to that sort of treatment. True, on his last visit to Russell Square, he had been informed that the ladies were out, but surely it was no more than proper to pay one's compliments at a party. "Miss Georgina, you are looking extremely well," he added, turning to the younger sister. The upturned eyes were unmistakably adoring as the girl smiled at him. Lord, she *was* a lovely sight!

"Thank you, Major Harcourt." Georgina flashed her sister a triumphant look. Constance had told her earlier, while they were dressing, that Georgina mustn't expect Major Harcourt to notice her again, as Papa had warned him off. Georgina, while deploring the effect of such horrid treatment on her poor sensitive major, had maintained that no warning could stop his attentions to her, and she had been right. They might deny her to him at home, but he couldn't help rushing to her side at the first opportunity. It was just like a book, Georgina thought. She wasn't certain yet what she ought to do to bring about her own happiness, but she was giving the matter careful study. And she was absolutely sure of one thing: this dark, brooding man loved her.

"Well, Major," Constance said tartly. "We won't detain you. Come, Georgina, I wish to say a word to Lady Anne. Lord Elliot." She smiled at the young man who hadn't left her side. "You'll excuse us?"

"Only for a short while, Miss Miller," said the young baron with a look full of tenderness. Odd how it didn't bother a man anymore when Lady Anne's name was mentioned. And it was all due to the angelic ways of Constance Miller, who had stood by a fellow in his darkest moments. Dashed comfortable sort of girl!

Lady Anne was glad to break away from her côterie of gentlemen to greet the Millers. "Well, my dear, and what do you think of our Maria's return to the land of the living?" she asked Constance.

"It's a very pleasant party. She looks so well, and from what you tell me of the fit of the dismals she went through, it's a wonder. But good heavens!" Constance's eyes, which had been haphazardly following Lord Elliot about the room, suddenly widened in disbelief. "Who, pray, do I see with Ginevra Johnson?"

Anne smiled. "That, my dear, is the newest *on-dit*. Nell Tabor and Maria have made it up."

"You don't mean it!" gasped Constance.

"To my mind, it has something to do with Barrett Johnson's influence over Nell," said Anne. "A good sort of young man."

"Yes, indeed," agreed Constance. "Lord Elliot is giving him the Shropshire living. They're great friends."

"Unusual, with one a Corinthian and one quite the reverse. Though I've seen Mr. Johnson sit a horse, and he does it tolerably. They're of an age, true, and often it takes nothing more to account for a friendship."

Constance made a small noise, midway between a gasp and a squeak.

"What was that?" queried Anne.

"Oh, nothing," answered Constance in a weak voice. It had just occurred to the elder Miss Miller that, if Barrett Johnson and Elliot were of an age, so were she and Nell Tabor. Of all the comments which Constance had been hearing concerning the match between Nell and the clergyman, not one of them had ridiculed the couple's disparate ages.

"You're quiet all of a sudden," remarked Anne.

"Not really. It's Georgina who's quiet," Constance said, trying to create a diversion. It was true that the younger Miss Miller, who had been present all along, had yet to speak a word.

"I'm thinking, Constance," said Georgina in an expressionless voice. Her eyes were on Major Harcourt, and she had an uncharacteristic frown on her face.

"Isn't it delightful that Miss Tabor and the comtesse are friends again?" demanded her sister. Constance's manner was suddenly vigilant as she recalled herself to her duty of quelling Georgina's attachment to Harcourt at all cost. The idiot child was actually staring openly at that useless man.

"Oh, yes, I suppose," said Georgina in the same careless tone.

"Well, child, I'm out of patience with you and no mistake," snapped Constance. "Do tell me when you're ready to end this senseless pining for one who has been declared ineligible, and we'll see what can be done. But don't remind me by your mooning manner that your first season has been a total waste of time."

Georgina flushed angrily, but she said nothing.

Anne observed the exchange between the sisters and guessed that the subject of their quarrel must be Major George Harcourt. The major certainly seemed fond of young Georgina. It was interesting to see what was becoming of Maria's and her own former admirers. (She had not failed to remark

Lord Elliot's obvious tendre for Constance.) Men were certainly changeable creatures, and Anne couldn't but wish Major Harcourt well, though such a match would be the ruin of Constance's hopes for Georgina. The major was a plain, modest sort of fellow, nothing if not respectable, but there was no prospect of a title. Anne smiled softly: neither had there been a title in the case of Phillip Renshaw.

As the evening wore on, Lord Elliot grew more and more restive. It was a famous thing to discuss his upcoming race with all the sporting men present—and there were a dashed lot of them, for a literary soirée!—but the baron had a nagging sense of some unfinished business. The race was to take place next day, when Wormington should arrive from Kent. What the devil had a fellow meant to do before tomorrow? Something important—His lordship's eye lit upon Miss Miller. Yes, that was it. Not leave oneself in suspense any longer. The driving would suffer for it.

"I say, Miss Miller, a word?" he asked, bowing before the lady.

Constance started and turned from her conversation with Eleanor Tabor. "Of course, my lord," she said. "Some private intelligence, I take it?"

"Something of that sort. Miss Tabor, excuse us?" Elliot led Constance to a fairly isolated corner of the drawing room.

"I hope nothing is wrong, my lord?" asked Constance. She searched the room for Georgina, ever her first thought when it appeared that something might be amiss. There was the child, thank goodness, safely talking to the comtesse and Sir Stephen Wrackham. Major Harcourt was with her too, but one couldn't very well keep him from Georgina every minute—though Papa had warned so sternly that Constance must take every care to do so.

"No, nothing's wrong," said Elliot, staring at the

lady in a way that made her blush. "Hope not, at least."

"Then what is it, please?" asked Constance with polite interest.

"It's very simple," declared the tall Corinthian. "Doesn't need much thought at all. A question to ask you, with a one-word answer. Hope it's the right word. Shouldn't like to think it wouldn't be, Miss Miller."

Constance looked her confusion and remained silent.

"Dash it all, the comtesse doesn't have a conservatory or an anteroom hard by, or anything of that sort," said Elliot with a frown at the crowds of people who, though not precisely observing him and his lady, *did* have the bad taste to be present. "Ought to have more privacy, but it can't be helped." He paused. "Likely we couldn't get more private anyhow, with that sister of yours clinging to you like a limpet."

"My lord, what are you talking about?" asked Constance in something very akin to exasperation.

The baron reddened. He examined his large hands, twisted his signet ring, and gasped. "Not brought that, either! Crack-brained thing to do."

"Lord Elliot," begged Constance.

Elliot looked full at Miss Miller, nodded his head in decision, and began, "Shouldn't like to live without you, Miss Miller—it's as simple as that. Beg you to accept my signet ring for the moment—bacon-brained as I am—left the diamond at home. That is, if you'll marry a fellow?" His gaze was suddenly appealing and quite humble. He glanced round the room to make sure no one was looking, then he pulled off his ring and held it out.

Constance was more shocked than she had been since Pamelà announced her engagement to Wormington. She put her hand in his and said, "Yes. I shouldn't at all like living without you."

Elliot's face broke into a smile. "Couldn't be better, then," he cried. "I knew we had much in common." He sighed. "I should have liked to have you alone — kiss you and all that. Your father agrees, you know. Nothing to do now but contrive to be alone for once in our lives."

Constance lowered her eyes demurely. "It's true that the comtesse has no conservatory, but if we're quite discreet and leave by separate doors, we might contrive to meet in the library."

"Capital idea," said Elliot heartily, shaking his betrothed by the hand. "Knew you had a head on your shoulders. Meet you there in five minutes." The baron was soon off across the room at top speed, leaving Constance to stare after him in wonderment.

Constance and Elliot had at least two interested observers in the persons of the Comtesse de Beaulieu and Sir Stephen Wrackham. Maria had noted Sir Stephen observing the couple's private and intimate-appearing talk, and her heart was heavy for him. She knew he cared for Constance, and she couldn't help thinking that the wretched girl was playing him and Elliot off against each other. Maria tried her best to keep the poor gentleman from a justifiable fit of the dismals.

She leaned toward the baronet's chair. "It's probably nothing, Sir Stephen," she said softly. Wrackham had long since turned his eyes from Constance back to herself, but the bemused expression on his face made it evident that he was still thinking of Miss Miller.

"Nothing, what?" agreed Sir Stephen with a cheerful nod of his head. He hadn't a notion of what the woman could be talking — must not have been paying proper attention. Her own fault, shouldn't rig herself out in such a way as to make a man lose himself in looking at her.

"No, not a thing, sir, I'm certain," said Maria with an encouraging look.

"Capital, then, no question," returned Sir Stephen, but he was still completely at sea. He smiled broadly to cover his confusion.

It was certainly no hard task to soothe this gentleman's jealous feelings, thought Maria. Constance was a bit of a monster to play fast and loose with someone so good and openhearted. Maria sighed and felt a tear well up in her eye.

"Something wrong, M'dame?" queried Sir Stephen anxiously. "Get you anything?" He searched the pocket of his coat for a certain small box, remembered himself, and smiled at his near mistake.

Maria returned his smile, her eyes only slightly wet. "No, nothing, Sir Stephen," she responded with another little sigh.

"What, my lady, has you looking so mischievous?" Phillip Renshaw asked his wife. He took her hand in his as they sat upon a sofa across the room from Maria and the baronet, but well within view of them.

Anne gazed at her husband. "Magic, my dear Phillip," she said mysteriously. "Magic."

Sometime later, Maria found herself startled out of her bemused observation of Sir Stephen, who was now across the room talking sports with some friends, when another large gentleman of her acquaintance bowed before her.

"Why, Mr. Bickerstaff." Her eyes widened. "I'm surprised to see you here this evening." Juliana

302

never came to Maria's soirées—though an invitation was always sent out of courtesy—and Maria couldn't imagine why Roger Bickerstaff should choose to attend at all, let alone without his wife. He was hardly known for his literary interests.

"I've a message for you, ma'am," replied the young man eagerly. "An important message. Privacy would help, you know."

"A message? Privacy?" Maria was completely at sea. "Sir, I can hardly leave the room with you."

"Well, can't be helped, then. Try and act like there's nothing amiss," said Mr. Bickerstaff.

Since nothing *was* amiss, as far as she knew, Maria stared with incomprehension at the man she had heard referred to as the worst sort of blockhead. She was beginning to think the appellation was deserved, but she said nothing.

Bickerstaff took this as encouragement to go on. He first cast a furtive look about the room, then spoke in a voice softer than his usual robust tones. "Ma'am, I've a message from the Regent."

Maria caught her breath but managed to retain her outward calm. Roger Bickerstaff, she knew, was a member of the Carlton House set and a minor cog in government. "Does this have anything to do with a subject Mr. Renshaw opened with me once before?" she asked dryly. Since that dreadful evening at Morland House when Phillip Renshaw had infuriated her with a "message from the Regent," she had tried to put the regrettable incident out of her mind—for Anne's sake as well as her own and Renshaw's. She had convinced herself that the prince would surely not pursue the matter once he knew that she was not interested in beginning a liaison with Lord Abdul as a service to the crown.

Bickerstaff nodded, pleased at her quick understanding. "Renshaw. That's so, ma'am. He kicked up such a dust last time, went on and on about

303

how he'd never insult you again, that I was given the job."

"Of insulting me," said Maria quietly. Phillip Renshaw rose up a notch in her estimation. At least *he* had regretted his actions.

"Quite so, ma'am." Bickerstaff seemed not to pick up her sarcastic tone. "You know m'wife. It has to be a friend of yours that speaks to you, so it don't look odd."

"I suspect, sir, that you're no friend of mine."

Bickerstaff took no umbrage at this. He merely nodded and said, "Acquaintance, then. Same thing." Maria wondered how Juliana could bear being married to such a strange young man. If he had any fine qualities, they were well hidden this evening.

"I'll get this out quick and be away before you know it," Bickerstaff went on. He glanced about the room, but no one approached them. "Do you remember, countess, how your aunt crossed swords with a shopkeeper a while ago?"

Maria stared. She had quite forgotten Aunt Kitty's scrape with that oily little blackmailer.

"Well, it's like this," Bickerstaff continued. "That shopkeeper cove may be thinking of pressing charges after all. Your aunt wouldn't like it, and neither would you. You know the penalty for thievery—death or transportation."

"I don't understand you, Mr. Bickerstaff. What on earth could this have to do with the Regent? Aunt Kitty was hit upon, you must know, by one of those horridly dishonest men who make their livings preying on the naïve. How could you have heard that the rascal was thinking of carrying out this farce? Though I do thank you for your concern, and I assure you that Sir William—"

"Ma'am," Bickerstaff interrupted. "We're thinking that the shopkeeper may yet let the matter drop, if you would find it in your heart to—er—do the po-

lite to a certain foreign emissary." To Maria's astonishment, he winked. "Shouldn't be too difficult,
should it? You like the man. Juliana says—"

"I do not care, sir, what Juliana says," snapped
Maria, her eyes flashing. She knew a threat when
she heard one. "Let me assure you, the emissary in
question no longer has an interest in me."

Bickerstaff frowned. "So Renshaw said, but none
of us could believe it. It *would* put a different com-
plexion on matters, of course, ma'am, if he don't
want you."

"He does not," said Maria. "I hope you'll convey
that message, sir, and that any danger to my aunt
will be averted."

"Convey the message. That's all I can do," said
Bickerstaff with a shrug. "Don't want you? You're
certain of that, ma'am? If that's the case, you're
right. No use seeing your aunt on trial. But better
be sure. I know you've quarrelled—that's all over
town—but a man can't stay angry at a dasher like
you, with all respect."

"Respect," said Maria, "is one thing you and your
prince do not understand. Good evening, Mr. Bickerstaff. I'm sure you have other parties to attend."

"As a matter of fact, ma'am, I'm late picking up
Juliana at the theatre. We're going on to a rout at
her father's," said Bickerstaff. "Many thanks for your
time. I'll be leaving."

Maria watched him go, unable to comprehend
how anyone could be that stupid. She trusted that
the matter of Lord Abdul would be cleared up in
the Regent's mind this time. They would surely not
involve poor Aunt Kitty! In the unlikely event her
aunt *were* put in danger, Maria resolved not to be
quiet about his highness's machinations. That
should scotch this wild talk of death or transportation. Over a woman's refusal to have an affair! Diplomacy was something Maria would never

understand. Nor did she wish to if it involved such intrigues.

Phillip Renshaw looked up from his conversation with his wife and saw Roger Bickerstaff leaving the room. Bickerstaff would never attend a literary soirée unless he were dragged there by main force, yet here he was. Surely the Regent wasn't still up to his antics, trying to push the Comtesse de Beaulieu into Lord Abdul's arms? Renshaw thought he had made it clear that Maria would have no part in the scheme.

"Excuse me, my love," he said to Anne. He rose and kissed her cheek. "I saw Bickerstaff going out — must catch up with him and ask him a thing or two. Business."

Anne was surprised. "Roger Bickerstaff was here? How distinctly odd."

"I'm hoping it's nothing more than odd," said Renshaw. He saw Maria de Beaulieu across the room, her face perplexed and worried, and was off after Bickerstaff in an instant.

Maria had managed to work herself into quite a state before Sir Stephen Wrackham came back to her side and claimed her attention. The baronet's sincere smiles and rough gallantries immediately cleared her mind of all thoughts of governmental skullduggery. How comfortable she would be when Lord Abdul had left the country for good.

Chapter Twenty-nine

"Broken!" exclaimed Sir Stephen Wrackham. "You don't say so."

"Do say so, Cap'n, with all respect," retorted Walker. "Had it this minute from Mr. Renshaw's man. A clean break, they say. Calls off the race."

Wrackham furrowed his dark brow. "I should say it would, what, Harcourt?"

The two had been sitting in Sir Stephen's rooms at Fenton's Hotel, whither they had repaired for liquid refreshment after Elliot and Wormington had set out in their curricles from Hyde Park Corner, Renshaw following on horseback to make an on-scene observation. It had been pure chance that they had garnered such early news of Elliot's mishap, for Sir Stephen's man Walker had been carrying a message to the Renshaws' and had got the story straight from a Renshaw stableboy.

"The boy isn't badly hurt, is he, man?" the major asked solemnly.

The former soldier shook his head. "No, sir, Major, sir. Clean break near the ankle it was. He's laid up in an inn on the Dover Road and can't be moved."

Harcourt cleared his throat. "Rotten luck," he remarked. He wondered secretly if his own jealousy of Elliot in the matter of Miss Georgina Miller had in some supernatural way contributed to the young Corinthian's fall. "Overturned his curricle?"

"They say so, sir," said Walker.

"They'll race another time," said Sir Stephen. "The

important thing now is that the lad's all right and tight. Let's go inquire of Renshaw."

"Excellent idea, Wrackham," agreed the major.

Wrackham and Harcourt soon presented themselves at the house in Mount Street and were ushered into a salon where Lord Wormington sat with Lady Anne and Renshaw.

"You've heard the news of Elliot's spill?" asked Renshaw. "My brother Wormington was just telling us the latest."

"What horrid luck for poor Elliot," sighed Lady Anne.

"Mad as fire, he is, and calling out for a vehicle to take him home," said young Wormington cheerfully. "Left him cursing the day he didn't check that wheel. You should have been there, Anne, to see him overturn. Would have thrown most any lady into the vapors, but I know you like that sort of thing."

"Alfred, I most certainly do not," the earl's elder sister told him sternly.

"Of course she doesn't," corroborated Renshaw with a reproving look at his new brother.

"Don't know her yet like I do, Renshaw," responded his lordship affably. "Haven't yet seen her in the field. Bruising rider for a woman, I always say."

"Diana," put in Sir Stephen with a smile in Lady Anne's direction.

The lady bowed in response to this compliment and turned back to her husband and brother. "Now, are both of you sure there is nothing Elliot needs? Does he have adequate care, and is the place comfortable?"

"A fine coaching inn, everything in the first style," said Renshaw. "You may be easy, Anne. The sawbones who set the thing says there'll be no problem. Only he mustn't be moved till the leg's well on the way to knitting, and that's driving the boy wild. He

308

wants to get back to London posthaste for some reason."

"Left him eating beefsteak and trying to bribe an ostler," chuckled Lord Wormington. "We've greased a few palms ourselves, though. Seen to it he won't be moved."

"I'm glad to hear it," said Anne. "And of course, Phillip, we'll call off the dinner party till poor Elliot is well. He can't attend in any case for some time, but it would seem cruel to be enjoying ourselves with our friend laid up in some out of the way corner of the world."

"It's not out of the way, Anne. It's right on the Dover Road," contradicted her brother.

"Elliot thought you might postpone our dinner, and told me you were to do no such thing," said Renshaw.

"How gallant of him to think of that," said Anne with a smile. "I must admit I'd hate to call off our first party, and as long as Elliot is in no real danger—"

Just then, the two Miss Millers were announced.

"Well, Lady Anne," began Constance, "we've come to see if you have news of this race of your brother's." Her eyes, taking a belated survey of the gentlemen in the room, lit upon the earl. "Why, brother Wormington," she said in shocked tones. "Was the race called off? I must say I'm just as glad to hear it, for I have no idea why you men must eternally be galloping about the countryside for no reason."

"Constance, my dear, there's been a little accident," said Anne, looking keenly at her sister-in-law.

Constance sat down quite suddenly in the chair nearest to her hand and stared at Wormington. "The accident wasn't to yourself, sir?"

"No, sister Constance. Elliot took the spill this time, worse luck for him," responded the young man. "He won't be walking for some time, I daresay. But

309

then I hear he broke the other leg three years ago in that famous race he had over to Bath, and he was up and about in jig time, though he finished out the race with the leg—er, hanging, as it were."

"Good God," said Constance, turning white. "Anne, is it bad?"

"Not at all. The gentlemen have just been telling me that Elliot is in very good spirits," said Lady Anne, and she shot her brother a murderous look. "He's young, and it's a clean break. Why, I broke my own leg when I was little, falling out of a tree down in the country, and there's nothing wrong with it to-day."

"Not a thing," corroborated Renshaw, taking the opportunity to seize his lady's hand

"I broke my leg during the war," put in Major Harcourt. He had come to uncharacteristic life upon Georgina Miller's entrance. He now stole a look at her, though his remark had been addressed to her sister. "Not even limping on it now," he added.

"Oh, how painful it must have been," said Georgina with a speaking look.

"Georgina," said Constance tightly. "It isn't Major Harcourt's long-ago injury which is in question, but the present one of Lord Elliot."

"Don't snap so, Constance," retorted the younger girl.

The others in the room were at pains not to notice the sisters' bickering, and a strained silence was the result.

"Well," Sir Stephen Wrackham finally said, "Elliot is a strong lad. Be back on his feet in no time."

Constance turned to the baronet. "You think so, sir?"

"No question," responded Sir Stephen with an encouraging smile.

"The only problem seems to be that Elliot is bored

and wanting to get back to town," put in Anne. "When he is better, you gentlemen must go down and cheer him."

"No question. I was about to suggest that very thing," said Sir Stephen. "Famous idea, what, Harcourt? Not today or tomorrow. The boy's doubtless more knocked up than he thinks. Must make a point, though, to go and see him soon."

"That would be very kind," said Constance. She was in a quandary. No one but she, Elliot, and Papa was aware of their betrothal as yet, and she supposed that—now that the baron was laid up—any announcement had best be delayed. Very well, she wouldn't even tell her sister. She wasn't in charity with the girl anyhow, for Georgina's behavior over Major Harcourt remained as foolish as ever. Constance sighed. It was nothing less than tragic for poor Elliot to be all alone at some strange inn, unable to move. She must write to him as soon as she returned to Russell Square. And she would contrive to send him some sporting journals and things. How she wished she could be there herself to cheer him!

"I do hope you don't think it heartless of Phillip and me to give our dinner as planned, " Anne said to Constance. "Elliot has sent word that he doesn't want us to change our plans on his account."

Constance, starting back to reality, agreed that there would be no reason in the world to do such a thing.

The callers soon dispersed, leaving the Renshaws to entertain their brother Womrington and to urge him, though unsuccessfully, to remain the night with them.

"Must hurry off, can't stay," responded the young earl with a slight show of regret. "Pamela won't have me gone for long. Can't say I blame her, with no one but m'mother to bear her company. Pamela needs a bit more companionship."

"I should think so," said Renshaw, whose mind still recoiled at the thought of the senior Lady Wormington. It was a true blessing that the formidable dowager had remained to sulk in the country after his wedding to Lady Anne.

Sir Stephen Wrackham strolled back to Fenton's in an indecisive mood. Of course it wasn't the thing to go calling on M'dame la Countess now, when one would have no choice but to tell her the news about Elliot. She was a delicate lady, and the intelligence might well overset her. She had seemed lately to be on the edge of tears at the least little thing. Hadn't yet recovered her old spirits. That Abdul character must have hurt her badly when he suddenly stopped his marked attentions. Sir Stephen could not but think that the comtesse was better off out of sight of the foreign gentleman. There was something definitely havey-cavey about that man. Sir Stephen was a man of the world, and he assumed that Lord Abdul's late neglect of the comtesse merely meant that he was absorbed in a mistress.

As if mere thoughts of the diplomat could make the man appear, Sir Stephen ran into Lord Abdul just inside the portals of Fenton's.

"Sir Stephen. A pleasure," said Abdul. He smiled.

"Not heard the news, Abdul?" Wrackham returned bluntly. "Know you had money on Elliot. The boy cracked up on the road, broke a leg—called off the race."

"Nothing more serious, I hope?" Abdul asked with every appearance of honest concern. "The young man is strong."

"Clean break, no problem," elaborated Sir Stephen. "He'll be back on his feet in no time. I'm minded of the time just before Waterloo, m'self and a friend drove out from Brussels — Belgium, y'know — not planning to race, but —"

"I'm pleased to hear that it's nothing worse than a broken leg," cut in Lord Abdul. "I am quitting the country shortly, and I'd hate to leave any of my English friends in less than good health."

"Leaving?" queried Sir Stephen.

"Yes, on Monday," replied Lord Abdul with a bow. "That gives my servants three days besides this to prepare me. My business is concluded, and I would be off."

"Only natural," nodded Sir Stephen. "Get back to the family."

"To be sure. And lately I have also discovered that the frivolity of your London life is wearing," said Abdul with a mysterious glint in his eye. "I would return to my own country."

"No question, admire a man for such a sentiment," said Sir Stephen. He tried unsuccessfully to hide his own relief that Lord Abdul would soon be physically unable to do any sort of unkindness to the Comtesse de Beaulieu. "Monday, what? Sailing out of Dover?"

"Folkestone, Sir Stephen. I find it more convenient to my purposes," responded the Persian gentleman.

"Not at all amiss to sail out of Folkestone," agreed the baronet.

When the gentlemen parted, Sir Stephen returned to his rooms.

"A lot of bustling about among those foreign men of M'lord Abdul's, Cap'n," Walker informed his master as the baronet settled himself into a large chair. "They're leaving tomorrow."

"Monday," Sir Stephen corrected his man. He wondered if he shouldn't call on the comtesse after all.

"They said tomorrow, sir, Friday," contradicted Walker, who never did scruple to defend his own

313

opinion. "Packing up already."

"They're getting a start on things for Monday, then," said Sir Stephen. "Spoke to Abdul m'self just now, and he told me Monday. Not likely he'd mistake."

"Not likely, Cap'n," said Walker, deferring to rank with a shrug. "Servants told me Friday. Don't sound at all like Monday, do it, though they do talk odd." The old soldier's tone was disapproving.

"Foreigners," said Sir Stephen.

"That would account for it, Cap'n," agreed his man. "Wouldn't like to trust them to get *me* to Dover."

"Folkestone," corrected Sir Stephen.

"Dover, beg pardon, sir," said the servant.

"Folkestone, man!" said Sir Stephen. "Talked to m'lord Abdul just now, Walker. He told me Folkestone and told me Monday. No question." His black brows knotted dangerously.

"Not meaning to contradict you, Cap'n," said the man respectfully. "Repeating what I've heard. Friday. Dover."

Sir Stephen's laugh rang out. "Walker, my man, we mustn't quarrel over servants' chatter. What say to a small wager on the matter? A guinea, no more."

Walker's eyes lit up at this, and the bargain was concluded. "You can be sure I'll watch 'em ever so careful, cap'n."

"You may do that. Folkestone, Dover—no harm in either place. The man's going." Sir Stephen found his spirits lifting at the mere idea of Abdul's imminent departure.

"As you say, Cap'n," contested Walker. He left the room with a new spring in his step, thinking of lightening his master's purse come Monday—Saturday morning, rather—for a man knew what a man had heard.

Sir Stephen sat for a bit in thoughtful silence and

then went out again into the bright spring day, his step directed toward Curzon Street. He had decided that the news of Elliot's spill should come to Maria de Beaulieu's ears from a friend who could break it to her carefully. One wouldn't want her to hear it out in the shops. It might not come amiss to drop a word in her ear about Lord Abdul's departure as well. She could very well take that news hard, close as she had once been to the foreign gentleman.

Chapter Thirty

"Phillip, what do you think? Should I have taken Constance's advice and redecorated Renshaw House before entertaining?" asked Lady Anne.

"Anne, by all means do so," answered Renshaw. "I can have the painters here within the hour. New furnishings will be a little harder to come by, but I'm sure our guests will be reasonable and wait in the street until we're ready."

"My love, you'll be the death of me," laughed Anne. "And I'm perfectly happy with your own taste. I have more important things to do than to contend with all the problems of redecoration." She sighed, as though the weight of the world were on her shoulders.

"What is it, dear Anne?" queried Renshaw with a keen look.

"Oh, nothing that can be helped." She sighed a second time. "It's just that Maria can't be present tonight, and I'm a little disappointed that she's not to share in my first party. But I understand that it wouldn't have been at all the thing not to have invited Lord Abdul—he's such a great friend of yours—and so it can't be helped."

Renshaw nodded. For a brief instant, he had been afraid that the Comtesse de Beaulieu had hinted to Anne about his own excrable behavior in delivering that "message" from his superiors. Each day, he came more and more to realize he had been a cad. Instead of blindly knuckling under to the demands of others, he should have refused to act, in his capacity as Madame's friend. On the other hand, look what had happened when he *had* refused: that blundering fool Bickerstaff had been delegated the task. When Renshaw questioned him after Maria's party, Roger Bickerstaff had proudly described the part he'd played. The threat to Miss Torrington was a particularly sickening detail, and Renshaw was resolved to see that nothing came of it.

He knew that, after the dinner party, he must confess all to his wife—his own actions as well as Bickerstaff's. Anne would undoubtedly be upset, might even treat him to a display of temper she hadn't had to resort to so far in their married life, and there was no use in getting her hackles up before her first entertainment as a matron.

"Look at it this way, my love," said Renshaw. "Abdul told me today that he's leaving on Monday to return to his homeland. This is Friday. He'll soon be out of the comtesse's way for good."

"Well, that *is* splendid news," returned Anne. "Not that your friend won't be missed. He is certainly the most attentive and complimentary gentleman that I or any other lady in town has met of late."

"My dear, you'll arouse my jealousy, and that would never do just before our first dinner party," laughed Renshaw.

Several hours later, the party underway, Anne had to admit that she was a wonderful hostess despite the fact that domestic arrangements bored her: she had left everything to the discretion of the housekeeper and the chef. As the new mistress of Renshaw House sat with the ladies in the drawing room—Renshaw and the male guests were still at their wine—she could think of only two flaws in her otherwise perfect evening. One was the unfortunate absence of Maria, and the other was that the Miller sisters were up to their usual quarreling.

"But Constance, I wasn't casting sheep's eyes at anyone at all at table," insisted Georgina in her high, matter-of-fact voice.

"Indeed you were, and no mistake," returned her sister. Constance's voice had an extra sharpness tonight, and she was uncomfortably aware that her black mood was as much due to her worry over Lord Elliot as to her concern for Georgina's behavior. But she couldn't seem to stop herself from scolding her sister, who, in all justice, was still being foolish and needed a talking-to.

"My dears, I'm glad the three of us are sitting a little to one side. Couldn't we speak of something else?" suggested Anne softly.

"Lady Anne, Constance wishes to take me to task, and we can't stop her," said Georgina with an injured look.

"Georgina, I beg you not to make such accusations," retorted Constance.

"The gentlemen are coming, ladies," put in Anne. Her sharp ears had detected Sir Stephen Wrackham's booming voice in the distance. "They mustn't think anything is amiss with the two of you."

"As indeed nothing is," remarked Georgina coolly. She then turned to observe the gentlemen's entrance with her eye out for Major Harcourt. It was most important that she find a moment to speak to him in private.

Anne was also determined to speak to one gentleman in particular, although in her case the lucky male was not George Harcourt but Sir Stephen Wrackham. She sailed across the room and cornered the baronet just as he was about to offer his snuff box to none other than Lord Abdul.

"Dear Sir Stephen," she said. "You're enjoying my little party?" She included the foreign gentleman in her smile, but in such a way as to convey that she would prefer not to converse with him. Abdul accordingly bowed and turned toward a group of ladies.

"No question, m'lady, no question," responded Sir Stephen. "Not quite a full turnout?"

"I suppose you're referring to the absence of the Comtesse de Beaulieu," said Anne. She raised her voice just enough so that the retreating Lord Abdul might hear. "She's indisposed. A terrible thing! I wouldn't have had my closest friend miss this gathering for the world."

"Not serious?" asked Sir Stephen in alarm.

"Oh, no, she sent a message that she had the headache or something of that sort," replied her ladyship with a speaking look. "Of course, Miss Katherine Torrington stayed at home with her niece, and Sir William sent his regrets, so my poor little table was quite small."

"Plenty of people, all the same," said Sir Stephen.

"To be sure," said Anne. "But to return to Maria— she hasn't been in the best of spirits lately, and she tells me you've been most kind in visiting her often. It means a lot to Maria to have such a disinterested friend as yourself."

"Disinterested?" Sir Stephen repeated the word in perplexity.

"Yes, my dear sir. You know how it is with the usual run of gentlemen. They tend to flirt with a lady instead of being plainly useful and companionable as you have done," Lady Anne elaborated with a wise smile.

"Useful," said Sir Stephen. "Companionable." He seemed to have a need to repeat the words to give them meaning. Staring at Lady Anne, he then confided, "Most one can hope, to be of use. Not a lit'ry man."

"Few are, Sir Stephen," countered the lady. "You have many excellent qualities, though, that would cause any lady to admire you. Loyalty, for one."

"Yes, quite, I must admit it, very loyal. Not difficult." Sir Stephen straightened to his full considerable height.

"And there are many other things about you. You're a titled landowner, you move in the first circles, and there is nothing wrong with your connections," Anne went on boldly. "Not that we are talking of eligibility for *marriage*, of course, and I won't embarrass you by doing so. But you mustn't be so diffident that you consider your own friendship to be worthy any less than that of a more literary gentleman, and so I've brought forward the reasons that several ladies have had for setting their caps at you."

"Several ladies?" Sir Stephen's face reddened

Anne's charming laugh rang out. "Why, certainly," she said shrewdly. "But of course you've been too busy to notice such things, haven't you, sir?"

Sir Stephen frowned in thought. "Beg your pardon, Lady Anne. Not meaning to be rude, but are you driving at something? Not catching it. Not clever, you know."

Anne sighed. This was more difficult than she had thought. "Sir, I will be plain. I would not, mind you, if I didn't have your true interests at heart." She paused dramatically and looked up at her large companion. "You want Maria, and out of diffidence you hesitate. She wants you, but she is very French sometimes, Sir Stephen, and the French are notoriously lacking in imagination." She held up her hand as Sir Stephen opened an astonished mouth to speak. "Now don't tell me some Banbury tale about only wanting to be her friend, for I have eyes in my head and I've seen the looks you give her. What is more, I know you've been sending her white roses for weeks." This last remark was only conjecture. Anne paused to observe the effect of her words.

Sir Stephen Wrackham's stare was so totally blank, Anne feared for a moment that she had gone too far. At last he spoke. "Wants me?" he muttered. "No question?"

"Sir, if there were any such thing as a question, be

320

assured I would have kept out of this, where I know I belong," said the lady. "And now, if you'll excuse me, I'll leave you to your thoughts." After pressing his large hand in both of hers, Anne drifted into the crowd. She felt as if a gigantic weight had been lifted from her. Now let Maria and Sir Stephen work the rest of the spell. Lady Anne Renshaw had done her bit.

As she moved among the guests, Anne was startled by a most unfamiliar sound, one she couldn't quite identify and which she knew she had never heard before. She turned round and stared. It was Major George Harcourt, and he was actually laughing.

"You little hoyden," he said between chuckles to Georgina Miller. "I wouldn't have believed it possible."

"I don't care what you call me, sir, but do lower your voice," was Miss Georgina's murmured answer.

Anne shrugged and moved away, thinking only of Maria's affairs. A small wedding would be the thing, and a honeymoon to Paris—though visiting the Beaulieus in just this circumstance might be awkward. No, Italy would be better. And Maria must be married in a pale shade of nile green, her best color. There was much to arrange.

At evening's end, a very high-spirited Sir Stephen Wrackham approached Lord Abdul in the street outside the Renshaw residence. "Walk back to Fenton's together?" he suggested.

The foreign gentleman jumped. Sir Stephen's voice had been even louder than usual, and his manner was nearly boisterous. "No, my dear sir. Obliged, of course, but I am going on to Watier's," Abdul said.

"Famous idea! A great one! Go along with you," cried Sir Stephen, very easy to please.

The Persian hesitated, leaned toward Sir Stephen with a conspiratorial look. "The thing is, sir, I'm going to see a lady. You understand. You who are a man of the world yourself."

"Traffic with the muslin company, what? Understand perfectly," said Sir Stephen with a broad wink. "Not at all the thing to leave the country without a fond farewell."

"Sir, you do understand," answered Lord Abdul. "I mean to see that a certain — fair Cyprian — doesn't soon forget me."

"Not wanting to intrude on a scene like that," said Sir Stephen, and the two men parted with a friendly handshake.

Sir Stephen reached his rooms treading on air, or very nearly. Lady Anne's words were still ringing in his ears, and he could scarcely wait for the morrow, when he planned to visit Maria de Beaulieu and observe for himself if there were anything more than friendship in her manner toward him. That such a thing should be true was more than he dared hope, but working in his favor was the fact that Lady Anne Renshaw would never intentionally steer him wrong. Such a fine sportswoman would never mislead a man. B'gad, it was hours till morning, and even more hours till it would be seemly to call upon the comtesse. Sir Stephen jovially tossed his things to his waiting valet and entered his sitting room.

"Your foreign friend takes a strange way of traveling, Cap'n, sir," remarked the servant as he deftly caught his master's hat and gloves.

"Walker, what the devil have you been drinking?" countered Sir Stephen, casting himself into a chair which gave out a warning creak under his weight.

"Leaving by night," said Walker. "Havey-cavey sort of a thing, all respect."

"M'lord Abdul? He's leaving Monday, Walker," Sir Stephen informed his man. He let his mind wander to dreams of the morrow: declarations of love, clasping a certain delicate female form to his bosom . . .

"Leaving tonight, sir," contradicted the manservant smugly. "I'll be troubling you for that guinea we wagered on the matter."

Sir Stephen sat up straight. "Tonight?" he repeated, frowning. He looked sternly at his valet. "Sure of it?"

Walker nodded. "Saw them loading up the carriage just this evening. Sent on a load of baggage a few hours ago. T'other coach took off just before you came in, Cap'n. Watching from the window I was, thinking of my guinea, and also that I wasn't sorry to see the backs of them heathen servants of your friend's, Cap'n. All respect."

The baronet's brows came together. "Wanting to see a lady? It couldn't be," he muttered. His mind wandered back to the sly hesitation in Abdul's voice when he had identified his fair one as a Cyprian.

"Something about a lady, sir?" queried the helpful Walker.

"Impossible — still, no harm in being sure," continued Sir Stephen to himself. "Better be safe than sorry. No question." He got up with a sudden movement that made the chair creak again and grabbed for his hat. "Going out for a walk," he informed the startled servant. "Be back as soon as I can. Wait up. I may need something done. Likely not, but wait up."

"Right you are, Cap'n," said Walker. He looked wistfully after his master as the baronet's long strides took him down the hall with astonishing quickness. The matter of the guinea would have to wait till morning.

Chapter Thirty-one

All was quiet in the house in Russell Square as Constance crept down the staircase to the front hall, followed by a timid maidservant who carried a bandbox and valise. In her own hand, Constance clutched a note which she meant to leave on Papa's desk in the study. It briefly informed him of her whereabouts and assured him that she was holding strictly to the rules of propriety. Gathering her traveling cloak more securely around her, Constance wondered if the footman had indeed dared to obey her at the risk of Papa's displeasure. If so, had he been able to procure a hackney coach and have it waiting on the corner? It was most unpleasant to have to travel in a hack post chaise, but it wasn't very far to the inn where Elliot lay.

Constance whispered to the maid to wait in the hall, then stole to the study and softly opened the oak door. All was darkness, but she remembered very well where things were, and it was but a short way to Papa's desk. She had only to drop the letter and then turn round and leave again. . . .

As Constance approached the desk, she gasped. There was another cloaked figure in the room, bending over the desk, and this other let out a little squeal.

"Georgina!" whispered Constance, her heart beginning to beat again. "What are you doing here?"

"You can't stop me, Constance," responded her sister in her high, little voice. "How in heaven's name did you guess I was here?"

Constance grasped the dim figure of her sister by the shoulders, shocked to feel that the girl was wrapped in an outdoor garment. She propelled her to a spot in the room where a beam from the street-lamp came though a shutter. "Now tell me what you're about," she whispered.

The girl's face was now dim, but recognizable, and her eyes were sly. "I'll tell you," she said, a hand reaching out to touch the folds of her older sister's cloak, "if you'll tell me."

Constance squirmed, but she made one more attempt at sisterly authority. "My dear, you ought to be in bed, and if you don't tell me what you're doing here, I'll send for Papa."

"Shall *you* send for Papa?" asked Georgina. "Or shall *I?*"

The elder Miss Miller sighed in exasperation. "Georgina, I'm not doing anything improper, whereas I suspect that you are throwing your cap over the windmill and playing the fool. Now tell me what is going on."

Georgina wrenched herself free from her sister's grip, crossed to her Papa's desk, and dropped a sealed note there. Then she returned to Constance's side and whispered, "If you must know, I'm eloping. And I'm glad of the chance to say goodbye to you, sister. Now, if you'll excuse me, the coach must be waiting outside."

Constance thought uncomfortably of her own hack post chaise. If it had come, would it still be waiting after this delay? At the moment, the ruin of Georgina's young life was more important. "Is it permissible to ask you, Miss, with whom you're eloping?"

"You don't need to ask, for you know I love only one man, and that is George Harcourt," said Georgina dramatically. The shaft of light which cut across the room revealed her face in a fond expression. "And the poor man will be worried something is wrong," she added. "He didn't think much of this scheme, you know. He was sure something would go amiss."

"As indeed something has," said Constance. "If you think that I'm going to allow you to wreck your life and all our hopes for you, then you don't know me as well as you ought."

Georgina sighed. "Constance, how dare you say that to me, after sneaking in here in the middle of the night to lay a letter on Papa's desk—and dressed in a cloak. It doesn't show good judgment on your part. I might easily set an alarm to have *you* found, you know. But there is one thing I don't understand."

Constance averted her eyes. "And that is?"

"With whom are you eloping?" asked Georgina. "Never tell me it's Sir Stephen Wrackham."

"I'm not eloping at all," said Constance with dignity. "I hope that I'm more sensible of what is due to the family."

"But, Constance—"

"Child, I'm going away to care for a friend who needs me. I know that Papa would never let me go, but I'm taking every care to travel properly, with my maid. I simply feel it's best to be gone before Papa discovers me."

Georgina smiled wisely and shook her head.

"Now go up to bed at once, child," ventured Constance. The note of authority was clear in her softened voice. "And then I'll be off."

"It's Lord Elliot, isn't it?" asked the younger girl. "But why run off to marry him? Papa would surely approve the match, and besides you know Lord Elliot can't be moved. You won't get very far with him."

"It happens that Elliot and I are betrothed, and I'm merely going to him to take care of him," said Constance, blushing. "He mustn't be left alone in that horrid, strange inn. And as I'm taking pains to be proper about the thing, there's no need for you to plague me."

Georgina hugged her sister impulsively. "Oh, Constance, I'm so happy for you. Do you truly love Lord Elliot?"

Constance returned the embrace, tears forming in her eyes. "I truly do," she choked.

"Then you must understand my situation," said Georgina eagerly. "Major Harcourt and I simply must be together. Papa will never approve, and it's years till I'm of age."

"So you're going off to Gretna Green?" Constance made herself sound as cold and disapproving as possible. "Georgina, the major can't be a true gentleman if he would consent, at his age—which, by the way, is twice yours—to take you off like this. How would you live?"

"Major Harcourt isn't a pauper, Constance," said Georgina. "He hasn't got a title, and he isn't wealthy, but he has a good enough income, and a house in Sussex that his mother lives in. He can take care of me."

"From what I have seen," said Constance wryly, "it will be more a case of you taking care of *him*."

"Yes, I am looking forward to that," sighed Georgina.

"You're such a fool," Constance shot back. "Do but think!"

"I've been doing nothing but think, and very hard, ever since I met the major, and I'm tired of it," said Georgina. "I want to be comfortable, Constance."

"I can't let you do this," Constance said. But how indeed could she stop the girl without raising the house and curtailing her own plans? She would surely go mad if she couldn't be with Elliot soon.

"You have no choice, sister," answered the young girl. "Now do excuse me. I must go."

"Child, he won't be able to support you in any style at all," warned Constance, wishing that the chit cared more for luxuries.

"I care nothing for that, but I've thought of it all the same," said Georgina. She picked up a valise which lay by the desk. "I'm not such a fool as to be off without my jewels."

Constance had to admire the child's practicality.

"Now, do let's go outside," said Georgina. "I've seen to it that the side door was left unbarred. We could never get out through the front, you know. Come! And wish me happy, Constance."

"I can't do so in good conscience," said Constance severely, "but I'll come out with you and have speech with this George Harcourt. He *is* escorting you, isn't he? Or are the two of you to meet in Scotland?"

"Constance, don't be ridiculous. How would the poor major ever find me?" laughed Georgina. "Now let's go."

The sisters tiptoed out of the study, paused in the front hall to collect Miss Miller's frightened abigail, and made their way through the side door without incident. Outside, a worried footman informed Constance that the coach was waiting. Relieved that her own plan was so well in train, the elder sister sent her maid to wait in the chaise, then turned to where two figures were embracing in the shadows of the Miller residence.

"Well, Major," she said acidly. "What does this mean?"

Harcourt clutched tightly at Georgina. His face was paler than usual in the wavering lamplight. "Miss Miller, your sister and I must be married for our own happiness, and we shall be," he said. "When the idea was put to me at the party tonight, I was as shocked as you must be, but it's the only way. Your father has given us no choice."

"Georgina will be twenty-one in three years' time," said Constance. "Wouldn't a true gentleman wait for her?"

"My dear Miss Miller, anything can happen in three years," said the major. "Another war, for in-

stance. Would you deny us three years of life together?"

"Major Harcourt, there was never anyone like you
for looking on the dark side of things," snapped Constance. "I can't approve of this."

"Neither can you stop it, ma'am," responded the
major.

"My champion," sighed his young beloved. "See,
Constance. He does take every care of me."

"He's taking every care to ruin you, you widgeon,"
Constance shot back.

"By the way, Miss Miller," put in the major. His
normally brooding eyes took on a lively gleam. "I
notice you're dressed for traveling."

"Yes, she's going off to Elliot's inn to nurse him.
Papa would never let her go even though they are
engaged, and she's in as much danger as we are,"
Georgina said in a rush.

"Oh, Georgina," sighed her sister. "Can you really
expect me to let you go like this?" She turned to the
gentleman. "Major, I appeal to your sense of honor."

"Miss Miller, Miss Georgina will soon be my wife,
and she will have every honor due to her," said Harcourt.

"Constance," urged Georgina, touching her sister's
arm. "You understand. I know you do."

Constance couldn't deny that, in fact, she did. But
all her ambitions for Georgina had been wasted, and
she disliked waste. "There could have been so much
more for you, my dear," she said miserably.

"A title and a loveless marriage?" snorted
Georgina. "I'm much too selfish to sacrifice myself
like that. Besides, you and Pamela have caught titles."

At this stage of the argument, Major Harcourt interrupted his betrothed to say farewell and to demand
Miss Miller's blessing. "I don't like to take Georgina
away without some show of approval from her family.
And we must be going now," he explained with a
nervous look around.

"My blessing?" said Constance. She paused significantly and stared at the two in the dim, shifting light. It was impossible! What if she did give the alarm, and Georgina's plans were foiled? The child would pine away in her chamber — for Papa would lock her in — and with her dramatic inclinations, she'd probably go into a decline or make drastic attempts at escape. Constance suddenly knew she couldn't do such a thing to her little sister.

"Are the two of you really determined?" she pleaded. "You've had some time now. Haven't you thought better of it?"

The major's jaw was set stubbornly, and he looked positively fierce. "We're determined," he said. "Your blessing, Miss Miller," he repeated, glancing at Georgina.

"You must take every care of her, sir," said Constance, choking back a sob. "She is so young."

"She's years older than you or I, you know," laughed the major.

Georgina ran up to Constance and threw her arms around her. "I'll write to you from Scotland, sister. My love to Mama and Papa. You and Elliot will come to visit us, won't you?"

"Oh, Georgina," sighed Constance.

"And never think it was your fault, for not taking better care of me," added Georgina. "You don't have the power to stop love, you know."

"Major, promise me one thing," said Constance, and she gave her sister a final squeeze.

"Anything, Miss Miller," offered Harcourt.

"Don't let the child read any more of those horrid romantic novels," said his sister-to-be. "I'd hate for her to pick up more ideas than she has already."

There was a general laugh and some hurried waves and whispers before Constance Miller separated from the couple to steal away to her own traveling coach.

330

Chapter Thirty-two

Maria stretched her slippered feet out to the grate in her boudoir. The June night was cool, and the fire made her feel pleasantly wicked. Throughout her Philadelphia childhood, her father had strictly forbidden the building of fires in June. It had been a needed measure of economy, and Maria always hated pinching pennies. To order a fire whenever she wanted, in whatever room she pleased, still gave the luxurious Comtesse de Beaulieu a guilty thrill.

She bent her head to her lapdesk once more. She had been making great progress with her novel this evening. Aunt Kitty had decided on an early night, and Maria had used the unexpected solitude well. She had thought of a new character and spent the time going over her manuscript to write him in. How thankful she was for this occupation on an evening which would otherwise have been spent brooding over Anne's party and the dismal fact that she, Anne's closest friend, could not be present. Though Anne didn't know it, Maria had a double reason for not attending: not only did she wish to avoid Lord Abdul, but she wasn't yet certain of her ability to deal with Phillip Renshaw. Her relief on finding that he had refused to convey the Regent's threat had been considerable — she didn't have to think too badly of Anne's husband. Still, she felt Renshaw ought to have made his superiors understand beyond a doubt that Lord Abdul no longer admired her. The whole embarrassing incident with Bickerstaff might have been avoided.

Maria was stacking up a pile of scribbled pages when the door opened. "Yes?" she said without turning round. It would undoubtedly be Hester, with her mistress's bedtime cordial of warm wine-and-water.

"Madame," said a familiar voice. "May I beg a moment of your time?"

Maria caught her breath and whirled about on her long chair. Lord Abdul was standing before her. As she watched, he closed the door and came forward. He was in full evening dress, with jewels and diplomatic orders flashing on his black-clothed chest. And his smile — why should he be smiling at all, let alone in such an intimate, insinuating way? At their last meeting, he had looked angry enough to throttle her.

"Sir," said Maria. Her voice came out in a whisper, and she cleared her throat. "What are you doing here? Who let you in?"

Abdul waved his hand. "No matter. Menials can be bought. My greatest desire, Madame, was to see you before I depart the country. To make my peace, as it were. I could not let a little thing like a closed house stop me, could I?"

"Apparently not." Maria regained the power of motion and quickly set her papers and desk on the carpet. She rose and held out her hand, wishing she were not clad in her favorite flimsy dressing gown of fawn-colored silk and lace. Well, her costume could not be helped, and she must keep her dignity in any case. What was she to do about the servants? She had no idea how to find out which of them had done this, and the alternative — to send away every one of them on the morrow — would be quite inconvenient. "I would be glad to be friends again, sir, and I bid you godspeed on your journey," she said in the formal tone of a distant acquaintance.

Abdul took her hand, capturing it in both his own. He had removed his gloves, and the warmth of his

332

skin was unnerving. "May I sit with you a moment?" He managed to look quite humble. "Only to talk a bit before I go. I'm off this very night, and you have been so special to me, Madame—though I realize that what I wanted for us can never be—"

"I would really prefer that you go," Maria interrupted, averting her eyes. His had wandered in the old way to her half-exposed bosom, and what had once excited and flattered her now made her very uneasy. He didn't have the manner of someone come to take a platonic farewell of a friend, though Maria was a bit mollified when she remembered that he tended to gaze in that raking way at every female, with the possible exception of Miss Ginevra Johnson.

"Please, only a moment of your time, *ma chère madame?*"

"Well—" Maria hesitated, her eye on the bell rope near the door. What if she were to call the servants? Would they even come? Abdul had obviously paid them off already. Doubtless her best plan would be to sit down for a moment, give him a glass of wine, and hope he would soon take his leave. "Do sit down, milord." She indicated the sofa near the door. "I'll find you a glass, and we can drink to your safe journey."

The only beverage in Maria's boudoir was a decanter of some sickly sweet wine which its owner never touched, but which was suitable for lady visitors thrown into the vapors. Aunt Kitty liked it. Maria poured some of this treat into two tiny, gold-stemmed glasses and carried them to the couch. She apologized prettily for being able to offer Abdul nothing better. "But I'm vexed with my servants for the moment, sir, and I don't care to see any one of them. They were quite wrong to let you in, though I do admit that, from what has gone before, they might well have expected me to welcome you to a private interview. My fault, as our whole misunderstanding has been."

Her words were sincere. Maria's days of serious thought had brought her to the inescapable conclusion that, had she not first moved to flirt with this enticing stranger, nothing would have happened—no threat from the Regent, no disappointment for Abdul, and no unhappiness for herself. And though she longed to find out if he had been party to Bickerstaff's threat of danger to Aunt Kitty, she couldn't imagine how to approach the subject.

Abdul shrugged, and accepted the glass. "You English. Servants are nothing. Sit down beside me, and we will drink to my safe journey. And to your long and happy life, Madame."

Maria sat at the opposite end of the velvet-covered sofa, the end nearest the bell rope. She accepted his offer to hold her glass of wine while she settled herself, then made sure to spread her lacy draperies in such a way as to preclude her male guest moving nearer. The more she thought about it, the more she was inclined to forgive Abdul's breaking in on her like this. It could be that he had no knowledge of the Regent's schemes, and the culture he came from could easily explain his oddly casual attitude about bribing another's staff. She knew him well enough to understand that beneath his romantic veneer was a pragmatism that even she could not match. He had simply taken what he considered an ordinary way to achieve his objective. Maria accepted the wineglass back from him and offered him a distant but friendly smile.

"To your safe journey, milord." She raised the glass.

"And to your happiness, madame," he countered. They drank down the wine.

Maria nearly choked on the sickening stuff. "*Mon Dieu*, no wonder I never drink this." She fumbled for the bell. "I must see to it that Roy brings you something else. Some good brandy, perhaps?"

"Ah, no, *ma chère,* there is no need," said Abdul, coming closer to stay her hand. "We have had our toast. But, madame—is something amiss?"

Maria had put her hand to her head, which was suddenly swimming. "I—it's merely the wine. I'm not used to that sort. Sir, I must ask that you leave. I'm not well." Indeed, she felt so far from well that she only hoped he would be out of the room before she fell victim to an attack of nausea.

Abdul was all solicitude. He moved closer and put an arm around her shoulders at the moment they sagged. "Madame? Are you revived?"

He rang the bell.

The house in Mount Street was cleared of the last guest, Lord Westhill, who had stayed and chattered until both his host and hostess were obviously fatigued. Lady Anne Renshaw leaned happily against her husband as his arms circled round her. "A success, Phillip." She smiled into his face and was surprised to find it solemn. "Why, what ails you, my love? I suppose you're tired? A lot of clattering jaws, to be sure, but that is society. I must say it was delightful to be in control for once. I spent too many years as my mama's subordinate in the social waters."

"Anne," said Renshaw, "I must speak to you."

Mystified, Anne followed him across the drawing room. The ornately furnished place had the empty look common to a room after a party, and their footsteps seemed almost to echo as Renshaw led the way to a satin-striped sofa.

"I've meant for some time to confess to you a dreadful thing I did. I thought myself forced by my connection to the foreign office, you see. You and I have talked about the possibility of going abroad, of my taking another position, perhaps following in my father's footsteps. Well, Anne, I've changed my mind about that, for if this is diplomacy, I wish nothing whatever to do with it."

"Phillip," said Anne with concern. She was struck by the earnest and pleading expression in his blue eyes. "What in the world are you talking about?"

Renshaw hesitated, then continued. "I'd give anything not to have to tell you this, my dear, but the situation has gone beyond my duties to the government. Our love for each other, our trust—those are at stake now. I can't keep secrets from you, even when those secrets may make you hate me."

"Hate you?" Anne's voice was incredulous, and she laid her hand on his arm.

He took that hand in his own and kissed it. "It's about your friend Maria. I suspect she was not only avoiding Lord Abdul by staying home from our party. I'm certain she had no wish to see me—or Roger Bickerstaff, for that matter."

Anne's eyes widened. For one instant, she thought that perhaps Phillip and Maria had been intriguing behind her back. But what on earth did Bickerstaff have to do with anything? Before she could question her husband further, a tap came at the door, and the butler entered with a silver salver whereon reposed a sealed note.

"Delivered a moment ago by special messenger, sir."

Renshaw ripped open the letter and scanned the message; there was no salutation and no signature, but he believed he recognized the writing as that of the Regent's personal secretary.

You would do great service to the crown if you would keep your lady from Curzon Street for the next couple of days. We have arranged to give our visitor a very pretty present in leave-taking.

"Phillip," said Anne in the sternest tone she had used since their marriage. "I demand to know what is happening."

Renshaw handed over the letter and proceeded to tell her as much as he himself understood.

Chapter Thirty-three

Walking to Curzon Street, Sir Stephen Wrackham didn't know exactly what he suspected, but he had to at least stroll past the Beaulieu house to see for himself that all was well. Lord Abdul's remark about going to see a lady, coupled with his lie about leaving on Monday rather than Friday, did not bode well. Wrackham had asked the management of Fenton's and found that the diplomat had indeed paid his shot and departed. If the foreigner meant to try anything desperate, it mustn't be at the expense of Maria de Beaulieu. Sir Stephen clenched his fists angrily, and as he strode toward his destination, his face was dark with anticipatory rage.

When he turned Maria's corner, a strange sight met his eyes. A traveling coach was pulled up to her door, and Lord Abdul was just stepping into it. Another male figure — a servant, from the look of him — descended the steps of the house. In the light of the streetlamp, Sir Stephen thought he saw the glint of gold changing hands. The first thought that came to the baronet's mind was the the foreign gentleman had doubtless tried to see Maria on his way out of town and been denied. But why, in that case, had the servant pocketed anything? As the coach pulled away, the baronet broke into a run.

Mr. Roy was not yet up the steps of the house when he felt his shoulders seized by a large, powerful pair of hands. A mustachioed face with a terrifying expression in its odd, light eyes glared down at him.

"I would see your mistress, man," Sir Stephen Wrackham said through clenched teeth.

"Retired for the night, sir," the butler managed to return civilly, though he was shivering under the large man's grip.

"Wake her," said the gentleman. "I've an important message."

"Impossible, sir. Madame left strict orders that she was not to be disturbed." A note of slyness was now evident in Roy's dignified voice.

"Wake her!" Sir Stephen said tightly, and he thrust the man aside. Roy scrambled up the steps to the entrance, but the intruder was in the hall before the door could be barricaded. "Which door upstairs?" inquired the baronet as he started up the staircase. "I'll find her m'self, no question, but I don't like to disturb Miss Torrington."

"Sir, I can't allow this. Come down and I—I will send to Madame," ventured Roy in his most conciliative tone.

Sir Stephen turned on the stairs and came back down. "Send, then."

Roy quaked but otherwise didn't move.

"Send," repeated the deep, booming voice of Sir Stephen Wrackham. He took a threatening step toward the servant.

"Oh, please don't harm him, sir," cried a shrill female voice. Sir Stephen turned to see a youngish lady's maid spring out from behind the baize door at the rear of the hall. The woman flung herself between Sir Stephen and Roy.,

"What the devil?" Sir Stephen demanded.

"I told him it was wrong," gasped the female with tears in her eyes. "He's always hated her. I didn't want to help them. But don't you see, sir, there was nothing I could do. I love him!" Her gaze turned fondly to the unprepossessing figure of the butler.

"Hester, you fool," muttered that individual. He

339

backed farther away from Sir Stephen.

"Speak, woman, where's your mistress? What is all this?"

"Keep quiet," Mr. Roy countered.

Sir Stephen, his expression one of naked fury, once more started toward the man, but the maid threw herself in the way yet again, and the baronet stopped and looked down at her. "The truth, woman, or I'll have it out of his hide," he warned. The female might as well believe that he would lay hands on a servant. Anything to loosen her tongue.

"Lord Abdul took Madame away," cried the terrified Hester. "She was drugged and couldn't help it. He—I—Mr. Roy—" She burst into tears.

Roy gave Hester's arm a shake. "Blast you, woman, you know she went willingly," he hissed. "She'll be back in a few days. Forget your lame attempts to save her reputation."

"Willingly!" exclaimed Sir Stephen. "See you in hell for that!" He moved toward the butler and was on the point of throttling the man when he remembered himself. "Where?" he asked urgently.

By this time, Roy's jaw was set in stubbornness. He now realized that he was in no physical danger from the gentleman. "Where Madame chooses to go is her own business," he stated. "She did not impart her destination to us, as she didn't wish to make this journey public. Her reputation, sir."

Sir Stephen turned to Hester. "Do you know anything, woman?" As she shook her head in fright, he added, "I'll pay you well for what you know. Seems to be the thing. Nothing, you say? A fine lot of servants. Probably make off with the silver when I leave."

Nevertheless, he did leave, and immediately. The heavy door of the Beaulieu residence slammed forcefully behind him.

Roy spent several minutes berating Hester, then

sent her away in tears to her lady's dressing room. He was wiping his clammy forehead with a large pocket handkerchief, thinking grateful thoughts of his near escape, when another knock sounded at the door. The butler undid the latch cautiously.

"Where is she?" snapped Phillip Renshaw, and when Roy hesitated, he forced his way inside.

Mr. Roy gave a heavy sigh and thanked the stars that this gentleman was at least not so large as Madame's other savior.

As his massive black stallion galloped through the night, Sir Stephen had something like leisure to think about the arrangements he had made. He was headed along the Dover Road, which he considered the most likely direction for Abdul to have taken. Sir William Torrington, to whose house Sir Stephen had gone immediately upon leaving Curzon Street, had insisted on searching along the Folkestone Road himself after sending members of his staff to the Beaulieu home to keep a watch on Roy and Hester and guard the safety of Miss Torrington. Sir William had applauded the care Wrackham was taking of Maria's reputation, as witnessed by the man's decision not to go outside the lady's family for help.

Sir Stephen's jaw was set, and his thoughts were running wild. The image of Maria drugged, helpless, and in the clutches of the madman Abdul was driving him to distraction. Wrackham had formulated a plot in his own mind, and what he had come up with angered him greatly: the foreign villain was abducting Maria de Beaulieu, taking her out of England, no doubt with the ultimate lewd design of shutting her up in the harem he must preside over in his own country. The man would pay dearly for the cruelties of which he had already been guilty, but if Sir Stephen could help it, the lady would suffer nothing more than an uncomfortable coach ride.

Miles flew by without a sign of the eastern gentleman and his retinue. The black stallion was a prime 'un, quite up to Sir Stephen's weight, but the animal was nevertheless winded when the baronet halted at an inn about an hour out of London.

"A coach?" he asked of the first ostler he met in the yard. He threw the boy his reins as he dismounted. "Foreign man, dark—passed by not long ago?"

The lad hadn't yet opened his mouth to answer when Sir Stephen perceived that a coach was even now drawn up before the inn. What was more, at its side in the light of a lantern, lurked the sinister figure of Lord Abdul! The baronet strode across the yard, pushed aside the foreign gentleman—for indeed it was he—and forced his way into the coach.

Maria lay unconscious on the carriage squabs, her face pale as death. Sir Stephen held her close for a moment, made sure she was breathing regularly, and laid her gently down again. He descended from the vehicle to face Lord Abdul.

"You must forgive Madame," said that gentleman. "She was overtired by the journey and has fallen asleep."

"You don't say so," said Sir Stephen.

"She'll be sorry to have missed you, but you may speak to her in town when she returns from this little farewell interlude that she and I have planned," continued Abdul smoothly.

"*She* planned!" roared Sir Stephen. Without further ado, his right fist flew out and landed the foreign gentleman unconscious on the ground. Sir Stephen then stepped back into the coach and emerged with Maria in his arms.

The innkeeper, several of his underlings, the coachman, and a small dark man (who appeared to be a personal servant of Lord Abdul's) were by now witnessing the scene with lively interest. "Private

342

room," muttered Sir Stephen in the direction of the landlord.

"Yes, sir," said the innkeeper, and he hurried into the building in the wake of the large gentleman. "Shall it be the room that was bespoken for the lady and her other escort, the one you flattened?" The man hesitated. "Not a thing I allow," he ventured, "having a mill in the yard, that is. Bad for business as a rule. But I see you are a man of means, sir, who will pay me well for any inconvenience. Shall it be the room bespoke for the other gentleman, sir? Our best bedchamber—"

"One more word in that vein," said Sir Stephen in a dangerously calm voice, "and I'll land you where I've landed him. A private parlor for the lady's comfort, man! A maidservant with blankets. Brandy. A fire. All that sort of thing."

"At once, sir," agreed the host with a timid bow. He called out to his staff.

At that moment, a hack post chaise rolled up, and a lady dressed in the first style of elegance descended, accompanied by a neat maidservant. The innkeeper hurried out once more.

"Madam," he began heartily, hoping that this prosperous-looking female wouldn't notice the unconscious man who lay not a yard from her well-shod feet.

But it would seem she already had. "Lord Abdul!" gasped Constance Miller, kneeling before the motionless figure. She never thought her nursing talents would be called into play before she had even reached Elliot. "Innkeeper, what has happened?" she asked.

"Oh, gentlemen in their cups, you know, Madam," he said in an offhand manner. "Nothing serious. He's known to you, then?"

"Slightly," said Constance, and she stood up. If Abdul were merely drunk—and how he could be foxed in the middle of the night miles outside London was a problem she could not begin to fathom—it was important that she be well out of his sight by the time he recovered his senses, lest he bear a tale back to town with him. "I am betrothed to Lord Elliot," she announced with no little touch of pride, "and I've come to nurse him. The baron is here, isn't he?"

"This very inn, Madam. The young gentleman has been with us at least two days," answered the landlord. "Shall I take you to him?"

"No, don't disturb his rest," replied Constance. "Just show me to a room for me and my maid."

The innkeeper considered this carefully. "My best bedchamber and sitting room are free, Madam, should they suit your taste." He glanced at their intended tenant, the unconscious man on the ground.

"I'm sure they will do very well, and I would be shown up at once," said Constance with a sigh of relief, for she was suddenly very tired. Then she hesitated. "These rooms are at a distance from Lord Elliot's, are they not?"

The landlord grew even more obsequious in recognition of the lady's respectability. His forehead nearly scraped the ground as he said, "Oh, staircases and corridors by the dozens, madam, you need have no fear. May I show you up?"

Constance gratefully followed him, her maid trailing behind.

Lord Abdul was rising shakily to his feet with the aid of his man, when another coach rattled into the yard and Phillip Renshaw jumped out. "Abdul! So Wrackham found you."

"He did," replied the foreign gentleman, rubbing his jaw.

Before further words could be exchanged, Lady Anne followed Renshaw out of the coach. Abdul's eyes widened at sight of her, resplendent in her evening finery with a velvet cloak thrown carelessly over her shoulders. He smiled slightly at the anger blazing in her eyes.

"Lord Abdul," said Anne, "you are no gentleman." He bowed.

Renshaw said, "And to think, my lord, I never quite believed that you were privy to the Regent's plans for your — er — happiness."

"As it happens, I was not," said Abdul. "Until last night, when word was quite subtly brought to me that a room at this inn was ready for my reception, and that Madame de Beaulieu would not be searched for should she decide to visit out of town for a few days." He hesitated, then added, "I had already thought to buy her staff, thinking of my convenience during what I had hoped would be an enjoyable connection. In short, I was tempted, Renshaw. Now you say that there has been some other sort of activity in my behalf? Concerning the woman, that is?"

"The woman!" cried Anne. "How dare you?"

Renshaw saw no harm in relating to Lord Abdul the suggestions and threats that Maria had suffered in recent weeks. Anne glared at Abdul and her husband in turn.

At the end of the recital, Abdul shook his head. "Your prince! A finger in every pie, is that not the expression? This does clear up the mystery, though, of her refusal. She has her pride. If the good man had kept out of my business, I should have had her."

"Don't be so sure of that!" snapped Lady Anne. "She's in love with someone else. Is she inside?" Without waiting for an answer from Abdul, Anne swept into the hostelry and was led to the best private parlour, where an unconscious Maria lay upon a settle. Sir Stephen Wrackham was kneeling at her side.

He rose at sight of Lady Anne, who said, "Oh, no, Sir Stephen, don't get up. How is she?"

"Breathes normally, but she must have had quite a dose of it. Laudanum, I think." The baronet took Lady Anne's advice and kept his station beside Maria. "She should come round. How do you happen to be here, ma'am?"

Anne hesitated. The story of Renshaw's involvement in Maria's plight not only sounded fantastic, but she didn't want to anger Sir Stephen by repeating it. She saw no reason to cause a rift between the two men, so she countered, "What about you, sir? How did you find out Maria was in danger?"

Sir Stephen told a rambling tale involving, as far as Anne could tell, his valet, a vague feeling of uneasiness about Maria, and Lord Abdul's suspicious ways. Anne concluded that his rescue of Maria had been a lucky accident.

"Sir, I thought Maria might need my help or my company, but I can see now that it's unnecessary. You have the matter well in hand," she said, deciding on the spot to turn the accident to account.

"Lady Anne! Another woman's the very thing. You'll be chaperone. I'm a single man, you know. Wouldn't leave me, would you, to ride off in a closed carriage with her?"

"An excellent idea," said Anne with a smile. "I couldn't have thought up a better arrangement had I plotted for months. Do use your opportunity, Sir Stephen. Oh—and see she wakes up before the ride is over. Otherwise, why bother?"

Sir Stephen looked shocked for an instant, but he soon directed a knowing smile at Lady Anne. Then he returned his attention to Maria.

Lady Anne, pleased at the baronet's protective air, wandered back out to the shadowy yard. There she came upon her husband, staring after an elaborate coach which was just disappearing out the gates of the inn.

"Was that Lord Abdul?" asked Anne, and Renshaw

346

nodded. "Drat! I had a thousand things left to say to him — all uncomplimentary."

Her husband turned to face her with a crooked smile that made him look more boyish than ever. "You're foiled in that plan. He's gone back to Persia. But I stand ready, my lady, to take the worst tongue-lashing of my life. I must compliment you, by the way, on your reticence throughout this adventure."

"I was worried about Maria," said Anne. "Do you know your friend Sir Stephen is at her side? She's quite safe now, and I can return my attention to myself — and you. How could you, Phillip? And as for his highness — words fail me."

"As our foreign friend observed, our prince does like to have a hand in everything," said Renshaw. "But I'm more to blame than he in this case. I ought to have made certain that the comtesse would never be bothered again. Instead — well, I can only guess what a man of Bickerstaff's tact and address must have said to her."

Anne nodded soberly.

Her silence seemed to urge Renshaw to further words. "My dear, you can't call me worse names than I've already called myself, but you are welcome to try. The important thing is for us to come through this and for you to trust me in the future. You have my word that there will be no more secrets between us, and if we someday end up in some post or other — in Russia or China or right in town — my duty to my office will never come before my duty to myself. And to you."

Anne kept silent a moment. Never had Renshaw spoken to her with such fervor. "I'm glad, Phillip," she said finally. "You've been very wrong, but I can't be angry with you. And I expect Maria will have to forgive someone of your charm. Perhaps we do belong in the diplomatic corps."

Renshaw kissed his wife gently, brushing back her

disheveled raven curls. "Perhaps Madame de Beaulieu will forgive me in her happiness at her approaching wedding. You did say that my friend Wrackham is with her now?"

Maria's eyes opened, and she looked about her in consternation. A rough, heavy cloak was wrapped around her, and she appeared to be jolting along in a closed carriage. Most extraordinary of all, she was tightly clasped in someone's arms. A wary look out of the corner of one eyes disclosed a grim, mustachioed countenance. "Sir Stephen!" Maria gasped.

"Awake, are you?" the gentleman asked cheerfully. "Damned good thing. I was beginning to think he'd given you something odd. Foreign, you know. You're awake, though. Capital." He gave a contented sigh and smiled down at his companion, enfolding her most closely against his chest in a matter-of-fact manner.

"But, sir." Maria drew herself gently away. "Please explain this to me. What on earth am I doing here? I—I was at home." Her thoughts turned back to the last thing she remembered. The late visit from Lord Abdul, a sudden feeling of faintness, and then— "Drugged?" she asked. "Lord Abdul?"

Sir Stephen's conversation was often lengthy, but this explanation was one he could give in relatively few words. "Drugged," he said. "Abducted you, M'dame. Taking you off out of the country. Not like it in a harem, what? I brought you back."

Maria considered the baronet's version of what sounded like a horrid adventure. And she had slept through it! "I doubt, Sir Stephen," she said with the sigh of a woman who knows the ways of the world, "that Abdul planned to abduct me out of England. He wouldn't have to. I believe he only wanted to take me off somewhere to . . ." Her voice drifted off as she searched for a genteel way to mention the one-time seduction she was certain had been Abdul's idea. Had Abdul had help in his plans for her? She would probably never know, and she preferred it that way. Though not an intimate of the Regent's, she was bound to see him from time to time, and she would rather not be obliged to fight back her anger.

"He wanted you, no question," Sir Stephen said. He gave her shoulder an awkward pat. "Safe now, though. All right and tight."

These encouraging words put Maria perilously near tears. She impulsively clasped her rescuer's hand in hers and kissed it. "Thank you very much, Sir Stephen."

He kissed her hand in return, giving her a keen look. Dawn was breaking, and Maria could see his eyes quite clearly in the light coming through the chaise window. "Pleasure to serve a lady," he said.

This statement made Maria burst into hot tears and cry as if her heart would break. After the first bleak moments had passed in rueful sobbing, she realized that she was in Sir Stephen's arms again. At this show of kindly consideration, she sobbed even more bitterly into his shoulder and clutched at his coatfront.

"Safe," he murmured into her ear. "Not to worry. You're overwrought, M'dame."

Maria continued to cry, but more quietly. It hurt her so to be comforted by this gentleman, of all people. She knew that all she could ask for was comfort. She must remember her limitations, the limitations of a woman who was *not* a lady, who was considered fair game not only for leering advances, but for country inn seductions as well. Maria worked herself into quite a bleak state as she sniffled into the rumpled evening coat of her rescuer, a respectable and upstanding man who must never find out that she cared for him.

"Not lit'ry." His voice interrupted her glum thoughts. "Not a large estate. Only a baronet. You ought to have a duke."

Maria's weeping ceased immediately, and she stared at Sir Stephen. "Sir, what are you saying?"

"We'll marry," said Sir Stephen. "Special license, down to Snowfield, not a large wedding—unless that's what you'd like." He patted her shoulder again.

"But Sir Stephen," said Maria, "we can never be married."

The baronet's response was to grasp her even tighter and kiss her quite thoroughly.

She drew back in wonder. "What can this mean?"

Sir Stephen's eyes narrowed momentarily as he searched his own mind. This was a matter he had given much serious thought over the past few hours. "Magic?" he suggested with a smile.

Maria sighed, shook her head, and nestled against his chest. She returned to reason only because Sir Stephen seemed to be insisting, as he stroked her half-undone hair, that he intended to marry her the next day.

"You can't, sir," she said with all the firmness she could summon up. Then another thought struck her. "Miss Miller!"

"Lay you a wager she makes Elliot a tenant for life within the year," countered the gentleman.

"Lord Elliot? So he is serious about her. . . ."

"Besides, I've not been hanging about Miss Miller lately," added Sir Stephen. "Not the thing when I'm in love with you."

With a large effort of will, Maria forced her conscience to remain in control in the face of this happy declaration. "Sir Stephen," she said in a tone of finality, "you can't marry a woman like me. I don't think you realize. It isn't done."

"Love me?" queried the baronet with a wistful look.

"Oh, yes! I adore you, and I have for a longer time than I suspected," said Maria, almost in exasperation. "But marriage is at issue here."

"Married tomorrow," said Sir Stephen. "Special license. Nothing easier."

Maria sighed. "Sir, I can't marry you. I think too highly of you. Don't think my latest little adventure will remain a secret. Everyone will talk. What would your friends say if they found you had married someone so notorious?"

"They'll say I'm a lucky man," replied the baronet. "Be notorious together, what?"

Maria closed her eyes and took a deep breath. "Sir Stephen," she said, in one final attempt to save his good name, "you are under no obligation. You must not do this out of chivalry."

"Must marry, you know that," Sir Stephen continued in his no-nonsense voice. "Love you. Not a lit'ry man, true, but we ought to have a famous life, Maria. Famous life."

He felt a small hand on his shoulder, and the lady reached up to kiss his ear as his arms tightened about her once more.

"No question," said the Comtesse de Beaulieu.